Collected Short Stories
Featuring
Doctor John Thorndyke
Volume 1

Collected Short Stories Featuring Doctor John Thorndyke

Fifteen Criminal Investigations of an Edwardian Forensic Scientist

Volume 1

R. Austin Freeman

LEONAUR

Collected Short Stories Featuring
Doctor John Thorndyke
Fifteen Criminal Investigations of an Edwardian Forensic Scientist
Volume 1
by R. Austin Freeman

FIRST EDITION IN THIS FORMAT

Leonaur is an imprint
of Oakpast Ltd

ISBN: 978-1-916535-90-9 (hardcover)
ISBN: 978-1-916535-91-6 (softcover)

http://www.leonaur.com

Publisher's Notes

The views expressed in this book are not necessarily
those of the publisher.

Contents

A Case of Premeditation

The wine merchant who should supply a consignment of *petit vin* to a customer who had ordered, and paid for, a vintage wine, would render himself subject to unambiguous comment. Nay! more; he would be liable to certain legal penalties. And yet his conduct would be morally indistinguishable from that of the railway company which, having accepted a first-class fare, inflicts upon the passenger that kind of company which he has paid to avoid. But the corporate conscience, as Herbert Spencer was wont to explain, is an altogether inferior product to that of the individual.

Such were the reflections of Mr. Rufus Pembury when, as the train was about to move out of Maidstone (West) station, a coarse and burly man (clearly a denizen of the third-class) was ushered into his compartment by the guard. He had paid the higher fare, not for cushioned seats, but for seclusion or, at least, select companionship. The man's entry had deprived him of both, and he resented it.

But if the presence of this stranger involved a breach of contract, his conduct was a positive affront—an indignity; for, no sooner had the train started than he fixed upon Mr. Pembury a gaze of impertinent intensity, and continued thereafter to regard him with a stare as steady and unwinking as that of a Polynesian idol.

It was offensive to a degree, and highly disconcerting withal. Mr. Pembury fidgeted in his seat with increasing discomfort and rising temper. He looked into his pocket-book, read one or two letters and sorted a collection of visiting-cards. He even thought of opening his umbrella. Finally, his patience exhausted and his wrath mounting to boiling-point, he turned to the stranger with frosty remonstrance.

"I imagine, sir, that you will have no difficulty in recognising me, should we ever meet again—which God forbid."

"I should recognise you among ten thousand," was the reply, so unexpected as to leave Mr. Pembury speechless.

"You see," the stranger continued impressively, "I've got the gift of faces. I never forget."

"That must be a great consolation," said Pembury.

"It's very useful to me," said the stranger, "at least, it used to be, when I was a warder at Portland—you remember me, I dare say: my name is Pratt. I was assistant-warder in your time. God-forsaken hole, Portland, and mighty glad I was when they used to send me up to town on reckernizing duty. Holloway was the house of detention then, you remember; that was before they moved to Brixton."

Pratt paused in his reminiscences, and Pembury, pale and gasping with astonishment, pulled himself together.

"I think," said he, "you must be mistaking me for someone else."

"I don't," replied Pratt. "You're Francis Dobbs, that's who you are. Slipped away from Portland one evening about twelve years ago. Clothes washed up on the Bill next day. No trace of fugitive. As neat a mizzle as ever I heard of. But there are a couple of photographs and a set of fingerprints at the Habitual Criminals Register. P'r'aps you'd like to come and see 'em?"

"Why should I go to the Habitual Criminals Register?" Pembury demanded faintly.

"Ah! Exactly. Why should you? When you are a man of means, and a little judiciously invested capital would render it unnecessary?"

Pembury looked out of the window, and for a minute or more preserved a stony silence. At length he turned suddenly to Pratt. "How much?" he asked.

"I shouldn't think a couple of hundred a year would hurt you," was the calm reply.

Pembury reflected awhile. "What makes you think I am a man of means?" he asked presently.

Pratt smiled grimly. "Bless you, Mr. Pembury," said he, "I know all about you. Why, for the last six months I have been living within half-a-mile of your house."

"The devil you have!"

"Yes. When I retired from the service, General O'Gorman engaged me as a sort of steward or caretaker of his little place at Baysford—he's very seldom there himself—and the very day after I came down, I met you and spotted you, but, naturally, I kept out of sight myself. Thought I'd find out whether you were good for anything before I spoke, so

I've been keeping my ears open and I find you are good for a couple of hundred."

There was an interval of silence, and then the ex-warder resumed—"That's what comes of having a memory for faces. Now there's Jack Ellis, on the other hand; he must have had you under his nose for a couple of years, and yet he's never twigged—he never will either," added Pratt, already regretting the confidence into which his vanity had led him.

"Who is Jack Ellis?" Pembury demanded sharply.

"Why, he's a sort of supernumerary at the Baysford Police Station; does odd jobs; rural detective, helps in the office and that sort of thing. He was in the Civil Guard at Portland, in your time, but he got his left forefinger chopped off, so they pensioned him, and, as he was a Baysford man, he got this billet. But he'll never reckernize you, don't you fear."

"Unless you direct his attention to me," suggested Pembury.

"There's no fear of that," laughed Pratt. "You can trust me to sit quiet on my own nest-egg. Besides, we're not very friendly. He came nosing round our place after the parlour-maid—him a married man, mark you! But I soon boosted him out, I can tell you; and Jack Ellis don't like me now."

"I see," said Pembury reflectively; then, after a pause, he asked: "Who is this General O'Gorman? I seem to know the name."

"I expect you do," said Pratt. "He was governor of Dartmoor when I was there—that was my last billet—and, let me tell you, if he'd been at Portland in your time, you'd never have got away."

"How is that?"

"Why, you see, the general is a great man on bloodhounds. He kept a pack at Dartmoor and, you bet, those lags knew it. There were no attempted escapes in those days. They wouldn't have had a chance."

"He has the pack still, hasn't he?" asked Pembury.

"Rather. Spends any amount of time on training 'em, too. He's always hoping there'll be a burglary or a murder in the neighbourhood so as he can try 'em, but he's never got a chance yet. P'r'aps the crooks have heard about 'em. But, to come back to our little arrangement: what do you say to a couple of hundred, paid quarterly, if you like?"

"I can't settle the matter off-hand," said Pembury. "You must give me time to think it over."

"Very well," said Pratt. "I shall be back at Baysford tomorrow evening. That will give you a clear day to think it over. Shall I look in at your place tomorrow night?"

"No," replied Pembury; "you'd better not be seen at my house, nor I at yours. If I meet you at some quiet spot, where we shan't be seen, we can settle our business without any one knowing that we have met. It won't take long, and we can't be too careful."

"That's true," agreed Pratt. "Well, I'll tell you what. There's an avenue leading up to our house; you know it, I expect. There's no lodge, and the gates are always ajar, excepting at night. Now I shall be down by the six-thirty at Baysford. Our place is a quarter of an hour from the station. Say you meet me in the avenue at a quarter to seven."

"That will suit me," said Pembury; "that is, if you are sure the bloodhounds won't be straying about the grounds."

"Lord bless you, no!" laughed Pratt. "D'you suppose the general lets his precious hounds stray about for any casual crook to feed with poisoned sausage? No, they're locked up safe in the kennels at the back of the house. Hallo! This'll be Swanley, I expect. I'll change into a smoker here and leave you time to turn the matter over in your mind. So long. Tomorrow evening in the avenue at a quarter to seven. And, I say, Mr. Pembury, you might as well bring the first instalment with you—fifty, in small notes or gold."

"Very well," said Mr. Pembury. He spoke coldly enough, but there was a flush on his cheeks and an angry light in his eyes, which, perhaps, the ex-warder noticed; for when he had stepped out and shut the door, he thrust his head in at the window and said threateningly—

"One more word, Mr. Pembury-Dobbs: no hanky-panky, you know. I'm an old hand and pretty fly, I am. So don't you try any chickery-pokery on me. That's all." He withdrew his head and disappeared, leaving Pembury to his reflections.

The nature of those reflections—if some telepathist transferring his attention for the moment from hidden courtyards or missing thimbles to more practical matters—could have conveyed them into the mind of Mr. Pratt, would have caused that quondam official some surprise and, perhaps, a little disquiet. For long experience of the criminal, as he appears when in durance, had produced some rather misleading ideas as to his behaviour when at large. In fact, the ex-warder had considerably under-estimated the ex-convict.

Rufus Pembury, to give his real name—for Dobbs was literally a *nom de guerre*—was a man of strong character and intelligence. So much so that, having tried the criminal career and found it not worth pursuing, he had definitely abandoned it. When the cattle-boat that

10

picked him up off Portland Bill had landed him at an American port, he brought his entire ability and energy to bear on legitimate commercial pursuits, and with such success that, at the end of ten years, he was able to return to England with a moderate competence. Then he had taken a modest house near the little town of Baysford, where he had lived quietly on his savings for the last two years, holding aloof without much difficulty from the rather exclusive local society; and here he might have lived out the rest of his life in peace but for the unlucky chance that brought the man Pratt into the neighbourhood. With the arrival of Pratt his security was utterly destroyed.

There is something eminently unsatisfactory about a blackmailer. No arrangement with him has any permanent validity. No undertaking that he gives is binding. The thing which he has sold remains in his possession to sell over again. He pockets the price of emancipation, but retains the key of the fetters. In short, the blackmailer is a totally impossible person.

Such were the considerations that had passed through the mind of Rufus Pembury, even while Pratt was making his proposals; and those proposals he had never for an instant entertained. The ex-warder's advice to him to "turn the matter over in his mind" was unnecessary. For his mind was already made up. His decision was arrived at in the very moment when Pratt had disclosed his identity. The conclusion was self-evident. Before Pratt appeared he was living in peace and security. While Pratt remained, his liberty was precarious from moment to moment. If Pratt should disappear, his peace and security would return. Therefore Pratt must be eliminated.

It was a logical consequence.

The profound meditations, therefore, in which Pembury remained immersed for the remainder of the journey, had nothing whatever to do with the quarterly allowance; they were concerned exclusively with the elimination of ex-warder Pratt.

Now Rufus Pembury was not a ferocious man. He was not even cruel. But he was gifted with a certain magnanimous cynicism which ignored the trivialities of sentiment and regarded only the main issues. If a wasp hummed over his tea-cup, he would crush that wasp; but not with his bare hand. The wasp carried the means of aggression. That was the wasp's look-out. His concern was to avoid being stung.

So it was with Pratt. The man had elected, for his own profit, to threaten Pembury's liberty. Very well. He had done it at his own risk. That risk was no concern of Pembury's. His concern was his own safety.

When Pembury alighted at Charing Cross, he directed his steps (after having watched Pratt's departure from the station) to Buckingham Street, Strand, where he entered a quiet private hotel. He was apparently expected, for the manageress greeted him by his name as she handed him his key.

"Are you staying in town, Mr. Pembury?" she asked.

"No," was the reply. "I go back tomorrow morning, but I may be coming up again shortly. By the way, you used to have an encyclopaedia in one of the rooms. Could I see it for a moment?"

"It is in the drawing-room," said the manageress. "Shall I show you—but you know the way, don't you?"

Certainly Mr. Pembury knew the way. It was on the first floor; a pleasant old-world room looking on the quiet old street; and on a shelf, amidst a collection of novels, stood the sedate volumes of *Chambers's Encyclopaedia*.

That a gentleman from the country should desire to look up the subject of "hounds" would not, to a casual observer, have seemed unnatural. But when from hounds the student proceeded to the article on blood, and thence to one devoted to perfumes, the observer might reasonably have felt some surprise; and this surprise might have been augmented if he had followed Mr. Pembury's subsequent proceedings, and specially if he had considered them as the actions of a man whose immediate aim was the removal of a superfluous unit of the population.

Having deposited his bag and umbrella in his room, Pembury set forth from the hotel as one with a definite purpose; and his footsteps led, in the first place, to an umbrella shop on the Strand, where he selected a thick rattan cane. There was nothing remarkable in this, perhaps; but the cane was of an uncomely thickness and the salesman protested. "I like a thick cane," said Pembury.

"Yes, sir; but for a gentleman of your height" (Pembury was a small, slightly-built man) "I would venture to suggest—?"

"I like a thick cane," repeated Pembury. "Cut it down to the proper length and don't rivet the ferrule on. I'll cement it on when I get home."

His next investment would have seemed more to the purpose, though suggestive of unexpected crudity of method. It was a large Norwegian knife. But not content with this he went on forthwith to a second cutler's and purchased a second knife, the exact duplicate of the first. Now, for what purpose could he want two identically similar knives? And why not have bought them both at the same shop? It was highly mysterious.

Shopping appeared to be a positive mania with Rufus Pembury. In the course of the next half-hour he acquired a cheap hand-bag, an artist's black-japanned brush-case, a three-cornered file, a stick of elastic glue and a pair of iron crucible-tongs. Still insatiable, he repaired to an old-fashioned chemist's shop in a by-street, where he further enriched himself with a packet of absorbent cotton-wool and an ounce of permanganate of potash; and, as the chemist wrapped up these articles, with the occult and necromantic air peculiar to chemists, Pembury watched him impassively.

"I suppose you don't keep musk?" he asked carelessly.

The chemist paused in the act of heating a stick of sealing-wax, and appeared as if about to mutter an incantation. But he merely replied: "No, sir. Not the solid musk; it's so very costly. But I have the essence."

"That isn't as strong as the pure stuff, I suppose?"

"No," replied the chemist, with a cryptic smile, "not so strong, but strong enough. These animal perfumes are so very penetrating, you know; and so lasting. Why, I venture to say that if you were to sprinkle a table-spoonful of the essence in the middle of St. Paul's, the place would smell of it six months hence."

"You don't say so!" said Pembury. "Well, that ought to be enough for anybody. I'll take a small quantity, please, and, for goodness' sake, see that there isn't any on the outside of the bottle. The stuff isn't for myself, and I don't want to go about smelling like a civet cat."

"Naturally you don't, sir," agreed the chemist. He then produced an ounce bottle, a small glass funnel and a stoppered bottle labelled "*Ess. Moschi*," with which he proceeded to perform a few trifling feats of legerdemain.

"There, sir," said he, when he had finished the performance, "there is not a drop on the outside of the bottle, and, if I fit it with a rubber cork, you will be quite secure."

Pembury's dislike of musk appeared to be excessive, for, when the chemist had retired into a secret cubicle as if to hold converse with some familiar spirit (but actually to change half-a-crown), he took the brush-case from his bag, pulled off its lid, and then, with the crucible-tongs, daintily lifted the bottle off the counter, slid it softly into the brush-case, and, replacing the lid, returned the case and tongs to the bag. The other two packets he took from the counter and dropped

13

into his pocket, and, when the presiding wizard, having miraculously transformed a single half-crown into four pennies, handed him the product, he left the shop and walked thoughtfully back towards the Strand. Suddenly a new idea seemed to strike him. He halted, considered for a few moments and then strode away northward to make the oddest of all his purchases.

The transaction took place in a shop in the Seven Dials, whose strange stock-in-trade ranged the whole zoological gamut, from water-snails to Angora cats. Pembury looked at a cage of guinea-pigs in the window and entered the shop.

"Do you happen to have a dead guinea-pig?" he asked.

"No; mine are all alive," replied the man, adding, with a sinister grin: "But they're not immortal, you know."

Pembury looked at the man distastefully. There is an appreciable difference between a guinea-pig and a blackmailer. "Any small mammal would do," he said.

"There's a dead rat in that cage, if he's any good," said the man. "Died this morning, so he's quite fresh."

"I'll take the rat," said Pembury; "he'll do quite well."

The little corpse was accordingly made into a parcel and deposited in the bag, and Pembury, having tendered a complimentary fee, made his way back to the hotel.

After a modest lunch he went forth and spent the remainder of the day transacting the business which had originally brought him to town. He dined at a restaurant and did not return to his hotel until ten o'clock, when he took his key, and tucking under his arm a parcel that he had brought in with him, retired for the night.

But before undressing—and after locking his door—he did a very strange and unaccountable thing. Having pulled off the loose ferrule from his newly-purchased cane, he bored a hole in the bottom of it with the spike end of the file. Then, using the latter as a broach, he enlarged the hole until only a narrow rim of the bottom was left. He next rolled up a small ball of cotton-wool and pushed it into the ferrule; and having smeared the end of the cane with elastic glue, he replaced the ferrule, warming it over the gas to make the glue stick.

When he had finished with the cane, he turned his attention to one of the Norwegian knives. First, he carefully removed with the file most of the bright, yellow varnish from the wooden case or handle.

Then he opened the knife, and, cutting the string of the parcel that he had brought in, took from it the dead rat which he had bought at

14

the zoologist's. Laying the animal on a sheet of paper, he cut off its head, and, holding it up by the tail, allowed the blood that oozed from the neck to drop on the knife, spreading it over both sides of the blade and handle with his finger.

Then he laid the knife on the paper and softly opened the window. From the darkness below came the voice of a cat, apparently perfecting itself in the execution of chromatic scales; and in that direction Pembury flung the body and head of the rat, and closed the window. Finally, having washed his hands and stuffed the paper from the parcel into the fire-place, he went to bed.

But his proceedings in the morning were equally mysterious. Having breakfasted betimes, he returned to his bedroom and locked himself in. Then he tied his new cane, handle downwards, to the leg of the dressing-table. Next, with the crucible-tongs, he drew the little bottle of musk from the brush-case, and, having assured himself, by sniffing at it, that the exterior was really free from odour, he withdrew the rubber cork. Then, slowly and with infinite care, he poured a few drops—perhaps half-a-teaspoonful—of the essence on the cotton-wool that bulged through the hole in the ferrule, watching the absorbent material narrowly as it soaked up the liquid.

When it was saturated he proceeded to treat the knife in the same fashion, letting fall a drop of the essence on the wooden handle—which soaked it up readily. This done, he slid up the window and looked out. Immediately below was a tiny yard in which grew, or rather survived, a couple of faded laurel bushes. The body of the rat was nowhere to be seen; it had apparently been spirited away in the night. Holding out the bottle, which he still held, he dropped it into the bushes, flinging the rubber cork after it.

His next proceeding was to take a tube of Vaseline from his dressing-bag and squeeze a small quantity onto his fingers. With this he thoroughly smeared the shoulder of the brush-case and the inside of the lid, so as to ensure an air-tight joint. Having wiped his fingers, he picked the knife up with the crucible-tongs, and, dropping it into the brush-case, immediately pushed on the lid. Then he heated the tips of the tongs in the gas flame to destroy the scent, packed the tongs and brush-case in the bag, untied the cane—carefully avoiding contact with the ferrule—and, taking up the two bags, went out, holding the cane by its middle.

There was no difficulty in finding an empty compartment, for first-class passengers were few at that time in the morning. Pembury waited on the platform until the guard's whistle sounded, when he stepped into the compartment, shut the door and laid the cane on the seat with its ferrule projecting out of the off-side window, in which position it remained until the train drew up in Baysford station.

Pembury left his dressing-bag at the cloak-room, and, still grasping the cane by its middle, he sallied forth. The town of Baysford lay some half-a-mile to the east of the station; his own house was a mile along the road to the west; and half-way between his house and the station was the residence of General O'Gorman. He knew the place well. Originally a farmhouse, it stood on the edge of a great expanse of flat meadows and communicated with the road by an avenue, nearly three hundred yards long, of ancient trees. The avenue was shut off from the road by a pair of iron gates, but these were merely ornamental, for the place was unenclosed and accessible from the surrounding meadows—indeed, an indistinct footpath crossed the meadows and intersected the avenue about half-way up.

On this occasion Pembury, whose objective was the avenue, elected to approach it by the latter route; and at each stile or fence that he surmounted, he paused to survey the country. Presently the avenue arose before him, lying athwart the narrow track, and, as he entered it between two of the trees, he halted and looked about him.

He stood listening for a while. Beyond the faint rustle of leaves no sound was to be heard. Evidently there was no one about, and, as Pratt was at large, it was probable that the general was absent.

And now Pembury began to examine the adjacent trees with more than a casual interest. The two between which he had entered were respectively an elm and a great pollard oak, the latter being an immense tree whose huge, warty bole divided about seven feet from the ground into three limbs, each as large as a fair-sized tree, of which the largest swept outward in a great curve half-way across the avenue. On this patriarch Pembury bestowed especial attention, walking completely round it and finally laying down his bag and cane (the latter resting on the bag with the ferrule off the ground) that he might climb up, by the aid of the warty outgrowths, to examine the crown; and he had just stepped up into the space between the three limbs, when the creaking of the iron gates was followed by a quick step in the avenue. Hastily he let himself down from the tree, and, gathering up his possessions, stood close behind the great bole.

"Just as well not to be seen," was his reflection, as he hugged the tree closely and waited, peering cautiously round the trunk. Soon a streak of moving shadow heralded the stranger's approach, and he moved round to keep the trunk between himself and the intruder. On the footsteps came, until the stranger was abreast of the tree; and when he had passed Pembury peeped round at the retreating figure. It was only the postman, but then the man knew him, and he was glad he had kept out of sight.

Apparently the oak did not meet his requirements, for he stepped out and looked up and down the avenue. Then, beyond the elm, he caught sight of an ancient pollard hornbeam—a strange, fantastic tree whose trunk widened out trumpet-like above into a broad crown, from the edge of which multitudinous branches uprose like the limbs of some weird hamadryad.

That tree he approved at a glance, but he lingered behind the oak until the postman, returning with brisk step and cheerful whistle, passed down the avenue and left him once more in solitude. Then he moved on with a resolute air to the hornbeam.

The crown of the trunk was barely six feet from the ground. He could reach it easily, as he found on trying. Standing the cane against the tree—ferrule downwards, this time—he took the brush-case from the bag, pulled off the lid, and, with the crucible-tongs, lifted out the knife and laid it on the crown of the tree, just out of sight, leaving the tongs also invisible—still grasping the knife. He was about to replace the brush-case in the bag, when he appeared to alter his mind.

Sniffing at it, and finding it reeking with the sickly perfume, he pushed the lid on again and threw the case up into the tree, where he heard it roll down into the central hollow of the crown. Then he closed the bag, and, taking the cane by its handle, moved slowly away in the direction whence he had come, passing out of the avenue between the elm and the oak.

His mode of progress was certainly peculiar. He walked with excessive slowness, trailing the cane along the ground, and every few paces he would stop and press the ferrule firmly against the earth, so that, to any one who should have observed him, he would have appeared to be wrapped in an absorbing reverie.

Thus he moved on across the fields, not, however, returning to the high road, but crossing another stretch of fields until he emerged into a narrow lane that led out into the High Street. Immediately opposite to the lane was the police station, distinguished from the adjacent cottages only by its lamp, its open door and the notices pasted up outside. Straight across the road Pembury walked, still trailing the cane, and halted at the station door to read the notices, resting his cane on the doorstep as he did so. Through the open doorway he could see a man writing at a desk. The man's back was towards him, but, presently, a movement brought his left hand into view, and Pembury noted that the forefinger was missing. This, then, was Jack Ellis, late of the Civil Guard at Portland.

Even while he was looking the man turned his head, and Pembury recognised him at once. He had frequently met him on the road between Baysford and the adjoining village of Thorpe, and always at the same time. Apparently Ellis paid a daily visit to Thorpe—perhaps to receive a report from the rural constable—and he started between three and four and returned between seven and a quarter past.

Pembury looked at his watch. It was a quarter past three. He moved away thoughtfully (holding his cane, now, by the middle), and began to walk slowly in the direction of Thorpe—westward.

For a while he was deeply meditative, and his face wore a puzzled frown. Then, suddenly, his face cleared and he strode forward at a brisker pace. Presently he passed through a gap in the hedge, and, walking in a field parallel with the road, took out his purse—a small pigskin pouch.

Having frugally emptied it of its contents, excepting a few shillings, he thrust the ferrule of his cane into the small compartment ordinarily reserved for gold or notes.

And thus he continued to walk on slowly, carrying the cane by the middle and the purse jammed on the end.

At length he reached a sharp double curve in the road whence he could see back for a considerable distance; and here opposite a small opening, he sat down to wait. The hedge screened him effectually from the gaze of passers-by—though these were few enough—without interfering with his view.

A quarter of an hour passed. He began to be uneasy. Had he been mistaken? Were Ellis's visits only occasional instead of daily, as he had thought? That would be tiresome though not actually disastrous. But at this point in his reflections a figure came into view, advancing along the road with a steady swing. He recognised the figure. It was Ellis.

But there was another figure advancing from the opposite direction: a labourer, apparently. He prepared to shift his ground, but another glance showed him that the labourer would pass first. He waited. The labourer came on and, at length, passed the opening, and, as he did so, Ellis disappeared for a moment in a bend of the road. Instantly

Pembury passed his cane through the opening in the hedge, shook off the purse and pushed it into the middle of the foot-way. Then he crept forward, behind the hedge, towards the approaching official, and again sat down to wait. On came the steady tramp of the unconscious Ellis, and, as it passed, Pembury drew aside an obstructing branch and peered out at the retreating figure. The question now was, would Ellis see the purse? It was not a very conspicuous object.

The footsteps stopped abruptly. Looking out, Pembury saw the police official stoop, pick up the purse, examine its contents and finally stow it in his trousers pocket. Pembury heaved a sigh of relief; and, as the dwindling figure passed out of sight round a curve in the road, he rose, stretched himself and strode away briskly.

Near the gap was a group of ricks, and, as he passed them, a fresh idea suggested itself. Looking round quickly he passed to the farther side of one and, thrusting his cane deeply into it, pushed it home with a piece of stick that he picked up near the rick, until the handle was lost among the straw. The bag was now all that was left, and it was empty—for his other purchases were in the dressing-bag, which, by the way, he must fetch from the station. He opened it and smelt the interior, but, though he could detect no odour, he resolved to be rid of it if possible.

As he emerged from the gap a wagon jogged slowly past. It was piled high with sacks, and the tail-board was down. Stepping into the road, he quickly overtook the wagon, and, having glanced round, laid the bag lightly on the tail-board. Then he set off for the station.

On arriving home he went straight up to his bedroom, and, ringing for his housekeeper, ordered a substantial meal. Then he took off his clothes and deposited them, even to his shirt, socks and necktie, in a trunk, wherein his summer clothing was stored with a plentiful sprinkling of *naphthol* to preserve it from the moth. Taking the packet of permanganate of potash from his dressing-bag, he passed into the adjoining bathroom, and, tipping the crystals into the bath, turned on the water.

Soon the bath was filled with a pink solution of the salt, and into this he plunged, immersing his entire body and thoroughly soaking his hair. Then he emptied the bath and rinsed himself in clear water, and, having dried himself, returned to the bedroom and dressed himself in fresh clothing. Finally he took a hearty meal, and then lay down on the sofa to rest until it should be time to start for the rendezvous.

Half-past six found him lurking in the shadow by the station-approach, within sight of the solitary lamp. He heard the train come in, saw the stream of passengers emerge, and noted one figure detach itself from the throng and turn on to the Thorpe road. It was Pratt, as the lamplight showed him; Pratt, striding forward to the meeting-place with an air of jaunty satisfaction and an uncommonly creaky pair of boots.

Pembury followed him at a safe distance, and rather by sound than sight, until he was well past the stile at the entrance to the footpath. Evidently he was going on to the gates. Then Pembury vaulted over the stile and strode away swiftly across the dark meadows.

When he plunged into the deep gloom of the avenue, his first act was to grope his way to the hornbeam and slip his hand up onto the crown and satisfy himself that the tongs were as he had left them. Reassured by the touch of his fingers on the iron loops, he turned and walked slowly down the avenue. The duplicate knife—ready opened—was in his left inside breast-pocket, and he fingered its handle as he walked.

Presently the iron gate squeaked mournfully, and then the rhythmical creak of a pair of boots was audible, coming up the avenue. Pembury walked forward slowly until a darker smear emerged from the surrounding gloom, when he called out—

"Is that you, Pratt?"

"That's me," was the cheerful, if ungrammatical response, and, as he drew nearer, the ex-warder asked: "Have you brought the rhino, old man?"

The insolent familiarity of the man's tone was agreeable to Pembury: it strengthened his nerve and hardened his heart. "Of course," he replied; "but we must have a definite understanding, you know."

"Look here," said Pratt, "I've got no time for jaw. The General will be here presently; he's riding over from Bingfield with a friend. You hand over the dibs and we'll talk some other time."

"That is all very well," said Pembury, "but you must understand—?" He paused abruptly and stood still. They were now close to the hornbeam, and, as he stood, he stared up into the dark mass of foliage.

"What's the matter?" demanded Pratt. "What are you staring at?" He, too, had halted and stood gazing intently into the darkness.

Then, in an instant, Pembury whipped out the knife and drove it, with all his strength, into the broad back of the ex-warder, below the left shoulder-blade.

With a hideous yell Pratt turned and grappled with his assailant. A

20

powerful man and a competent wrestler, too, he was far more than a match for Pembury unarmed, and, in a moment, he had him by the throat. But Pembury clung to him tightly, and, as they trampled to and fro and round and round, he stabbed again and again with the viciousness of a scorpion, while Pratt's cries grew more gurgling and husky. Then they fell heavily to the ground, Pembury underneath. But the struggle was over. With a last bubbling groan, Pratt relaxed his hold and in a moment grew limp and inert. Pembury pushed him off and rose, trembling and breathing heavily.

But he wasted no time. There had been more noise than he had bargained for. Quickly stepping up to the hornbeam, he reached up for the tongs. His fingers slid into the looped handles; the tongs grasped the knife, and he lifted it out from its hiding-place and carried it to where the corpse lay, depositing it on the ground a few feet from the body. Then he went back to the tree and carefully pushed the tongs over into the hollow of the crown.

At this moment a woman's voice sounded shrilly from the top of the avenue.

"Is that you, Mr. Pratt?" it called.

Pembury started and then stepped back quickly, on tiptoe, to the body. For there was the duplicate knife. He must take that away at all costs.

The corpse was lying on its back. The knife was underneath it, driven in to the very haft. He had to use both hands to lift the body, and even then he had some difficulty in disengaging the weapon. And, meanwhile, the voice, repeating its question, drew nearer.

At length he succeeded in drawing out the knife and thrust it into his breast-pocket. The corpse fell back, and he stood up gasping.

"Mr. Pratt! Are you there?" The nearness of the voice startled Pembury, and, turning sharply, he saw a light twinkling between the trees. And then the gates creaked loudly and he heard the crunch of a horse's hoofs on the gravel.

He stood for an instant bewildered—utterly taken by surprise. He had not reckoned on a horse. His intended flight across the meadows towards Thorpe was now impracticable. If he were overtaken he was lost, for he knew there was blood on his clothes and his hands were wet and slippery—to say nothing of the knife in his pocket.

But his confusion lasted only for an instant. He remembered the oak tree; and, turning out of the avenue, he ran to it, and, touching it as little as he could with his bloody hands, climbed quickly up into the crown. The great horizontal limb was nearly three feet in diameter, and, as he lay out on it, gathering his coat closely round him, he was quite invisible from below.

He had hardly settled himself when the light which he had seen came into full view, revealing a woman advancing with a stable lantern in her hand. And, almost at the same moment, a streak of brighter light burst from the opposite direction. The horseman was accompanied by a man on a bicycle.

The two men came on apace, and the horseman, sighting the woman, called out: "Anything the matter, Mrs. Parton?" But, at that moment, the light of the bicycle lamp fell full on the prostrate corpse. The two men uttered a simultaneous cry of horror; the woman shrieked aloud: and then the horseman sprang from the saddle and ran forward to the body.

"Why," he exclaimed, stooping over it, "it's Pratt;" and, as the cyclist came up and the glare of his lamp shone on a great pool of blood, he added: "There's been foul play here, Hanford."

Hanford flashed his lamp around the body, lighting up the ground for several yards.

"What is that behind you, O'Gorman?" he said suddenly; "isn't it a knife?" He was moving quickly towards it when O'Gorman held up his hand.

"Don't touch it!" he exclaimed. "We'll put the hounds onto it. They'll soon track the scoundrel, whoever he is. By God! Hanford, this fellow has fairly delivered himself into our hands." He stood for a few moments looking down at the knife with something uncommonly like exultation, and then, turning quickly to his friend, said: "Look here, Hanford; you ride off to the police station as hard as you can pelt. It is only three-quarters of a mile; you'll do it in five minutes. Send or bring an officer and I'll scour the meadows meanwhile. If I haven't got the scoundrel when you come back, we'll put the hounds onto this knife and run the beggar down."

"Right," replied Hanford, and without another word he wheeled his machine about, mounted and rode away into the darkness.

"Mrs. Parton," said O'Gorman, "watch that knife. See that nobody touches it while I go and examine the meadows."

"Is Mr. Pratt dead, sir?" whimpered Mrs. Parton.

"Gad! I hadn't thought of that," said the general. "You'd better have a look at him; but mind! nobody is to touch that knife or they will confuse the scent."

He scrambled into the saddle and galloped away across the meadows in the direction of Thorpe; and, as Pembury listened to the diminuendo of the horse's hoofs, he was glad that he had not attempted to escape; for that was the direction in which he had meant to go, and he would surely have been overtaken.

As soon as the general was gone, Mrs. Parton, with many a terror-stricken glance over her shoulder, approached the corpse and held the lantern close to the dead face. Suddenly she stood up, trembling violently, for footsteps were audible coming down the avenue. A familiar voice reassured her.

"Is anything wrong, Mrs. Parton?" The question proceeded from one of the maids who had come in search of the elder woman, escorted by a young man, and the pair now came out into the circle of light.

"Good God!" ejaculated the man. "Who's that?"

"It's Mr. Pratt," replied Mrs. Parton. "He's been murdered."

The girl screamed, and then the two domestics approached on tiptoe, staring at the corpse with the fascination of horror.

"Don't touch that knife," said Mrs. Parton, for the man was about to pick it up. "The general's going to put the bloodhounds onto it."

"Is the general here, then?" asked the man; and, as he spoke, the drumming of hoofs, growing momentarily louder, answered him from the meadow.

O'Gorman reined in his horse as he perceived the group of servants gathered about the corpse. "Is he dead, Mrs. Parton?" he asked.

"I am afraid so, sir," was the reply.

"Ha! Somebody ought to go for the doctor; but not you, Bailey. I want you to get the hounds ready and wait with them at the top of the avenue until I call you."

He was off again into the Baysford meadows, and Bailey hurried away, leaving the two women staring at the body and talking in whispers.

Pembury's position was cramped and uncomfortable. He dared not move, hardly dared to breathe, for the women below him were not a dozen yards away; and it was with mingled feelings of relief and apprehension that he presently saw from his elevated station a group of lights approaching rapidly along the road from Baysford. Presently they were hidden by the trees, and then, after a brief interval, the whirr of wheels sounded on the drive and streaks of light on the tree-trunks announced the new arrivals. There were three bicycles, ridden respectively by Mr. Hanford, a police inspector and a sergeant; and, as they drew up, the general came thundering back into the avenue.

"Is Ellis with you?" he asked, as he pulled up.

"No, sir," was the reply. "He hadn't come in from Thorpe when we left. He's rather late tonight."

"Have you sent for a doctor?"

"Yes, sir, I've sent for Dr. Hills," said the inspector, resting his bicycle against the oak. Pembury could smell the reek of the lamp as he crouched. "Is Pratt dead?"

"Seems to be," replied O'Gorman, "but we'd better leave that to the doctor. There's the murderer's knife. Nobody has touched it. I'm going to fetch the bloodhounds now."

"Ah! that's the thing," said the inspector. "The man can't be far away." He rubbed his hands with a satisfied air as O'Gorman cantered away up the avenue.

In less than a minute there came out from the darkness the deep baying of a hound followed by quick footsteps on the gravel. Then into the circle of light emerged three sinister shapes, loose-limbed and gaunt, and two men advancing at a shambling trot.

"Here, inspector," shouted the general, "you take one; I can't hold 'em both."

The inspector ran forward and seized one of the leashes, and the general led his hound up to the knife, as it lay on the ground. Pembury, peering cautiously round the bough, watched the great brute with almost impersonal curiosity; noted its high poll, its wrinkled forehead and melancholy face as it stooped to snuff suspiciously at the prostrate knife.

For some moments the hound stood motionless, sniffing at the knife; then it turned away and walked to and fro with its muzzle to the ground. Suddenly it lifted its head, bayed loudly, lowered its muzzle and started forward between the oak and the elm, dragging the general after it at a run.

The inspector next brought his hound to the knife, and was soon bounding away to the tug of the leash in the general's wake.

"They don't make no mistakes, they don't," said Bailey, addressing the gratified sergeant, as he brought forward the third hound; "you'll see—?" But his remark was cut short by a violent jerk of the leash, and the next moment he was flying after the others, followed by Mr. Hanford.

The sergeant daintily picked the knife up by its ring, wrapped it in his handkerchief and bestowed it in his pocket. Then he ran off after the hounds.

Pembury smiled grimly. His scheme was working out admirably in spite of the unforeseen difficulties. If those confounded women would only go away, he could come down and take himself off while the course was clear. He listened to the baying of the hounds, gradually growing fainter in the increasing distance, and cursed the dilatoriness of the doctor. Confound the fellow! Didn't he realise that this was a case of life or death?

Suddenly his ear caught the tinkle of a bicycle bell; a fresh light appeared coming up the avenue and then a bicycle swept up swiftly to the scene of the tragedy, and a small elderly man jumped down by the side of the body. Giving his machine to Mrs. Parton, he stooped over the dead man, felt the wrist, pushed back an eyelid, held a match to the eye and then rose. "This is a shocking affair, Mrs. Parton," said he. "The poor fellow is quite dead. You had better help me to carry him to the house. If you two take the feet I will take the shoulders."

Pembury watched them raise the body and stagger away with it up the avenue. He heard their shuffling steps die away and the door of the house shut. And still he listened. From far away in the meadows came, at intervals, the baying of the hounds. Other sounds there was none. Presently the doctor would come back for his bicycle, but, for the moment, the coast was clear. Pembury rose stiffly. His hands had stuck to the tree where they had pressed against it, and they were still sticky and damp. Quickly he let himself down to the ground, listened again for a moment, and then, making a small circuit to avoid the lamplight, softly crossed the avenue and stole away across the Thorpe meadows.

The night was intensely dark, and not a soul was stirring in the meadows. He strode forward quickly, peering into the darkness and stopping now and again to listen; but no sound came to his ears, save the now faint baying of the distant hounds. Not far from his house, he remembered, was a deep ditch spanned by a wooden bridge, and towards this he now made his way; for he knew that his appearance was such as to convict him at a glance.

Arrived at the ditch, he stooped to wash his hands and wrists; and, as he bent forward, the knife fell from his breast-pocket into the shallow water at the margin. He groped for it, and, having found it, drove it deep into the mud as far out as he could reach. Then he wiped his hands on some water-weed, crossed the bridge and started homewards.

He approached his house from the rear, satisfied himself that his housekeeper was in the kitchen, and, letting himself in very quiet-ly with his key, went quickly up to his bedroom. Here he washed thoroughly—in the bath, so that he could get rid of the discoloured water—changed his clothes and packed those that he took off in a portmanteau.

By the time he had done this the gong sounded for supper. As he took his seat at the table, spruce and fresh in appearance, quietly cheerful in manner, he addressed his housekeeper. "I wasn't able to finish my business in London," he said. "I shall have to go up again tomorrow."

"Shall you come home the same day?" asked the housekeeper.

"Perhaps," was the reply, "and perhaps not. It will depend on cir-cumstances."

He did not say what the circumstances might be, nor did the housekeeper ask. Mr. Pembury was not addicted to confidences. He was an eminently discreet man: and discreet men say little.

PART 2. RIVAL SLEUTH-HOUNDS
(Related by Christopher Jervis, M.D.)

The half-hour that follows breakfast, when the fire has, so to speak, got into its stride, and the morning pipe throws up its clouds of in-cense, is, perhaps, the most agreeable in the whole day. Especially so when a sombre sky, brooding over the town, hints at streets pervaded by the chilly morning air, and hoots from protesting tugs upon the river tell of lingering mists, the legacy of the lately-vanished night.

The autumn morning was raw: the fire burned jovially. I thrust my slippered feet towards the blaze and meditated, on nothing in par-ticular, with cat-like enjoyment. Presently a disapproving grunt from Thorndyke attracted my attention, and I looked round lazily. He was extracting, with a pair of office shears, the readable portions of the morning paper, and had paused with a small cutting between his fin-ger and thumb. "Bloodhounds again," said he. "We shall be hearing presently of the revival of the ordeal by fire."

"And a deuced comfortable ordeal, too, on a morning like this," I said, stroking my legs ecstatically. "What is the case?"

He was about to reply when a sharp rat-tat from the little brass knocker announced a disturber of our peace. Thorndyke stepped over to the door and admitted a police inspector in uniform, and I stood up, and, presenting my dorsal aspect to the fire, prepared to combine bodily comfort with attention to business.

"I believe I am speaking to Dr. Thorndyke," said the officer, and, as Thorndyke nodded, he went on: "My name, sir, is Fox, Inspector Fox of the Baysford Police. Perhaps you've seen the morning paper?"

Thorndyke held up the cutting, and, placing a chair by the fire, asked the inspector if he had breakfasted.

"Thank you, sir, I have," replied Inspector Fox. "I came up to town by the late train last night so as to be here early, and stayed at an hotel. You see, from the paper, that we have had to arrest one of our own men. That's rather awkward, you know, sir."

"Very," agreed Thorndyke.

"Yes; it's bad for the force and bad for the public too. But we had to do it. There was no way out that we could see. Still, we should like the accused to have every chance, both for our sake and his own, so the chief constable thought he'd like to have your opinion on the case, and he thought that, perhaps, you might be willing to act for the defence."

"Let us have the particulars," said Thorndyke, taking a writing-pad from a drawer and dropping into his armchair. "Begin at the beginning," he added, "and tell us all you know."

"Well," said the inspector, after a preliminary cough, "to begin with the murdered man: his name is Pratt. He was a retired prison warder, and was employed as steward by General O'Gorman, who is a retired prison governor—you may have heard of him in connection with his pack of bloodhounds. Well, Pratt came down from London yesterday evening by a train arriving at Baysford at six-thirty. He was seen by the guard, the ticket collector and the outside porter. The porter saw him leave the station at six-thirty-seven. General O'Gorman's house is about half-a-mile from the station.

"At five minutes to seven the general and a gentleman named Hanford and the general's housekeeper, a Mrs. Parton, found Pratt lying dead in the avenue that leads up to the house. He had apparently been stabbed, for there was a lot of blood about, and a knife—a Norwegian knife—was lying on the ground near the body. Mrs. Parton had thought she heard someone in the avenue calling out for help, and, as Pratt was just due, she came out with a lantern. She met the general and Mr. Hanford, and all three seem to have caught sight of the body at the same moment. Mr. Hanford cycled down to us, at once, with the news; we sent for a doctor, and I went back with Mr. Hanford and took a sergeant with me.

"We arrived at twelve minutes past seven, and then the general, who had galloped his horse over the meadows each side of the avenue without having seen anybody, fetched out his bloodhounds and led them up to the knife. All three hounds took up the scent at once—I held the leash of one of them—and they took us across the meadows without a pause or a falter, over stiles and fences, along a lane, out into the town, and then, one after the other, they crossed the road in a bee-line to the police station, bolted in at the door, which stood open, and made straight for the desk, where a supernumerary officer, named El-lis, was writing. They made a rare to-do, struggling to get at him, and it was as much as we could manage to hold them back. As for Ellis, he turned as pale as a ghost."

"Was any one else in the room?" asked Thorndyke.

"Oh, yes. There were two constables and a messenger. We led the hounds up to them, but the brutes wouldn't take any notice of them. They wanted Ellis."

"And what did you do?"

"Why, we arrested Ellis, of course. Couldn't do anything else—especially with the general there."

"What had the general to do with it?" asked Thorndyke.

"He's a J.P. and a late governor of Dartmoor, and it was his hounds that had run the man down. But we must have arrested Ellis in any case."

"Is there anything against the accused man?"

"Yes, there is. He and Pratt were on distinctly unfriendly terms. They were old comrades, for Ellis was in the Civil Guard at Portland when Pratt was warder there—he was pensioned off from the service because he got his left forefinger chopped off—but lately they had had some unpleasantness about a woman, a parlour-maid of the general's. It seems that Ellis, who is a married man, paid the girl too much attention—or Pratt thought he did—and Pratt warned Ellis off the premises. Since then they had not been on speaking terms."

"And what sort of a man is Ellis?"

"A remarkably decent fellow he always seemed; quiet, steady, good-natured; I should have said he wouldn't have hurt a fly. We all liked him—better than we liked Pratt, in fact; poor Pratt was what you'd call an old soldier—sly, you know, sir—and a bit of a sneak."

"You searched and examined Ellis, of course?"

"Yes. There was nothing suspicious about him except that he had two purses. But he says he picked up one of them? a small, pigskin pouch—on the footpath of the Thorpe road yesterday afternoon; and there's no reason to disbelieve him. At any rate, the purse was not Pratt's."

Thorndyke made a note on his pad, and then asked: "There were no bloodstains or marks on his clothing?"

"No. His clothing was not marked or disarranged in any way."

"Any cuts, scratches or bruises on his person?"

"None whatever," replied the inspector.

"At what time did you arrest Ellis?"

"Half-past seven exactly."

"Have you ascertained what his movements were? Had he been near the scene of the murder?"

"Yes; he had been to Thorpe and would pass the gates of the avenue on his way back. And he was later than usual in returning, though not later than he has often been before."

"And now, as to the murdered man: has the body been examined?"

"Yes; I had Dr. Hills's report before I left. There were no less than seven deep knife-wounds, all on the left side of the back. There was a great deal of blood on the ground, and Dr. Hills thinks Pratt must have bled to death in a minute or two."

"Do the wounds correspond with the knife that was found?"

"I asked the doctor that, and he said 'Yes,' though he wasn't going to swear to any particular knife. However, that point isn't of much importance. The knife was covered with blood, and it was found close to the body."

"What has been done with it, by the way?" asked Thorndyke.

"The sergeant who was with me picked it up and rolled it in his handkerchief to carry in his pocket. I took it from him, just as it was, and locked it in a dispatch-box."

"Has the knife been recognised as Ellis's property?"

"No, sir, it has not."

"Were there any recognisable footprints or marks of a struggle?" Thorndyke asked.

The inspector grinned sheepishly. "I haven't examined the spot, of course, sir," said he, "but, after the general's horse and the bloodhounds and the general on foot and me and the gardener and the sergeant and Mr. Hanford had been over it twice, going and returning, why, you see, sir—?"

"Exactly, exactly," said Thorndyke. "Well, inspector, I shall be pleased to act for the defence; it seems to me that the case against Ellis is in some respects rather inconclusive."

The inspector was frankly amazed. "It certainly hadn't struck me in that light, sir," he said.

"No? Well, that is my view; and I think the best plan will be for me to come down with you and investigate matters on the spot."

The inspector assented cheerfully, and, when we had provided him with a newspaper, we withdrew to the laboratory to consult time-tables and prepare for the expedition.

"You are coming, I suppose, Jervis?" said Thorndyke.

"If I shall be of any use," I replied.

"Of course you will," said he. "Two heads are better than one, and, by the look of things, I should say that ours will be the only ones with any sense in them. We will take the research case, of course, and we may as well have a camera with us. I see there is a train from Charing Cross in twenty minutes."

For the first half-hour of the journey Thorndyke sat in his corner, alternately conning over his notes and gazing with thoughtful eyes out of the window. I could see that the case pleased him, and was careful not to break in upon his train of thought. Presently, however, he put away his notes and began to fill his pipe with a more companionable air, and then the inspector, who had been wriggling with impatience, opened fire.

"So you think, sir, that you see a way out for Ellis?"

"I think there is a case for the defence," replied Thorndyke. "In fact, I call the evidence against him rather flimsy."

The inspector gasped. "But the knife, sir? What about the knife?"

"Well," said Thorndyke, "what about the knife? Whose knife was it? You don't know. It was covered with blood. Whose blood? You don't know. Let us assume, for the sake of argument, that it was the murderer's knife. Then the blood on it was Pratt's blood. But if it was Pratt's blood, when the hounds had smelt it they should have led you to Pratt's body, for blood gives a very strong scent. But they did not. They ignored the body. The inference seems to be that the blood on the knife was not Pratt's blood."

The inspector took off his cap and gently scratched the back of his head. "You're perfectly right, sir," he said. "I'd never thought of that. None of us had."

"Then," pursued Thorndyke, "let us assume that the knife was Pratt's. If so, it would seem to have been used in self-defence. But this was a Norwegian knife, a clumsy tool—not a weapon at all—which takes an appreciable time to open and requires the use of two free hands. Now, had Pratt both hands free? Certainly not after the attack had commenced. There were seven wounds, all on the left side of the back; which indicates that he held the murderer locked in his arms and that the murderer's arms were around him. Also, incidentally, that the murderer is right-handed. But, still, let us assume that the knife was Pratt's. Then the blood on it was that of the murderer. Then the murderer must have been wounded. But Ellis was not wounded. Then Ellis is not the murderer. The knife doesn't help us at all."

The inspector puffed out his cheeks and blew softly. "This is getting out of my depth," he said. "Still, sir, you can't get over the bloodhounds. They tell us distinctly that the knife is Ellis's knife and I don't see any answer to that."

"There is no answer because there has been no statement. The bloodhounds have told you nothing. You have drawn certain inferences from their actions, but those inferences may be totally wrong and they are certainly not evidence."

"You don't seem to have much opinion of bloodhounds," the inspector remarked.

"As agents for the detection of crime," replied Thorndyke, "I regard them as useless. You cannot put a bloodhound in the witness-box. You can get no intelligible statement from it. If it possesses any knowledge, it has no means of communicating it. The fact is," he continued, "that the entire system of using bloodhounds for criminal detection is based on a fallacy. In the American plantations these animals were used with great success for tracking runaway slaves. But the slave was a known individual. All that was required was to ascertain his whereabouts. That is not the problem that is presented in the detection of a crime. The detective is not concerned in establishing the whereabouts of a known individual, but in discovering the identity of an unknown individual. And for this purpose bloodhounds are useless. They may discover such identity, but they cannot communicate their knowledge. If the criminal is unknown, they cannot identify him: if he is known, the police have no need of the bloodhound.

"To return to our present case," Thorndyke resumed, after a pause; "we have employed certain agents—the hounds—with whom we are not *en rapport*, as the spiritualists would say; and we have no 'medium.' The hound possesses a special sense—the olfactory—which in man is quite rudimentary. He thinks, so to speak, in terms of smell, and his thoughts are untranslatable to beings in whom the sense of smell is undeveloped. We have presented to the hound a knife, and he discovers in it certain odorous properties; he discovers similar or related odorous properties in a tract of land and a human individual—Ellis. We cannot verify his discoveries or ascertain their nature.

"What remains? All that we can say is that there appears to exist some odorous relation between the knife and the man Ellis. But until we can ascertain the nature of that relation, we cannot estimate its evidential value or bearing. All the other 'evidence' is the product of your imagination and that of the general. There is, at present, no case against Ellis."

"He must have been pretty close to the place when the murder happened," said the inspector.

"So, probably, were many other people," answered Thorndyke; "but had he time to wash and change? Because he would have needed it."

"I suppose he would," the inspector agreed dubiously.

"Undoubtedly. There were seven wounds which would have taken some time to inflict. Now we can't suppose that Pratt stood passively while the other man stabbed him. Indeed, as I have said, the position of the wounds shows that he did not. There was a struggle. The two men were locked together. One of the murderer's hands was against Pratt's back; probably both hands were, one clasping and the other stabbing. There must have been blood on one hand and probably on both. But you say there was no blood on Ellis, and there doesn't seem to have been time or opportunity for him to wash."

"Well, it's a mysterious affair," said the inspector; "but I don't see how you are going to get over the bloodhounds."

Thorndyke shrugged his shoulders impatiently. "The bloodhounds are an obsession," he said. "The whole problem really centres around the knife. The questions are, Whose knife was it? and what was the connection between it and Ellis? There is a problem, Jervis," he continued, turning to me, "that I submit for your consideration. Some of the possible solutions are exceedingly curious."

As we set out from Baysford station, Thorndyke looked at his watch and noted the time. "You will take us the way that Pratt went," he said.

"As to that," said the inspector, "he may have gone by the road or by the footpath; but there's very little difference in the distance."

Turning away from Baysford, we walked along the road westward, towards the village of Thorpe, and presently passed on our right a stile at the entrance to a footpath.

"That path," said the inspector, "crosses the avenue about halfway up. But we'd better keep to the road." A quarter of a mile further on we came to a pair of rusty iron gates one of which stood open, and, entering, we found ourselves in a broad drive bordered by two rows of trees, between the trunks of which a long stretch of pasture meadows could be seen on either hand. It was a fine avenue, and, late in the year as it was, the yellowing foliage clustered thickly overhead.

When we had walked about a hundred and fifty yards from the gates, the inspector halted.

"This is the place," he said; and Thorndyke again noted the time.

"Nine minutes exactly," said he. "Then Pratt arrived here about fourteen minutes to seven, and his body was found at five minutes to seven—nine minutes after his arrival. The murderer couldn't have been far away then."

"No, it was a pretty fresh scent," replied the inspector. "You'd like to see the body first, I think you said, sir?"

"Yes; and the knife, if you please."

"I shall have to send down to the station for that. It's locked up in the office."

He entered the house, and, having dispatched a messenger to the police station, came out and conducted us to the outbuilding where the corpse had been deposited. Thorndyke made a rapid examination of the wounds and the holes in the clothing, neither of which presented anything particularly suggestive. The weapon used had evidently been a thick-backed, single-edged knife similar to the one described, and the discolouration around the wounds indicated that the weapon had a definite shoulder like that of a Norwegian knife, and that it had been driven in with savage violence.

"Do you find anything that throws any light on the case?" the inspector asked, when the examination was concluded.

"That is impossible to say until we have seen the knife," replied Thorndyke; "but while we are waiting for it, we may as well go and look at the scene of the tragedy. These are Pratt's boots, I think?" He lifted a pair of stout laced boots from the table and turned them up to inspect the soles.

"Yes, those are his boots," replied Fox, "and pretty easy they'd have been to track, if the case had been the other way about. Those Blakey's protectors are as good as a trademark."

"We'll take them, at any rate," said Thorndyke; and, the inspector having taken the boots from him, we went out and retraced our steps down the avenue.

The place where the murder had occurred was easily identified by a large dark stain on the gravel at one side of the drive, half-way between two trees—an ancient pollard hornbeam and an elm. Next to the elm was a pollard oak with a squat, warty bole about seven feet high, and three enormous limbs, of which one slanted half-way across the avenue; and between these two trees the ground was covered with the tracks of men and hounds superimposed upon the hoof-prints of a horse.

"Where was the knife found?" Thorndyke asked.

The inspector indicated a spot near the middle of the drive, almost opposite the hornbeam and Thorndyke, picking up a large stone, laid it on the spot. Then he surveyed the scene thoughtfully, looking up and down the drive and at the trees that bordered it, and, finally, walked slowly to the space between the elm and the oak, scanning the ground as he went. "There is no dearth of footprints," he remarked grimly, as he looked down at the trampled earth.

"No, but the question is, whose are they?" said the inspector.

"Yes, that is the question," agreed Thorndyke; "and we will begin the solution by identifying those of Pratt."

"I don't see how that will help us," said the inspector. "We know he was here."

Thorndyke looked at him in surprise, and I must confess that the foolish remark astonished me too, accustomed as I was to the quick-witted officers from Scotland Yard.

"The hue and cry procession," remarked Thorndyke, "seems to have passed out between the elm and the oak; elsewhere the ground seems pretty clear." He walked round the elm, still looking earnestly at the ground, and presently continued: "Now here, in the soft earth bordering the turf, are the prints of a pair of smallish feet wearing pointed boots; a rather short man, evidently, by the size of foot and length of stride, and he doesn't seem to have belonged to the procession.

"But I don't see any of Pratt's; he doesn't seem to have come off the hard gravel." He continued to walk slowly towards the hornbeam with his eyes fixed on the ground. Suddenly he halted and stooped with an eager look at the earth; and, as Fox and I approached, he stood up and pointed. "Pratt's footprints—faint and fragmentary, but unmistakable. And now, inspector, you see their importance. They furnish the time factor in respect of the other footprints. Look at this one and then look at that." He pointed from one to another of the faint impressions of the dead man's foot.

"You mean that there are signs of a struggle?" said Fox.

"I mean more than that," replied Thorndyke. "Here is one of Pratt's footprints treading into the print of a small, pointed foot; and there at the edge of the gravel is another of Pratt's nearly obliterated by the tread of a pointed foot. Obviously the first pointed footprint was made before Pratt's, and the second one after his; and the necessary inference is that the owner of the pointed foot was here at the same time as Pratt."

"Then he must have been the murderer!" exclaimed Fox.

"Presumably," answered Thorndyke; "but let us see whither he went. You notice, in the first place, that the man stood close to this tree"—he indicated the hornbeam—"and that he went towards the elm. Let us follow him. He passes the elm, you see, and you will observe that these tracks form a regular series leading from the hornbeam and not mixed up with the marks of the struggle. They were, therefore, probably made after the murder had been perpetrated. You will also notice that they pass along the backs of the trees—outside the avenue, that is; what does that suggest to you?"

"It suggests to me," I said, when the inspector had shaken his head hopelessly, "that there was possibly someone in the avenue when the man was stealing off."

"Precisely," said Thorndyke. "The body was found not more than nine minutes after Pratt arrived here. But the murder must have taken some time. Then the housekeeper thought she heard someone calling and came out with a lantern, and, at the same time, the general and Mr. Hanford came up the drive. The suggestion is that the man sneaked along outside the trees to avoid being seen. However, let us follow the tracks. They pass the elm and they pass on behind the next tree; but wait! There is something odd here." He passed behind the great pollard oak and looked down at the soft earth by its roots.

"Here is a pair of impressions much deeper than the rest, and they are not a part of the track since their toes point towards the tree. What do you make of that?" Without waiting for an answer he began closely to scan the bole of the tree and especially a large, warty protuberance about three feet from the ground. On the bark above this was a vertical mark, as if something had scraped down the tree, and from the wart itself a dead twig had been newly broken off and lay upon the ground. Pointing to these marks Thorndyke set his foot on the protuberance, and, springing up, brought his eye above the level of the crown, whence the great boughs branched off.

"Ah!" he exclaimed. "Here is something much more definite."

With the aid of another projection, he scrambled up into the crown of the tree, and, having glanced quickly round, beckoned to us. I stepped up on the projecting lump and, as my eyes rose above the crown, I perceived the brown, shiny impression of a hand on the edge. Climbing into the crown, I was quickly followed by the inspector, and we both stood up by Thorndyke between the three boughs. From where we stood we looked on the upper side of the great limb that swept out across the avenue; and there on its lichen-covered surface, we saw the imprints in reddish-brown of a pair of open hands.

"You notice," said Thorndyke, leaning out upon the bough, "that he is a short man; I cannot conveniently place my hands so low. You also note that he has both forefingers intact, and so is certainly not Ellis."

"If you mean to say, sir, that these marks were made by the murderer," said Fox, "I say it's impossible. Why, that would mean that he was here looking down at us when we were searching for him with the hounds. The presence of the hounds proves that this man could not have been the murderer."

"On the contrary," said Thorndyke, "the presence of this man with bloody hands confirms the other evidence, which all indicates that the hounds were never on the murderer's trail at all. Come now, inspector, I put it to you: Here is a murdered man; the murderer has almost certainly blood upon his hands; and here is a man with bloody hands, lurking in a tree within a few feet of the corpse and within a few minutes of its discovery (as is shown by the footprints); what are the reasonable probabilities?"

"But you are forgetting the bloodhounds, sir, and the murderer's knife," urged the inspector.

"Tut, tut, man!" exclaimed Thorndyke; "those bloodhounds are a positive obsession. But I see a sergeant coming up the drive, with the knife, I hope. Perhaps that will solve the riddle for us."

The sergeant, who carried a small dispatch-box, halted opposite the tree in some surprise while we descended, when he came forward with a military salute and handed the box to the inspector, who forthwith unlocked it, and, opening the lid, displayed an object wrapped in a pocket-handkerchief.

"There is the knife, sir," said he, "just as I received it. The handkerchief is the sergeant's."

Thorndyke unrolled the handkerchief and took from it a large-sized Norwegian knife, which he looked at critically and then handed to me. While I was inspecting the blade, he shook out the handkerchief and, having looked it over on both sides, turned to the sergeant.

"At what time did you pick up this knife?" he asked.

"About seven-fifteen, sir; directly after the hounds had started. I was careful to pick it up by the ring, and I wrapped it in the handkerchief at once."

"Seven-fifteen," said Thorndyke. "Less than half-an-hour after the murder. That is very singular. Do you observe the state of this handkerchief? There is not a mark on it. Not a trace of any bloodstain; which proves that when the knife was picked up, the blood on it was already dry. But things dry slowly, if they dry at all, in the saturated air of an autumn evening. The appearances seem to suggest that the blood on the knife was dry when it was thrown down. By the way, sergeant, what do you scent your handkerchief with?"

"Scent, sir!" exclaimed the astonished officer in indignant accents; "me scent my handkerchief! No, sir, certainly not. Never used scent in my life, sir."

Thorndyke held out the handkerchief, and the sergeant sniffed at it incredulously. "It certainly does seem to smell of scent," he admitted, "but it must be the knife." The same idea having occurred to me, I applied the handle of the knife to my nose and instantly detected the sickly-sweet odour of musk.

"The question is," said the inspector, when the two articles had been tested by us all, "was it the knife that scented the handkerchief or the handkerchief that scented the knife?"

"You heard what the sergeant said," replied Thorndyke. "There was no scent on the handkerchief when the knife was wrapped in it. Do you know, inspector, this scent seems to me to offer a very curious suggestion. Consider the facts of the case: the distinct trail leading straight to Ellis, who is, nevertheless, found to be without a scratch or a spot of blood; the inconsistencies in the case that I pointed out in the train, and now this knife, apparently dropped with dried blood on it and scented with musk.

"To me it suggests a carefully-planned, coolly-premeditated crime. The murderer knew about the general's bloodhounds and made use of them as a blind. He planted this knife, smeared with blood and tainted with musk, to furnish a scent. No doubt some object, also scented with musk, would be drawn over the ground to give the trail. It is only a suggestion, of course, but it is worth considering."

"But, sir," the inspector objected eagerly, "if the murderer had handled the knife, it would have scented him too."

"Exactly; so, as we are assuming that the man is not a fool, we may assume that he did not handle it. He will have left it here in readiness, hidden in some place whence he could knock it down, say, with a stick, without touching it."

"Perhaps in this very tree, sir," suggested the sergeant, pointing to the oak.

"No," said Thorndyke, "he would hardly have hidden in the tree where the knife had been. The hounds might have scented the place instead of following the trail at once. The most likely hiding-place for the knife is the one nearest the spot where it was found." He walked over to the stone that marked the spot, and looking round, continued: "You see, that hornbeam is much the nearest, and its flat crown would be very convenient for the purpose—easily reached even by a short man, as he appears to be. Let us see if there are any traces of it. Perhaps you will give me a 'back up', sergeant, as we haven't a ladder."

The sergeant assented with a faint grin, and stooping beside the tree in an attitude suggesting the game of leapfrog, placed his hands firmly on his knees. Grasping a stout branch, Thorndyke swung himself up on the sergeant's broad back, whence he looked down into the crown of the tree. Then, parting the branches, he stepped onto the ledge and disappeared into the central hollow.

When he re-appeared he held in his hands two very singular objects: a pair of iron crucible-tongs and an artist's brush-case of black-japanned tin. The former article he handed down to me, but the brush-case he held carefully by its wire handle as he dropped to the ground.

"The significance of these things is, I think, obvious," he said. "The tongs were used to handle the knife with and the case to carry it in, so that it should not scent his clothes or bag. It was very carefully planned."

"If that is so," said the inspector, "the inside of the case ought to smell of musk."

"No doubt," said Thorndyke; "but before we open it, there is a rather important matter to be attended to. Will you give me the Vitogen powder, Jervis?"

I opened the canvas-covered "research case" and took from it an object like a diminutive pepper-caster—an iodo-form dredger in fact—and handed it to him. Grasping the brush-case by its wire handle, he sprinkled the pale yellow powder from the dredger freely all round the pull-off lid, tapping the top with his knuckles to make the fine particles spread. Then he blew off the superfluous powder, and the two police officers gave a simultaneous gasp of joy; for now, on the black background, there stood out plainly a number of finger-prints, so clear and distinct that the ridge-pattern could be made out with perfect ease.

"These will probably be his right hand," said Thorndyke. "Now for the left." He treated the body of the case in the same way, and, when he had blown off the powder, the entire surface was spotted with yellow, oval impressions. "Now, Jervis," said he, "if you will put on a glove and pull off the lid, we can test the inside."

There was no difficulty in getting the lid off, for the shoulder of the case had been smeared with Vaseline—apparently to produce an airtight joint—and, as it separated with a hollow sound, a faint, musky odour exhaled from its interior.

"The remainder of the inquiry," said Thorndyke, when I pushed the lid on again, "will be best conducted at the police station, where, also, we can photograph these fingerprints."

"The shortest way will be across the meadows," said Fox; "the way the hounds went."

By this route we accordingly travelled, Thorndyke carrying the brush-case tenderly by its handle.

"I don't quite see where Ellis comes in in this job," said the inspector, as we walked along, "if the fellow had a grudge against Pratt. They weren't chums."

"I think I do," said Thorndyke. "You say that both men were prison officers at Portland at the same time. Now doesn't it seem likely that this is the work of some old convict who had been identified—and perhaps blackmailed—by Pratt, and possibly by Ellis too? That is where the value of the finger-prints comes in. If he is an old 'lag' his prints will be at Scotland Yard. Otherwise they are not of much value as a clue."

"That's true, sir," said the inspector. "I suppose you want to see Ellis."

"I want to see that purse that you spoke of, first," replied Thorndyke. "That is probably the other end of the clue."

As soon as we arrived at the station, the inspector unlocked a safe and brought out a parcel. "These are Ellis's things," said he, as he unfastened it, "and that is the purse."

He handed Thorndyke a small pigskin pouch, which my colleague

39

opened, and having smelt the inside, passed to me. The odour of musk was plainly perceptible, especially in the small compartment at the back.

"It has probably tainted the other contents of the parcel," said Thorndyke, sniffing at each article in turn, "but my sense of smell is not keen enough to detect any scent. They all seem odourless to me, whereas the purse smells quite distinctly. Shall we have Ellis in now?"

The sergeant took a key from a locked drawer and departed for the cells, whence he presently re-appeared accompanied by the prisoner—a stout, burly man, in the last stage of dejection.

"Come, cheer up, Ellis," said the inspector. "Here's Dr. Thorndyke come down to help us and he wants to ask you one or two questions."

Ellis looked piteously at Thorndyke, and exclaimed: "I know nothing whatever about this affair, sir, I swear to God I don't."

"I never supposed you did," said Thorndyke. "But there are one or two things that I want you to tell me. To begin with, that purse: where did you find it?"

"On the Thorpe road, sir. It was lying in the middle of the footway."

"Had any one else passed the spot lately? Did you meet or pass anyone?"

"Yes, sir, I met a labourer about a minute before I saw the purse. I can't imagine why he didn't see it."

"Probably because it wasn't there," said Thorndyke. "Is there a hedge there?"

"Yes, sir; a hedge on a low bank."

"Ha! Well, now, tell me: is there any one about here whom you knew when you and Pratt were together at Portland? Any old lag—to put it bluntly—whom you and Pratt have been putting the screw on."

"No, sir, I swear there isn't. But I wouldn't answer for Pratt. He had a rare memory for faces."

Thorndyke reflected. "Were there any escapes from Portland in your time?" he asked.

"Only one—a man named Dobbs. He made off to the sea in a sudden fog and he was supposed to be drowned. His clothes washed up on the Bill, but not his body. At any rate, he was never heard of again."

"Thank you, Ellis. Do you mind my taking your fingerprints?"

"Certainly not, sir," was the almost eager reply; and the office inking-pad being requisitioned, a rough set of finger-prints was produced; and when Thorndyke had compared them with those on the brush-case and found no resemblance, Ellis returned to his cell in quite buoyant spirits.

Having made several photographs of the strange fingerprints, we returned to town that evening, taking the negatives with us; and while we waited for our train, Thorndyke gave a few parting injunctions to the inspector. "Remember," he said, "that the man must have washed his hands before he could appear in public. Search the banks of every pond, ditch and stream in the neighbourhood for footprints like those in the avenue; and, if you find any, search the bottom of the water thoroughly, for he is quite likely to have dropped the knife into the mud."

The photographs, which we handed in at Scotland Yard that same night, enabled the experts to identify the fingerprints as those of Francis Dobbs, an escaped convict. The two photographs—profile and full-face—which were attached to his record, were sent down to Baysford with a description of the man, and were, in due course, identified with a somewhat mysterious individual, who passed by the name of Rufus Pembury and who had lived in the neighbourhood as a private gentleman for some two years. But Rufus Pembury was not to be found either at his genteel house or elsewhere. All that was known was, that on the day after the murder, he had converted his entire "personalty" into "bearer securities," and then vanished from mortal ken. Nor has he ever been heard of to this day.

"And, between ourselves," said Thorndyke, when we were discussing the case some time after, "he deserved to escape. It was clearly a case of blackmail, and to kill a blackmailer—when you have no other defence against him—is hardly murder. As to Ellis, he could never have been convicted, and Dobbs, or Pembury, must have known it. But he would have been committed to the Assizes, and that would have given time for all traces to disappear. No, Dobbs was a man of courage, ingenuity and resource; and, above all, he knocked the bottom out of the great bloodhound superstition."

A Message from the Deep Sea

The Whitechapel Road, though redeemed by scattered relics of a more picturesque past from the utter desolation of its neighbour the Commercial Road, is hardly a gay thoroughfare. Especially at its eastern end, where its sordid modernity seems to reflect the colourless lives of its inhabitants, does its grey and dreary length depress the spirits of the wayfarer. But the longest and dullest road can be made delightful by sprightly discourse seasoned with wit and wisdom, and so it was that, as I walked westward by the side of my friend John Thorndyke, the long, monotonous road seemed all too short.

We had been to the London Hospital to see a remarkable case of acromegaly, and, as we returned, we discussed this curious affection, and the allied condition of gigantism, in all their bearings, from the origin of the "Gibson chin" to the physique of Og, King of Bashan.

"It would have been interesting," Thorndyke remarked as we passed up Aldgate High Street, "to have put one's finger into His Majesty's pituitary fossa—after his decease, of course. By the way, here is Harrow Alley; you remember Defoe's description of the dead-cart waiting out here, and the ghastly procession coming down the alley." He took my arm and led me up the narrow thoroughfare as far as the sharp turn by the "Star and Still" public-house, where we turned to look back.

"I never pass this place," he said musingly, "but I seem to hear the clang of the bell and the dismal cry of the carter—"

He broke off abruptly. Two figures had suddenly appeared framed in the archway, and now advanced at headlong speed. One, who led, was a stout, middle-aged Jewess, very breathless and dishevelled; the other was a well-dressed young man, hardly less agitated than his companion. As they approached, the young man suddenly recognised my colleague, and accosted him in agitated tones.

"I've just been sent for to a case of murder or suicide. Would you mind looking at it for me, sir? It's my first case, and I feel rather nervous."

Here the woman darted back, and plucked the young doctor by the arm.

"Hurry! hurry!" she exclaimed, "don't stop to talk." Her face was as white as lard, and shiny with sweat; her lips twitched, her hands shook, and she stared with the eyes of a frightened child.

"Of course I will come, Hart," said Thorndyke; and, turning back, we followed the woman as she elbowed her way frantically among the foot-passengers.

"Have you started in practice here?" Thorndyke asked as we hurried along.

"No, sir," replied Dr. Hart; "I am an assistant. My principal is the police-surgeon, but he is out just now. It's very good of you to come with me, sir."

"Tut, tut," rejoined Thorndyke. "I am just coming to see that you do credit to my teaching. That looks like the house."

We had followed our guide into a side street, halfway down which we could see a knot of people clustered round a doorway. They watched us as we approached, and drew aside to let us enter. The woman whom we were following rushed into the passage with the same headlong haste with which she had traversed the streets, and so up the stairs. But as she neared the top of the flight she slowed down suddenly, and began to creep up on tiptoe with noiseless and hesitating steps. On the landing she turned to face us, and pointing a shaking forefinger at the door of the back room, whispered almost inaudibly, "She's in there," and then sank half-fainting on the bottom stair of the next flight.

I laid my hand on the knob of the door, and looked back at Thorndyke. He was coming slowly up the stairs, closely scrutinizing floor, walls, and handrail as he came. When he reached the landing, I turned the handle, and we entered the room together, closing the door after us. The blind was still down, and in the dim, uncertain light nothing out of the common was, at first, to be seen. The shabby little room looked trim and orderly enough, save for a heap of cast-off feminine clothing piled upon a chair. The bed appeared undisturbed except by the half-seen shape of its occupant, and the quiet face, dimly visible in its shadowy corner, might have been that of a sleeper but for its utter stillness and for a dark stain on the pillow by its side.

Dr. Hart stole on tiptoe to the bedside, while Thorndyke drew up the blind; and as the garish daylight poured into the room, the young surgeon fell back with a gasp of horror.

"Good God!" he exclaimed; "poor creature! But this is a frightful thing, sir!"

The light streamed down upon the white face of a handsome girl of twenty-five, a face peaceful, placid, and beautiful with the austere and almost unearthly beauty of the youthful dead. The lips were slightly parted, the eyes half closed and drowsy, shaded with sweeping lashes; and a wealth of dark hair in massive plaits served as a foil to the translucent skin.

Our friend had drawn back the bedclothes a few inches, and now there was revealed, beneath the comely face, so serene and inscrutable, and yet so dreadful in its fixity and waxen pallor, a horrible, yawning wound that almost divided the shapely neck.

Thorndyke looked down with stern pity at the plump white face.

"It was savagely done," said he, "and yet mercifully, by reason of its very savagery. She must have died without waking."

"The brute!" exclaimed Hart, clenching his fists and turning crimson with wrath. "The infernal cowardly beast! He shall hang! By God, he shall hang!" In his fury the young fellow shook his fists in the air, even as the moisture welled up into his eyes.

Thorndyke touched him on the shoulder. "That is what we are here for, Hart," said he. "Get out your notebook;" and with this he bent down over the dead girl.

At the friendly reproof the young surgeon pulled himself together, and, with open notebook, commenced his investigation, while I, at Thorndyke's request, occupied myself in making a plan of the room, with a description of its contents and their arrangements. But this occupation did not prevent me from keeping an eye on Thorndyke's movements, and presently I suspended my labours to watch him as, with his pocket-knife, he scraped together some objects that he had found on the pillow.

"What do you make of this?" he asked, as I stepped over to his side. He pointed with the blade to a tiny heap of what looked like silver sand, and, as I looked more closely, I saw that similar particles were sprinkled on other parts of the pillow.

"Silver sand!" I exclaimed. "I don't understand at all how it can have got there. Do you?"

Thorndyke shook his head. "We will consider the explanation

later," was his reply. He had produced from his pocket a small metal box which he always carried, and which contained such requisites as cover-slips, capillary tubes, moulding wax, and other "diagnostic materials." He now took from it a seed-envelope, into which he neatly shovelled the little pinch of sand with his knife. He had closed the envelope, and was writing a pencilled description on the outside, when we were startled by a cry from Hart.

"Good God, sir! Look at this! It was done by a woman!"

He had drawn back the bedclothes, and was staring aghast at the dead girl's left hand. It held a thin tress of long, red hair.

Thorndyke hastily pocketed his specimen, and, stepping round the little bedside table, bent over the hand with knitted brows. It was closed, though not tightly clenched, and when an attempt was made gently to separate the fingers, they were found to be as rigid as the fingers of a wooden hand. Thorndyke stooped yet more closely, and, taking out his lens, scrutinized the wisp of hair throughout its entire length.

"There is more here than meets the eye at the first glance," he remarked. "What say you, Hart?" He held out his lens to his quondam pupil, who was about to take it from him when the door opened, and three men entered. One was a police-inspector, the second appeared to be a plain-clothes officer, while the third was evidently the divisional surgeon.

"Friends of yours, Hart?" inquired the latter, regarding us with some disfavour.

Thorndyke gave a brief explanation of our presence to which the newcomer rejoined:

"Well, sir, your *locus standi* here is a matter for the inspector. My assistant was not authorized to call in outsiders. You needn't wait, Hart."

With this he proceeded to his inspection, while Thorndyke withdrew the pocket-thermometer that he had slipped under the body, and took the reading.

The inspector, however, was not disposed to exercise the prerogative at which the surgeon had hinted; for an expert has his uses.

"How long should you say she'd been dead, sir?" he asked affably.

"About ten hours," replied Thorndyke.

The inspector and the detective simultaneously looked at their watches. "That fixes it at two o'clock this morning," said the former. "What's that, sir?"

The surgeon was pointing to the wisp of hair in the dead girl's hand.

"My word!" exclaimed the inspector. "A woman, eh? She must be a tough customer. This looks like a soft job for you, sergeant."

"Yes," said the detective. "That accounts for that box with the hassock on it at the head of the bed. She had to stand on them to reach over. But she couldn't have been very tall."

"She must have been mighty strong, though," said the inspector; "why, she has nearly cut the poor wench's head off." He moved round to the head of the bed, and, stooping over, peered down at the gaping wound. Suddenly he began to draw his hand over the pillow, and then rub his fingers together. "Why," he exclaimed, "there's sand on the pillow—silver sand! Now, how can that have come there?"

The surgeon and the detective both came round to verify this discovery, and an earnest consultation took place as to its meaning.

"Did you notice it, sir?" the inspector asked Thorndyke.

"Yes," replied the latter; "it's an unaccountable thing, isn't it?"

"I don't know that it is, either," said the detective, he ran over to the washstand, and then uttered a grunt of satisfaction. "It's quite a simple matter, after all, you see," he said, glancing complacently at my colleague. "There's a ball of sand-soap on the washstand, and the basin is full of blood-stained water. You see, she must have washed the blood off her hands, and off the knife, too—a pretty cool customer she must be—and she used the sand-soap. Then, while she was drying her hands, she must have stood over the head of the bed, and let the sand fall on to the pillow. I think that's clear enough."

"Admirably clear," said Thorndyke; "and what do you suppose was the sequence of events?"

The gratified detective glanced round the room. "I take it," said he, "that the deceased read herself to sleep. There is a book on the table by the bed, and a candlestick with nothing in it but a bit of burnt wick at the bottom of the socket. I imagine that the woman came in quietly, lit the gas, put the box and the hassock at the bed-head, stood on them, and cut her victim's throat. Deceased must have waked up and clutched the murderess's hair—though there doesn't seem to have been much of a struggle; but no doubt she died almost at once. Then the murderess washed her hands, cleaned the knife, tidied up the bed a bit, and went away. That's about how things happened, I think, but how she got in without anyone hearing, and how she got out, and where she went to, are the things that we've got to find out."

"Perhaps," said the surgeon, drawing the bedclothes over the corpse, "we had better have the landlady in and make a few inquiries." He glanced significantly at Thorndyke, and the inspector coughed behind his hand. My colleague, however, chose to be obtuse to these hints: opening the door, he turned the key backwards and forwards several times, drew it out, examined it narrowly, and replaced it.

"The landlady is outside on the landing," he remarked, holding the door open.

Thereupon the inspector went out, and we all followed to hear the result of his inquiries.

"Now, Mrs. Goldstein," said the officer, opening his notebook, "I want you to tell us all that you know about this affair, and about the girl herself. What was her name?"

The landlady, who had been joined by a white-faced, tremulous man, wiped her eyes, and replied in a shaky voice: "Her name, poor child, was Minna Adler. She was a German. She came from Bremen about two years ago. She had no friends in England—no relatives, I mean. She was a waitress at a restaurant in Fenchurch Street, and a good, quiet, hard-working girl."

"When did you discover what had happened?"

"About eleven o'clock. I thought she had gone to work as usual, but my husband noticed from the back yard that her blind was still down. So I went up and knocked, and when I got no answer, I opened the door and went in, and then I saw—" Here the poor soul, overcome by the dreadful recollection, burst into hysterical sobs.

"Her door was unlocked, then; did she usually lock it?"

"I think so," sobbed Mrs. Goldstein. "The key was always inside."

"And the street door; was that secure when you came down this morning?"

"It was shut. We don't bolt it because some of the lodgers come home rather late."

"And now tell us, had she any enemies? Was there anyone who had a grudge against her?"

"No, no, poor child! Why should anyone have a grudge against her? No, she had no quarrel—no real quarrel—with anyone; not even with Miriam."

"Miriam!" inquired the inspector. "Who is she?"

"That was nothing," interposed the man hastily. "That was not a quarrel."

"Just a little unpleasantness, I suppose, Mr. Goldstein?" suggested the inspector.

"Just a little foolishness about a young man," said Mr. Goldstein. "That was all. Miriam was a little jealous. But it was nothing."

"No, no. Of course. We all know that young women are apt to—"

A soft footstep had been for some time audible, slowly descending the stair above, and at this moment a turn of the staircase brought the newcomer into view. And at that vision the inspector stopped short as if petrified, and a tense, startled silence fell upon us all. Down the remaining stairs there advanced towards us a young woman, powerful though short, wild-eyed, dishevelled, horror-stricken, and of a ghastly pallor: and her hair was a fiery red.

Stock still and speechless we all stood as this apparition came slowly towards us; but suddenly the detective slipped back into the room, closing the door after him, to reappear a few moments later holding a small paper packet, which, after a quick glance at the inspector, he placed in his breast pocket.

"This is my daughter Miriam that we spoke about, gentlemen," said Mr. Goldstein. "Miriam, those are the doctors and the police."

The girl looked at us from one to the other. "You have seen her, then," she said in a strange, muffled voice, and added: "She isn't dead, is she? Not really dead?" The question was asked in a tone at once coaxing and despairing, such as a distracted mother might use over the corpse of her child. It filled me with vague discomfort, and, unconsciously, I looked round towards Thorndyke.

To my surprise he had vanished.

Noiselessly backing towards the head of the stairs, where I could command a view of the hall, or passage, I looked down, and saw him in the act of reaching up to a shelf behind the street door. He caught my eye, and beckoned, whereupon I crept away unnoticed by the party on the landing. When I reached the hall, he was wrapping up three small objects, each in a separate cigarette-paper; and I noticed that he handled them with more than ordinary tenderness.

"We didn't want to see that poor devil of a girl arrested," said he, as he deposited the three little packets gingerly in his pocket-box. "Let us be off." He opened the door noiselessly, and stood for a moment, turning the latch backwards and forwards, and closely examining its bolt.

I glanced up at the shelf behind the door. On it were two flat china candlesticks, in one of which I had happened to notice, as we came in, a short end of candle lying in the tray, and I now looked to see if that was what Thorndyke had annexed; but it was still there.

I followed my colleague out into the street, and for some time we walked on without speaking. "You guessed what the sergeant had in that paper, of course," said Thorndyke at length.

"Yes. It was the hair from the dead woman's hand; and I thought that he had much better have left it there."

"Undoubtedly. But that is the way in which well-meaning policemen destroy valuable evidence. Not that it matters much in this particular instance; but it might have been a fatal mistake."

"Do you intend to take any active part in this case?" I asked.

"That depends on circumstances. I have collected some evidence, but what it is worth I don't yet know. Neither do I know whether the police have observed the same set of facts; but I need not say that I shall do anything that seems necessary to assist the authorities. That is a matter of common citizenship."

The inroads made upon our time by the morning's adventures made it necessary that we should go each about his respective business without delay; so, after a perfunctory lunch at a tea-shop, we separated, and I did not see my colleague again until the day's work was finished, and I turned into our chambers just before dinner-time.

Here I found Thorndyke seated at the table, and evidently full of business. A microscope stood close by, with a condenser throwing a spot of light on to a pinch of powder that had been sprinkled on to the slide; his collecting-box lay open before him, and he was engaged, rather mysteriously, in squeezing a thick white cement from a tube on to three little pieces of moulding-wax.

"Useful stuff, this Fortafix," he remarked; "it makes excellent casts, and saves the trouble and mess of mixing plaster, which is a consideration for small work like this. By the way, if you want to know what was on that poor girl's pillow, just take a peep through the microscope. It is rather a pretty specimen."

I stepped across, and applied my eye to the instrument. The specimen was, indeed, pretty in more than a technical sense. Mingled with crystalline grains of quartz, glassy spicules, and water-worn fragments of coral, were a number of lovely little shells, some of the texture of fine porcelain, others like blown Venetian glass.

"These are *Foraminifera!*" I exclaimed.

"Yes."

"Then it is not silver sand, after all?"

"Certainly not."

"But what is it, then?"

Thorndyke smiled. "It is a message to us from the deep sea, Jervis; from the floor of the Eastern Mediterranean."

"And can you read the message?"

"I think I can," he replied, "but I shall know soon, I hope."

I looked down the microscope again, and wondered what message these tiny shells had conveyed to my friend. Deep-sea sand on a dead woman's pillow! What could be more incongruous? What possible connection could there be between this sordid crime in the east of London and the deep bed of the "tideless sea"?

Meanwhile Thorndyke squeezed out more cement on to the three little pieces of moulding-wax (which I suspected to be the objects that I had seen him wrapping up with such care in the hall of the Goldsteins' house); then, laying one of them down on a glass slide, with its cemented side uppermost, he stood the other two upright on either side of it. Finally he squeezed out a fresh load of the thick cement, apparently to bind the three objects together, and carried the slide very carefully to a cupboard, where he deposited it, together with the envelope containing the sand and the slide from the stage of the microscope.

He was just locking the cupboard when a sharp rat-tat on our knocker sent him hurriedly to the door. A messenger-boy, standing on the threshold, held out a dirty envelope.

"Mr. Goldstein kept me a awful long time, sir," said he; "I haven't been a-loitering."

Thorndyke took the envelope over to the gas-light, and, opening it, drew forth a sheet of paper, which he scanned quickly and almost eagerly; and, though his face remained as inscrutable as a mask of stone, I felt a conviction that the paper had told him something that he wished to know.

The boy having been sent on his way rejoicing, Thorndyke turned to the bookshelves, along which he ran his eye thoughtfully until it alighted on a shabbily-bound volume near one end. This he reached down, and as he laid it open on the table, I glanced at it, and was surprised to observe that it was a bi-lingual work, the opposite pages being apparently in Russian and Hebrew.

"The Old Testament in Russian and Yiddish," he remarked, noting my surprise. "I am going to get Polton to photograph a couple of specimen pages—is that the postman or a visitor?"

It turned out to be the postman, and as Thorndyke extracted from the letter-box a blue official envelope, he glanced significantly at me.

"This answers your question, I think, Jervis," said he. "Yes; coroner's subpoena and a very civil letter: 'sorry to trouble you, but I had no choice under the circumstances'—of course he hadn't—'Dr. Davidson has arranged to make the autopsy tomorrow at 4 p.m., and I should be glad if you could be present. The mortuary is in Barker Street, next to the school.' Well, we must go, I suppose, though Davidson will probably resent it." He took up the Testament, and went off with it to the laboratory.

We lunched at our chambers on the following day, and, after the meal, drew up our chairs to the fire and lit our pipes. Thorndyke was evidently preoccupied, for he laid his open notebook on his knee, and, gazing meditatively into the fire, made occasional entries with his pencil as though he were arranging the points of an argument. Assuming that the Aldgate murder was the subject of his cogitations, I ventured to ask:

"Have you any material evidence to offer the coroner?"

He closed his notebook and put it away. "The evidence that I have," he said, "is material and important; but it is disjointed and rather inconclusive. If I can join it up into a coherent whole, as I hope to do before I reach the court, it will be very important indeed—but here is my invaluable familiar, with the instruments of research." He turned with a smile towards Polton, who had just entered the room, and master and man exchanged a friendly glance of mutual appreciation. The relations of Thorndyke and his assistant were a constant delight to me: on the one side, service, loyal and whole-hearted; on the other, frank and full recognition.

"I should think those will do, sir," said Polton, handing his principal a small cardboard box such as playing-cards are carried in. Thorndyke pulled off the lid, and I then saw that the box was fitted internally with grooves for plates, and contained two mounted photographs. The latter were very singular productions indeed; they were copies each of a page of the Testament, one Russian and the other Yiddish; but the lettering appeared white on a black ground, of which it occupied only quite a small space in the middle, leaving a broad black margin. Each photograph was mounted on a stiff card, and each card had a duplicate photograph pasted on the back.

Thorndyke exhibited them to me with a provoking smile, holding them daintily by their edges, before he slid them back into the grooves of their box.

"We are making a little digression into philology, you see," he remarked, as he pocketed the box. "But we must be off now, or we shall keep Davidson waiting. Thank you, Polton."

The District Railway carried us swiftly eastward, and we emerged from Aldgate Station a full half-hour before we were due. Nevertheless, Thorndyke stepped out briskly, but instead of making directly for the mortuary, he strayed off unaccountably into Mansell Street, scanning the numbers of the houses as he went. A row of old houses, picturesque but grimy, on our right seemed specially to attract him, and he slowed down as we approached them.

"There is a quaint survival, Jervis," he remarked, pointing to a crudely painted, wooden effigy of an Indian standing on a bracket at the door of a small old-fashioned tobacconist's shop. We halted to look at the little image, and at that moment the side door opened, and a woman came out on to the doorstop, where she stood gazing up and down the street.

Thorndyke immediately crossed the pavement, and addressed her, apparently with some question, for I heard her answer presently: "A quarter-past six is his time, sir, and he is generally punctual to the minute."

"Thank you," said Thorndyke; "I'll bear that in mind;" and, lifting his hat, he walked on briskly, turning presently up a side-street which brought us out into Aldgate. It was now but five minutes to four, so we strode off quickly to keep our tryst at the mortuary; but although we arrived at the gate as the hour was striking, when we entered the building we found Dr. Davidson hanging up his apron and preparing to depart.

"Sorry I couldn't wait for you," he said, with no great show of sincerity, "but a postmortem is a mere farce in a case like this; you have seen all that there was to see. However, there is the body; Hart hasn't closed it up yet."

With this and a curt "good-afternoon" he departed.

"I must apologise for Dr. Davidson, sir," said Hart, looking up with a vexed face from the desk at which he was writing out his notes.

"You needn't," said Thorndyke; "you didn't supply him with manners; and don't let me disturb you. I only want to verify one or two points."

Accepting the hint, Hart and I remained at the desk, while Thorndyke, removing his hat, advanced to the long slate table, and bent over its burden of pitiful tragedy. For some time he remained motionless, running his eye gravely over the corpse, in search, no doubt, of bruises and indications of a struggle. Then he stooped and narrowly examined the wound, especially at its commencement and end. Suddenly he drew nearer, peering intently as if something had attracted his attention, and having taken out his lens, fetched a small sponge, with which he dried an exposed process of the spine. Holding his lens before the dried spot, he again scrutinized it closely, and then, with a scalpel and forceps, detached some object, which he carefully washed, and then once more examined through his lens as it lay in the palm of his hand. Finally, as I expected, he brought forth his "collecting-box," took from it a seed-envelope, into which he dropped the object—evidently something quite small—closed up the envelope, wrote on the outside of it, and replaced it in the box.

"I think I have seen all that I wanted to see," he said, as he pocketed the box and took up his hat. "We shall meet tomorrow morning at the inquest." He shook hands with Hart, and we went out into the relatively pure air.

On one pretext or another, Thorndyke lingered about the neighbourhood of Aldgate until a church bell struck six, when he bent his steps towards Harrow Alley. Through the narrow, winding passage he walked, slowly and with a thoughtful mien, along Little Somerset Street and out into Mansell Street, until just on the stroke of a quarter-past we found ourselves opposite the little tobacconist's shop.

Thorndyke glanced at his watch and halted, looking keenly up the street. A moment later he hastily took from his pocket the cardboard box, from which he extracted the two mounted photographs which had puzzled me so much. They now seemed to puzzle Thorndyke equally, to judge by his expression, for he held them close to his eyes, scrutinizing them with an anxious frown, and backing by degrees into the doorway at the side of the tobacconist's. At this moment I became aware of a man who, as he approached, seemed to eye my friend with some curiosity and more disfavour; a very short, burly young man, apparently a foreign Jew, whose face, naturally sinister and unprepossessing, was further disfigured by the marks of smallpox.

"Excuse me," he said brusquely, pushing past Thorndyke; "I live here."

"I am sorry," responded Thorndyke. He moved aside, and then suddenly asked: "By the way, I suppose you do not by any chance understand Yiddish?"

"Why do you ask?" the newcomer demanded gruffly.

"Because I have just had these two photographs of lettering given

54

to me. One is in Greek, I think, and one in Yiddish, but I have forgotten which is which." He held out the two cards to the stranger, who took them from him, and looked at them with scowling curiosity.

"This one is Yiddish," said he, raising his right hand, "and this other is Russian, not Greek." He held out the two cards to Thorndyke, who took them from him, holding them carefully by the edges as before.

"I am greatly obliged to you for your kind assistance," said Thorndyke; but before he had time to finish his thanks, the man had entered, by means of his latchkey, and slammed the door.

Thorndyke carefully slid the photographs back into their grooves, replaced the box in his pocket, and made an entry in his notebook.

"That," said he, "finishes my labours, with the exception of a small experiment which I can perform at home. By the way, I picked up a morsel of evidence that Davidson had overlooked. He will be annoyed, and I am not very fond of scoring off a colleague; but he is too uncivil for me to communicate with."

★★★★★★★★

The coroner's subpoena had named ten o'clock as the hour at which Thorndyke was to attend to give evidence, but a consultation with a well-known solicitor so far interfered with his plans that we were a quarter of an hour late in starting from the Temple. My friend was evidently in excellent spirits, though silent and preoccupied, from which I inferred that he was satisfied with the results of his labours; but, as I sat by his side in the hansom, I forbore to question him, not from mere unselfishness, but rather from the desire to hear his evidence for the first time in conjunction with that of the other witnesses.

The room in which the inquest was held formed part of a school adjoining the mortuary. Its vacant bareness was on this occasion enlivened by a long, baize-covered table, at the head of which sat the coroner, while one side was occupied by the jury; and I was glad to observe that the latter consisted, for the most part, of genuine working men, instead of the stolid-faced, truculent "professional jurymen" who so often grace these tribunals.

A row of chairs accommodated the witnesses, a corner of the table was allotted to the accused woman's solicitor, a smart dapper gentleman in gold pince-nez, a portion of one side to the reporters, and several ranks of benches were occupied by a miscellaneous assembly representing the public.

There were one or two persons present whom I was somewhat

surprised to see. There was, for instance, our pock-marked acquaintance of Mansell Street, who greeted us with a stare of hostile surprise; and there was Superintendent Miller of Scotland Yard, in whose manner I seemed to detect some kind of private understanding with Thorndyke. But I had little time to look about me, for when we arrived, the proceedings had already commenced. Mrs. Goldstein, the first witness, was finishing her recital of the circumstances under which the crime was discovered, and, as she retired, weeping hysterically, she was followed by looks of commiseration from the sympathetic jurymen.

The next witness was a young woman named Kate Silver. As she stepped forward to be sworn she flung a glance of hatred and defiance at Miriam Goldstein, who, white-faced and wild of aspect, with her red hair streaming in dishevelled masses on to her shoulders, stood apart in custody of two policemen, staring about her as if in a dream.

"You were intimately acquainted with the deceased, I believe?" said the coroner.

"I was. We worked at the same place for a long time—the Empire Restaurant in Fenchurch Street—and we lived in the same house. She was my most intimate friend."

"Had she, as far as you know, any friends or relations in England?"

"No. She came to England from Bremen about three years ago. It was then that I made her acquaintance. All her relations were in Germany, but she had many friends here, because she was a very lively, amiable girl."

"Had she, as far as you know, any enemies—any persons, I mean, who bore any grudge against her and were likely to do her an injury?"

"Yes. Miriam Goldstein was her enemy. She hated her."

"You say Miriam Goldstein hated the deceased. How do you know that?"

"She made no secret of it. They had had a violent quarrel about a young man named Moses Cohen. He was formerly Miriam's sweetheart, and I think they were very fond of one another until Minna Adler came to lodge at the Goldsteins' house about three months ago. Then Moses took a fancy to Minna, and she encouraged him, although she had a sweetheart of her own, a young man named Paul Petrofsky, who also lodged in the Goldsteins' house. At last Moses broke off with Miriam, and engaged himself to Minna. Then Miriam was furious, and complained to Minna about what she called her perfidious conduct; but Minna only laughed, and told her she could have

Petrofsky instead."

"And what did Minna say to that?" asked the coroner.

"She was still more angry, because Moses Cohen is a smart, good-looking young man, while Petrofsky is not much to look at. Besides, Miriam did not like Petrofsky; he had been rude to her, and she had made her father send him away from the house. So they were not friends, and it was just after that that the trouble came."

"The trouble?"

"I mean about Moses Cohen. Miriam is a very passionate girl, and she was furiously jealous of Minna, so when Petrofsky annoyed her by taunting her about Moses Cohen and Minna, she lost her temper, and said dreadful things about both of them."

"As, for instance—?"

"She said that she would kill them both, and that she would like to cut Minna's throat."

"When was this?"

"It was the day before the murder."

"Who heard her say these things besides you?"

"Another lodger named Edith Bryant and Petrofsky. We were all standing in the hall at the time."

"But I thought you said Petrofsky had been turned away from the house."

"So he had, a week before; but he had left a box in his room, and on this day he had come to fetch it. That was what started the trouble. Miriam had taken his room for her bedroom, and turned her old one into a workroom. She said he should not go to her room to fetch his box."

"And did he?"

"I think so. Miriam and Edith and I went out, leaving him in the hall. When we came back the box was gone, and, as Mrs. Goldstein was in the kitchen and there was nobody else in the house, he must have taken it."

"You spoke of Miriam's workroom. What work did she do?"

"She cut stencils for a firm of decorators."

Here the coroner took a peculiarly shaped knife from the table before him, and handed it to the witness.

"Have you ever seen that knife before?" he asked.

"Yes. It belongs to Miriam Goldstein. It is a stencil-knife that she used in her work."

This concluded the evidence of Kate Silver, and when the name of the next witness, Paul Petrofsky, was called, our Mansell Street friend came forward to be sworn. His evidence was quite brief, and merely corroborative of that of Kate Silver, as was that of the next witness, Edith Bryant. When these had been disposed of, the coroner announced:

"Before taking the medical evidence, gentlemen, I propose to hear that of the police-officers, and first we will call Detective-Sergeant Alfred Bates."

The sergeant stepped forward briskly, and proceeded to give his evidence with official readiness and precision.

"I was called by Constable Simmonds at eleven-forty-nine, and reached the house at two minutes to twelve in company with Inspector Harris and Divisional Surgeon Davidson. When I arrived Dr. Hart, Dr. Thorndyke, and Dr. Jervis were already in the room. I found the deceased woman, Minna Adler, lying in bed with her throat cut. She was dead and cold. There were no signs of a struggle, and the bed did not appear to have been disturbed. There was a table by the bedside on which was a book and an empty candlestick. The candle had apparently burnt out, for there was only a piece of charred wick at the bottom of the socket. A box had been placed on the floor at the head of the bed and a hassock stood on it. Apparently the murderer had stood on the hassock and leaned over the head of the bed to commit the murder. This was rendered necessary by the position of the table, which could not have been moved without making some noise and perhaps disturbing the deceased. I infer from the presence of the box and hassock that the murderer is a short person."

"Was there anything else that seemed to fix the identity of the murderer?"

"Yes. A tress of a woman's red hair was grasped in the left hand of the deceased."

As the detective uttered this statement, a simultaneous shriek of horror burst from the accused woman and her mother. Mrs. Goldstein sank half-fainting on to a bench, while Miriam, pale as death, stood as one petrified, fixing the detective with a stare of terror, as he drew from his pocket two small paper packets, which he opened and handed to the coroner.

"The hair in the packet marked A," said he, "is that which was found in the hand of the deceased; that in the packet marked B is the hair of Miriam Goldstein."

Here the accused woman's solicitor rose. "Where did you obtain the hair in the packet marked B?" he demanded.

"I took it from a bag of combings that hung on the wall of Miriam Goldstein's bedroom," answered the detective.

"I object to this," said the solicitor. "There is no evidence that the hair from that bag was the hair of Miriam Goldstein at all."

Thorndyke chuckled softly. "The lawyer is as dense as the policeman," he remarked to me in an undertone. "Neither of them seems to see the significance of that bag in the least."

"Did you know about the bag, then?" I asked in surprise.

"No. I thought it was the hair-brush."

I gazed at my colleague in amazement, and was about to ask for some elucidation of this cryptic reply, when he held up his finger and turned again to listen.

"Very well, Mr. Horwitz," the coroner was saying, "I will make a note of your objection, but I shall allow the sergeant to continue his evidence."

The solicitor sat down, and the detective resumed his statement.

"I have examined and compared the two samples of hair, and it is my opinion that they are from the head of the same person. The only other observation that I made in the room was that there was a small quantity of silver sand sprinkled on the pillow around the deceased woman's head."

"Silver sand!" exclaimed the coroner. "Surely that is a very singular material to find on a woman's pillow?"

"I think it is easily explained," replied the sergeant. "The washhand basin was full of bloodstained water, showing that the murderer had washed his—or her—hands, and probably the knife, too, after the crime. On the washstand was a ball of sand-soap, and I imagine that the murderer used this to cleanse his—or her—hands, and, while drying them, must have stood over the head of the bed and let the sand sprinkle down on to the pillow."

"A simple but highly ingenious explanation," commented the coroner approvingly, and the jurymen exchanged admiring nods and nudges.

"I searched the rooms occupied by the accused woman, Miriam Goldstein, and found there a knife of the kind used by stencil cutters, but larger than usual. There were stains of blood on it which the accused explained by saying that she cut her finger some days ago. She admitted that the knife was hers."

This concluded the sergeant's evidence, and he was about to sit down when the solicitor rose.

"I should like to ask this witness one or two questions," said he, and the coroner having nodded assent, he proceeded: "Has the finger of the accused been examined since her arrest?"

"I believe not," replied the sergeant. "Not to my knowledge, at any rate."

The solicitor noted the reply, and then asked: "With reference to the silver sand, did you find any at the bottom of the wash-hand basin?"

The sergeant's face reddened. "I did not examine the wash-hand basin," he answered.

"Did anybody examine it?"

"I think not."

"Thank you." Mr. Horwitz sat down, and the triumphant squeak of his quill pen was heard above the muttered disapproval of the jury.

"We shall now take the evidence of the doctors, gentlemen," said the coroner, "and we will begin with that of the divisional surgeon. You saw the deceased, I believe, Doctor," he continued, when Dr. Davidson had been sworn, "soon after the discovery of the murder, and you have since then made an examination of the body?"

"Yes. I found the body of the deceased lying in her bed, which had apparently not been disturbed. She had been dead about ten hours, and rigidity was complete in the limbs but not in the trunk. The cause of death was a deep wound extending right across the throat and dividing all the structures down to the spine. It had been inflicted with a single sweep of a knife while deceased was lying down, and was evidently homicidal. It was not possible for the deceased to have inflicted the wound herself. It was made with a single-edged knife, drawn from left to right; the assailant stood on a hassock placed on a box at the head of the bed and leaned over to strike the blow. The murderer is probably quite a short person, very muscular, and right-handed. There was no sign of a struggle, and, judging by the nature of the injuries, I should say that death was almost instantaneous. In the left hand of the deceased was a small tress of a woman's red hair. I have compared that hair with that of the accused, and am of opinion that it is her hair."

"You were shown a knife belonging to the accused?"

"Yes; a stencil-knife. There were stains of dried blood on it which I have examined and find to be mammalian blood. It is probably human blood, but I cannot say with certainty that it is."

"Could the wound have been inflicted with this knife?"

"Yes, though it is a small knife to produce so deep a wound. Still, it is quite possible."

The coroner glanced at Mr. Horwitz. "Do you wish to ask this witness any questions?" he inquired.

"If you please, sir," was the reply. The solicitor rose, and, having glanced through his notes, commenced: "You have described certain blood-stains on this knife. But we have heard that there was blood-stained water in the wash-hand basin, and it is suggested, most reasonably, that the murderer washed his hands and the knife. But if the knife was washed, how do you account for the bloodstains on it?"

"Apparently the knife was not washed, only the hands."

"But is not that highly improbable?"

"No, I think not."

"You say that there was no struggle, and that death was practically instantaneous, but yet the deceased had torn out a lock of the murderess's hair. Are not those two statements inconsistent with one another?"

"No. The hair was probably grasped convulsively at the moment of death. At any rate, the hair was undoubtedly in the dead woman's hand."

"Is it possible to identify positively the hair of any individual?"

"No. Not with certainty. But this is very peculiar hair."

The solicitor sat down, and, Dr. Hart having been called, and having briefly confirmed the evidence of his principal, the coroner announced: "The next witness, gentleman, is Dr. Thorndyke, who was present almost accidentally, but was actually the first on the scene of the murder. He has since made an examination of the body, and will, no doubt, be able to throw some further light on this horrible crime."

Thorndyke stood up, and, having been sworn, laid on the table a small box with a leather handle. Then, in answer to the coroner's questions, he described himself as the lecturer on Medical Jurisprudence at St. Margaret's Hospital, and briefly explained his connection with the case. At this point the foreman of the jury interrupted to ask that his opinion might be taken on the hair and the knife, as these were matters of contention, and the objects in question were accordingly handed to him.

"Is the hair in the packet marked A in your opinion from the same person as that in the packet marked B?" the coroner asked.

"I have no doubt that they are from the same person," was the reply.

"Will you examine this knife and tell us if the wound on the deceased might have been inflicted with it?"

Thorndyke examined the blade attentively, and then handed the knife back to the coroner.

"The wound might have been inflicted with this knife," said he, "but I am quite sure it was not."

"Can you give us your reasons for that very definite opinion?"

"I think," said Thorndyke, "that it will save time if I give you the facts in a connected order." The coroner bowed assent, and he proceeded: "I will not waste your time by reiterating facts already stated. Sergeant Bates has fully described the state of the room, and I have nothing to add on that subject. Dr. Davidson's description of the body covers all the facts: the woman had been dead about ten hours, the wound was unquestionably homicidal, and was inflicted in the manner that he has described. Death was apparently instantaneous, and I should say that the deceased never awakened from her sleep."

"But," objected the coroner, "the deceased held a lock of hair in her hand."

"That hair," replied Thorndyke, "was not the hair of the murderer. It was placed in the hand of the corpse for an obvious purpose; and the fact that the murderer had brought it with him shows that the crime was premeditated, and that it was committed by someone who had had access to the house and was acquainted with its inmates."

As Thorndyke made this statement, coroner, jurymen, and spectators alike gazed at him in open-mouthed amazement. There was an interval of intense silence, broken by a wild, hysteric laugh from Mrs. Goldstein, and then the coroner asked:

"How did you know that the hair in the hand of the corpse was not that of the murderer?"

"The inference was very obvious. At the first glance the peculiar and conspicuous colour of the hair struck me as suspicious. But there were three facts, each of which was in itself sufficient to prove that the hair was probably not that of the murderer.

"In the first place there was the condition of the hand. When a person, at the moment of death, grasps any object firmly, there is set up a condition known as cadaveric spasm. The muscular contraction passes immediately into *rigor mortis,* or death-stiffening, and the object remains grasped by the dead hand until the rigidity passes off. In this case the hand was perfectly rigid, but it did not grasp the hair at all. The little tress lay in the palm quite loosely and the hand was only partially closed. Obviously the hair had been placed in it after death.

The other two facts had reference to the condition of the hair itself. Now, when a lock of hair is torn from the head, it is evident that all the roots will be found at the same end of the lock. But in the present instance this was not the case; the lock of hair which lay in the dead woman's hand had roots at both ends, and so could not have been torn from the head of the murderer. But the third fact that I observed was still more conclusive. The hairs of which that little tress was composed had not been pulled out at all. They had fallen out spontaneously. They were, in fact, shed hairs—probably combings. Let me explain the difference.

When a hair is shed naturally, it drops out of the little tube in the skin called the root sheath, having been pushed out by the young hair growing up underneath; the root end of such a shed hair shows nothing but a small bulbous enlargement—the root bulb. But when a hair is forcibly pulled out, its root drags out the root sheath with it, and this can be plainly seen as a glistening mass on the end of the hair. If Miriam Goldstein will pull out a hair and pass it to me, I will show you the great difference between hair which is pulled out and hair which is shed."

The unfortunate Miriam needed no pressing. In a twinkling she had tweaked out a dozen hairs, which a constable handed across to Thorndyke, by whom they were at once fixed in a paper-clip. A second clip being produced from the box, half a dozen hairs taken from the tress which had been found in the dead woman's hand were fixed in it. Then Thorndyke handed the two clips, together with a lens, to the coroner.

"Remarkable!" exclaimed the latter, "and most conclusive." He passed the objects on to the foreman, and there was an interval of silence while the jury examined them with breathless interest and much facial contortion.

"The next question," resumed Thorndyke, "was, Whence did the murderer obtain these hairs? I assumed that they had been taken from Miriam Goldstein's hair-brush; but the sergeant's evidence makes it pretty clear that they were obtained from the very bag of combings from which he took a sample for comparison."

"I think, Doctor," remarked the coroner, "you have disposed of the hair clue pretty completely. May I ask if you found anything that might throw any light on the identity of the murderer?"

"Yes," replied Thorndyke, "I observed certain things which determine the identity of the murderer quite conclusively." He turned a significant glance on Superintendent Miller, who immediately rose, stepped quietly to the door, and then returned, putting something into his pocket. "When I entered the hall," Thorndyke continued, "I noted the following facts: Behind the door was a shelf on which were two china candlesticks. Each was fitted with a candle, and in one was a short candle-end, about an inch long, lying in the tray. On the floor, close to the mat, was a spot of candle-wax and some faint marks of muddy feet. The oil-cloth on the stairs also bore faint footmarks, made by wet goloshes. They were ascending the stairs, and grew fainter towards the top.

"There were two more spots of candle-wax on the stairs, and one on the handrail; a burnt end of a wax match halfway up the stairs, and another on the landing. There were no descending footmarks, but one of the spots of wax close to the balusters had been trodden on while warm and soft, and bore the mark of the front of the heel of a golosh descending the stairs. The lock of the street door had been recently oiled, as had also that of the bedroom door, and the latter had been unlocked from outside with a bent wire, which had made a mark on the key. Inside the room I made two further observations. One was that the dead woman's pillow was lightly sprinkled with sand, somewhat like silver sand, but greyer and less gritty. I shall return to this presently.

"The other was that the candlestick on the bedside table was empty. It was a peculiar candlestick, having a skeleton socket formed of eight flat strips of metal. The charred wick of a burnt-out candle was at the bottom of the socket, but a little fragment of wax on the top edge showed that another candle had been stuck in it and had been taken out, for otherwise that fragment would have been melted. I at once thought of the candle-end in the hall, and when I went down again I took that end from the tray and examined it.

"On it I found eight distinct marks corresponding to the eight bars of the candlestick in the bedroom. It had been carried in the right hand of some person, for the warm, soft wax had taken beautifully clear impressions of a right thumb and forefinger. I took three moulds of the candle-end in moulding wax, and from these moulds have made this cement cast, which shows both the fingerprints and the marks of the candlestick." He took from his box a small white object, which he handed to the coroner.

"And what do you gather from these facts?" asked the coroner.

"I gather that at about a quarter to two on the morning of the crime, a man (who had, on the previous day visited the house to obtain the tress of hair and oil the locks) entered the house by means of a latchkey. We can fix the time by the fact that it rained on that morning from half-past one to a quarter to two, this being the only rain that has fallen for a fortnight, and the murder was committed at about two o'clock.

"The man lit a wax match in the hall and another halfway up the stairs. He found the bedroom door locked, and turned the key from outside with a bent wire. He entered, lit the candle, placed the box and hassock, murdered his victim, washed his hands and knife, took the candle-end from the socket and went downstairs, where he blew out the candle and dropped it into the tray.

"The next clue is furnished by the sand on the pillow. I took a little of it, and examined it under the microscope, when it turned out to be deep-sea sand from the Eastern Mediterranean. It was full of the minute shells called '*Foraminifera*,' and as one of these happened to belong to a species which is found only in the Levant, I was able to fix the locality."

"But this is very remarkable," said the coroner. "How on earth could deep-sea sand have got on to this woman's pillow?"

"The explanation," replied Thorndyke, "is really quite simple. Sand of this kind is contained in considerable quantities in Turkey sponges. The warehouses in which the sponges are unpacked are often strewn with it ankle deep; the men who unpack the cases become dusted over with it, their clothes saturated and their pockets filled with it. If such a person, with his clothes and pockets full of sand, had committed this murder, it is pretty certain that in leaning over the head of the bed in a partly inverted position he would have let fall a certain quantity of the sand from his pockets and the interstices of his clothing.

"Now, as soon as I had examined this sand and ascertained its nature, I sent a message to Mr. Goldstein asking him for a list of the persons who were acquainted with the deceased, with their addresses and occupations. He sent me the list by return, and among the persons mentioned was a man who was engaged as a packer in a wholesale sponge warehouse in the Minories. I further ascertained that the new season's crop of Turkey sponges had arrived a few days before the murder.

"The question that now arose was, whether this sponge-packer was the person whose fingerprints I had found on the candle-end. To settle this point, I prepared two mounted photographs, and having contrived to meet the man at his door on his return from work, I induced him to look at them and compare them. He took them from me, holding each one between a forefinger and thumb. When he returned them to me, I took them home and carefully dusted each on both sides with a certain surgical dusting-powder. The powder adhered to the places where his fingers and thumbs had pressed against the photographs, showing the fingerprints very distinctly. Those of the right hand were identical with the prints on the candle, as you will see if you compare them with the cast." He produced from the box the photograph of the Yiddish lettering, on the black margin of which there now stood out with startling distinctness a yellowish-white print of a thumb.

Thorndyke had just handed the card to the coroner when a very singular disturbance arose. While my friend had been giving the latter part of his evidence, I had observed the man Petrofsky rise from his seat and walk stealthily across to the door. He turned the handle softly and pulled, at first gently, and then with more force. But the door was locked. As he realised this, Petrofsky seized the handle with both hands and tore at it furiously, shaking it to and fro with the violence of a madman, and his shaking limbs, his starting eyes, glaring insanely at the astonished spectators, his ugly face, dead white, running with sweat and hideous with terror, made a picture that was truly shocking.

Suddenly he let go the handle, and with a horrible cry thrust his hand under the skirt of his coat and rushed at Thorndyke. But the superintendent was ready for this. There was a shout and a scuffle, and then Petrofsky was born down, kicking and biting like a maniac, while Miller hung on to his right hand and the formidable knife that it grasped.

"I will ask you to hand that knife to the coroner," said Thorndyke, when Petrofsky had been secured and handcuffed, and the superintendent had readjusted his collar. "Will you kindly examine it, sir," he continued, "and tell me if there is a notch in the edge, near to the point—a triangular notch about an eighth of an inch long?"

The coroner looked at the knife, and then said in a tone of surprise: "Yes, there is. You have seen this knife before, then?"

"No, I have not," replied Thorndyke. "But perhaps I had better continue my statement. There is no need for me to tell you that the fingerprints on the card and on the candle are those of Paul Petrofsky; I will proceed to the evidence furnished by the body.

"In accordance with your order, I went to the mortuary and examined the corpse of the deceased. The wound has been fully and accurately described by Dr. Davidson, but I observed one fact which I presume he had overlooked. Embedded in the bone of the spine—in the left transverse process of the fourth vertebra—I discovered a small particle of steel, which I carefully extracted."

He drew his collecting-box from his pocket, and taking from it a seed-envelope, handed the latter to the coroner. "That fragment of steel is in this envelope," he said, "and it is possible that it may correspond to the notch in the knife-blade."

Amidst an intense silence the coroner opened the little envelope, and let the fragment of steel drop on to a sheet of paper. Laying the knife on the paper, he gently pushed the fragment towards the notch. Then he looked up at Thorndyke.

"It fits exactly," said he.

There was a heavy thud at the other end of the room and we all looked round.

Petrofsky had fallen on to the floor insensible.

★★★★★★★★

"An instructive case, Jervis," remarked Thorndyke, as we walked homewards—"a case that reiterates the lesson that the authorities still refuse to learn."

"What is that?" I asked.

"It is this. When it is discovered that a murder has been committed, the scene of that murder should instantly become as the Palace of the Sleeping Beauty. Not a grain of dust should be moved, not a soul should be allowed to approach it, until the scientific observer has seen everything in situ and absolutely undisturbed. No tramplings of excited constables, no rummaging by detectives, no scrambling to and fro of bloodhounds. Consider what would have happened in this case if we had arrived a few hours later. The corpse would have been in the mortuary, the hair in the sergeant's pocket, the bed rummaged and the sand scattered abroad, the candle probably removed, and the stairs covered with fresh tracks.

"There would not have been the vestige of a clue."

"And," I added, "the deep sea would have uttered its message in vain."

A Sower of Pestilence

The affectionate relations that existed between Thorndyke and his devoted follower, Polton, were probably due, at least in part, to certain similarities in their characters. Polton was an accomplished and versatile craftsman, a man who could do anything, and do it well; and Thorndyke has often said that if he had not been a man of science, he would, by choice, have been a skilled craftsman. Even as things were, he was a masterly manipulator of all instruments of research, and a good enough workman to devise new appliances and processes and to collaborate with his assistant in carrying them out.

Such a collaboration was taking place when the present case opened. It had occurred to Thorndyke that lithography might be usefully applied to medico-legal research, and on this particular morning he and Polton were experimenting in the art of printing from the stone. In the midst of their labours the bell from our chambers below was heard to ring, and Polton, reluctantly laying down the inking roller and wiping his hands on the southern aspect of his trousers, departed to open the door.

"It's a Mr. Rabbage," he reported on his return. "Says he has an appointment with you, sir."

"So he has," said Thorndyke. "And, as I under stand that he is going to offer us a profound mystery for solution, you had better come down with me, Jervis, and hear what he has to say."

Mr. Rabbage turned out to be a elderly gentleman who, as we entered, peered at us through a pair of deep, concave spectacles and greeted us "with a smile that was childlike and bland." Thorndyke looked him over and adroitly brought him to the point.

"Yes," said Mr. Rabbage, "it is really a most mysterious affair that has brought me here. I have already laid it before a very talented detective officer whom I know slightly—a Mr. Badger; but he frankly admitted that it was beyond him and strongly advised me to consult you."

"Inspector Badger was kind enough to pay me a very handsome compliment," said Thorndyke.

"Yes. He said that you would certainly be able to solve this mystery without any difficulty. So here I am. And perhaps I had better explain who I am, in case you don't happen to know my name. I am the director of the St. Francis Home of Rest for aged, invalid and destitute cats: an institution where these deserving animals are enabled to convert the autumn of their troubled lives into a sort of Indian summer of comfort and repose. The home is, I may say, my own venture. I support it out of my own means. But I am open to receive contributions; and to that end there is secured to the garden railings a large box with a wide slit and an inscription inviting donations of money, of articles of value, or of food or delicacies for the inmates."

"And do you get much?" I asked.

"Of money," he replied, "very little. Of articles of value, none at all. As to gifts of food, they are numerous, but they often display a strange ignorance of the habits of the domestic cat. Such things, for instance, as pickles and banana-skins, though doubtless kindly meant, are quite unsuitable as diet. But the most singular donation that I have ever received was that which I found in the box the day before yesterday. There were a number of articles, but all apparently from the same donor; and their character was so mysterious that I showed them to Mr. Badger, as I have told you, who was as puzzled as I was and referred me to you. The collection comprised three ladies' purses, a morocco-leather wallet and a small aluminium case. I have brought them with me to show you."

"What did the purses contain?" Thorndyke asked.

"Nothing," replied Mr. Rabbage, gazing at us with wide-open eyes. "They were perfectly empty. That is the astonishing circumstance."

"And the leather wallet?"

"Empty, too, excepting for a few odd papers."

"And the aluminium case?"

"Ah!" exclaimed Mr. Rabbage, "that was the most amazing of all. It contained a number of glass tubes! and those tubes contained—now, what do you suppose?" He paused impressively, and then, as neither of us offered a suggestion, be answered his own question. "Fleas and lice! Yes, actually! Fleas and lice! Isn't that an extraordinary donation?"

"It is certainly," Thorndyke agreed. "Anyone might have known

70

that, with a houseful of cats, you could produce your own fleas."

"Exactly," said Mr. Rabbage. "That is what instantly occurred to me, and also, I may say, to Mr. Badger. But let me show you the things."

He produced from a hand-bag and spread out on the table a collection of articles which were, evidently, the "husks" of the gleanings of some facetious pickpocket, to whom Mr. Rabbage's donation-box must have appeared as a perfect God-send. Thorndyke picked up the purses, one after the other, and having glanced at their empty interiors, put them aside. The letter-wallet he looked through more attentively, but without disturbing its contents, and then he took up and opened the aluminium case. This certainly was a rather mysterious affair. It opened like a cigarette case. One side was fitted with six glass specimen-tubes, each provided with a well-fitting parchment cap, perforated with a number of needle-holes; and of the six tubes, four contained fleas—about a dozen in each tube—some of which were dead, but others still alive, and the remaining two lice, all of which were dead. In the opposite side of the case, secured with a catch, was a thin celluloid note-tablet on which some numbers had been written in pencil.

"Well," said Mr. Rabbage, when the examination was finished, "can you offer any solution of the mystery?"

Thorndyke shook his head gravely. "Not offhand," he replied. "This is a matter which will require careful consideration. Leave these things with me for further examination and I will let you know, in the course of a few days, what conclusion we arrive at."

"Thank you," said Mr. Rabbage, rising and holding out his hand. "You have my address, I think."

He glanced at his watch, snatched up his hand-bag and darted to the door; and a moment later we heard him bustling down the stairs in the hurried, strenuous manner that is characteristic of persons who spend most of their lives doing nothing.

"I'm surprised at you, Thorndyke," I said when he had gone, "encouraging that ass, Badger, in his silly practical jokes. Why didn't you tell this old nincompoop that he had just got a pick-pocket's leavings and have done with it?"

"For the reason, my learned brother, that I haven't done with it. I am a little curious as to whose pocket has been picked, and what that person was doing with a collection of fleas and lice."

"I don't see that it is any business of yours," said I. "And as to the vermin, I should suggest that the owner of the case is an entomologist

71

who specialises in *epizoa*. Probably he is collecting varieties and races."

"And how," asked Thorndyke, opening the case and handing it to me, "does my learned friend account for the faint scent of aniseed that exhales from this collection?"

"I don't account for it at all," said I. "It is a nasty smell. I noticed it when you first opened the case. I can only suppose that the flea-merchant likes it, or thinks that the fleas do."

"The latter seems the more probable," said Thorndyke, "for you notice that the odour seems to principally from the parchment caps of the four tubes that contain fleas. The caps of the louse tubes don't seem to be scented. And now let us have a little closer look at the letter-wallet."

He opened the wallet and took out its contents, which were unilluminating enough. Apparently it had been gutted by the pickpocket and only the manifestly valueless articles left. One or two bills, recording purchases at shops, a time-table, a brief letter in French, without its envelope and bearing neither address, date, nor signature, and a set of small maps mounted on thin card: this was the whole collection, and not one of the articles appeared to furnish the slightest clue to the identity of the owner.

Thorndyke looked at the letter curiously and read it aloud.

"It is just a little singular," he remarked, "that this note should be addressed to nobody by name, should bear neither address, date, nor signature, and should have had its envelope removed. There is almost an appearance of avoiding the means of identification. Yet the matter is simple and innocent enough: just an appointment to meet at the Mile End Picture Palace. But these maps are more interesting; in fact, they are quite curious."

He took them out of the wallet—lifting them carefully by the edges, I noticed—and laid them out on the table. There were seven cards, and each had a map, or rather a section, pasted on both sides. The sections had been cut out of a street map of London, and as each card was three inches by four and a half, each section represented an area of one mile by a mile and a half. They had been very carefully prepared neatly stuck on the cards and varnished, and every section bore a distinguishing letter. But the most curious feature was a number of small circles drawn in pencil on various parts of the maps, each circle enclosing a number.

"What do you make of those circles, Thorndyke?" I asked.

"One can only make a speculative hypothesis," he replied. "I am disposed to associate them with the fleas and lice. You notice that the maps all represent the most squalid parts of East London—Spitalfields, Bethnal Green, Whitechapel, and so forth, where the material would be plentiful; and you also notice that the celluloid tablet in the insect case bears a number of pencilled jottings that might refer to these maps. Here, for instance, is a note, 'B 21 a + b—,' and you observe that each entry has an a and a b with either a plus or a minus sign. Now, if we assume that a means fleas and b lice, or *vice versa*, the maps and the notes together might form a record of collections or experiments with a geographical basis."

"They might," I agreed, "but there isn't a particle of evidence that they do. It is a most fantastic hypothesis. We don't know, and we have no reason to suppose, that the insect-case and the wallet were the property of the same person. And we have no means of finding out whether they were or were not."

"There I think you do us an injustice, Jervis," said he. "Are we not lithographers?"

"I don't see where the lithography comes in," said I.

"Then you ought to. This is a test case. These maps are varnished, and are thus virtually lithographic transfer paper; and the celluloid tablet also has a non-absorbent surface. Now, if you handle transfer paper carelessly when drawing on it, you are apt to find, when you have transferred to the stone, that your finger prints ink up, as well as the drawing. So it is possible that if we put these maps and the note-tablet on the stone, we may be able to ink up the prints of the fingers that have handled them and so prove whether they were or were not the same fingers."

"That would be interesting as an experiment," said I, "though I don't see that it matters two straws whether they were the same or not."

"Probably it doesn't," he replied, "though it may. But we have a new method and we may as well try it."

We took the things up to the laboratory and explained the problem to Polton, who entered into the inquiry with enthusiasm. Producing from a cupboard a fresh stone, he picked the maps out of the wallet one by one (with a pair of watchmaker's tweezers) and fell to work forthwith on the task of transferring the invisible—and possibly non-existent—fingerprints from the maps and the note-tablet to the stone. I watched him go through the various processes in his neat, careful, dexterous fashion and hoped that all his trouble would not be in vain. Nor was it; for when he began cautiously ink up the stone, it was evident that something was there, though it was not so evident what that something was. Presently, however, the vague markings took more definite shape, and now could be recognised eight rather confused masses of fingerprints, badly smeared, some incomplete, and all mixed up and superimposed so as to make the identification of any one print almost an impossibility.

Thorndyke looked them over dubiously. "It is a dreadful muddle," said he, "but I think we can pick out the prints well enough for identification if that should be necessary. Which of these is the notes tablet, Polton?"

"The one in the right-hand top corner, sir," was the reply.

"Ah!" said Thorndyke, "then that answers our question. Confused as the impressions are, you can see quite plainly that the left thumb is the same thumb as that on the maps."

"Yes," I agreed after making the comparison, "there is not much doubt that they are the same. And now the question is, what about it?"

"Yes," said Thorndyke; "that is the question." And with this we retired from the laboratory, leaving Polton joyfully pulling off proofs.

During the next few days I had a vague impression that my colleague was working at this case, though with what object I could not imagine. Mr. Rabbage's problem was too absurd to take seriously, and Thorndyke was beyond working out cases, as he used to at one time, for the sake of mere experience. However, a day or two later, a genuine case turned up and occupied our attention to some purpose.

It was about six in the evening when Mr. Nicholas Balcombe called on us by appointment, and proceeded, in a business-like fashion, to state his case.

"I was advised by my friend Stalker, of the Griffin Life Assurance Office, to consult you," said he. "Stalker tells me that you have got him out of endless difficulties, and I am hoping that you will be able to help me out of mine, though they are not so clearly within your province as Stalker's. But you will know about that better than I do.

"I am the manager of Rutherford's Bank—the Cornhill Branch—and I have just had a very alarming experience. The day before yesterday, about three in the afternoon, a deed-box was handed in with a note from one of our customers—Mr. Pilcher, the solicitor, of Pilcher, Markham and Sudburys—asking us to deposit it in our strong-room and give the bearer a receipt for it. Of course this was done, in the ordinary way of business; but there was one exceptional circumstance that turns out to have been, as it would appear, providential. Owing to the increase of business our strong-room had become insufficient for our needs, and we have lately had a second one built on the most modern lines and perfectly fire-proof. This had not been taken into use when Pilcher's deed-box arrived, but as the old room was very full, I opened the new room and saw the deed-box deposited in it.

"Well, nothing happened up to the time that I left the bank, but about two o'clock in the morning the night watchman noticed a smell of burning, and on investigating, located the smell as apparently proceeding from the door of the new strong-room. He at once reported to the senior clerk, whose turn it was to sleep on the premises, and the latter at once telephoned to the police station. In a few minutes a police officer arrived with a couple of firemen and a hand-extinguisher. The clerk took them down to the strong-room and unlocked the door. As soon as it was opened, a volume of smoke and fumes burst out, and then they saw the deed-box—or rather the distorted remains of it—lying on the floor. The police took possession of what was left, but a very cursory examination on the spot showed that the box was, in effect, an incendiary bomb, with a slow time fuse or some similar arrangement."

"Was any damage done?" Thorndyke asked.

"Mercifully, no," replied Mr. Balcombe. "But just think of what might have happened! If I had put the box in the old strong-room it is certain that thousands of pounds' worth of valuable property would have been destroyed. Or again, if instead of an incendiary bomb the box had contained a high explosive, the whole building would probably have been blown to pieces."

"What explanation does Pilcher give?"

"A very simple one. He knows nothing about it. The note was a forgery; and on the firm's headed paper, or a perfect imitation of it. And mind you," Mr. Balcombe continued, "my experience is not a solitary one. I have made private inquiries of other bank managers, and I find that several of them have been subjected to similar outrages, some with serious results. And probably there are more. They don't talk about these things, you know. Then there are those fires: the great timber fire at Stepney, and those big warehouse fires near the London Docks; there is something queer about them. It looks as if some gang was at work for purposes of pure mischief and destruction."

"You have consulted the police, of course?"

"Yes. And they know something, I feel sure. But they are extremely reticent; so I suppose they don't know enough. At any rate, I should like you to investigate the case independently and so would my directors. The position is most alarming."

"Could you let me see Pilcher's letter?" Thorndyke asked.

"I have brought it with me," said Balcombe. "Thought you would probably want to examine it. I will leave it with you; and if we can give you any other information or assistance, we shall be only too glad."

"Was the box brought by hand?" inquired Thorndyke.

"Yes," replied Balcombe, "but I didn't see the bearer. I can get you a description from the man who received the package, if that would be any use."

"We may as well have it," said Thorndyke, "and the name and address of the person giving it, in case he is wanted as a witness."

"You shall have it," said Balcombe, rising and picking up his hat. "I will see to it myself. And you will let me know, in due course, if any information comes to hand?"

Thorndyke gave the required promise and our client took his leave.

"Well," I said with a laugh, as the brisk footsteps died away on the stairs, "you have had a very handsome compliment paid you. Our friend seems to think that you are one of those master craftsmen who can make bricks, not only without straw, but without clay. There's absolutely nothing to go on."

"It is certainly rather in the air," Thorndyke agreed. "There is this letter and the description of the man who left the packet, when we get it, and neither of them is likely to help us much."

He looked over the letter and its envelope, held the former up to the light and then handed them to me.

"We ought to find out whether this is Pilcher's own paper or an imitation," said I, when I had examined the letter and envelope without finding anything in the least degree distinctive or characteristic; "because, if it is their paper, the unknown man must have had some sort of connection with their establishment or staff."

"There must have been some sort of connection in any case," said Thorndyke. "Even an imitation implies possession of an original. But you are quite right. It is a line of inquiry, and practically the only one that offers."

The inquiry was made on the following day, and the fact clearly established that the paper was Pitcher's paper, but the ink was not their ink. The handwriting appeared to be disguised, and no one connected with the firm was able to recognise it. The staff, even to the caretaker, were all eminently respectable and beyond suspicion of being implicated in an affair of the kind.

"But after all," said Mr. Pitcher, "there are a hundred ways in which a sheet of paper may go astray if anyone wants it: at the printer's, the stationer's, or even in this office—for the paper is always in the letter-rack on the table."

Thus our only clue—if so it could be called—came to an end, and I waited with some curiosity to see what Thorndyke would do next. But so far as I could see, he did nothing, nor did he make any reference to this obscure case during the next few days. We had a good deal of other work on hand, and I assumed that this fully occupied his attention.

One evening, about a week later, he made the first reference to the case and a very mysterious communication it seemed to me.

"I have projected a little expedition for tomorrow," said he. "I am proposing to spend the day, or part of it, in the pastoral region of Bethnal Green."

"In connection with any of our cases?" I asked.

"Yes," he replied. "Balcombe's. I have been making some cautious inquiries with Polton's assistance, principally among hawkers and coffee-shop keepers, and I think I have struck a promising track."

"What kind of inquiries have you been making?" said I.

"I have been looking for a man, or men, engaged in giving street entertainments. That is what our data seemed to suggest, among other possibilities."

"Our data!" I exclaimed. "I didn't know we had any."

"We had Balcombe's account of the attempt to burn the bank. That gave us some hint as to the kind of man to look for. And there were certain other data, which my learned friend may recall."

"I don't recall anything suggesting a street entertainer," said I.

"Not directly," he replied. "It was one of several hypotheses, but it is probably the correct one, as I have heard of such a person as I had assumed, and have ascertained where he is likely to be found on certain days. Tomorrow I propose to go over his beat in the hope of getting a glimpse of him. If you think of coming with me, I may remind you that it is not a dressy neighbourhood."

On the following morning we set forth about ten o'clock, and as raiment which is inconspicuous at Bethnal Green may be rather noticeable in the Temple, we slipped out by the Tudor Street gate and made our way to Blackfriars Station. In place of the usual "research-case," I noticed that Thorndyke was carrying a somewhat shabby wood-fibre *attaché* case, and that he had no walking-stick. We got out at Aldgate and presently struck up Vallance Street in the direction of Bethnal Green; and by the brisk pace and the direct route adopted, I judged that Thorndyke had a definite objective. However, when we entered the maze of small streets adjoining the Bethnal Green Road, our pace was reduced to a saunter, and at corners and crossroads Thorndyke halted from time to time to look along the streets; and occasionally he referred to a card which he produced from his pocket, on which were written the names of streets and days of the week.

A couple of hours passed in this apparently aimless perambulation of the back streets.

"It doesn't look as if you were going to have much luck," I remarked, suppressing a yawn. "And I am not sure that we are not, in our turn, being 'spotted'. I have noted a man—a small, shabby-looking fellow, apparently keeping us in view from a distance, though I don't see him at the moment."

"It is quite likely," said Thorndyke. "This is a shady neighbourhood, and any native could see that we don't belong to it. Good morning! Taking a little fresh air?"

The latter question was addressed to a man who was standing at the door of a small coffee-shop, having apparently come to the surface for a "breather."

"Dunno about fresh," was the reply, "but it's the best there is. By the by, I saw one of them blokes what I was a-tellin' you about go by just now. Foreigner with the rats. If you want to see him give a show, I expect you'll find him in that bit of waste ground off Bolter's Rents."

"Bolter's Rents?" Thorndyke repeated. "Is that a turning out of Salcombe Street?"

"Quite right," was the reply. "Halfway up on the right-hand side."

Thanking our informant, Thorndyke strode off up the street, and as we turned the next corner I glanced back. At the moment, the small man whom I had noticed before stepped out of a doorway and came after us at a pace suggesting anxiety not to lose sight of us.

Bolter's Rents turned out to be a wide paved alley, one side of which opened into a patch of waste ground where a number of old houses had been demolished. This space had an unspeakably squalid appearance; for not only had the debris of the demolished houses been left in unsavoury heaps, but the place had evidently been adopted by the neighbourhood as a general dumping-ground for household refuse. The earth was strewn with vegetable, and even animal, leavings; flies and bluebottles hummed around and settled in hundreds on the garbage, and the air was pervaded by an odour like that of an old-fashioned brick dust-bin.

But in spite of these trifling disadvantages, a considerable crowd had collected, mainly composed of women and children; and at the centre of the crowd a man was giving an entertainment with a troupe of performing rats. We had sauntered slowly up the Rents and now halted to look on. At the moment, a white rat was climbing a pole at the top of which a little flag was stuck in a socket. We watched him rapidly climb the pole, seize the flagstaff in his teeth, lift it out of the socket, climb down the pole and deliver the flag to his master. Then a little carriage was produced and the rat harnessed into it, another white rat being dressed in a cloak and placed in the seat, and the latter—introduced to the audience as Lady Murphy—was taken for a drive round the stage.

While the entertainment was proceeding I inspected the establishment and its owner. The stage was composed of light hinged boards opened out on a small four-wheeled hand-cart, apparently home-made. At one end was a largish cage, divided by a wire partition into two parts, one of which contained a number of white and piebald rats, while the inmates of the other compartment were all wild rats; but not, I noted, the common brown or Norway rat, but the old-fashioned British black rat. I remarked upon the circumstance to Thorndyke.

"Yes," he said, "they were probably caught locally. The sewers here will be inhabited by brown rats, but the houses, in an old neighbourhood like this, will be infested principally by the black rat. What do you make of the exhibitor?"

I had already noticed him, and now unobtrusively examined him again. He was a medium-sized man with a sallow complexion, dark, restless eyes—which frequently wandered in our direction—a crop of stiff, bushy, upstanding hair—he wore no hat—and a ragged beard.

"A Slav of some kind, I should think," was my reply; "a Russian, or perhaps a Lett. But that beard is not perfectly convincing."

"No," Thorndyke agreed, "but it is a good make up. Perhaps we had better move on now; we have a deputy, you observe."

As he spoke, the small man whom I had observed following us strolled up the Rents; and as he drew nearer, revealed to my astonished gaze no less a person than our ingenious laboratory assistant, Polton.

Strangely altered, indeed, was our usually neat and spruce artificer with his seedy clothing and grubby hands; but as he sauntered up, profoundly unaware of our existence, a faint reminiscence of the familiar crinkly smile stole across his face.

We were just moving off when a chorus of shrieks mingled with laughter arose from the spectators, who hastily scattered right and left, and I had a momentary glimpse of a big black rat bounding across the space, to disappear into one of the many heaps of debris. It seemed that the exhibitor had just opened the cage to take out a black rat when one of the waiting performers—presumably a new recruit—had seized the opportunity to spring out and escape.

"Well," a grinning woman remarked to me, genially, "there's plenty more where that one came from. You should see this place on a moonlight night! Fair alive with 'em it is."

We sauntered up the Rents and along the cross street at the top; and as we went, I reflected on the very singular inquiry in which Thorndyke seemed to be engaged. The rat-tamer's appearance was suspicious. He didn't quite look the part, and his beard was almost certainly a make-up—and a skilful one, too, for it was no mere "property" beard; and the restless, furtive eyes, and a certain suppressed excitement in his bearing, hinted at something more than met the eye. But if this was Mr. Balcombe's incendiary, how had Thorndyke arrived at his identity, and, above all, by what process of reasoning had he contrived to associate the bank outrage with performing rats? That he had done so, his systematic procedure made quite clear. But how? It had seemed to me that we had not a single fact on which to start an investigation.

We had walked the length of the cross street, and had halted before turning, when a troop of children emerged from the Rents. Then came the exhibitor, towing his cart, with the cage shrouded in a cloth, then more children, and finally, at a little distance, Polton, slouching along idly but keeping the cart in view.

"I think," said Thorndyke, "it would be instructive, as a study in urban sanitation, to have a look round the scene of the late exhibition."

We retraced our steps down Bolter's Rents, now practically deserted, and wandered around the patch of waste land and in among the piles of bricks and rotting timber where the houses had been pulled down.

"Your lady friend was right," said Thorndyke. "This is a perfect Paradise for rats. Convenient residences among the ruins and unlimited provisions to be had for the mere picking up."

"Apparently you were right, too," said I, "as to the species inhabiting these eligible premises. That seems to be a black rat," and I pointed to a deceased specimen that lay near the entrance to a burrow.

Thorndyke stooped over the little corpse, and after a brief inspection, drew a glove on his right hand.

"Yes," he said, "this is a typical specimen of *Mus rattus*, though it is unusually light in colour. I think it will be worth taking away to examine at our leisure."

Glancing round to see that we were unobserved, he opened his *attaché* case and took from it a largish tin canister and removed the lid—which, I noted, was anointed at the joint with Vaseline. Stooping, he picked up the dead rat by the tail with his gloved fingers dropped it into the canister, clapped on the lid, and replaced it in the *attaché* case. Then he pulled off the glove and threw it on a rubbish heap.

"You are mighty particular," said I.

"A dead rat is a dirty thing," said he, "and it was only an old glove."

On our way home I made various cautious attempt to extract from Thorndyke some hint as to the purpose of his investigation and his mode of procedure. But I could extract nothing from him beyond certain generalities.

"When a man," said he, "introduces an incendiary bomb into the strong-room of a bank, we may reasonably inquire as to his motives. And when we have reached the fairly obvious conclusion as to what those motives must be, we may ask ourselves what kind of conduct such motives will probably generate; that is, what sort of activities will be likely to be associated with such motives and with the appropriate state of mind. And when we have decided on that, too, we may look for a person engaged in those activities; and if we find such a person we may consider that we have a *prima facie* case. The rest is a matter of verification."

"That is all very well, Thorndyke," I objected, "but if I find a man trying to set fire to a bank, I don't immediately infer that his customary occupation is exhibiting performing rats in a back street of Bethnal Green."

Thorndyke laughed quietly. "My learned friend's observation is perfectly just. It is not a universal rule. But we are dealing with a specific case in which certain other facts are known to us. Still, the connection, if there is one, has yet to be established. This exhibitor may turn out not to be Balcombe's man after all."

"And if he is not?"

"I think we shall want him all the same; but I shall know better in a couple of hours' time."

What transpired during those two hours I did not discover at the time, for I had an engagement to dine with some legal friends and must needs hurry away as soon as I had purified myself from the effects of our travel in the unclean East. When I returned to our chambers, about half-past ten, I found Thorndyke seated in his easy chair immersed in a treatise on old musical instruments. Apparently he had finished with the case.

"How did Polton get on?" I asked.

"Admirably," replied Thorndyke. "He shadowed our entertaining friend from Bethnal Green to a by street in Ratcliff, where he apparently resides. But he did more than that. We had made up a little book of a dozen leaves of transfer paper in which I wrote in French some infallible rules for taming rats. Just as the man was going into his house, Polton accosted him and asked him for an expert opinion on these directions. The foreign gentleman was at first impatient and huffy, but when he had glanced at the book, he became interested, and a good deal amused, and finally read the whole set of rules through attentively. Then he handed the book back to Polton and recommended him to follow the rules carefully, offering to supply him with a few rats to experiment on, an offer which Polton asked him to hold over for a day or two.

"As soon as he got home, Polton dismembered the book and put the leaves down on the stone, with this result."

He took from his pocket-book a number of small pieces of paper, each of which was marked more or less distinctly with lithographed reproductions of fingerprints, and laid them on the table. I looked through them attentively, and with a faint sense of familiarity.

"Isn't that left thumb," said I, "rather similar to the print on the maps from Mr. Rabbage's letter wallet?"

"It is identical," he replied. "Here are the proofs of the map-prints and the note-tablet. If you compare them you can see that not only the left thumb but the other prints are the same in all."

Careful comparison showed that this was so.

"But," I exclaimed, "I don't understand this at all. These are the finger-prints of Mr. Rabbage's mysterious entomologist. I thought you were looking for Balcombe's man."

"My impression," he replied "is that they are the same person, though the evidence is far from conclusive. But we shall soon know. I have sworn an information against the foreign gent, and Miller has arranged to raid the house at Ratcliff early tomorrow and as it promises to be a highly interesting event, I propose to be present. Shall I have the pleasure of my learned friend's company?"

"Most undoubtedly," I replied, "though I am absolutely in the dark as to the meaning of the whole affair."

"Then," said Thorndyke, "I recommend you to go over the history of both cases systematically in the interval."

Six o'clock on the following morning found us in an empty house in Old Gravel Lane, Ratcliff, in company with Superintendent Miller and three stalwart plain clothes men, awaiting the report of a patrol. We were all dressed in engineers' overalls, reeking with *naphthalin*. Our trousers were tucked into our socks, and socks and boots were thickly smeared with vaseline, as were our wrists, around which our sleeves were bound closely with tape. These preparations, together with an automatic pistol served out to each of us, gave me some faint inkling of the nature of the case, though it was still very confused in my mind.

About a quarter-past six a messenger arrived and reported that the house which was to be raided was open. Thereupon Miller and one of his men set forth, and the rest of us followed at short intervals. On arriving at the house, which was but a short distance from our rendezvous, we found a stolid plain-clothes man guarding the open door and a frowsy-looking woman, who carried a jug of milk, angrily demanding in very imperfect English to be allowed to pass into her house. Pushing past the protesting housekeeper, we entered the grimy passage, where Miller was just emerging from a ground-floor room.

"That is the woman's quarters," said he, "and the kitchen seems to be a sort of rat-menagerie. We'd better try the first-floor."

He led the way up the stairs, and when he reached the landing he tried the handle of the front room. Finding the door locked or bolted, he passed on to the back room and tried the door of that, with the same result. Then, holding up a warning finger, he proceeded to whistle a popular air in a fine, penetrating tone, and to perform a double shuffle on the bare floor.

Almost immediately an angry voice was heard in the front room, and slippered feet padded quickly across the floor. Then a bolt was drawn noisily, the door flew open, and for an instant I had a view of the rat-show man, clothed in a suit of very soiled pyjamas. But it was only for an instant. Even as our eyes met, he tried to slam the door to, and failing—in consequence of an intruding constabulary foot—he sprang back, leaped over a bed and darted through a communicating doorway into the back room and shut and bolted the door.

"That's unfortunate," said Miller. "Now we're going to have trouble."

The superintendent was right. On the first attempt to force the door, a pistol-shot from within blew a hole in the top panel and made a notch in the ear of the would-be invader. The latter replied through the hole, and there followed a sort of snarl and the sound of a shattered bottle. Then, as the constable stood aside and shot after shot came from within, the door became studded with ragged holes. Meanwhile Miller, Thorndyke and I tiptoed out on the landing, and taking as long a run as was possible, flung ourselves, simultaneously on the back-room door. The weight of three large men was too much for the crazy woodwork. As we fell on it together, there was a bursting crash, the hinges tore away, the door flew inwards, and we staggered into the room.

It was a narrow shave for some of us. Before we could recover our footing, the showman had turned with his pistol pointing straight at Miller's head. A bare instant before it exploded, Thorndyke, whose momentum had carried him half-way across the room, caught it with an upward snatch, and its report was followed by a harmless shower of plaster from the ceiling. Immediately our quarry changed his tactics. Leaving the pistol in Thorndyke's grasp, he darted across the room towards a work-bench on which stood a row of upright, cylindrical tins. He was in the act of reaching out for one of these when Thorndyke grasped his pyjamas between the shoulders and dragged him back, while Miller rushed forward and seized him.

For a few moments there was a frantic and furious struggle, for the fellow fought with hands and feet and teeth with the ferocity of a wild cat, and, overpowered as he was, still strove to drag his captors towards the bench. Suddenly, once more, a pistol-shot rang out, and then all was still. By accident or design the struggling man had got hold of the pistol that Thorndyke still grasped and pressed the trigger, and the bullet had entered his own head just above the ear.

"Pooh!" exclaimed Miller, rising and wiping his forehead, "that was a near one. If you hadn't stopped him, doctor, we'd all have gone up like rockets."

"You think those things are bombs, then?" said I.

"Think!" he repeated. "I removed two exactly like them from the General Post Office, and they turned out to be charged with T.N.T.

And those square ones on the shelf are twin brothers of the one that went off in Rutherford's Bank."

As we were speaking, I happened to glance round at the doorway, and there, to my surprise, was the woman whom we had seen below, still holding the jug of milk and staring in with an expression of horror at the dead revolutionary. Thorndyke also observed her, and stepping across to where she stood, asked: "Can you tell me if there has been, or is now, anyone sick in this house?

"Yes," the woman replied, without removing her eyes from the dead man. "Dere is a chentleman sick upstairs. I haf not seen him. He used to look after him," and she nodded to the dead body of the showman.

"I think we will go up and have a look at this sick gentleman," said Thorndyke. "You had better not come, Miller."

We started together up the stairs, and as we went I asked: "Do you suppose this is a case of plague?"

"No," he replied. "I fancy the plague department is in the kitchen; but we shall see."

He looked round the landing which we had now reached and then opened the door of the front room, Immediately I was aware of a strange, intensely fetid odour, and glancing into the room, I perceived a man lying, apparently in a state of stupor, in a bed covered with indescribably filthy bedclothes. Thorndyke entered and approached the bed, and I followed. The light was rather dim, and it was not until we were quite close that I suddenly recognised the disease.

"Good God!" I exclaimed, "it is typhus!"

"Yes," said Thorndyke; "and look at the bed clothes, and look at the poor devil's neck. We can see now how that villain collected his specimens."

I stooped over the poor, muttering, unconscious wretch and was filled with horror. Bedclothes, pillow and patient were all alike crawling with vermin.

★★★★★★★★

"Of course," I said as we walked homewards, "I see the general drift of this case, but what I can't under stand is how you connected up the facts."

"Well," replied Thorndyke, "let us set out the argument and trace the connections. The starting-point was the aluminium case that Mr. Rabbage brought us. Those tubes of fleas and lice were clearly an abnormal phenomenon. They might, as you suggested, have belonged to a scientific collector; but that was not probable. The fleas were alive, and were meant to remain alive, as the perforated caps of the tubes proved, And the lice had merely died, as lice quickly do if they are not fed. They did not appear to have been killed. But against your view there were two very striking facts, one of which I fancy you did not observe. The fleas were not the common human flea; they were Asiatic rat-fleas."

"You are quite right," I admitted. "I did not notice that."

"Then," he continued, "there was the aniseed with which the parchment caps of the tubes were scented. Now aniseed is irresistible to rats. It is an infallible bait. But it is not specially attractive to fleas. What then was the purpose of the scent? The answer, fantastic as it was, had to be provisionally accepted because it was the only one that suggested itself. If one of these tubes had been exposed to rats—dropped down a rat-hole, for instance—it is certain that the rats would have gnawed off the parchment cap. Then the fleas would have been liberated, and as they were rat-fleas, they would have immediately fastened upon the rats. The tubes, therefore, appeared to be an apparatus for disseminating rat-fleas.

"But why should anyone want to disseminate rat-fleas? That question at once brought into view another striking fact, Here, in these tubes, were rat-fleas and body-lice: both carriers of deadly disease. The rat-flea is a carrier of plague; the body-louse is a carrier of typhus. It was an impressive coincidence. It suggested that the dissemination of rat-fleas might be really the dissemination of plague; and if the lice were distributed, too, that might mean the distribution of typhus.

"And now consider the maps. The circles on them all marked old slum-areas tenanted by low-class aliens. But old slums abound in rats; and low-class aliens abound in body-lice. Here was another coincidence. Then there was the note-tablet bearing numbers associated with the letters a and b and plus and minus signs. The letters a and b might mean rat and louse or plague and typhus, and the plus and minus might mean a success or a failure to produce an outbreak of disease. That was merely speculative, but it was quite consistent.

"So far we were dealing with a hypothesis based on simple observation. But that hypothesis could be proved or disproved. The question was: Were these insects infected insects, or were they not? To settle this I took one flea from each of the four tubes and 'sowed' it on agar, with the result that from each flea I got a typical culture of plague *bacillus*, which I verified with Haffkine's 'Stalactite test.' I also examined one louse from each of the two tubes, and in each case got a definite typhus reaction. So the insects were infected and the hypothesis was confirmed.

"The next thing was to find the owner of the tubes. Now the circles on the maps indicated some sort of activity, presumably connected with rats and carried on in these areas.

"I visited those areas and got into conversation with the inhabitants on the subject of rats, rat-catchers, rat pits, sewermen, and everything bearing on rats; and at length I heard of an exhibitor of performing rats. You know the rest. We found the man, we observe that all his rats, excepting the tame white ones, were black rats—the special plague-carrying species—and we found on this spot a dead rat, which I ascertained on examining the body, had died of plague. Finally there was Polton's little book giving us the finger prints of the owner of the aluminium case. That completed the identification; and inquiries at the Local Government Board showed that cases of plague and typhus had occurred in the marked areas."

"Had not the authorities taken any steps in the matter?" I asked.

"Oh, yes," he replied. "They had carried out an energetic rat campaign in the London Docks, the likeliest source of infection. Naturally, they would not think of a criminal lunatic industriously sowing plague broadcast."

"Then how did you connect this man with the bank outrage?"

"I never did, very conclusively," he replied. "It was mostly a matter of inference. You see, the two crimes were essentially similar. They were varieties of the same type. Both were cases of idiotic destructiveness, and the agent in each was evidently a moral imbecile who was a professed enemy of society. Such persons are rare in this country, and when they occur are usually foreigners, most commonly Russians, or East Europeans of some kind. The only actual clue was the date on Pilcher's letter, the rather peculiar figures of which were extraordinarily like those on the maps and the note-tablet. Still, it was little more than a guess, though it happens to have turned out correct."

"And how do you suppose this fellow avoided getting plague and typhus himself?"

"It was quite likely that he had had both. But he could easily avoid the typhus by keeping himself clean and his clothing disinfected; and as to the plague, he could have used Haffkine's plague-prophylactic and given it to the woman. Clearly it would not have suited him to have a case of plague in the house and have the health officer inspecting the premises."

That was the end of the case, unless I should include in the history a very handsome fee sent to my colleague by the President of the Local Government Board.

"I think we have earned it," said Thorndyke; "and yet I am not sure that Mr. Rabbage is not entitled to a share."

And in fact, when that benevolent person called a few days later to receive a slightly ambiguous report and tender his fee, he departed beaming, bearing a donation wherewith to endow an additional bed, cot, or basket, in the St. Francis Home of Rest.

Gleanings From the Wreckage

There was a time, and not so very long ago, when even the main streets of London, after midnight, were as silent as—not the grave; that is an unpleasant simile. Besides, who has any experience of conditions in the grave? But they were nearly as silent as the streets of a village. Then the nocturnal pedestrian could go his way encompassed and soothed by quiet, which was hardly disturbed by the rumble of a country wagon wending to market or the musical tinkle of the little bells on the collar of the hansom-cab horse sedately drawing some late reveller homeward.

Very different is the state of those streets nowadays. Long after the hour when the electric trams have ceased from troubling and the motor omnibuses are at rest, the heavy road transport from the country thunders through the streets; the air is rent by the howls of the electric hooter, and belated motor-cyclists fly past, stuttering explosively like perambulant Lewis guns with an inexhaustible charge.

"Let us get into the by-streets," said Thorndyke, as a car sped past us uttering sounds suggestive of a dyspeptic dinosaur. "We don't want our conversation seasoned with mechanical objurgations. In the back-streets it is still possible to hear oneself speak and forget the march of progress."

We turned into a narrow by-way with the confidence of the born and bred Londoner in the impossibility of losing our direction, and began to thread the intricate web of streets in the neighbourhood of a canal.

"It is a remarkable thing," Thorndyke resumed *anon*, "that every new application of science seems to be designed to render the environment of civilised man more and more disagreeable. If the process goes much farther, as it undoubtedly will, we shall presently find ourselves looking back wistfully at the Stone-Age as the golden age of human comfort."

At this point his moralising was cut short by a loud, sharp explosion. We both stopped and looked about from the parapet of the bridge that we were crossing.

"Quite like old times," Thorndyke remarked. "Carries one back to 1915, when friend Fritz used to call on us. Ah! There is the place; the top story of that tall building across the canal." He pointed as he spoke to a factory-like structure, from the upper windows of which a lurid light shone and rapidly grew brighter.

"It must be down the next turning," said I, quickening my pace.

But he restrained me, remarking: "There is no hurry. That was the sound of high explosive, and those flames suggest nitro compounds burning. *Festina lente.* There may be some other packets of high explosives."

He had hardly finished speaking when a flash of dazzling violet light burst from the burning building. The windows flew out bodily, the roof opened in places, and almost at the same moment the clang of a violent explosion shook the ground under our feet, a puff of wind stirred our hair, and then came a clatter of falling glass and slates.

We made our way at a leisurely pace towards the scene of the explosion, through streets lighted up by the ruddy glare from the burning factory. But others were less cautious. In a few minutes the street was filled by one of those crowds which, in London, seem mysteriously to spring up in an instant where but a moment before not a person was to be seen. Before we had reached the building, a fire-engine had rumbled past us, and already a sprinkling of policemen had appeared as if, like the traditional frogs, they had dropped from the clouds.

In spite of the ferocity of its outbreak, the fire seemed to be no great matter, for even as we looked and before the fire-hose was fully run out, the flames began to die down. Evidently, they had been dealt with by means of extinguishers within the building, and the services of the engine would not be required after all. Noting this flat ending to what had seemed so promising a start, we were about to move off and resume our homeward journey when I observed a uniformed inspector who was known to us, and who, observing us at the same instant, made his way towards us through the crowd.

"You remind me, sir," said he, when he had wished us good-evening, "of the stories of the vultures that make their way in the sky from nowhere when a camel drops dead in the desert. I don't mean anything uncomplimentary," he hastened to add. "I was only thinking of the wonderful instinct that has brought you to this very spot at this identical moment, as if you had smelt a case afar off."

"Then your imagination has misled you," said Thorndyke, "for I haven't smelt a case, and I don't smell one now. Fires are not in my province."

"No, sir," replied the inspector, "but bodies are, and the fireman tells me that there is a dead man up there—or at least the remains of one. I am going up to inspect. Do you care to come up with me?"

Thorndyke considered for a moment, but I knew what his answer would be, and I was not mistaken.

"As a matter of professional interest, I should," he replied, "but I don't want to be summoned as a witness at the inquest."

"Of course you don't, sir," the inspector agreed, "and I will see that you are not summoned, unless an expert witness is wanted. I need not mention that you have been here; but I should be glad of your opinion for my own guidance in investigating the case."

He led us through the crowd to the door of the building, where we were joined by a fireman—whose helmet I should have liked to borrow—by whom we were piloted up the stairs. Half up we met the night-watchman, carrying an exhausted extinguisher and a big electric lantern, and he joined our procession, giving us the news as we ascended.

"It's all safe up above," said he, "excepting the roof; and that isn't so very much damaged. The big windows saved it. They blew out and let off the force of the explosion. The floor isn't damaged at all. It's girder and concrete. But poor Mr. Manford caught it properly. He was fairly blown to bits."

"Do you know how it happened?" the inspector asked.

"I don't," was the reply. "When I came on duty Mr. Manford was up there in his private laboratory. Soon afterwards a friend of his—a foreign gentleman of the name of Bilsky—came to see him. I took him up, and then Mr. Manford said he had some business to do, and after that he had got a longish job to do and would be working late. So he said I might turn in and he would let me know when he had finished. And he did let me know with a vengeance, poor chap. I lay down in my clothes, and I hadn't been asleep above a couple of hours when some noise woke me up.

"Then there came a most almighty bang. I rushed for an extinguisher and ran upstairs, and there I found the big laboratory all ablaze, the windows blown out and the ceiling down. But it wasn't so bad as it looked. There wasn't very much stuff up there; only the experimental stuff, and that burned out almost at once. I got the rest of the fire out in a few minutes."

"What stuff is it that you are speaking of?" the inspector asked.

"Celluloid, mostly, I think," replied the watchman. "They make films and other celluloid goods in the works. But Mr. Manford used to do experiments in the material up in his laboratory. This time he was working with alloys, melting them on the gas furnace. Dangerous thing to do with all that inflammable stuff about. I don't know what there was up there, exactly. Some of it was celluloid, I could see by the way it burned, but the Lord knows what it was that exploded. Some of the raw stuff, perhaps."

At this point we reached the top floor, where a door blown off its hinges and a litter of charred wood fragments filled the landing. Passing through the yawning doorway, we entered the laboratory and looked on a hideous scene of devastation. The windows were mere holes, the ceiling a gaping space fringed with black and ragged lathing, through which the damaged roof was visible by the light of the watchman's powerful lantern. The floor was covered with the fallen plaster and fragments of blackened woodwork, but its own boards were only slightly burnt in places, owing, no doubt, to their being fastened directly to the concrete which formed the actual floor.

"You spoke of some human remains," said the inspector.

"Ah!" said the watchman, "you may well say 'remains'. Just come here." He led the way over the rubbish to a corner of the laboratory, where he halted and threw the light of his lantern down on a brownish, dusty, globular object that lay on the floor half buried in plaster. "That's all that's left of poor Mr. Manford; that and a few other odd pieces. I saw a hand over the other side."

Thorndyke picked up the head and placed it on the blackened remnant of a bench, where, with the aid of the watchman's lantern and the inspection lamp which I produced from our research-case, he examined it curiously. It was extremely, but unequally, scorched. One ear was completely shrivelled, and most of the face was charred to the bone. But the other ear was almost intact; and though most of the hair was burned away to the scalp, a tuft above the less damaged ear was only singed, so that it was possible to see that the hair had been black, with here and there a stray white hair.

Thorndyke made no comments, but I noticed that he examined the gruesome object minutely, taking nothing for granted. The inspector noticed this, too; and when the examination was finished, looked at him inquiringly.

"Anything abnormal, sir?" he asked.

"No," replied Thorndyke; "nothing that is not accounted for by fire and the explosion. I see he had no natural teeth, so he must have worn a complete set of false teeth. That should help in the formal identification, if the plates are not completely destroyed."

"There isn't much need for identification," said the watchman, "seeing that there was nobody in the building but him and me. His friend went away about half-past twelve. I heard Mr. Manford let him out."

"The doctor means at the inquest," the inspector explained. "Somebody has got to recognise the body if possible."

He took the watchman's lantern, and throwing its light on the floor, began to search among the rubbish. Very soon he disinterred from under a heap of plaster the headless trunk. Both legs were attached, though the right was charred below the knee and the foot blown off, and one complete arm. The other arm—the right—was intact only to the elbow. Here, again, the burning was very unequal.

In some parts the clothing had been burnt off or blown away completely; in others, enough was left to enable the watchman to recognise it with certainty. One leg was much more burnt than the other; and whereas the complete arm was only scorched, the dismembered one was charred almost to the bone. When the trunk had been carried to the bench and laid there beside the head, the lights were turned on it for Thorndyke to make his inspection.

"It almost seems," said the police officer, as the hand was being examined, "as if one could guess how he was standing when the explosion occurred. I think I can make out finger-marks—pretty dirty ones, too—on the back of the hand, as if he had been standing with his hands clasped together behind him while he watched something that he was experimenting with." The inspector glanced for confirmation at Thorndyke, who nodded approvingly.

"Yes," he said, "I think you are right. They are very indistinct, but the marks are grouped like fingers. The small mark near the wrist suggests a little finger and the separate one near the knuckle looks like a fore-finger, while the remaining two marks are close together." He turned the hand over and continued "And there, in the palm, just between the roots of the third and fourth fingers, seems to be the trace of a thumb. But they are all very faint. You have a quick eye, inspector."

The gratified officer, thus encouraged, resumed his explorations among the debris in company with the watchman—the fireman had retired after a professional look round—leaving Thorndyke to continue his examination of the mutilated corpse, at which I looked on unsympathetically. For we had had a long day and I was tired and longing to get home. At length I drew out my watch, and with a portentous yawn, entered a mild protest.

"It is nearly two o'clock," said I. "Don't you think we had better be getting on? This really isn't any concern of ours, and there doesn't seem to be anything in it, from our point of view."

"Only that we are keeping our intellectual joints supple," Thorndyke replied with a smile. "But it is getting late. Perhaps we had better adjourn the inquiry."

At this moment, however, the inspector discovered the missing forearm—completely charred—with the fingerless remains of the hand, and almost immediately afterwards the watchman picked up a dental plate of some white metal, which seemed to be practically uninjured. But our brief inspection of these objects elicited nothing of interest, and having glanced at them, we took our departure, avoiding on the stairs an eager reporter, all agog for "copy."

A few days later we received a visit, by appointment, from a Mr. Herdman, a solicitor who was unknown to us and who was accompanied by the widow of Mr. James Manford, the victim of the explosion. In the interval the inquest had been opened but had been adjourned for further examination of the premises and the remains. No mention had been made of our visit to the building, and so far as I knew nothing had been said to anybody on the subject.

Mr. Herdman came to the point with business directness.

"I have called," he said, "to secure your services, if possible, in regard to the matter of which I spoke in my letter. You have probably seen an account of the disaster in the papers?"

"Yes," replied Thorndyke. "I read the report of the inquest."

"Then you know the principal facts. The inquest, as you know, was adjourned for three weeks. When it is resumed; I should like to retain you to attend on behalf of Mrs. Manford."

"To watch the case on her behalf?" Thorndyke suggested.

"Well, not exactly," replied Herdman. "I should ask you to inspect the premises and the remains of poor Mr. Manford, so that, at the adjourned inquest, you could give evidence to the effect that the explosion and the death of Mr. Manford were entirely due to accident."

"Does anyone say that they were not?" Thorndyke asked.

"No, certainly not," Mr. Herdman replied hastily. "Not at all. But I happened, quite by chance, to see the manager of the 'Pilot' Insurance Society, on another matter, and I mentioned the case of Mr. Manford. He then let drop a remark which made me slightly uneasy. He observed that there was a suicide clause in the policy, and that the possibility of suicide would have to be ruled out before the claim could be settled. Which suggested a possible intention to contest the claim."

"But," said Thorndyke, "I need not point out to you that if he sets up the theory of suicide, it is for him to prove it, not for you to disprove it. Has anything transpired which would lend colour to such a suggestion?"

"Nothing material," was the reply. "But we should feel more happy if you could be present and give positive evidence that the death was accidental."

"That," said Thorndyke, "would be hardly possible. But my feeling is that the suicide question is negligible. There is nothing to suggest it, so far as I know. Is there anything known to you?"

The solicitor glanced at his client and replied somewhat evasively: "We are anxious to secure ourselves. Mrs. Manford is left very badly off, unless there is some personal property that we don't know about. If the insurance is not paid, she will be absolutely ruined. There isn't enough to pay the debts. And I think the suicide question might be raised—even successfully—on several points. Manford had been rather queer lately: jumpy and rather worried. Then, he was under notice to terminate his engagement at the works. His finances were in a confused state; goodness knows why, for he had a liberal salary. And then there was some domestic trouble. Mrs. Manford had actually consulted me about getting a separation. Some other woman, you know."

"I should like to forget that," said Mrs. Manford; "and it wasn't that which worried him. Quite the contrary. Since it began he had been quite changed. So smart in his dress and so particular in his appearance. He even took to dyeing his hair. I remember that he opened a fresh bottle of dye the very morning before his death and took no end of trouble putting it on. It wasn't that entanglement that made him jumpy. It was his money affairs. He had too many irons in the fire."

Thorndyke listened with patient attention to these rather irrelevant details and inquired: "What sort of irons?"

"I will tell you," said Herdman. "About three months ago he had need for two thousand pounds; for what purpose, I can't say, but Mrs.

Manford thinks it was to invest in certain valuables that he used to purchase from time to time from a Russian dealer named Bilsky. At any rate, he got this sum on short loan from a Mr. Clines, but meanwhile arranged for a longer loan with a Mr. Elliott on a note of hand and an agreement to insure his life for the amount.

"As a matter of fact, the policy was made out in Elliott's name, he having proved an insurable interest. So if the insurance is paid, Elliott is settled with. Otherwise the debt falls on the estate, which would be disastrous; and to make it worse, the day before his death, he drew out five hundred pounds—nearly the whole balance—as he was expecting to see Mr. Bilsky, who liked to be paid in banknotes. He did see him, in fact, at the laboratory, but they couldn't have done any business, as no jewels were found."

"And the bank-notes?"

"Burned with the body, presumably. He must have had them with him."

"You mentioned," said Thorndyke, "that he occasionally bought jewels from this Russian. What became of them?"

"Ah!" replied Herdman, "there is a gleam of hope there. He had a safe deposit somewhere. We haven't located it yet, but we shall. There may be quite a nice little nest-egg in it. But meanwhile there is the debt to Elliott. He wrote to Manford about it a day or two ago. You have the letter, I think," he added, addressing Mrs. Manford, who thereupon produced two envelopes from her handbag and laid them on the table.

"This is Mr. Elliott's letter," she said. "Merely a friendly reminder, you see, telling him that he is just off to the Continent and that he has given his wife a power of attorney to act in his absence."

Thorndyke glanced through the letter and made a few notes of its contents. Then he looked inquiringly at the other envelope.

"That," said Mrs. Manford, "'is a photograph of my husband. I thought it might help you if you were going to examine the body."

As Thorndyke drew the portrait out and regarded it thoughtfully, I recalled the shapeless, blackened fragments of its subject; and when he passed it to me, I inspected it with a certain grim interest, and mentally compared it with those grisly remains. It was a commonplace face, rather unsymmetrical—the nose was deflected markedly to the left, and the left eye had a pronounced divergent squint. The bald head, with an abundant black fringe and an irregular scar on the side of the forehead, sought compensation in a full beard and moustache, both apparently jet-black. It was not an attractive countenance, and it was not improved by a rather odd-shaped ear—long, lobeless, and pointed above, like the ear of a satyr.

"I realise your position," said Thorndyke, "but I don't quite see what you want of me. If," he continued, addressing the solicitor, "you had thought of my giving *ex parte* evidence, dismiss the idea. I am not a witness-advocate. All I can undertake to do is to investigate the case and try to discover what really happened. But in that case, whatever I may discover I shall disclose to the coroner. Would that suit you?"

The lawyer looked doubtful and rather glum, but Mrs. Manford interposed, firmly: "Why not? We are not proposing any deception, but I am certain that he did not commit suicide. I agree unreservedly to what you propose."

With this understanding—which the lawyer was disposed to boggle at—our visitors took their leave. As soon as they were gone, I gave utterance to the surprise with which I had listened to Thorndyke's proposal.

"I am astonished at your undertaking this case. Of course, you have given them fair warning, but still, it will be unpleasant if you have to give evidence unfavourable to your client."

"Very," he agreed. "But what makes you think I may have to?"

"Well, you seem to reject the probability of suicide, but have you forgotten the evidence at the inquest?"

"Perhaps I have," he replied blandly. "Let us go over it again."

I fetched the report from the office, and spreading it out on the table began to read it aloud. Passing over the evidence of the inspector and the fireman, I came to that of the night-watchman.

"Shortly after I came on duty at ten o'clock, a foreign, gentleman named Bilsky called to see Mr. Manford. I knew him by sight, because he had called once or twice before at about the same time. I took him up to the laboratory, where Mr. Manford was doing something with a big crucible on the gas furnace. He told me that he had some business to transact with Mr. Bilsky and when he had finished he would let him out. Then he was going to do some experiments in making alloys, and as they would probably take up most of the night he said I might as well turn in. He said he would call me when he was ready to go.

"So I told him to be careful with the furnace and not set the place on fire and burn me in my bed, and then I went downstairs. I had a look round to see that everything was in order, and then I took off my boots and laid down. About half-past twelve I heard Mr. Manford and Bilsky come down. I recognised Mr. Bilsky by a peculiar cough that he had and by the sound of his stick and his limping tread—he had something the matter with his right foot and walked quite lame."

"You say that the deceased came down with him," said the coroner. "Are you quite sure of that?"

"Well, I suppose Mr. Manford came down with him, but I can't say I actually heard him."

"You did not hear him go up again?"

"No, I didn't. But I was rather sleepy and I wasn't listening very particular. Well, then I went to sleep and slept till about half-past one, when some noise woke me. I was just getting up to see what it was when I heard a tremendous bang, right overhead. I ran down and turned the gas off at the main and then I got a fire extinguisher and ran up to the laboratory. The place seemed to be all in a blaze, but it wasn't much of a fire after all, for by the time the fire engines arrived I had got it practically out."

The witness then described the state of the laboratory and the finding of the body, but as this was already known to us, I passed on to the evidence of the next witness, the superintendent of the fire brigade, who had made a preliminary inspection of the premises. It was a cautious statement and subject to the results of a further examination; but clearly the officer was not satisfied as to the cause of the outbreak. There seemed to have been two separate explosions, one near a cupboard and another—apparently the second—in the cupboard itself; and there seemed to be a burned track connecting the two spots. This might have been accidental or it might have been arranged. Witness did not think that the explosive was celluloid. It seemed to be a high explosive of some kind. But further investigations were being made.

The superintendent was followed by Mrs. Manford, whose evidence was substantially similar to what she and Mr. Herdman had told us, and by the police surgeon, whose description of the remains conveyed nothing new to us. Finally, the inquest was adjourned for three weeks to allow of further examination of the premises and the remains.

"Now," I said, as I folded up the report, "I don't see how you are able to exclude suicide. If the explosion was arranged to occur when Manford was in the laboratory, what object, other than suicide, can be imagined?"

Thorndyke looked at me with an expression that I knew only too well. "Is it impossible," he asked, "to imagine that the object might have been homicide?"

"But," I objected, "there was no one there but Manford—after Bilsky left."

"Exactly," he agreed, dryly; "after Bilsky left. But up to that time there were two persons there."

I must confess that I was startled, but as I rapidly reviewed the circumstances I perceived the cogency of Thorndyke's suggestion. Bilsky had been present when Manford dismissed the night-watchman. He knew that there would be no interruption. The inflammable and explosive materials were there, ready to his hand. Then Bilsky had gone down to the door alone instead of being conducted down and let out; a very striking circumstance, this. Again, no jewels had been found though the meeting had been ostensibly for the purpose of a deal; and the bank-notes had vanished utterly. This was very remarkable. In view of the large sum, it was nearly certain that the notes would be in a close bundle, and we all know how difficult it is to burn tightly-folded paper. Yet they had vanished without leaving a trace. Finally, there was Bilsky himself. Who was he? Apparently a dealer in stolen property—a hawker of the products of robbery and murder committed during the revolution.

"Yes," I admitted, "the theory of homicide is certainly tenable. But unless some new facts can be produced, it must remain a matter of speculation."

"I think, Jervis," he rejoined, "you must be overlooking the facts that are known to us. We were there. We saw the place within a few minutes of the explosion and we examined the body. What we saw established a clear presumption of homicide, and what we have heard this, morning confirms it. I may say that I communicated my suspicions the very next day to the coroner and to Superintendent Miller."

"Then you must have seen more than I did," I began. But he shook his head and cut short my protestations.

"You saw what I saw, Jervis, but you did not interpret its meaning. However, it is not too late. Try to recall the details of our adventure and what our visitors have told us. I don't think you will then entertain the idea of suicide."

I was about to put one or two leading questions, but at this moment footsteps became audible ascending our stairs. The knock which followed informed me that our visitor was Superintendent Miller, and I rose to admit him.

"Just looked in to report progress," he announced as he subsided into an armchair. "Not much to report, but what there is supports your view of the case. Bilsky has made a clean bolt. Never went home to his hotel. Evidently meant to skedaddle, as he has left nothing of any value behind. But it was a stupid move, for it would have raised suspicion in any case. The notes were a consecutive batch. All the numbers are known, but, of course, none of them have turned up yet. We have made inquiries about Bilsky, and gather that he is a shady character; practically a fence who deals in the jewellery stolen from those unfortunate Russian aristocrats. But we shall have him all right. His description has been circulated at all the seaports and he is an easy man to spot with his lame foot and his stick and a finger missing from his right hand."

Thorndyke nodded, and seemed to reflect for a moment. Then he asked: "Have you made any other inquiries?"

"No; there is nothing more to find out until we get hold of our man, and when we do, we shall look to you to secure the conviction. I suppose you are quite certain as to your facts?"

Thorndyke shook his head with a smile.

"I am never certain until after the event. We can only act on probabilities."

"I understand," said the superintendent, casting a sly look at me; "but your probabilities are good enough for me."

With this, he picked up his hat and departed, leaving us to return to the occupations that our visitors had interrupted.

I heard no more of the Manford case for about a week, and assumed that Thorndyke's interest in it had ceased. But I was mistaken, as I discovered when he remarked casually one evening: "No news of Bilsky, so far; and time is running on. I am proposing to make a tentative move in a new direction." I looked at him inquiringly, and he continued: "It appears, 'from information received,' that Elliott had some dealings with him, so I propose to call at his house tomorrow and see if we can glean any news of the lost sheep."

"But Elliott is abroad," I objected.

"True; but his wife isn't; and she evidently knows all about his affairs. I have invited Miller to come with me in case he would like to put any questions; and you may as well come, too, if you are free."

It did not sound like a very thrilling adventure, but one never knew with Thorndyke. I decided to go with him, and at that the matter dropped, though I speculated a little curiously on the source of the information. So, apparently, had the superintendent, for when he arrived on the following morning he proceeded to throw out a few cautious feelers, but got nothing for his pains beyond vague generalities.

"It is a purely tentative proceeding," said Thorndyke, "and you mustn't be disappointed if nothing comes of it."

"I shall be, all the same," replied Miller, with a sly glance at my senior, and with this we set forth on our quest.

The Elliotts' house was, as I knew, in some part of Wimbledon, and thither we made our way by train. From the station we started along a wide, straight main street from which numbers of smaller streets branched off. At the corner of one of these I noticed a man standing, apparently watching our approach; and something in his appearance seemed to me familiar. Suddenly he took off his hat, looked curiously into its interior, and put it on again. Then he turned about and walked quickly down the side street.

I looked at his retreating figure as we crossed the street, wondering who he could be. And then it flashed upon me that the resemblance was to a certain ex-sergeant Barber whom Thorndyke occasionally employed for observation duties. Just as I reached this conclusion, Thorndyke halted and looked about him doubtfully.

"I am afraid we have come too far," said he. "I fancy we ought to have gone down that last turning." We accordingly faced about and walked back to the corner, where Thorndyke read out the name, Mendoza Avenue.

"Yes," he said, "this is the way," and we thereupon turned down the Avenue, following it to the bottom, where it ended in a cross-road, the name of which, Berners Park, I recognised as that which I had seen on Elliott's letter.

"Sixty-four is the number," said Thorndyke, "so as this corner house is forty-six and the next is forty-eight, it will be a little way along on this side, just about where you can see that smoke—which, by the way, seems to be coming out of a window."

"Yes, by Jove!" I exclaimed. "The staircase window, apparently. Not our house, I hope!"

But it was. We read the number and the name, 'Green Bushes', on the gate as we came up to it, and we hurried up the short path to the door. There was no knocker, but when Miller fixed his thumb on the bell-push, we heard a loud ringing within. But there was no response; and meanwhile the smoke poured more and more densely out of the open window above.

"Rum!" exclaimed Miller, sticking to the bell-push like a limpet.

"House seems to be empty."

"I don't think it is." Thorndyke replied calmly.

The superintendent looked at him with quick suspicion, and then glanced at the ground-floor window.

"That window is unfastened," said he, "and here comes a constable."

Sure enough, a policeman was approaching quickly, looking up at the houses. Suddenly he perceived the smoke and quickened his pace, arriving just as Thorndyke had pulled down the upper window-sash and was preparing to climb over into the room. The constable hailed him sternly, but a brief explanation from Miller reduced the officer to a state of respectful subservience, and we all followed Thorndyke through the open window, from which smoke now began to filter.

"Send the constable upstairs to give the alarm," Thorndyke instructed Miller in a low tone. The order was given without question, and the next moment the officer was bounding up the stairs, roaring like a whole fire brigade. Meanwhile, the superintendent browsed along the hall through the dense smoke, sniffing inquisitively, and at length approached the street door. Suddenly, from the heart of the reek, his voice issued in tones of amazement.

"Well, I'm hanged! It's a plumber's smoke-rocket. Some fool has stuck it through into the letter-cage!"

In the silence which followed this announcement I heard an angry voice from above demand: "What is all this infernal row about? And what are you doing here?"

"Can't you see that the house is on fire?" was the constable's, stern rejoinder. "You'd better come down and help to put it out."

The command was followed by the sound of descending footsteps, on which Thorndyke ran quickly up the stairs, followed by the superintendent and me. We met the descending party on the landing, opposite a window, and here we all stopped, gazing at one another with mutual curiosity. The man who accompanied the constable looked distinctly alarmed—as well he might—and somewhat hostile.

"Who put that smoke in the hall?" Miller demanded fiercely. "And why didn't you come down when you heard us ringing the bell?"

"I don't know what you a talking about." the man replied sulkily, "or what business this is of yours. Who are you? And what are you doing in my house?"

"In your house?" repeated Thorndyke. "Then you will be Mr. Elliott?"

The man turned a startled glance on him and replied angrily: "Never you mind who I am. Get out of this house."

"But I do mind who you are," Thorndyke rejoined mildly. "I came here to see Mr. Elliott. Are you Mr. Elliott?

"No, I am not. Mr. Elliott is abroad. If you like to send a letter here for him, I will forward it when I get his address."

While this conversation had been going on, I had been examining the stranger, not without curiosity. For his appearance was somewhat unusual. In the first place, he wore an unmistakable wig, and his shaven face bore an abundance of cuts and scratches, suggesting a recently and unskilfully mown beard. His spectacles did not disguise a pronounced divergent squint of the left eye; but what specially caught my attention was the ear—large ear, lobeless and pointed at the tip like the ear of a satyr. As I looked at this, and at the scraped face, the squint and the wig, a strange suspicion flashed into my mind; and then, as I noted that the nose was markedly deflected to the left, I turned to glance at Thorndyke.

"Would you mind telling us your name?" the latter asked blandly.

"My name is—is—Johnson; Frederick Johnson."

"Ah," said Thorndyke. "I thought it was Manford—James Manford—and I think so still. I suggest that you have a scar on the right side of your forehead, just under the wig. May we see?"

As Thorndyke spoke the name, the man turned a horrible livid grey and started back as if to retreat up the stairs. But the constable blocked the way; and as the man was struggling to push past, Miller adroitly snatched off the wig; and there, on the forehead, was the telltale scar.

For an appreciable time we all stood stock-still like the figures of a tableau. Then Thorndyke turned to the superintendent.

"I charge this man, James Manford, with the murder of Stephan Bilsky."

Again there was a brief interval of intolerable silence. In the midst of it, we heard the street door open and shut, and a woman's voice called up the stairs: "Whatever is all this smoke? Are you up there, Jim?"

I pass over the harrowing details of the double arrest. I am not a policeman, and to me such scenes are intensely repugnant. But we must needs stay until two taxis and four constables had conveyed the prisoners away from the still reeking house to the caravanserai of the law. Then, at last, we went forth with relief into the fresh air and bent our steps towards the station.

"I take it," Miller said reflectively, "that you never suspected Bilsky?"

"I did at first. But when Mrs. Manford and the solicitor told their tale I realised that he was the victim and that Manford must be the murderer."

"Let us have the argument," said I. "It is obvious that I have been a blockhead, but I don't mind our old friend here knowing it."

"Not a blockhead, Jervis," he corrected. "You were half asleep that night and wholly uninterested. If you had been attending to the matter, you would have observed several curious and anomalous appearances. For instance, you would have noticed that the body was, in parts, completely charred, and brittle. Now we saw the outbreak of the fire and we found it extinguished when we reached the building. Its duration was a matter of minutes; quite insufficient to reduce a body to that state.

"For, as you know, a human body is an extremely incombustible thing. The appearance suggested the destruction of a body which had been already burnt; and this suggestion was emphasised by the curiously unequal distribution of the charring. The right hand was burnt to a cinder and blown to pieces. The left hand was only scorched. The right foot was utterly destroyed, but the left foot was nearly intact. The face was burned away completely, and yet there were parts of the head where the hair was only singed.

"Naturally, with these facts in mind, I scrutinised those remains narrowly. And presently something much more definite and sinister came to light. On the left hand, there was a faint impression of another hand—very indistinct and blurred, but still unmistakably a hand."

"I remember," said I, "the inspector pointed it out as evidence that the deceased had been standing with his hands clasped before or behind him; and I must admit that it seemed a reasonable inference."

"So it did, because you were both assuming that the man had been alone and that it must therefore have been the impression of his own hand. For that reason, neither of you looked at it critically. If you had, you would have seen at once that it was the impression of a left hand."

"You are quite right," I confessed ruefully. "As the man was stated to have been alone, the hand impression did not interest me. And it was a mere group of smudges, after all. You are sure that it was a left hand?"

"Quite," he replied. "Blurred as the smudges were, one could make out the relative lengths of the fingers. And there was the thumb mark at the distal end of the palm, but pointing to the outer side of the hand. Try how you may, you can't get a right hand into that position.

"Well, then, here was a crucial fact. The mark of a left hand on a left hand proved the presence of a second person, and at once raised a strong presumption of homicide, especially when considered in conjunction with the unaccountable state of the body. During the evening, a visitor had come and gone, and on him—Bilsky—the suspicion naturally fell. But Mrs. Manford unwittingly threw an entirely new light on the case. You remember she told us that her husband had opened a new bottle of hair dye on the very morning before the explosion and had applied it with unusual care. Then his hair was dyed. But the hair of the corpse was not dyed. Therefore the corpse was not the corpse of Manford. Further, the presumption of murder applied now to Manford, and the body almost certainly was that of Bilsky."

"How did you deduce that the hair of the corpse was not dyed?" I asked.

"I didn't deduce it at all. I observed it. You remember a little patch of hair above the right ear, very much singed but still recognisable as hair? Well, in that patch I made out distinctly two or three white hairs. Naturally, when Mrs. Manford spoke of the dye, I recalled those white hairs, for though you may find silver hairs among the gold, you don't find them among the dyed. So the corpse could not be Manford's and was presumably that of Bilsky.

"But the instant that this presumption was made, a quantity of fresh evidence arose to support it. The destruction of the body was now understandable. Its purpose was to prevent identification. The parts destroyed were the parts that had to be destroyed for that purpose: the face was totally unrecognisable, and the right hand and right foot were burnt and shattered to fragments. But these were Bilsky's personal marks. His right hand was mutilated and his right foot deformed. And the fact that the false teeth found were undoubtedly Manford's was conclusive evidence of the intended deception.

"Then there were those very queer financial transactions, of which my interpretation was this: Manford borrowed two thousand pounds from Clines. With this he opened an account in the name of Elliott. As Elliott, he lent himself two thousand pounds which he repaid Clines—subject to an insurance of his life for that amount, taken out in Elliott's name."

"Then he would have gained nothing," I objected.

"On the contrary, he would have stood to gain two thousand pounds on proof of his own death. That, I assumed, was his scheme: to murder Bilsky, to arrange for Bilsky's corpse to personate his own, and then, when the insurance was paid, to abscond the company of some woman this sum, with the valuables that he had taken from Bilsky, and the five hundred pounds that he had withdrawn from the bank.

"But this was only theory. It had to be tested; and as we had Elliott's address, I did the only thing that was possible. I employed our friend, ex-Sergeant Barber, to watch the house. He took lodgings in a house nearly opposite and kept up continuous observation, which soon convinced him that there was someone on the premises besides Mrs. Elliott. Then, late one night, he saw a man come out and walk away quickly. He followed the man for some distance, until the stranger turned back and began to retrace his steps. Then Barber accosted him, asking for a direction, and carefully inspecting him. The man's appearance tallied exactly with the description that I had given—I had assumed that he would probably shave off his beard—and with the photograph; so Barber, having seen him home, reported to me. And that is the whole story."

"Not quite the whole," said Miller, with a sly grin. "There is that smoke-rocket. If it hadn't been for the practical joker who slipped that through the letter-slit, we could never have got into that house. I call it a most remarkable coincidence."

"So do I," Thorndyke agreed, without moving a muscle; "but there is a special providence that watches over medical jurists."

We were silent for a few moments. Then I remarked: "This will come as a terrible shock to Mrs. Manford."

"I am afraid it will," Thorndyke agreed. "But it will be better for her than if Manford had absconded with this woman, taking practically every penny that he possessed with him. She stood to lose a worthless husband in either event. At least we have saved her from poverty. And, knowing the facts, we were morally and legally bound to further the execution of justice."

"A very proper sentiment," said the superintendent, "though I am not quite clear as to the legal aspects of that smoke-rocket."

Mr. Ponting's Alibi

Thorndyke looked doubtfully at the pleasant-faced athletic-look-ing clergyman who had just come in, bearing Mr. Brodribb's card as an explanatory credential.

"I don't quite see," said he, "why Mr. Brodribb sent you to me. It seems to be a purely legal matter which he could have dealt with himself, at least as well as I can."

"He appeared to think otherwise," said the clergyman. ("The Revd. Charles Meade" was written on the card.)

"At any rate," he added with a persuasive smile, "here I am, and I hope you are not going to send me away."

"I shouldn't offer that affront to my old friend Brodribb," replied Thorndyke, smiling in return; "so we may as well get to business, which, in the first place, involves the setting out of all the particulars. Let us begin with the lady who is the subject of the threats of which you spoke."

"Her name," said Mr. Meade, "is Miss Mlillicent Fawcett. She is a person of independent means, which she employs in works of charity. She was formerly a hospital sister, and she does a certain amount of voluntary work in the parish as a sort of district nurse. She has been a very valuable help to me and we have been close friends for several years; and I may add, as a very material fact, that she has consented to marry me in about two months' time. So that, you see, I am properly entitled to act on her behalf."

"Yes," agreed Thorndyke. "You are an interested party. And now, as to the threats. What do they amount to?"

"That," replied Meade, "I can't tell you. I gathered quite by chance, from some words that she dropped, that she had been threatened. But she was unwilling to say more on the subject, as she did not take the matter seriously. She is not at all nervous. However, I told her I was taking advice; and I hope you will be able to extract more details from her. For my own part, I am decidedly uneasy."

"And as to the person or persons who have uttered the threats. Who are they? and out of what circumstances have the threats arisen?"

"The person is a certain William Ponting, who is Miss Fawcett's stepbrother—if that is the right term. Her father married, as his second wife, a Mrs. Ponting, a widow with one son. This is the son. His mother died before Mr. Fawcett, and the latter, when he died, left his daughter, Millicent, sole heir to his property. That has always been a grievance to Ponting. But now he has another. Miss Fawcett made a will some years ago by which the bulk of her rather considerable property is left to two cousins, Frederick and James Barnett, the sons of her father's sister. A comparatively small amount goes to Ponting. When he heard this he was furious. He demanded a portion at least equal to the others, and has continued to make this demand from time to time. In fact, he has been extremely troublesome, and appears to be getting still more so. I gathered that the threats were due to her refusal to alter the will."

"But," said I, "doesn't he realise that her marriage will render that will null and void?"

"Apparently not," replied Meade; "nor, to tell the truth, did I realise it myself. Will she have to make a new will?"

"Certainly," I replied. "And as that new will may be expected to be still less favourable to him, that will presumably be a further grievance."

"One doesn't understand," said Thorndyke, "why he should excite himself so much about her will. What are their respective ages?"

"Miss Fawcett is thirty-six and Ponting is about forty."

"And what kind of man is he?" Thorndyke asked.

"A very unpleasant kind of man, I am sorry to say. Morose, rude, and violent-tempered. A spendthrift and a cadger. He has had quite a lot of money from Miss Fawcett—loans, which, of course, are never repaid. And he is none too industrious, though he has a regular job on the staff of a weekly paper. But he seems to be always in debt."

"We may as well note his address," said Thorndyke.

"He lives in a small flat in Bloomsbury—alone now, since he quarrelled with the man who used to share it with him. The address is 12 Borneo House, Devonshire Street."

"What sort of terms is he on with the cousins, his rivals?"

"No sort of terms now," replied Meade. "They used to be great friends. So much so that he took his present flat to be near them—they live in the adjoining flat, number 12 Sumatra House. But since the trouble about the wills he is hardly on speaking terms with them."

"They live together, then?"

"Yes, Frederick and his wife and James, who is unmarried. They are rather a queer lot, too. Frederick is a singer on the variety stage, and James accompanies him on various instruments. But they are both sporting characters of a kind, especially James, who does a bit on the turf and engages in other odd activities. Of course, their musical habits are a grievance to Ponting. He is constantly making complaints of their disturbing him at his work."

Mr. Meade paused and looked wistfully at Thorndyke, who was making full notes of the conversation.

"Well," said the latter, "we seem to have got all the facts excepting the most important—the nature of the threats. What do you want us to do?"

"I want you to see Miss Fawcett—with me, if possible—and induce her to give you such details as would enable you to put a stop to the nuisance. You couldn't come tonight, I suppose? It is a beast of a night, but I would take you there in a taxi—it is only to Tooting Bec. What do you say?" he added eagerly, as Thorndyke made no objection. "We are sure to find her in, because her maid is away on a visit to her home and she is alone in the house."

Thorndyke looked reflectively at his watch.

"Half-past eight," he remarked, "and half an hour to get there. These threats are probably nothing but ill-temper. But we don't know. There may be something more serious behind them; and, in law as in medicine, prevention is better than a post-mortem. What do you say, Jervis?"

What could I say? I would much sooner have sat by the fire with a book than turn out into the murk of a November night. But I felt it necessary, especially as Thorndyke had evidently made up his mind. Accordingly I made a virtue of necessity; and a couple of minutes later we had exchanged the cosy room for the chilly darkness of Inner Temple Lane, up which the gratified parson was speeding ahead to capture a taxi. At the top of the Lane we perceived him giving elaborate instructions to a taxi-driver as he held the door of the cab open; and Thorndyke, having carefully disposed of his research-case—which, to my secret amusement, he had caught up, from mere force of habit, as we started—took his seat, and Meade and I followed.

As the taxi trundled smoothly along the dark streets, Mr. Meade filled in the details of his previous sketch, and, in a simple, manly, unaffected way dilated upon his good fortune and the pleasant future that lay before him. It was not, perhaps, a romantic marriage, he admitted; but Miss Fawcett and he had been faithful friends for years, and faithful friends they would remain till death did them part. So he ran on, now gleefully, now with a note of anxiety, and we listened by no means unsympathetically, until at last the cab drew up at a small, unpretentious house, standing in its own little grounds in a quiet suburban road.

"She is at home, you see," observed Meade, pointing to a lighted ground-floor window. He directed the taxi-driver to wait for the return journey, and striding up the path, delivered a characteristic knock at the door. As this brought no response, he knocked again and rang the bell. But still there was no answer, though twice I thought I heard the sound of a bolt being either drawn or shot softly. Again Mr. Meade plied the knocker more vigorously, and pressed the push of the bell, which we could hear ringing loudly within.

"This is very strange," said Meade, in an anxious tone, keeping his thumb pressed on the bell-push. "She can't have gone out and left the electric light on. What had we better do?"

"We had better enter without more delay," Thorndyke replied. "There were certainly sounds from within. Is there a side gate?"

Meade ran off towards the side of the house, and Thorndyke and I glanced at the lighted window, which was slightly open at the top.

"Looks a bit queer," I remarked, listening at the letter-box.

Thorndyke assented gravely, and at this moment Meade returned, breathing hard.

"The side gate is bolted inside," said he; and at this I recalled the stealthy sound of the bolt that I had heard. "What is to be done?"

Without replying, Thorndyke handed me his research-case, stepped across to the window, sprang up on the sill, drew down the upper sash and disappeared between the curtains into the room. A moment later the street door opened and Meade and I entered the hall. We glanced through the open doorway into the lighted room, and I noticed a heap of needlework thrown hastily on the dining-table. Then Meade switched on the hall light, and Thorndyke walked quickly past him to the half-open door of the next room. Before entering, he reached in and switched on the light; and as he stepped into the room he partly closed the door behind him.

"Don't come in here, Meade!" he called out. But the parson's eye, like my own, had seen something before the door closed: a great, dark stain on the carpet just within the threshold. Regardless of the admonition, he pushed the door open and darted into the room. Following him, I saw him rush forward, fling his arms up wildly, and with a dreadful, strangled cry, sink upon his knees beside a low couch on which a woman was lying.

"Merciful God!" he gasped. "She is dead! Is she dead, doctor? Can nothing be done?"

Thorndyke shook his head. "Nothing," he said in a low voice. "She is dead."

Poor Meade knelt by the couch, his hands clutching at his hair and his eyes riveted on the dead face, the very embodiment of horror and despair.

"God Almighty!" he exclaimed in the same strangled undertone. "How frightful! Poor, poor Millie! Dear, sweet friend!" Then suddenly—almost savagely—he turned to Thorndyke. "But it can't be, doctor! It is impossible—unbelievable. That, I mean!" and he pointed to the dead woman's right hand, which held an open razor.

Our poor friend had spoken my own thought. It was incredible that this refined, pious lady should have inflicted those savage wounds, that gaped scarlet beneath the waxen face. There, indeed, was the razor lying in her hand. But what was its testimony worth? My heart rejected it; but yet, unwillingly, I noted that the wounds seemed to support it; for they had been made from left to right, as they would have been if self-inflicted.

"It is hard to believe," said Thorndyke, "but there is only one alternative. Someone should acquaint the police at once."

"I will go," exclaimed Meade, starting up. "I know the way and the cab is there." He looked once more with infinite pity and affection at the dead woman. "Poor, sweet girl!" he murmured. "If we can do no more for you, we can defend your memory from calumny and call upon the God of Justice to right the innocent and punish the guilty."

With these words and a mute farewell to his dead friend, he hurried from the room, and immediately afterwards we heard the street door close.

As he went out, Thorndyke's manner changed abruptly. He had been deeply moved—as who would not have been—by this awful tragedy that had in a moment shattered the happiness of the genial, kindly parson. Now he turned to me with a face set and stern. "This is an abominable affair, Jervis," he said in an ominously quiet voice.

"You reject the suggestion of suicide, then?" said I, with a feeling of relief that surprised me.

"Absolutely," he replied. "Murder shouts at us from everything that meets our eye. Look at this poor woman, in her trim nurse's dress, with her unfinished needlework lying on the table in the next room and that preposterous razor loose in her limp hand. Look at the savage wounds. Four of them, and the first one mortal. The great bloodstain by the door, the great bloodstain on her dress from the neck to the feet. The gashed collar, the cap-string cut right through. Note that the bleeding had practically ceased when she lay down. That is a group of visible facts that is utterly inconsistent with the idea of suicide. But we are wasting time. Let us search the premises thoroughly. The murderer has pretty certainly got away, but as he was in the house when we arrived, any traces will be quite fresh."

As he spoke he took his electric lamp from the research-case and walked to the door.

"We can examine this room later," he said, "but we had better look over the house. If you will stay by the stairs and watch the front and back doors, I will look through the upper rooms."

He ran lightly up the stairs while I kept watch below, but he was absent less than a couple of minutes.

"There is no one there," he reported, "and as there is no basement we will just look at this floor and then examine the grounds."

After a rapid inspection of the ground-floor rooms, including the kitchen, we went out by the back door, which was unbolted, and inspected the grounds. These consisted of a largish garden with a small orchard at the side. In the former we could discover no traces of any kind, but at the end of the path that crossed the orchard we came an a possible clue. The orchard was enclosed by a five-foot fence, the top of which bristled with hooked nails; and at the point opposite to the path, Thorndyke's lantern brought into view one or two wisps of cloth caught on the hooks.

"Someone has been over here," said Thorndyke, "but as this is an orchard, there is nothing remarkable in the fact. However, there is no fruit on the trees now, and the cloth looks fairly fresh. There are two kinds, you notice: a dark blue and a black and white mixture of some kind."

"Corresponding, probably, to the coat and trousers," I suggested.

"Possibly," he agreed, taking from his pocket a couple of the little seed-envelopes of which he always carried a supply. Very delicately he picked the tiny wisps of cloth from the hooks and bestowed each kind in a separate envelope. Having pocketed these, he leaned over the fence and threw the light of his lamp along the narrow lane or alley that divided the orchard from the adjoining premises. It was ungravelled and covered with a growth of rank grass, which suggested that it was little frequented. But immediately below was a small patch of bare earth, and on this was a very distinct impression of a foot, covering several less distinct prints.

"Several people have been over here at different times," I remarked.

"Yes," Thorndyke agreed. "But that sharp footprint belongs to the last one over, and he is our concern. We had better not confuse the issues by getting over ourselves. We will mark the spot and explore from the other end." He laid his handkerchief over the top of the fence and we then went back to the house.

"You are going to take a plaster cast, I suppose?" said I; and as he assented, I fetched the research-case from the drawing-room. Then we fixed the catch of the front-door latch and went out, drawing the door to after us.

We found the entrance to the alley about sixty yards from the gate, and entering it, walked slowly forwards, scanning the ground as we went. But the bright lamplight showed nothing more than the vague marks of trampling feet on the grass until we came to the spot marked by the handkerchief on the fence.

"It is a pity," I remarked, "that this footprint has obliterated the others."

"On the other hand," he replied, "this one, which is the one that interests us, is remarkably clear and characteristic: a circular heel and a rubber sole of a recognisable pattern mended with a patch of cement paste. It is a footprint that could be identified beyond a doubt."

As he was speaking, he took from the research-case the water-bottle, plaster-tin, rubber mixing-bowl and spoon, and a piece of canvas with which to "reinforce" the cast. Rapidly, he mixed a bowlful—extra thick, so that it should set quickly and hard—dipped the canvas into it, poured the remainder into the footprint, and laid the canvas on it.

"I will get you to stay here, Jervis," said he, "until the plaster has set. I want to examine the body rather more thoroughly before the police arrive, particularly the back."

"Why the back?" I asked.

"Did not the appearance of the body suggest to you the advisability of examining the back?" he asked, and then, without waiting for a reply, he went off, leaving the inspection-lamp with me.

His words gave me matter for profound thought during my short vigil. I recalled the appearance of the dead woman very vividly—indeed, I am not likely ever to forget it—and I strove to connect that appearance with his desire to examine the back of the corpse. But there seemed to be no connection at all. The visible injuries were in front, and I had seen nothing to suggest the existence of any others. From time to time I tested the condition of the plaster, impatient to rejoin my colleague but fearful of cracking the thin cast by raising it prematurely. At length the plaster seemed to be hard enough, and trusting to the strength of the canvas, I prised cautiously at the edge, when, to my relief, the brittle plate came up safely and I lifted it clear. Wrapping it carefully in some spare rag, I packed it in the research-case, and then, taking this and the lantern, made my way back to the house.

When I had let down the catch and closed the front door, I went to the drawing-room, where I found Thorndyke stooping over the dark stain at the threshold and scanning the floor as if in search of something. I reported the completion of the cast and then asked him what he was looking for.

"I am looking for a button," he replied. "There is one missing from the back; the one to which the collar was fastened."

"Is it of any importance?" I asked.

"It is important to ascertain when and where it became detached," he replied. "Let us have the inspection-lamp."

I gave him the lamp, which he placed on the floor, turning it so that its beam of light travelled along the surface. Stooping to follow the light, I scrutinised the floor minutely but in vain.

"It may not be here at all," said I; but at that moment the bright gleam, penetrating the darkness under a cabinet, struck a small object close to the wall. In a moment I had thrown myself prone on the carpet, and reaching under the cabinet, brought forth a largish mother-of-pearl button.

"You notice," said Thorndyke, as he examined it, "that the cabinet is near the window, at the opposite end of the room to the couch. But we had better see that it is the right button."

He walked slowly towards the couch, still stooping and searching the floor with the light. The corpse, I noticed, had been turned on its side, exposing the back and the displaced collar. Through the strained button-hole of the latter Thorndyke passed the button without difficulty.

"Yes," he said, "that is where it came from. You will notice that there is a similar one in front. By the way," he continued, bringing the lamp close to the surface of the grey serge dress, "I picked off one or two hairs—animal hairs; cat and dog they looked like. Here are one or two more. Will you hold the lamp while I take them off?"

"They are probably from some pets of hers," I remarked, as he picked them off with his forceps and deposited them in one of the invaluable seed-envelopes. "Spinsters are a good deal addicted to pets, especially cats and dogs."

"Possibly," he replied. "But I could see none in front, where you would expect to find them, and there seem to be none on the carpet. Now let us replace the body as we found it and just have a look at our material before the police arrive. I expected them here before this."

We turned the body back into its original position, and taking the research-case and the lamp, went into the dining-room. Here Thorndyke rapidly set up the little travelling microscope, and bringing forth the seed-envelopes, began to prepare slides from the contents of some while I prepared the others. There was time only for a very hasty examination, which Thorndyke made as soon as the specimens were mounted.

"The clothing," he reported, with his eye at the microscope, "is woollen in both cases. Fairly good quality. The one a blue serge, apparently indigo dyed; the other a mixture of black and white, no other colour. Probably a fine tabby or a small shepherd's plaid."

"Serge coat and shepherd's plaid trousers," I suggested. "Now see what the hairs are." I handed him the slide, on which I had roughly mounted the collection in oil of lavender, and he placed it on the stage.

"There are three different kinds of hairs here," he reported, after a rapid inspection. "Some are obviously from a cat—a smoky Persian. Others are long, rather fine tawny hairs from a dog. Probably a Pekinese. But there are two that I can't quite place. They look like monkey's hairs, but they are a very unusual colour. There is a perceptible greenish tint, which is extremely uncommon in mammalian hairs. But I hear the taxi approaching. We need not be expansive to the local police as to what we have observed. This will probably be a case for the C.I.D."

I went out into the hall and opened the door as Meade came up the path, followed by two men; and as the latter came into the light, I was astonished to recognise in one of them our old friend, Detective-Superintendent Miller, the other being, apparently, the station super-intendent.

"We have kept Mr. Meade a long time," said Miller, "but we knew you were here, so the time wouldn't be wasted. Thought it best to get a full statement before we inspected the premises. How do, doctor?" he added, shaking hands with Thorndyke. "Glad to see you here. I suppose you have got all the facts. I understood so from Mr. Meade."

"Yes," replied Thorndyke, "we have all the antecedents of the case, and we arrived within a few minutes of the death of the deceased."

"Ha!" exclaimed Miller. "Did you? And I expect you have formed an opinion on the question as to whether the injuries were self-in-flicted?"

"I think," said Thorndyke, "that it would be best to act on the as-sumption that they were not—and to act promptly."

"Precisely," Miller agreed emphatically. "You mean that we had better find out at once where a certain person was at—What time did you arrive here?"

"It was two minutes to nine when the taxi stopped," replied Thorndyke; "and, as it is now only twenty-five minutes to ten, we have good time if Mr. Meade can spare us the taxi. I have the address."

"The taxi is waiting for you," said Mr. Meade, "and the man has been paid for both journeys. I shall stay here in case the superinten-dent wants anything." He shook our hands warmly, and as we bade him farewell and noted the dazed, despairing expression and lines of grief that had already eaten into the face that had been so blithe and hopeful, we both thought bitterly of the few fatal minutes that had made us too late to save the wreckage of his life.

We were just turning away when Thorndyke paused and again faced the clergyman. "Can you tell me," he asked, "whether Miss Faw-cett had any pets? Cats, dogs, or other animals?"

Meade looked at him in surprise, and Superintendent Miller seemed to prick up his ears. But the former answered simply: "No. She was not very fond of animals; she reserved her affections for men and women."

Thorndyke nodded gravely, and picking up the research-case walked slowly out of the room, Miller and I following.

As soon as the address had been given to the driver and we had taken our seats in the taxi, the superintendent opened the examination-in-chief.

"I see you have got your box of magic with you, doctor," he said, cocking his eye at the research-case. "Any luck?"

"We have secured a very distinctive footprint," replied Thorndyke, "but it may have no connection with the case."

"I hope it has," said Miller. "A good cast of a footprint which you can let the jury compare with the boot is first-class evidence." He took the cast, which I had produced from the research-case, and turning it over tenderly and gloatingly, exclaimed: "Beautiful! beautiful! Absolutely distinctive! There can't be another exactly like it in the world. It is as good as a fingerprint. For the Lord's sake take care of it. It means a conviction if we can find the boot."

The superintendent's efforts to engage Thorndyke in discussion were not very successful, and the conversational brunt was borne by me. For we both knew my colleague too well to interrupt him if he was disposed to be meditative. And such was now his disposition. Looking at him as he sat in his corner, silent but obviously wrapped in thought, I knew that he was mentally sorting out the data and testing the hypotheses that they yielded.

"Here we are," said Miller, opening the door as the taxi stopped. "Now what are we going to say? Shall I tell him who I am?"

"I expect you will have to," replied Thorndyke, "if you want him to let us in."

"Very well," said Miller. "But I shall let you do the talking, because I don't know what you have got up your sleeve."

Thorndyke's prediction was verified literally. In response to the third knock, with an *obbligato* accompaniment on the bell, wrathful footsteps—I had no idea footsteps could be so expressive—advanced rapidly along the lobby, the door was wrenched open—but only for a few inches—and an angry, hairy face appeared in the opening.

"Now then," the hairy person demanded, "what the deuce do you want?"

"Are you Mr. William Ponting?" the superintendent inquired.

"What the devil is that to do with you?" was the genial answer—in the Scottish mode.

"We have business," Miller began persuasively.

"So have I," the presumable Ponting replied, "and mine won't wait."

"But our business is very important," Miller urged.

"So is mine," snapped Ponting, and would have shut the door but for Miller's obstructing foot, at which he kicked viciously, but with unsatisfactory results, as he was shod in light slippers, whereas the superintendent's boots were of constabulary solidity.

"Now, look here," said Miller, dropping his conciliatory manner very completely, "you'd better stop this nonsense. I am a police officer, and I am going to come in;" and with this he inserted a massive shoulder and pushed the door open.

"Police officer, are you?" said Ponting. "And what might your business be with me?"

"That is what I have been waiting to tell you," said Miller. "But we don't want to do our talking here."

"Very well," growled Ponting. "Come in. But understand that I am busy. I've been interrupted enough this evening."

He led the way into a rather barely furnished room with a wide bay-window in which was a table fitted with a writing-slope and lighted by an electric standard lamp. A litter of manuscript explained the nature of his business and his unwillingness to receive casual visitors. He sulkily placed three chairs, and then, seating himself, glowered at Thorndyke and me.

"Are they police officers, too?" he demanded.

"No," replied Miller, "they are medical gentlemen. Perhaps you had better explain the matter, doctor," he added, addressing Thorndyke, who thereupon opened the proceedings.

"We have called," said he, "to inform you that Miss Millicent Fawcett died suddenly this evening."

"The devil!" exclaimed Ponting. "That's sudden with a vengeance. What time did this happen?"

"About a quarter to nine."

"Extraordinary!" muttered Ponting. "I saw her only the day before yesterday, and she seemed quite well then. What did she die of?"

"The appearances," replied Thorndyke, "suggest suicide."

"Suicide!" gasped Ponting. "Impossible! I can't believe it. Do you mean to tell me she poisoned herself?"

"No," said Thorndyke, "it was not poison. Death was caused by injuries to the throat inflicted with a razor."

"Good God!" exclaimed Ponting. "What a horrible thing! But," he added, after a pause, "I can't believe she did it herself, and I don't. Why should she commit suicide? She was quite happy, and she was just going to be married to that mealy-faced parson. And a razor, too! How do you suppose she came by a razor? Women don't shave. They smoke and drink and swear, but they haven't taken to shaving yet. I don't believe it. Do you?"

He glared ferociously at the superintendent who replied: "I am not sure that I do. There's a good deal in what you've just said, and the same objections had occurred to us. But you see, if she didn't do it herself, someone else must have done it, and we should like to find out who that someone is. So we begin by ascertaining where any possible persons may have been at a quarter to nine this evening."

Ponting smiled like an infuriated cat. "So you think me a possible person, do you?" said he.

"Everyone is a possible person," Miller replied blandly, "especially when he is known to have uttered threats."

The reply sobered Ponting considerably. For a few moments he sat, looking reflectively at the superintendent; then, in comparatively quiet tones, he said: "I have been working here since six o'clock. You can see the stuff for yourself, and I can prove that it has been written since six."

The superintendent nodded, but made no comment, and Ponting gazed at him fixedly, evidently thinking hard. Suddenly he broke into a harsh laugh.

"What is the joke?" Miller inquired stolidly.

"The joke is that I have got another alibi—a very complete one. There are compensations in every evil. I told you I had been interrupted in my work already this evening. It was those fools next door, the Barnetts—cousins of mine. They are musicians, save the mark! Variety stage, you know. Funny songs and jokes for mental defectives. Well, they practise their infernal ditties in their rooms, and the row comes into mine, and an accursed nuisance it is. However, they have agreed not to practise on Thursdays and Fridays—my busy nights— and usually they don't. But tonight, just as I was in the thick of my writing, I suddenly heard the most unholy din; that idiot, Fred Barnett, bawling one of his imbecile songs—'*When the pigs their wings have folded,*' and balderdash of that sort—and the other donkey accompanying him on the clarinet, if you please!

"I stuck it for a minute or two. Then I rushed round to their flat and raised Cain with the bell and knocker. Mrs. Fred opened the door, and I told her what I thought of it. Of course she was very apologetic, said they had forgotten that it was Thursday and promised that she would make her husband stop. And I suppose she did, for by the time I got back to my rooms the row had ceased. I could have punched the whole lot of them into a jelly, but it was all for the best as it turns out."

"What time was it when you went round there?" asked Miller.

"About five minutes past nine," replied Ponting. "The church bell had struck nine when the row began."

"Hm!" grunted Miller, glancing at Thorndyke. "Well, that is all we wanted to know, so we need not keep you from your work any longer."

He rose, and being let out with great alacrity, stumped down the stairs, followed by Thorndyke and me. As we came out into the street, he turned to us with a deeply disappointed expression.

"Well," he exclaimed, "this is a suck-in. I was in hopes that we had pounced on our quarry before he had got time to clear away the traces. And now we've got it all to do. You can't get round an alibi of that sort."

I glanced at Thorndyke to see how he was taking this unexpected check. He was evidently puzzled, and I could see by the expression of concentration in his face that he was trying over the facts and inferences in new combinations to meet this new position. Probably he had noticed, as I had, that Ponting was wearing a tweed suit, and that therefore the shreds of clothing from the fence could not be his unless he had changed. But the alibi put him definitely out of the picture, and, as Miller had said, we now had nothing to give us a lead.

Suddenly Thorndyke came out of his reverie and addressed the superintendent.

"We had better put this alibi on the basis of ascertained fact. It ought to be verified at once. At present we have only Ponting's unsupported statement."

"It isn't likely that he would risk telling a lie," Miller replied gloomily.

"A man who is under suspicion of murder will risk a good deal," Thorndyke retorted, "especially if he is guilty. I think we ought to see Mrs. Barnett before there is any opportunity of collusion."

"There has been time for collusion already," said Miller. "Still, you are quite right, and I see there is a light in their sitting-room, if that is it, next to Ponting's. Let us go up and settle the matter now. I shall leave you to examine the witness and say what you think it best to say."

We entered the building and ascended the stairs to the Barnetts' flat, where Miller rang the bell and executed a double knock. After a short interval the door was opened and a woman looked out at us inquisitively.

"Are you Mrs. Frederick Barnett?" Thorndyke inquired. The woman admitted her identity in a tone of some surprise, and Thorndyke explained: "We have called to make a few inquiries concerning your neighbour, Mr. Ponting, and also about certain matters relating to your family. I am afraid it is a rather unseasonable hour for a visit, but as the affair is of some importance and time is an object, I hope you will overlook that."

Mrs. Barnett listened to this explanation with a puzzled and rather suspicious air. After a few moments' hesitation, she said: "I think you had better see my husband, if you will wait here a moment I will go and tell him." With this, she pushed the door to, without actually closing it, and we heard her retire along the lobby, presumably to the sitting-room. For, during the short colloquy, I had observed a door at the end of the lobby, partly open, through which I could see the end of a table covered with a red cloth.

The "moment" extended to a full minute, and the superintendent began to show signs of impatience.

"I don't see why you didn't ask her the simple question straight out," he said, and the same question had occurred to me. But at this point footsteps were heard approaching, the door opened, and a man confronted us, holding the door open with his left hand, his right being wrapped in a handkerchief. He looked suspiciously from one to the other of us, and asked stiffly: "What is it that you want to know? And would you mind telling me who you are?"

"My name is Thorndyke," was the reply. "I am the legal adviser of the Reverend Charles Meade, and these two gentlemen are interested parties. I want to know what you can tell me of Mr. Ponting's recent movements—today, for instance. When did you last see him?"

The man appeared to be about to refuse any conversation, but suddenly altered his mind, reflected for a few moments, and then replied: "I saw him from my window at his—they are bay-windows—about half-past eight. But my wife saw him later than that. If you will come in she can tell you the time exactly." He led the way along the lobby with an obviously puzzled air. But he was not more puzzled than I, or than Miller, to judge by the bewildered glance that the superintendent cast at me, as he followed our host along the lobby.

I was still meditating on Thorndyke's curiously indirect methods when the sitting-room door was opened; and then I got a minor surprise of another kind. When I had last looked into the room, the table had been covered by a red cloth. It was now bare; and when we entered the room I saw that the red cover had been thrown over a side table, on which was some bulky and angular object. Apparently it had been thought desirable to conceal that object, whatever it was, and as we took our seats beside the bare table, my mind was busy with conjectures as to what that object could be.

Mr. Barnett repeated Thorndyke's question to his wife, adding: "I think it must have been a little after nine when Ponting came round. What do you say?"

"Yes," she replied, "it would be, for I heard it strike nine just before you began your practice, and he came a few minutes after."

"You see," Barnett explained, "I am a singer, and my brother, here, accompanies me on various instruments, and of course we have to practise. But we don't practise on the nights when Ponting is busy—Thursdays and Fridays—as he said that the music disturbed him. To-night, however, we made a little mistake. I happen to have got a new song that I am anxious to get ready—it has an illustrative accompaniment on the clarinet, which my brother will play. We were so much taken up with the new song that we all forgot what day of the week it was, and started to have a good practice. But before we had got through the first verse, Ponting came round, battering at the door like a madman. My wife went out and pacified him, and of course we shut down for the evening."

While Mr. Barnett was giving his explanation, I looked about the room with vague curiosity. Somehow—I cannot tell exactly how—I was sensible of something queer in the atmosphere of this place; of a certain indefinite sense of tension. Mrs. Barnett looked pale and flurried. Her husband, in spite of his volubility, seemed ill at ease, and the brother, who sat huddled in an easy-chair, nursing a dark-coloured Persian cat, stared into the fire, and neither moved nor spoke. And again I looked at the red table-cloth and wondered what it covered.

"By the way," said Barnett, after a brief pause, "what is the point of these inquiries of yours? About Ponting, I mean. What does it matter to you where he was this evening?"

As he spoke, he produced a pipe and tobacco-pouch, and proceeded to fill the former, holding it in his bandaged right hand and filling it with his left. The facility with which he did this suggested that he was left-handed, an inference that was confirmed by the ease with which he struck the match with his left hand, and by the fact that he wore a wrist-watch on his right wrist.

"Your question is a perfectly natural one," said Thorndyke. "The answer to it is that a very terrible thing has happened. Miss Millicent Fawcett, who is, I think, a connection of yours, met her death this evening under circumstances of grave suspicion. She died, either by her own hand or by the hand of a murderer, a few minutes before nine o'clock. Hence it has become I necessary to ascertain the whereabouts at that time of any persons on whom suspicion might reasonably fall."

"Good God!" exclaimed Barnett. "What a shocking thing!"

The exclamation was followed by a deep silence, amidst which I could hear the barking of a dog in an adjacent room, the unmistakable sharp, treble yelp of a Pekinese. And again I seemed to be aware of a strange sense of tension in the occupants of this room. On hearing Thorndyke's answer, Mrs. Barnett had turned deadly pale and let her head fall forward on her hand. Her husband had sunk on to a chair, and he, too, looked pale and deeply shocked, while the brother continued to stare silently into the fire.

At this moment Thorndyke astonished me by an exhibition of what seemed—under the tragic circumstances—the most outrageous bad manners and bad taste. Rising from his chair with his eyes fixed on a print which hung on the wall above the red-covered table, he said: "That looks like one of Cameron's etchings," and forthwith stepped across the room to examine it, resting his hand, as he leaned forward, on the object covered by the cloth.

"Mind where you are putting your hand, sir!" Fred Barnett called out, springing to his feet.

Thorndyke looked down at his hand, and deliberately raising a corner of the cloth, looked under. "There is no harm done," he remarked quietly, letting the cloth drop; and with another glance at the print, he went back to his chair.

Once more a deep silence fell upon the room, and I had a vague feeling that the tension had increased. Mrs. Barnett was as white as a ghost and seemed to catch at her breath. Her, husband watched her with a wild, angry expression and smoked furiously, while the super-intendent—also conscious of something abnormal in the atmosphere of the room—looked furtively from the woman to the man and from him to Thorndyke.

Yet again in the silence the shrill barking of the Pekinese dog broke out, and somehow that sound connected itself in my mind with the Persian cat that dozed on the knees of the immovable man by the fire. I looked at the cat and at the man, and even as I looked, I was startled by a most extraordinary apparition. Above the man's shoulder, slowly rose a little round head like the head of a diminutive, greenish-brown man. Higher and higher the tiny monkey raised itself, resting on its little hands to peer at the strangers. Then, with sudden coyness, like a shy baby, it popped down out of sight.

I was thunderstruck. The cat and the dog I had noted merely as a curious coincidence. But the monkey—and such an unusual monkey, too—put coincidences out of the question. I stared at the man in positive stupefaction. Somehow that man was connected with that unforgettable figure lying upon the couch miles away. But how? When that deed of horror was doing, he had been here in this very room. Yet, in some way, he had been concerned in it. And suddenly a suspicion dawned upon me that Thorndyke was waiting for the actual perpetrator to arrive.

"It is a most ghastly affair," Barnett repeated presently in a husky voice. Then, after a pause, he asked: "Is there any sort of evidence as to whether she killed herself or was killed by somebody else?"

"I think that my friend, here, Detective-Superintendent Miller, has decided that she was murdered." He looked at the bewildered superintendent, who replied with an inarticulate grunt.

"And is there any clue as to who the—the murderer may be? You spoke of suspected persons just now."

"Yes," replied Thorndyke, "there is an excellent clue, if it can only be followed up. We found a most unmistakable footprint; and what is more, we took a plaster cast of it. Would you like to see the cast?"

Without waiting for a reply, he opened the research-case and took out the cast, which he placed in my hands.

"Just take it round and show it to them," he said.

The superintendent had witnessed Thorndyke's amazing proceedings with an astonishment that left him speechless. But now he sprang to his feet, and, as I walked round the table, he pressed beside me to guard the precious cast from possible injury. I laid it carefully down on the table, and as the light fell on it obliquely, it presented a most striking appearance—that of a snow-white boot-sole on which the unshapely patch, the circular heel, and the marks of wear were clearly visible.

The three spectators gathered round, as near as the superintendent would let them approach, and I observed them closely, assuming that this incomprehensible move of Thorndyke's was a device to catch one or more of them off their guard. Fred Barnett looked at the cast stolidly enough, though his face had gone several shades paler, but Mrs. Barnett stared at it with starting eyeballs and dropped jaw—the very picture of horror and dismay. As to James Barnett, whom I now saw clearly for the first time, he stood behind the woman with a singularly scared and haggard face, and his eyes riveted on the white boot-sole. And now I could see that he wore a suit of blue serge and that the front both of his coat and waistcoat were thickly covered with the shed hairs of his pets.

There was something very uncanny about this group of persons gathered around that accusing footprint, all as still and rigid as statues and none uttering a sound. But something still more uncanny followed. Suddenly the deep silence of the room was shattered by the shrill notes of a clarinet, and a brassy voice burst forth:

"*When the pigs their wings have folded
And the cows are in their nest—*"

We all spun round in amazement, and at the first glance the mystery of the crime was solved. There stood Thorndyke with the red table-cover at his feet, and at his side, on the small table, a massively-constructed phonograph of the kind used in offices for dictating letters, but fitted with a convoluted metal horn in place of the rubber ear-tubes.

A moment of astonished silence was succeeded by a wild confusion. Mrs. Barnett uttered a piercing shriek and fell back on to a chair, her husband broke away and rushed at Thorndyke, who instantly gripped his wrist and pinioned him, while the superintendent, taking in the situation at a glance, fastened on the unresisting James and forced him down into a chair. I ran round, and having stopped the machine—for the preposterous song was hideously incongruous with the tragedy that was enacting—went to Thorndyke's assistance and helped him to remove his prisoner from the neighbourhood of the instrument.

"Superintendent Miller," said Thorndyke, still maintaining a hold on his squirming captive, "I believe you are a justice of the peace?"

"Yes," was the reply, "*ex officio.*"

"Then," said Thorndyke, "I accuse these three persons of being concerned in the murder of Miss Millicent Fawcett; Frederick Barnett as the principal who actually committed the murder, James Barnett as having aided him by holding the arms of the deceased, and Mrs. Barnett as an accessory before the fact in that she worked this phonograph for the purpose of establishing a false alibi."

"I knew nothing about it!" Mrs. Barnett shrieked hysterically. "They never told me why they wanted me to work the thing."

"We can't go into that now," said Miller. "You will be able to make your defence at the proper time and place. Can one of you go for assistance or must I blow my whistle?"

"You had better go, Jervis," said Thorndyke. "I can hold this man until reinforcements arrive. Send a constable up and then go on to the station. And leave the outer door ajar."

I followed these directions, and having found the police station, presently returned to the flat with four constables and a sergeant in two taxis.

When the prisoners had been removed, together with the three animals—the latter in charge of a zoophilist constable—we searched the bedrooms. Frederick Barnett had changed his clothing completely, but in a locked drawer—the lock of which Thorndyke picked neatly, to the superintendent's undisguised admiration—we found the discarded garments, including a pair of torn shepherd's plaid trousers, covered with blood stains, and a new, empty razor-case. These things, together with the wax cylinder of the phonograph, Miller made up into a neat parcel and took away with him.

"Of course," said I, as we walked homewards, "the general drift of this case is quite obvious. But it seemed to me that you went to the Barnetts' flat with a definite purpose already formed, and with a definite suspicion in your mind. Now, I don't see how you came to suspect the Barnetts."

"I think you will," he replied, "if you will recall the incidents in their order from the beginning, including poor Meade's preliminary statement. To begin with the appearances of the body: the suggestion of suicide was transparently false. To say nothing of its incongruity with the character and circumstances of the deceased and the very unlikely weapon used, there were the gashed collar and the cut cap-string. As you know, it is a well-established rule that suicides do not damage their clothing. A man who cuts his own throat doesn't cut his collar. He takes it off. He removes all obstructions. Naturally, for he wishes to complete the act as easily and quickly as possible, and he has time for preparation. But the murderer must take things as he finds them and execute his purpose as best he can.

"But further; the wounds were inflicted near the door, but the body was on the couch at the other end of the room. We saw, from the absence of bleeding, that she was dying—in fact, apparently dead—when she lay down. She must therefore have been carried to the couch after the wounds were inflicted.

"Then there were the blood-stains. They were all in front, and the blood had run down vertically. Then she must have been standing upright while the blood was flowing. Now there were four wounds, and the first one was mortal, it divided the common carotid artery and the great veins. On receiving that wound she would ordinarily have fallen down. But she did not fall, or there would have been a bloodstain across the neck. Why did she not fall? The obvious suggestion was that someone was holding her up. This suggestion was confirmed by the absence of cuts on her hands—which would certainly have been cut if someone bad not been holding them. It was further confirmed by the rough crumpling of the collar at the back: so rough that the button was torn off. And we found that button near the door.

"Further, there were the animal hairs. They were on the back only. There were none on the front—where they would have been if derived from the animals—or anywhere else. And we learned that she kept no animals. All these appearances pointed to the presence of two persons, one of whom stood behind her and held her arms while the other stood in front and committed the murder. The cloth on the fence supported this view, being probably derived from two different pairs of trousers. The character of the wounds made it nearly certain that the murderer was left-handed.

"While we were returning in the cab, I reflected on these facts and considered the case generally. First, what was the motive? There was nothing to suggest robbery, nor was it in the least like a robber's crime. What other motive could there be? Well, here was a comparatively rich woman who had made a will in favour of certain persons, and she was going to be married. On her marriage the will would automatically become void, and she was not likely to make another will so favourable to those persons. Here, then, was a possible motive, and that motive applied to Ponting, who had actually uttered threats and was obviously suspect.

"But, apart from those threats, Ponting was not the principal suspect, for he benefited only slightly under the will. The chief beneficiaries were the Barnetts, and Miss Fawcett's death would benefit them, not only by securing the validity of the will, but by setting the will into immediate operation. And there were two of them. They therefore fitted the circumstances better than Ponting did. And when we came to interview Ponting, he went straight out of the picture. His manuscript would probably have cleared him—with his editor's confirmation. But the other alibi was conclusive.

"What instantly struck me, however, was that Ponting's alibi was also an alibi for the Barnetts. But there was this difference: Ponting had been seen; the Barnetts had only been heard. Now, it has often occurred to me that a very effective false alibi could be worked with a gramophone or a phonograph—especially with one on which one can make one's own records. This idea now recurred to me; and at once it was supported by the appearance of an arranged effect. Ponting was known to be at work. It was practically certain that a blast of 'music' would bring him out. Then he would be available, if necessary, as a witness to prove an alibi. It seemed to be worth while to investigate.

"When we came to the flat we encountered a man with an injured hand—the right, it would have been more striking if it had been his left. But it presently turns out that he is left-handed; which is still more striking as a coincidence. This man is extraordinarily ready to answer questions which most persons would have refused to answer at all. Those answers contain the alibi.

"Then there was the incident of the table—I think you noticed it. That cover was on the large table when we arrived, but it was taken off and thrown over something, evidently to conceal it. But I need not pursue the details. When I had seen the cat, heard the dog, and then seen the monkey, I determined to see what was under the table-cover; and finding that it was a phonograph with the cylinder record still on the drum, I decided to 'go Nap' and chance making a mistake. For until we had tried the record, the alibi remained. If it had failed, I should have advised Miller to hold a boot parade. Fortunately we struck the right record and completed the case."

Mrs. Barnett's defence was accepted by the magistrate and the charge against her was dismissed. The other two were committed for trial, and in due course paid the extreme penalty. "Yet another illustration," was Thorndyke's comment, "of the folly of that kind of criminal who won't let well alone, and who will create false clues. If the Barnetts had not laid down those false tracks, they would probably never have been suspected. It was their clever alibi that led us straight to their door."

Pandora's Box

"I see our friend, S. Chapman, is still a defaulter," said I, as I ran my eye over the "personal" column of *The Times.*

Thorndyke looked up interrogatively.

"Chapman?" he repeated; "let me see, who is he?"

"The man with the box. I read you the advertisement the other day. Here it is again.

'If the box left in the luggage-room by S. Chapman is not claimed within a week from this date, it will be sold to defray expenses.—Alexander Butt, "Red Lion" Hotel, Stoke Varley, Kent.'

That sounds like an ultimatum; but it has been appearing at intervals for the last month. As the first notice expired about three weeks ago, the question is, why doesn't Mr. Butt sell the box and have done with it?"

"He may have some qualms as to the legality of the proceeding," said Thorndyke. "It would be interesting to know what expenses he refers to and what is the value of the box."

The latter question was resolved a day or two later by the appearance in our chambers of an agitated gentleman, who gave his name as George Chapman. After apologising for his unannounced visit he explained: "I have come to you on the advice of my solicitor and on behalf of my brother, Samuel, who has become involved in a most extraordinary and horrible set of complications. At present he is in custody of the police charged with an atrocious murder."

"That is certainly a rather serious complication," Thorndyke observed dryly. "Perhaps you had better give us an account of the circumstances—the whole set of circumstances, from the beginning."

"I will," said Mr. Chapman, "without any reservations. The only question is, which is the beginning? There are the business and the domestic affairs. Perhaps I had better begin with the business concerns.

My brother was a sort of travelling agent for a firm of manufacturing jewellers. He held a stock of the goods, which he used as samples for large orders, but in the case of small retailers he actually supplied the goods himself. When travelling, he usually carried his stock in a small Gladstone bag, but he kept the bulk of it in a safe in his house, and he used to go home at week-ends, or oftener, to replenish his travelling stock. Now, about two months ago he left home on a trip, but instead of taking a selection of his goods, he took the entire stock in a largish wooden box, leaving the safe empty.

"What he meant to do I don't know, and that's the fact. I offer no opinion. The circumstances were peculiar, as you will hear presently, and his proceedings were peculiar; for he went down to Stoke Varley—a village not far from Folkestone—put up at the 'Red Lion,' and deposited his box in the luggage-room that is kept for the use of commercial travellers; and then, after staying there for a few days, came up to London to make some arrangements for selling or letting his house—which, it seems, he had decided to leave. He came up in the evening, and the very next morning the first of his adventures befell, and a very alarming one it was.

"It appears that, as he was walking down a quiet street, he saw a lady's purse lying on the pavement. Naturally he picked it up, and as it contained nothing to show the name or address of the owner, he put it in his pocket, intending to hand it in at a police station. Shortly after this, he got into an omnibus, and a well-dressed woman entered at the same time and sat down next to him. Just as the conductor was coming in to collect the fares, the woman began to search her pocket excitedly, and then, turning to my brother, called on him loudly to return her purse. Of course, he said that he knew nothing about her purse, whereupon she roundly accused him of having picked her pocket, declaring to the conductor that she had felt him take out her purse, and demanding that the omnibus should be stopped and a policeman fetched.

"At this moment a policeman was seen on the pavement. The conductor stopped the omnibus and hailed the constable, who came, and having examined the floor of the vehicle without finding the missing purse, and taken the conductor's name and number, took my brother into custody and conducted him and the woman to the police station. Here the inspector took down from the woman a description of the stolen purse and its contents, which my brother, to his utter dismay, recognised as that of the purse which he had picked up and which was still in his pocket. Immediately, he gave the inspector an account of the incident and produced the purse; but it is hardly necessary to say that the inspector refused to take his explanation seriously.

"Then my brother did a thing which was natural enough, but which did not help him. Seeing that he was practically certain to be convicted—for there was really no answer to the charge—he gave a false name and refused his address. He was then locked up in a cell for the night, and the next morning was brought before the magistrate, who, having heard the evidence of the woman and the inspector and having listened without comment to my brother's story, committed him for trial at the Central Criminal Court, and refused bail. He was then removed to Brixton, where he was detained for nearly a month, pending the opening of the sessions.

"At length the day of his trial drew near. But it was then found that the woman who had accused him had left her lodgings and could not be traced. As there was no one to prosecute, and as the disappearance of the woman put a rather new light upon my brother's story, the case against him was allowed to drop, and he was released.

"He went home by train, and at the station he bought a copy of *The Times* to read on the way. Before opening it he chanced to run his eye over the 'personal' column, and there his attention was arrested by his own name in an advertisement—"

"Relating to a box?" said I.

"Precisely. Then you have seen it. Well, considering the value of the contents of that box, he was naturally rather anxious. At once he sent off a telegram saying that he would call on the following day before noon to claim the box and pay what was owing. And he did so. Yesterday morning he took an early train down to Stoke Varley and went straight to the 'Red Lion.' On his arrival he was asked to step into the coffee-room, which he did; and there he found three police officers, who forthwith arrested him on a charge of murder. But before going into the particular that charge I had better give you an account of his domestic affairs on which this incredible and horrible accusation turns.

"My brother, I am sorry to say, was living with a woman who was not his wife. He had originally intended to marry her, but his association with her—which lasted over several years—did not encourage that intention. She was a terrible woman, and she led him a terrible life. Her temper was ungovernable; and when she had taken too much to drink—which was a pretty frequent occurrence—she was not only noisy and quarrelsome, but physically violent as well. Her antecedents were disreputable—she had been connected with the seamy side of the music-hall stage; her associations were disreputable; she brought questionable women to my brother's house; she consorted with men of doubtful character, and her relations with them were equally doubtful. Indeed, with one of them, a man named Gamble, I should say that her relations were not doubtful at all, though I understand he was a married man.

"Well, my brother put up with her for years, living a life that cut him off from all decent society. But at last his patience gave way (and I may add that he made the acquaintance of a very desirable lady, who was willing to condone his past and marry him if he could secure a possible future). After a particularly outrageous scene, he ordered the woman—Rebecca Mings was her name—out of the house and declared their relationship at an end.

"But she refused to be shaken off. She kept possession of the street-door key, and she returned again and again, and made a public scandal. The last time she created such an uproar when the door was bolted against her that a crowd collected in the street and my brother was forced to let her in. She stayed with him some hours, alone in the house—for the only servant he had was a daily girl who left at three o'clock—and went away quite quietly about ten at night. But, although a good many people saw her go into the house, no one but my brother seems to have seen her leave it; a most disastrous circumstance, for, from the moment when she left the house, no one ever saw her again. She did not go to her lodgings that night. She disappeared utterly—until—but I must go back now to the 'Red Lion' at Stoke Varley.

"When my brother was arrested on the charge of having murdered Rebecca Mings, certain particulars were given to him; and when I went down there in response to a telegram, I gathered some more. The circumstances are these: About a fortnight after my brother had left to come to London, some of the 'commercials' who used the luggage-room complained of an unpleasant odour in it, which was presently traced to my brother's box. As that box appeared to have been abandoned, the landlord became suspicious, and communicated with the police. They telephoned to the London police, who found my brother's house shut up and his whereabouts unknown.

"Thereupon the local police broke open the box and found in it a woman's left arm and a quantity of bloodstained clothing. On which they caused the advertisement to be put in *The Times*, and meanwhile they made certain inquiries. It appeared that my brother had spent part of his time at Stoke Varley fishing in the little river. On learning this, the police proceeded to dredge the river, and presently they brought up a right arm—apparently the fellow of the one found in the box—and a leg divided into three parts, evidently a woman's. Now, as to the arm found in the box, there could be no question about its identity, for it bore a very distinct tattooed inscription consisting of the initials R. M. above a heart transfixed by an arrow, with the initials J. B. underneath.

"A few inquiries elicited the fact that the woman, Rebecca Mings, who had disappeared, bore such a tattooed mark on her left arm and certain persons who had known her, having been sworn to secrecy, were shown the arm, and recognised the mark without hesitation. Further inquiries showed that Rebecca Mings was last seen alive entering my brother's house, as I have described; and on this information the police broke into the house and searched it."

"Do you know if they found anything?" Thorndyke asked.

"I don't," replied Chapman, "but I infer that they did. The police at Stoke Varley were very courteous and kind, but they declined to give any particulars about the visit to the house. However, we shall hear at the inquest if they made any discoveries."

"And is that all that you have to tell us?" asked Thorndyke.

"Yes," was the reply, "and enough, too. I make no comment on my brother's story, and I won't ask whether you believe it. I don't expect you to. The question is whether you would undertake the defence. I suppose it isn't necessary for a lawyer to be convinced of his client's innocence in order to convince the jury."

"You are thinking of an advocate," said Thorndyke. "I am not an advocate, and I should not defend a man whom I believed to be guilty. The most that I can do is to investigate the case. If the result of the investigation is to confirm the suspicions against your brother, I shall, go no farther in the case. You will have to get an ordinary criminal barrister to defend your brother. If, on the other hand, I find reasonable grounds for believing him innocent, I will undertake the defence. What do you say to that?"

"I've no choice," replied Chapman; "and I suppose if you find all the evidence against him, the defence won't matter much."

"I am afraid that is so," said Thorndyke. "And, now there are one or two questions to be cleared up. First, does your brother offer any explanation of the presence of these remains in his box?"

"He supposes that somebody at the 'Red Lion' must have taken the jewellery out and put the remains in. Anyone could get access to the luggage-room by asking for the key at the office."

"Well," said Thorndyke, "that is conceivable. Then, as to the person who might have made this exchange. Is there anyone who had any reason for wishing to make away with deceased?"

"No," replied Chapman. "Plenty of people disliked her, but no one but my brother had any motive for getting rid of her."

"You spoke of a man with whom she was on somewhat intimate terms. There had been no quarrel or breach there, I suppose?"

"The man Gamble, you mean. No, I should say they were the best of friends. Besides, Gamble had no responsibilities in regard to her. He could have dropped her whenever he was tired of her."

"Do you know anything about him?" Thorndyke asked.

"Very little. He has been a rolling stone, and has been in all sorts of jobs, I believe. He was in the New Zealand trade for some time, and dealt in all sorts of things—among others, in smoked human heads; sold them to collectors and museums, I understand. So he would have had some previous experience," Chapman added with a faint grin.

"Not in dismemberment," said Thorndyke. "Those will have been ancient Maori heads—relics of the old head hunters. There are some in the Hunterian Museum. But, as you say, there seems to be no motive in Gamble's case, even if there had been the opportunity; whereas, in your brother's case, there seem to have been both the motive and the opportunity. I suppose your brother never threatened the deceased?"

"I am sorry to say he did," replied Chapman. "On several occasions, and before witnesses, too, he threatened to put her out of the way. Of course he never meant it—he was really the mildest of men. But it was a foolish thing to do and most unfortunate, as things have turned out."

"Well." said Thorndyke, "I will look into the matter and let you know what I think of it. It is unnecessary to remark that appearances are not very encouraging."

"No, I can see that," said Chapman, rising and producing his card-case. "But we must hope for the best." He laid his card on the table, and having shaken hands with us gloomily, took his departure.

"It doesn't do to take things at their face value," I remarked, when he had gone; "but I don't think we have ever had a more hopeless-looking case. All it wants to complete it is the discovery of remains in

Chapman's house."

"In that respect," said Thorndyke, "it may already be complete. But it hardly wants that finishing touch. On the evidence that we have, any jury would find a verdict of 'guilty' without leaving the box. The only question for us is whether the face value of the evidence is its real value. If it is, the defence will be a mere formality."

"I suppose," said I, "you will begin the investigation at Stoke Varley?"

"Yes," he replied. "We begin by checking the alleged facts. If they are really as stated, we shall probably need to go no farther. And we had better lose no time, as the remains may be moved into the jurisdiction of a London coroner, and we ought to see everything in situ as far as possible. I suggest that we postpone the rest of today's business and start at once, taking Scotland Yard on the way to get authority to inspect the remains and the premises."

In a few minutes we were ready for the expedition. While Thorndyke packed the "research-case" with the necessary instruments, I gave instructions to our laboratory assistant, Polton, as to what was to be done in our absence, and then, when we had consulted the time-table, we set forth by way of the Embankment.

At Scotland Yard, on inquiring for our friend, Superintendent Miller, we received the slightly unwelcome news that he was at Stoke Varley, inquiring into the case. However, the authorisation was given readily enough, and, armed with this, we made our way to Charing Cross Station, arriving there in good time to catch our train.

We had just given up our tickets and turned out into the pleasant station approach of Stoke Varley when Thorndyke gave a soft chuckle. I looked at him inquiringly, and he explained. "Miller has had a telegram, and we are going to have facilities, with a little supervision." Following the direction of his glance, I now observed the superintendent strolling towards us, trying to look surprised, but achieving only a somewhat sheepish grin.

"Well, I'm sure, gentlemen!" he exclaimed. "This is an unexpected pleasure. You don't mean to say you are engaged in this treasure-trove case?"

"Why not?" asked Thorndyke.

"Well, I'll tell you why not," replied Miller. "Because it's no go. You'll only waste your time and injure your reputation. I may as well let you know, in confidence, that we've been through Chapman's house in London. It wasn't very necessary; but still, if there was a vacancy in his coffin for one or two more nails, we've knocked them in."

"What did you find in his house?" Thorndyke asked.

"We found," replied Miller, "in a cupboard in his bedroom, a good-sized bottle of *hyoscine* tablets, about two-thirds full—one-third missing. No great harm in that; he might have taken 'em himself. But when we went down into the cellar, we noticed that the place smelt—well, a bit graveyardy, so to speak. So we had a look round. It was a stone-floored cellar, not very even, but so far as we could see, none of the flagstones seemed to have been disturbed. We didn't want the job of digging the whole of them up, so I just filled a bucket with water and poured it over the floor. Then I watched.

"In less than a minute one big flagstone near the middle went nearly dry, while the water still stood on all the others. 'What O!' says I. 'Loose earth underneath here.' So we got a crow-bar and prised up that big flag; and sure enough, underneath it we found a good-sized bundle done up in a sheet. I won't go into unpleasant particulars—not that it would upset you, I suppose—but that bundle contained human remains."

"Any bones?" inquired Thorndyke.

"No. Mostly in'ards and some skin from the front of the body. We handed them over to the Home Office experts, and they examined them and made an analysis. Their report states that the remains are those of a woman of about thirty-five—that was about Mings' age—and that the various organs contained a large quantity of *hyoscine*; more than enough to have caused death. So there you are. If you are going to conduct the defence, you won't get much glory from it."

"It is very good of you, Miller," said Thorndyke, "to have given us this private information. It is very helpful, though I have not undertaken the defence. I have merely come down to check the facts and see if there is any material for a defence. And I shall go through the routine, as I am here. Where are the remains?"

"In the mortuary. I'll show you the way, and as I happen to have the key in my pocket, I can let you in."

We passed through the outskirts of the village, gathering a small train of stealthy followers, who dogged us to the door of the mortuary and hungrily watched us as the superintendent let us in and locked the door after us.

"There you are," said Miller, indicating the slate table on which the remains lay, covered by a sheet soaked in an antiseptic. "I've seen all I want to see." And he retired into a corner and lit his pipe.

The remnants of mortality, disclosed by the removal of the sheet, were dreadfully suggestive of crime in its most brutal and horrible form, but they offered little information. The dismemberment had been manifestly rude and unskilful, and the remains were clearly those of a woman of medium size and apparently in the prime of life. The principal interest centred in the left arm, the waxen skin of which bore a very distinct tattoo-mark, consisting of the initials R. M. over a very symmetrical heart, transfixed by an arrow, beneath which were the initials J. B.

The letters were Roman capitals about half an inch high, well-formed and finished with serifs, and the heart and arrow quite well drawn. I looked reflectively at the device, standing out in dull blue from its ivory-like background, and speculated vaguely as to who J. B. might have been and how many predecessors and successors he had had. And then my interest waned, and I joined the superintendent in the corner. It was a sordid case, and a conviction being a foregone conclusion, it did not seem to call for further attention.

Thorndyke, however, seemed to think otherwise. But that was his way. When he was engaged in an investigation he put out of his mind everything that he had been told and began from the very beginning. That was what he was doing now. He was inspecting these remains as if they had been the remains of some unidentified person. He made, and noted down, minute measurements of the limbs; he closely examined every square inch of surface; he scrutinised each finger separately, and then with the aid of his portable inking-plate and roller, took a complete set of fingerprints.

He measured all the dimensions of the tattoo-marks with a delicate calliper-gauge, and then examined the marks themselves, first with a common lens and then with the high-power Coddington. The principles that he laid down in his lectures at the hospital were: "Accept no statement without verification; observe every fact independently for yourselves; and keep an open mind." And, certainly, no one ever carried out more conscientiously his own precepts.

"Do you know, Dr. Jervis," the superintendent whispered to me as Thorndyke brought his Coddington to bear on the tattoo-marks, "I believe this lens business is becoming a habit with the doctor. It's my firm conviction that if somebody were to blow up the Houses of Parliament, he'd go and examine the ruins through a magnifying glass. Just look at him poring over those tattooed letters that you could read plainly twenty feet away!"

Meanwhile, Thorndyke, unconscious of these criticisms, placidly continued his inspection. From the table, with its gruesome burden, he transferred his attention to the box, which had been placed on a bench by the window, examining it minutely inside and out; feeling with his fingers the dark grey paint with which it was coated and the white-painted initials, "S. C.," on the lid, which he also measured carefully. He even copied into his note book the maker's name, which was stamped on a small brass label affixed to the inside of the lid, and the name of the lock-maker, and inspected the screws which had drawn from the wood when it was forced open.

At length he put away his notebook, closed the research-case and announced that he had finished, adding the inquiry: "How do you get to the 'Red Lion' from here?"

"It's only a few minutes' walk," said Miller. "I'll show you the way. But you're wasting your time, doctor, you are indeed. You see," he continued, when he had locked up the mortuary and pocketed the key, "that suggestion of Chapman's is ridiculous on the face of it. Just imagine a man bringing a portmanteau full of human remains into the luggage-room of a commercial hotel, opening it and opening another's man's box, and swapping the contents of the one for the other with the chance of one of the commercials coming in at any moment. Supposing one of 'em had, what would he have had to say? 'Hallo!' says the baggy, 'you seem to have got somebody's arm in your box.'

"'So I have,' says Chapman. 'I expect it's my wife's. Careless woman! must have dropped it in when she was packing the box.' Bah! It's a fool's explanation. Besides, how could he have got Chapman's box open? We couldn't. It was a first-class lock. We had to break it open, but it hadn't been broken open before. No, sir, that cat won't jump. Still, you needn't take my word for it. Here is the place, and here is Mr. Butt, himself, standing at his own front door looking as pleasant as the flowers in May, like the lump of sugar that you put in a fly-trap to induce 'em to walk in."

The landlord, who had overheard—without difficulty—the concluding passage of Miller's peroration, smiled genially; and when the purpose of the visit had been explained, suggested a "modest quencher" in the private parlour as an aid to conversation.

"I wanted," said Thorndyke, waiving the suggestion of the 'quencher,' "to ascertain whether Chapman's theory of an exchange of contents could be seriously entertained."

Well, sir," said the landlord, "the fact is that it couldn't. That room is a public room, and people may be popping in there at any time all day. We don't usually keep it locked. It isn't necessary. We know most of our customers, and the contents of the packages that are stowed in the room are principally travellers' samples of no considerable value. The thing would have been impossible in the daytime, and we lock the room up at night."

"Have you had any strangers staying with you in the interval between Chapman's going away and the discovery of the remains?"

"Yes. There was a Mr. Doler; he had two cabin trunks: and a uniform case which went to the luggage-room. And then there was a lady, Mrs. Murchison. She had a lot of stuff in there: a small, flat trunk, a hat-box, and a big dress-basket—one of these great basket pantechnicons that ladies take about with them. And there was another gentleman—I forget his name, but you will see it in the visitors' book—he had a couple of largish portmanteaux in there. Perhaps you would like to see the book?"

"I should," said Thorndyke, and when the book was produced and the names of the guests pointed out, he copied the entries into his notebook, adding the particulars of their luggage.

"And now, sir," said Miller, "I suppose you won't be happy until you've seen the room itself?"

"Your insight is really remarkable, superintendent," my colleague replied. "Yes, I should like to see the room."

There was little enough to see, however, when we arrived there. The key was in the door, and the latter was not only unlocked but stood ajar; and when we pushed it open and entered we saw a small room, empty save for a collection of portmanteaux, trunks, and Gladstone bags. The only noteworthy fact was that it was at the end of a corridor, covered with linoleum, so that anyone inside would have a few seconds' notice of another person's approach.

But evidently that would have been of little use in the alleged circumstances. For the hypothetical criminal must have emptied Chapman's box of the jewellery before he could put the incriminating objects into it; so that, apart from the latter, the arrival of an inopportune visitor would have found him apparently in the act of committing a robbery. The suggestion was obviously absurd.

"By the way," said Thorndyke, as we descended the stairs, "where is the central character of this drama—Chapman? He is not here, I suppose?"

"Yes, he is," replied Miller. "He is committed for trial, but we are keeping him here until we know where the inquest is to be held. You would probably like to have a few words with him? Well, I'll take you along to the police station and tell them who you are, and then perhaps you would like to come back here and have some lunch or dinner before you return to town."

I warmly seconded the latter proposal, and the arrangement having been made, we set forth for the police station, which we gathered from Miller was incorporated with a small local prison. Here we were shown into what appeared to be a private office, and presently a sergeant entered, ushering in a man whom we at once recognised from his resemblance to our client, Mr. George Chapman, disguised though it was by his pallor, his unshaven face, and his air of abject misery. The sergeant, having announced him by name, withdrew with the superintendent and locked the door on the outside.

As soon as we were alone, Thorndyke rapidly acquainted the prisoner with the circumstances of his brother's visit and then continued: "Now, Mr. Chapman, you want me to undertake your defence. If I do so, I must have all the facts. If there is anything known to you that your brother has not told me, I ask you to tell it to me without reservation."

Chapman shook his head wearily.

"I know nothing more than you know," said he. "The whole affair is a mystery that I can make nothing of. I don't expect you to believe me. Who would, with all this evidence against me? But I swear to God that I know nothing of this abominable crime. When I brought that box down here, it contained my stock of jewellery and nothing else; and after I put it in the luggage-room, I never opened it."

"Do you know of anybody who might have had a motive for getting rid of Rebecca Mings?"

"Not a soul," replied Chapman. "She led me the devil's own life, but she was popular enough with her own friends. And she was an attractive woman in her way: a fine, well-built woman, rather big—she stood five-feet-seven—with a good complexion and very handsome golden hair. Such as her friends were—they were a shady lot—I think they were fond of her, and I don't believe she had any enemies."

"Some *hyoscine* was found in your house," said Thorndyke. "Do you know anything about it?"

"Yes. I got it when I suffered from neuralgia. But I never took any. My doctor heard about it and sent me to the dentist. The bottle was never opened. It contained a hundred tablets."

"And with regard to the box," said Thorndyke. "Had you had it long?"

"Not very long. I bought it at Fletchers, in Holborn, about six months ago."

"And you have nothing more to tell us?"

"No," he replied. "I wish I had;" and then, after a pause, he asked with a wistful look at Thorndyke: "Are you going to undertake my defence, sir? I can see that there is very little hope, but I should like to be given just a chance."

I glanced at Thorndyke, expecting at the most a cautious and conditional reply. To my astonishment he answered: "There is no need to take such a gloomy view of the case, Mr. Chapman. I shall undertake the defence, and I think you have quite a fair chance of an acquittal."

On this amazing reply I reflected, not without some self-condemnation, during our walk to the hotel and the meal that preceded our departure. For it was evident that I had missed something vital. Thorndyke was a cautious man and little given to making promises or forecasts of results. He must have picked up some evidence of a very conclusive kind; but what that evidence could be, I found it impossible to imagine. The superintendent, too, was puzzled, I could see, for Thorndyke made no secret of his intention to go on with the case. But Miller's delicate attempts to pump him came to nothing; and when he had escorted us to the station and our train moved off, I could see him standing on the platform, gently scratching the back of his head and gazing speculatively at our retreating carriage.

As soon as we were clear of the station, I opened my attack.

"What on earth," I demanded, "did you mean by giving that poor devil, Chapman, hopes of acquittal? I can't see that he has a dog's chance."

Thorndyke looked at me gravely.

"My impression is, Jervis." he said, "that you have not kept an open mind in this case. You have allowed yourself to fall under the suggestive influence of the obvious; whereas the function of the investigator is to consider the possible alternatives of the obvious inference. And you have not brought your usual keen attention to bear on the facts. If you had considered George Chapman's statement attentively you would have noticed that it contained some very curious and significant suggestions; and if you had examined those dismembered remains critically, you would have seen that they confirmed those suggestions in a very remarkable manner."

"As to George Chapman's statement," said I, "the only suggestive point that I recall is the reference to those Maori heads. But, as you, yourself, pointed out, the dealers in those heads don't do the dismemberment."

Thorndyke shook his head a little impatiently.

"Tut, tut, Jervis," said he, "that isn't the point at all. Any fool can cut up a dead body as this one has been cut up. The point is that that statement, carefully considered, yields a definite and consistent alternative to the theory that Samuel Chapman killed this woman and dismembered her body; and that alternative theory is supported by the appearance of these remains. I think you will see the point if you recall Chapman's statement, and reflect on the possible bearing of the various incidents that he described."

In this, however, Thorndyke was unduly optimistic. I recalled the statement completely enough, and reflected on it frequently and profoundly during the next few days; but the more I thought of it the more conclusive did the case against the accused appear.

Meanwhile, my colleague appeared to be taking no steps in the matter, and I assumed that he was waiting for the inquest. It is true that, when, on one occasion, he had accompanied me towards the City, and leaving me in Queen Victoria Street disappeared into the premises of Messrs. Burden Brothers, lock manufacturers, I was inclined to associate his proceedings with his minute examination of the lock at Stoke Varley. And, again, when our laboratory assistant, Polton, was seen to issue forth, top-hatted and armed with an umbrella and an *attaché*-case, I suspected some sort of "private inquiries," possibly connected with the case.

But from Thorndyke I could get no information at all. My tentative "pumpings" elicited one unvarying reply. "You have the facts, Jervis. You heard George Chapman's statement, and you have seen the remains. Give me a reasonable theory and I will discuss it with pleasure." And that was how the matter remained. I had no reasonable theory—other than that of the police—and there was accordingly no discussion.

On a certain evening, a couple of days before the inquest—which had been postponed in the hope that some further remains might be discovered—I observed signs of an expected visitor: a small table placed by the supernumerary arm-chair and furnished with a tray bearing a siphon, a whisky-decanter and a box of cigars. Thorndyke caught my inquiring glance at these luxuries, for which neither of us had any use, and proceeded to explain.

"I have asked Miller to look in this evening—he is due now. I have been working at this Chapman case, and, as it is now complete, I propose to lay my cards on the table."

"Is that safe?" said I. "Supposing the police still go for a conviction and try to forestall your evidence?"

"They won't," he replied. "They couldn't. And it would be most improper to let the case go for trial on a false theory. But here is Miller; and a mighty twitter he is in, I have no doubt."

He was. Without even waiting for the customary cigar, he plumped down into the chair, and dragging a letter from his pocket, fixed a glare of astonishment on my placid colleague.

"This letter of yours, sir," said he, "is perfectly incomprehensible to me. You say that you are prepared to put us in possession of the facts of this Chapman case. But we are in possession of the facts already. We are absolutely certain of a conviction. Let me remind you, sir, of what those facts are. We have got a dead body which has been identified beyond all doubt. Part of that body was found in a box which is the property of Samuel Chapman, which was brought by him and deposited by him at the 'Red Lion' Hotel.

"Another part of that body was found in his dwelling-house. A supply of poison—an uncommon poison, too—similar to that which killed the dead person, has also been found in his house; and the dead body is that of a woman with whom Chapman was known to be on terms of enmity and whom he has threatened, in the presence of witnesses, to kill. Now, sir, what have you got to say to those facts?"

Thorndyke regarded the agitated detective with a quiet smile. "My comments, Miller," said he, "can be put in a nut-shell. You have got the wrong man, you have got the wrong box, and you have got the wrong body."

The superintendent was thunderstruck, and no wonder. So was I. As to Miller, he drew himself forward until he was sitting on the extreme edge of the chair, and for some moments stared at my impassive colleague in speechless amazement. At length he burst out: "But, my dear sir! This is sheer nonsense—at least, that's what it sounds like, though I know it can't be. Let's begin with the body. You say it's the wrong one."

"Yes. Rebecca Mings was a biggish woman. Her height was five-feet-seven. This woman was not more than five-feet-four."

"Bah!" exclaimed Miller. "You can't judge to an inch or two from parts of a dismembered body. You are forgetting the tattoo-mark. That clenches the identity beyond any possible doubt."

"It does, indeed," said Thorndyke. "That is the crucial evidence. Rebecca Mings had a certain tattoo mark on her left forearm. This woman had not."

"Had not!" shrieked Miller, coming yet farther forward on his chair. (I expected, every moment, to see him sitting on the floor.) "Why, I saw it; and so did you."

"I am speaking of the woman, not of the body," said Thorndyke. "The mark that you saw was a post-mortem tattoo-mark. It was made after death. But the fact that it was made after death is good evidence, that it was not there during life."

"Moses!" exclaimed the superintendent. "This is a facer. Are you perfectly sure it was done after death?"

"Quite sure. The appearance, through a powerful lens, is unmistakable. Tattoo-marks are made, as you know, of course, by painting Indian ink on the skin and pricking it in with fine needles. In the living skin the needle-wounds heal up at once and disappear, but in the dead skin the needle-holes remain unclosed and can be easily seen with a lens. In this case the skin had been well washed and the surface pressed with some smooth object; but the holes were plainly visible and the ink was still in them."

"Well, I'm sure!" said Miller. "I never heard of tattooing a dead body before."

"Very few people have, I expect," said Thorndyke. "But there is one class of persons who know all about it: the persons who deal in Maori heads."

"Indeed?" queried Miller. "How does it concern them?"

"Those heads are usually elaborately tattooed, and the value of a head depends on the quality of the tattooing. Now, when those heads became objects of trade, the dealers conceived the idea of touching up defective specimens by additional tattooing on the dead head, and from this they proceeded to obtain heads which had no tattoo-marks, and turn them into tattooed heads."

"Well, to be sure," said the superintendent, with a grin, "what wicked men there are in the world, aren't there, Dr. Jervis?"

I murmured a vague assent, but I was principally conscious of a desire to kick myself for having failed to pick this invaluable clue out of George Chapman's statement.

"And now," said Miller, "we come to the box. How do you know it is the wrong one?"

"That," replied Thorndyke, "is proved even more conclusively. The original box was made by Fletchers, in Holborn. It was sold to Chapman, and his initials painted on it, on the 9th of last April. I have seen the entry in the day-book. The locks of these boxes are made by Burden Brothers of Queen Victoria Street, and as they are quite high-class locks each is given a registered number, which is stamped on the lock. The number on the box that you have is 5007, and Burden's books show that it was made and sold to Fletchers about the middle of July—the sale was dated the 13th. Therefore this can not be Chapman's box."

"Apparently not," Miller agreed. "But whose box is it? And what has become of Chapman's box?"

"That," replied Thorndyke, "was presumably taken away in Mrs. Murchison's dress-basket."

"Then who the deuce is Mrs. Murchison?" demanded the superintendent.

"I should say," replied Thorndyke, "that she was formerly known as Rebecca Mings."

"The deceased!" exclaimed Miller, falling back in his chair with a guffaw. "My eye! What a lark it is! But she must have some sauce, to walk off with the jewellery and leave her own dismembered remains in exchange! By the way, whose remains are they?"

"We shall come to that presently," Thorndyke answered. "Now we have to consider the man you have in custody."

"Yes," agreed Miller, "we must settle about him. Of course if it isn't his box, and the body isn't Mings' body, that puts him out of it so far. But there are those remains that we dug up in his cellar. What about them?"

"That question," replied Thorndyke, "will, I think, be answered by a general review of the case. But I must, remind you that if the box is not Chapman's, it is some other person's; that is to say, that if Chapman goes out of the case, as to the Stoke Varley incidents, someone else comes in. So, if the body is not Mings' body, it is some other woman's, and that other woman must have disappeared. And now let us review the case as a whole.

"You know about the pocket-picking charge. It was obviously a false charge, deliberately prepared by 'planting' the purse; that is, it was a conspiracy. Now what was the object of this conspiracy? Clearly it was to get Chapman out of the way while the boxes were exchanged at Stoke Varley, and the remains deposited in the river and elsewhere. Then who were the conspirators—other than the agent who planted the purse?

"They—if there were more than one—must have had access to Mings, dead or alive, in order to make the exact copy, or tracing, of her tattoo-mark. They must have had some knowledge of the process of post-mortem tattooing. They must have had access to Chapman's house. And, since they had in their possession the dead body of a woman, they must have been associated with some woman who has disappeared.

"Who is there who answers this description? Well, of course, Mings had access to herself, though she could hardly have taken a tracing from her own arm, and she had access to Chapman's house, since she had possession of the latchkey. Then there is a man named Gamble, with whom Mings was on terms of great intimacy. Now Gamble was formerly a dealer in tattooed Maori heads, so he may be assumed to know something about post-mortem tattooing. And I have ascertained that Gamble's wife has disappeared from her usual places of resort. So here are two persons who, together, agree with the description of the conspirators. And now let us consider the train of events in connection with the dates.

"On July the 29th Chapman came to town from Stoke Varley. On the 30th he was arrested as a pick pocket. On the 31st he was committed for trial. On the 2nd of August Mrs. Gamble went away to the country. No one seems to have seen her go, but that is the date on which she is reported to have gone. On August the 5th Mrs. Murchison deposited at Stoke Varley a box which must have been purchased between the 13th of July and the 4th of August, and which contained a woman's arm. On the 14th of August that box was opened by the police. On the 18th human remains were discovered in Chapman's house. On the 27th Chapman was released from Brixton. On the 28th he was arrested for murder at Stoke Varley. I think, Miller, you will agree that that is a very striking succession of dates."

"Yes," Miller agreed. "It looks like a true bill. If you will give me Mr. Gamble's address, I'll call on him."

"I'm afraid you won't find him at home," said Thorndyke. "He has gone into the country, too; and I gather from his landlord, who holds a returned cheque, that Mr. Gamble's banking account has gone into the country with him."

"Then," said the superintendent "I suppose I must take a trip into the country, too."

"Well, Thorndyke," I said, as I laid down the paper containing the report of the trial of Gamble and Mings for the murder of Theresa Gamble, one morning about four months later, "you ought to be very highly gratified. After sentencing Gamble to death and Mings to fifteen years' penal servitude, the judge took the opportunity to compliment the police on their ingenuity in unravelling this crime, and the Home Office experts on their skill in detecting the counterfeit tattoo-marks. What do you think of that?"

"I think," replied Thorndyke, "that his lordship showed a very proper and appreciative spirit."

Percival Bland's Proxy

Mr. Percival Bland was a somewhat uncommon type of criminal. In the first place he really had an appreciable amount of commonsense. If he had only had a little more, he would not have been a criminal at all. As it was, he had just sufficient judgment to perceive that the consequences of unlawful acts accumulate as the acts are repeated; to realise that the criminal's position must, at length, become untenable; and to take what he considered fair precautions against the inevitable catastrophe.

But in spite of these estimable traits of character and the precautions aforesaid, Mr. Bland found himself in rather a tight place and with a prospect of increasing tightness. The causes of this uncomfortable tension do not concern us, and may be dismissed with the remark, that, if one perseveringly distributes flash Bank of England notes among the money-changers of the Continent, there will come a day of reckoning when those notes are tendered to the exceedingly knowing old lady who lives in Threadneedle Street.

Mr. Bland considered uneasily the approaching storm-cloud as he raked over the "miscellaneous property" in the Sale-rooms of Messrs. Plimpton. He was a confirmed frequenter of auctions, as was not unnatural, for the criminal is essentially a gambler. And criminal and gambler have one quality in common: each hopes to get something of value without paying the market price for it.

So Percival turned over the dusty oddments and his own difficulties at one and the same time. The vital questions were: When would the storm burst? And would it pass by the harbour of refuge that he had been at such pains to construct? Let us inspect that harbour of refuge.

A quiet flat in the pleasant neighbourhood of Battersea bore a name-plate inscribed, Mr. Robert Lindsay; and the tenant was known to the porter and the char woman who attended to the flat, as a fair-haired gentleman who was engaged in the book trade as a travelling agent, and was consequently a good deal away from home. Now Mr. Robert Lindsay bore a distinct resemblance to Percival Bland; which was not surprising seeing that they were first cousins (or, at any rate, they said they were; and we may presume that they knew). But they were not very much alike. Mr. Lindsay had flaxen, or rather sandy, hair; Mr. Bland's hair was black. Mr. Bland had a mole under his left eye; Mr. Lindsay had no mole under his eye—but carried one in a small box in his waistcoat pocket.

At somewhat rare intervals the cousins called on one another; but they had the very worst of luck, for neither of them ever seemed to find the other at home. And what was even more odd was that when-ever Mr. Bland spent an evening at home in his lodgings over the oil shop in Bloomsbury, Mr. Lindsay's flat was empty; and as sure as Mr. Lindsay was at home in his flat so surely were Mr. Bland's lodgings vacant for the time being. It was a queer coincidence, if anyone had noticed it; but nobody ever did.

However, if Percival saw little of his cousin, it was not a case of "out of sight, out of mind." On the contrary; so great was his solicitude for the latter's welfare that he not only had made a will constituting him his executor and sole legatee, but he had actually insured his life for no less a sum than three thousand pounds; and this will, together with the insurance policy, investment securities and other necessary docu-ments, he had placed in the custody of a highly respectable solicitor. All of which did him great credit. It isn't every man who is willing to take so much trouble for a mere cousin.

Mr. Bland continued his perambulations, pawing over the mis-cellaneous raffle from sheer force of habit, reflecting on the coming crisis in his own affairs, and on the provisions that he had made for his cousin Robert. As for the latter, they were excellent as far as they went, but they lacked definiteness and perfect completeness. There was the contingency of a "stretch," for instance; say fourteen years' penal servitude. The insurance policy did not cover that. And, mean-while, what was to become of the estimable Robert?

He had bruised his thumb somewhat severely in a screw-cutting lathe, and had abstractedly turned the handle of a bird-organ until politely requested by an attendant to desist, when he came upon a series of boxes containing, according to the catalogue, "a collection of surgical instruments the property of a lately deceased practitioner." To judge by the appearance of the instruments, the practitioner must have commenced practice in his early youth and died at a very advanced age. They were an uncouth set of tools, of no value whatever excepting as testimonials to the amazing tenacity of life of our ancestors; but Percival fingered them over according to his wont, working the handle of a complicated brass syringe and ejecting a drop of greenish fluid on to the shirt of a dressy Hebrew (who requested him to "point the dam' thing at thomeone elth nectht time"), opening musty leather cases, clicking off spring scarifiers and feeling the edges of strange, crooked, knives.

Then he came upon a largish black box, which, when he raised the lid, breathed out an ancient and fish-like aroma and exhibited a collection of bones, yellow, greasy and spotted in places with mildew. The catalogue described them as "a complete set of human osteology" but they were not an ordinary "student's set," for the bones of the hands and feet, instead of being strung together on cat-gut, were united by their original ligaments and were of an unsavoury brown colour.

"I thay, misther," expostulat the Hebrew, "shut that bocth. Thmellth like a blooming inquetht."

But the contents of the black box seemed to have a fascination for Percival. He looked in at those greasy remnants of mortality, at the brown and mouldy hands and feet and the skull that peeped forth eerily from the folds of a flannel wrapping; and they breathed out something more than that stale and musty odour. A suggestion—vague and general at first, but rapidly crystallising into distinct shape—seemed to steal out of the black box into his consciousness; a suggestion that somehow seemed to connect itself with his estimable cousin Robert.

For upwards of a minute he stood motionless, as one immersed in reverie, the lid poised in his hand and a dreamy eye fixed on the half skull. A stir in the room roused him. The sale was about to begin. The members of the knock-out and other *habitués* seated themselves on benches around a long, baize table; the attendants took possession of the first lots and opened their catalogues as if about to sing an introductory chorus; and a gentleman with a waxed moustache and a striking resemblance to His Late Majesty, the third Napoleon, having ascended to the rostrum bespoke the attention of the assembly by a premonitory tap with his hammer.

How odd are some of the effects of a guilty conscience! With what absurd self-consciousness do we read into the minds of others our own undeclared intentions, when those intentions are unlawful! Had

Percival Bland wanted a set of human bones for any legitimate purpose—such as anatomical study—he would have bought it openly and unembarrassed. Now, he found himself earnestly debating whether he should not bid for some of the surgical instruments, just for the sake of appearances; and there being little time in which to make up his mind—for the deceased practitioner's effects came first in the catalogue—he was already the richer by a set of cupping-glasses, a tooth-key, and an instrument of unknown use and diabolical aspect, before the fateful lot was called.

At length the black box was laid on the table, an object of obscene mirth to the knockers-out, and the auctioneer read the entry: "Lot seventeen; a complete set of human osteology. A very useful and valuable set of specimens, gentlemen."

He looked round at the assembly majestically, oblivious of sundry inquiries as to the identity of the deceased and the verdict of the coroner's jury, and finally suggested five shillings.

"Six," said Percival.

An attendant held the box open, and, chanting the mystic word "Loddlemen!" (which, being interpreted, meant "Lot, gentlemen"), thrust it under the rather bulbous nose of the smart Hebrew; who remarked that "they 'ummed a bit too much to thoot him" and pushed it away.

"Going at six shillings," said the auctioneer, reproachfully; and as nobody contradicted him, he smote the rostrum with his hammer and the box was delivered into the hands of Percival on the payment of that modest sum.

Having crammed the cupping-glasses, the tooth-key and the unknown instrument into the box, Percival obtained from one of the attendants a length of cord, with which he secured the lid. Then he carried his treasure out into the street, and, chartering a four-wheeler, directed the driver to proceed to Charing Cross Station. At the station he booked the box in the cloak (in the name of Simpson) and left it for a couple of hours; at the expiration of which he returned, and, employing a different porters had it conveyed to a hansom, in which it was borne to his lodgings over the oil-shop in Bloomsbury. There he, himself, carried it, unobserved, up the stairs, and, depositing it in a large cupboard, locked the door and pocketed the key.

And thus was the curtain rung down on the first act. The second act opened only a couple of days later, the office of call-boy—to pursue the metaphor to the bitter end—being discharged by a Belgian police official who emerged from the main entrance to the Bank of England. What should have led Percival Bland into so unsafe a neighbourhood it is difficult to imagine, unless it was that strange fascination that seems so frequently to lure the criminal to places associated with his crime. But there he was within a dozen paces of the entrance when the officer came forth, and mutual recognition was instant. Almost equally instantaneous was the self-possessed Percival's decision to cross the road.

It is not a nice road to cross. The old horse would condescend to shout a warning to the indiscreet wayfarer. Not so the modern chauffeur, who looks stonily before him and leaves you to get out of the way of Juggernaut. He knows his "exonerating" coroner's jury. At the moment, however, the procession of Juggernauts was at rest; but Percival had seen the presiding policeman turn to move away and he darted across the fronts of the vehicles even as they started.

The foreign officer followed. But in that moment the whole procession had got in motion. A motor omnibus thundered past in front of him; another was bearing down on him relentlessly. He hesitated, and sprang back; and then a taxi-cab, darting out from behind, butted him heavily, sending him sprawling in the road, whence he scrambled as best he could back on to the pavement.

Percival, meanwhile, had swung himself lightly on to the footboard of the first omnibus just as it was gathering speed. A few seconds saw him safely across at the Mansion House, and in a few more, he was whirling down Queen Victoria Street. The danger was practically over, though he took the precaution to alight at St. Paul's, and, crossing to Newgate Street, board another west-bound omnibus.

That night he sat in his lodgings turning over his late experience. It had been a narrow shave. That sort of thing mustn't happen again. In fact, seeing that the law was undoubtedly about to be set in motion, it was high time that certain little plans of his should be set in motion, too. Only, there was a difficulty; a serious difficulty. And as Percival thought round and round that difficulty his brows wrinkled and he hummed a soft refrain.

"Then is the time for disappearing,
Take a header—down you go—"

A tap at the door cut his song short. It was his landlady, Mrs. Brattle; a civil woman, and particularly civil just now. For she had a little request to make.

153

"It was about Christmas Night, Mr. Bland," said Mrs. Brattle. "My husband and me thought of spending the evening with his brother at Hornsey, and we were going to let the maid go home to her mother's for the night, if it wouldn't put you out."

"Wouldn't put me out in the least, Mrs. Brattle," said Percival.

"You needn't sit up for us, you see," pursued Mrs. Brattle, "if you just leave the side door unbolted. We shan't be home before two or three; but we'll come in quiet not to disturb you."

"You won't disturb me," Percival replied with a genial laugh. "I'm a sober man in general but 'Christmas comes but once a year'. When once I'm tucked up in bed, I shall take a bit of waking on Christmas Night."

Mrs. Brattle smiled indulgently. "And you won't feel lonely, all alone in the house?"

"Lonely!" exclaimed Percival. "Lonely! With a roaring fire, a jolly book, a box of good cigars and a bottle of sound port—ah, and a second bottle if need be. Not I."

Mrs. Brattle shook her head. "Ah," said she, "you bachelors! Well, well. It's a good thing to be independent," and with this profound reflection she smiled herself out of the room and descended the stairs.

As her footsteps died away Percival sprang from his chair and began excitedly to pace the room. His eyes sparkled and his face was wreathed with smiles. Presently he halted before the fireplace and, gazing into the embers, laughed aloud.

"Damn funny!" said he. "Deuced rich! Neat! Very neat! Ha! Ha!" And here he resumed his interrupted song:

"When the sky above is clearing,
When the sky above is clearing,
Bob up serenely, bob up serenely,
Bob up serenely from below!"

Which may be regarded as closing the first scene, of the second act.

During the few days that intervened before Christmas Percival went abroad but little; and yet he was a busy man. He did a little surreptitious shopping, venturing out as far as Charing Cross Road; and his purchases were decidedly miscellaneous. A porridge saucepan, a second-hand copy of *Gray's Anatomy*, a rabbit skin, a large supply of glue and upwards of ten pounds of shin of beef seems a rather odd assortment; and it was a mercy that the weather was frosty, for otherwise Percival's bedroom, in which these delicacies were deposited under

154

lock and key, would have yielded odorous traces of its wealth.

But it was in the long evenings that his industry was most conspicuous; and then it was that the big cupboard with the excellent lever lock, which he himself had fixed on, began to fill up with the fruits of his labours. In those evenings the porridge saucepan would simmer on the hob with a rich lading of good Scotch glue, the black box of the deceased practitioner would be hauled forth from its hiding-place, and the well-thumbed "Gray" laid open on the table.

It was an arduous business though; a stiffer task than he had bargained for. The right and left bones were so confoundedly alike, and the bones that joined were so difficult to fit together. However, the plates in "Gray" were large and very clear, so it was only a question of taking enough trouble.

His method of work was simple and practical. Having fished a bone out of the box, he would compare it with the illustrations in the book until he had identified it beyond all doubt, when he would tie on it a paper label with its name and side—right or left. Then he would search for the adjoining bone, and, having fitted the two together, would secure them with a good daub of glue and lay them in the fender to dry. It was a crude and horrible method of articulation that would have made a museum curator shudder.

But it seemed to answer Percival's purpose—whatever that may have been—for gradually the loose "items" came together into recognisable members such as arms and legs, the vertebra—which were, fortunately, strung in their order on a thick cord—were joined up into a solid backbone, and even the ribs, which were the toughest job of all, fixed on in some semblance of a thorax. It was a wretched performance. The bones were plastered with gouts of glue and yet would have broken apart at a touch. But, as we have said, Percival seemed satisfied, and as he was the only person concerned, there was no more to be said.

In due course, Christmas Day arrived. Percival dined with the Brattles at two, dozed after dinner, woke up for tea, and then, as Mrs. Brattle, in purple and fine raiment, came in to remove the tea-tray, he spread out on the table the materials for the night's carouse. A quarter of an hour later, the side slammed, and, peering out of the window, he saw the shopkeeper and his wife hurrying away up the gas-lit street towards the nearest omnibus route.

Then Mr. Percival Bland began his evening's entertainment; and a most remark entertainment it was, even for a solitary bachelor, left

alone in a house on Christmas Night. First, he took off his clothing and dressed himself in a fresh suit. Then, from the cupboard he
brought forth the reconstituted "set of osteology" and, laying the various members on the table, returned to the bedroom, whence he presently reappeared with a large, savoury parcel which he had disinterred
from a trunk. The parcel being opened revealed his accumulated purchases in the matter of shin of beef.

With a large knife, providently sharpened before hand, he cut the
beef into large, thin slices which he proceed to wrap around the various bones that formed the "complete set;" whereby their nakedness
was certainly mitigated though their attractiveness was by no means increased. Having thus "clothed the dry bones," he gathered up the scraps
of offal that were left, to be placed presently inside the trunk. It was an
extraordinary proceeding, but the next was more extraordinary still.

Taking up the newly clothed members one by one, he began very
carefully to insinuate them into the garments that he had recently
shed. It was a ticklish business, for the glued joints were as brittle as
glass. Very cautiously the legs were separately inducted, first into un-
derclothing and then into trousers, the skeleton feet were fitted with
the cast-off socks and delicately persuaded into the boots. The arms,
in like manner, were gingerly pressed into their various sleeves and
through the arm-holes of the waistcoat; and then came the most difficult task of all—to fit the garments on the trunk. For the skull and
ribs, secured to the back-bone with mere spots of glue, were ready to
drop off at a shake; and yet the garments had to be drawn over them
with the arms enclosed in the sleeves. But Percival managed it at last
by resting his "restoration" in the big, padded arm-chair and easing
the garments on inch by inch.

It now remained only to give the finishing touch; which was done
by cutting the rabbit-skin to the requisite shape and affixing it to the
skull with a thin coat of stiff glue; and when the skull had thus been
finished with a sort of crude, makeshift wig, its appearance was so
appalling as even to disturb the nerves of the matter-of-fact Percival.
However, this was no occasion for cherishing sentiment. A skull in
an extemporised wig or false scalp might be, and in fact was, a highly
unpleasant object; but so was a Belgian police officer.

Having finished the "restoration," Percival fetched the water-jug
from his bedroom, and, descending to the shop, the door of which
had been left unlocked, tried the taps of the various drums and bar-
rels until he came to the one which contained methylated spirit; and

from this he filled his jug and returned to the bedroom. Pouring the spirit out into the basin, he tucked a towel round his neck and filling his sponge with spirit proceeded very vigorously to wash his hair and eyebrows; and as, by degrees, the spirit in the basin grew dark and turbid, so did his hair and eyebrows grow lighter in colour until, after a final energetic rub with a towel, they had acquired a golden or sandy hue indistinguishable from that of the hair of his cousin Robert.

Even the mole under his eye was susceptible to the changing conditions, for when he had wetted it thoroughly with spirit, he was able, with the blade of a penknife to peel it off as neatly as if it had been stuck on with spirit-gum. Having done which, he deposited it in a tiny box which he carried in his waistcoat pocket.

The proceedings which followed were unmistakable as to their object. First he carried the basin of spirit through into the sitting-room and deliberately poured its contents on to the floor by the arm-chair. Then, having returned the basin to the bedroom, he again went down to the shop, where he selected a couple of galvanised buckets from the stock, filled them with paraffin oil from one of the great drums and carried them upstairs. The oil from one bucket he poured over the armchair and its repulsive occupant; the other bucket he simply emptied on the carpet, and then went down to the shop for a fresh supply.

When this proceeding had been repeated once or twice the entire floor and all the furniture were saturated, and such a reek of paraffin filled the air of the room that Percival thought it wise to turn out the gas. Returning to the shop, be poured a bucketful of oil over the stack of bundles of firewood, another over the counter and floor and a third over the loose articles on the walls and hanging from the ceiling. Looking up at the latter be now perceived a number of greasy patches where the oil had soaked through from the floor above, and some of these were beginning to drip on to the shop floor.

He now made his final preparations. Taking a bundle of "Wheel" firelighters, he made a small pile against the stack of firewood. In the midst of the firelighters he placed a ball of string saturated in paraffin; and in the central hole of the ball he stuck a half-dozen diminutive Christmas candles. This mine was now ready. Providing himself with a stock of firelighters, a few balls of paraffined string and a dozen or so of the little candles, he went upstairs to the sitting-room, which was immediately above the shop.

Here, by the glow of the fire, he built up one or two piles of firelighters around and partly under the arm-chair, placed the balls of string on the piles and stuck two or three bundles in each ball. Everything was now ready. Stepping into the bedroom, he took from the cupboard a spare overcoat, a new hat and a new umbrella—for he must leave his old hats, coat and umbrella in the hall. He put on the coat and hat, and, with the umbrella in his hand, returned to the sitting-room.

Opposite the armchair he stood awhile, irresolute, and a pang of horror shot through him. It was a terrible thing that he was going to do; a thing the consequences of which no one could foresee. He glanced furtively at the awful shape that sat huddled in the chair, its horrible head all awry and its rigid limbs sprawling in hideous grotesque deformity. It was but a dummy, a mere scarecrow; but yet, in the dim firelight, the grisly face under that horrid wig seemed to leer intelligently, to watch him with secret malice out of its shadowy eye-sockets, until he looked away with clammy skin and a shiver of half-superstitious terror.

But this would never do. The evening had run out, consumed by these engrossing labours; it was nearly eleven o'clock, and high time for him to be gone. For if the Brattles should return prematurely he was lost. Pulling himself together with an effort, he struck a match and lit the little candles one after the other. In a quarter of an hour or so, they would have burned down to the balls of string, and then—He walked quickly out of the room; but, at the door, he paused for a moment to look back at the ghastly figure, seated rigidly in the chair with the lighted candles at its feet, like some foul fiend appeased by votive fires. The unsteady flames threw flickering shadows on its face that made it seem to mow and gibber and grin in mockery of all his care and caution. So he turned and tremblingly ran down the stairs—opening the staircase window as he went. Running into the shop, he lit the candles there and ran out again, shutting the door after him.

Secretly and guiltily he crept down the hall, and opening the door a few inches peered out. A blast of icy wind poured in with a light powdering of dry snow. He opened his umbrella, flung open the door, looked up and down the empty street, stepped out, closed the door softly and strode away over the whitening pavement.

PART 2
(Related by Christopher Jervis, M.D.)

It was one of the axioms of medico-legal practice laid down by my colleague, John Thorndyke, that the investigator should be constantly on his guard against the effect of suggestion. Not only must all prejudices and preconceptions be avoided, but when information is received from outside, the actual, undeniable facts must be carefully sifted from the inferences which usually accompany them. Of the necessity for this precaution our insurance practice furnished an excellent instance in the case of the fire at Mr. Brattle's oil-shop.

The case was brought to our notice by Mr. Stalker of the Griffin Fire and Life Insurance Society a few days after Christmas. He dropped in, ostensibly to wish us a Happy New Year, but a discreet pause in the conversation on Thorndyke's part elicited a further purpose.

"Did you see the account of that fire in Bloomsbury?" Mr. Stalker asked.

"The oil-shop? Yes. But I didn't note any details, excepting that a man was apparently burnt to death and that the affair happened on the twenty-fifth of December."

"Yes, I know," said Mr. Stalker. "It seems uncharitable, but one can't help looking a little askance at these quarter-day fires. And the date isn't the only doubtful feature in this one; the Divisional Officer of the Fire Brigade, who has looked over the ruins, tells me that there are some appearances suggesting that the fire broke out in two different places—the shop and the first-floor room over it. Mind you, he doesn't say that it actually did. The place is so thoroughly gutted that very little is to be learned from it; but that is his impression; and it occurred to me that if you were to take a look at the ruins, your radiographic eye might detect something that he had overlooked."

"It isn't very likely," said Thorndyke. "Every man to his trade. The divisional officer looks at a burnt house with an expert eye, which I do not. My evidence would not carry much weight if you were contesting the claim."

"Perhaps not," replied Mr. Stalker, "and we are not anxious to contest the claim unless there is manifest fraud. Arson is a serious matter."

"It is wilful murder in this case," remarked Thorndyke.

"I know," said Stalker. "And that reminds me that the man who was burnt happens to have been insured in our office, too. So we stand a double loss."

"How much?" asked Thorndyke.

"The dead man, Percival Bland, had insured his life for three thousand pounds."

Thorndyke became thoughtful. The last statement had apparently made more impression on him than the former ones.

"If you want me to look into the case for you," said he, "you had better let me have all the papers connected with it, including the proposal forms."

Mr. Stalker smiled. "I thought you would say that—I know you of old, you see—so I slipped the papers in my pocket before coming here."

He laid the documents on the table and asked: "Is there anything that you want to know about the case?"

"Yes," replied Thorndyke. "I want to know all that you can tell me."

"Which is mighty little," said Stalker; "but such as it is, you shall have it.

"The oil-shop man's name is Brattle and the dead man, Bland, was his lodger. Bland appears to have been a perfectly steady, sober man in general; but it seems that he had announced his intention of spending a jovial Christmas Night and giving himself a little extra indulgence. He was last seen by Mrs. Brattle at about half-past six, sitting by a blazing fire, with a couple of unopened bottles of port on the table and a box of cigars. He had a book in his hand and two or three newspapers lay on the floor by his chair. Shortly after this, Mr. and Mrs. Brattle went out on a visit to Hornsey, leaving him alone in the house."

"Was there no servant?" asked Thorndyke.

"The servant had the day and night off duty to go to her mother's. That, by the way, looks a trifle fishy. However, to return to the Brattles; they spent the evening at Hornsey and did not get home until past three in the morning, by which time their house was a heap of smoking ruins. Mrs. Brattle's idea is that Bland must have drunk himself sleepy, and dropped one of the newspapers into the fender, where a chance cinder may have started the blaze. Which may or may not be the true explanation. Of course, an habitually sober man can get pretty mimsey on two bottles of port."

"What time did the fire break out?" asked Thorndyke.

"It was noticed about half-past eleven that flames were issuing from one of the chimneys, and the alarm was given at once. The first engine arrived ten minutes later, but, by that time, the place was roaring like a furnace. Then the water-plugs were found to be frozen hard, which caused some delay; in fact, before the engines were able to get to work the roof had fallen in, and the place was a mere shell. You know what an oil-shop is, when once it gets a fair start."

"And Mr. Bland's body was found in the ruins, I suppose?"

"Body!" exclaimed Mr. Stalker; "there wasn't much body! Just a few charred bones, which they dug out of the ashes next day."

"And the question of identity?"

"We shall leave that to the coroner. But there really isn't any question. To begin with, there was no one else in the house; and then the remains were found mixed up with the springs and castors of the chair that Bland was sitting in when he was last seen. Moreover, there were found, with the bones, a pocket knife, a bunch of keys and a set of steel waistcoat buttons, all identified by Mrs. Brattle as belonging to Bland. She noticed the cut steel buttons on his waistcoat when she wished him 'goodnight.'"

"By the way," said Thorndyke, "was Bland reading by the light of an oil lamp?"

"No," replied Stalker. "There was a two-branch gasalier with a porcelain shade to one burner, and he had that burner alight when Mrs. Brattle left."

Thorndyke reflectively picked up the proposal form, and, having glanced through it, remarked: "I see that Bland is described as unmarried. Do you know why he insured his life for this large amount?"

"No; we assumed that it was probably in connection with some loan that he had raised. I learn from the solicitor who notified us of the death, that the whole of Bland's property is left to a cousin—a Mr. Lindsay, I think. So the probability is that this cousin had lent him money. But it is not the life claim that is interesting us. We must pay that in any case. It is the fire claim that we want you to look into."

"Very well," said Thorndyke; "I will go round presently and look over the ruins, and see if I can detect any substantial evidence of fraud."

"If you would," said Mr. Stalker, rising to take his departure, "we should be very much obliged. Not that we shall probably contest the claim in any case."

When he had gone, my colleague and I glanced through the papers, and I ventured to remark: "It seems to me that Stalker doesn't quite appreciate the possibilities of this case."

"No," Thorndyke agreed. "But, of course, it is an insurance company's business to pay, and not to boggle at anything short of glaring fraud. And we specialists too," he added with a smile, "must beware of seeing too much. I suppose that, to a rhinologist, there is hardly such a thing as a healthy nose—unless it is his own—and the uric acid specialist is very apt to find the firmament studded with dumb-bell crystals. We mustn't forget that normal cases do exist, after all."

"That is true," said I; "but, on the other hand, the rhinologist's business is with the unhealthy nose, and our concern is with abnormal cases."

Thorndyke laughed. "'A Daniel come to judgement,'" said he. "But my learned friend is quite right. Our function is to pick holes. So let us pocket the documents and wend Bloomsbury way. We can talk the case over as we go."

We walked at an easy pace, for there was no hurry, and a little preliminary thought was useful. After a while, as Thorndyke made no remark, I reopened the subject.

"How does the case present itself to you?" I asked.

"Much as it does to you, I expect," he replied. "The circumstances invite inquiry, and I do not find myself connecting them with the shopkeeper. It is true that the fire occurred on quarter-day; but there is nothing to show that the insurance will do more than cover the loss of stock, chattels and the profits of trade. The other circumstances are much more suggestive. Here is a house burned down and a man killed. That man was insured for three thousand pounds, and, consequently, some person stands to gain by his death to that amount.

"The whole set of circumstances is highly favourable to the idea of homicide. The man was alone in the house when he died; and the total destruction of both the body and its surroundings seems to render investigation impossible. The cause of death can only be inferred; it cannot be proved; and the most glaring evidence of a crime will have vanished utterly. I think that there is a quite strong *prima facie* suggestion of murder. Under the known conditions, the perpetration of a murder would have been easy, it would have been safe from detection, and there is an adequate motive.

"On the other hand, suicide is not impossible. The man might have set fire to the house and then killed himself by poison or otherwise. But it is intrinsically less probable that a man should kill himself for another person's benefit than that he should kill another man for his own benefit.

"Finally, there is the possibility that the fire and the man's death were the result of accident; against which is the official opinion that the fire started in two places. If this opinion is correct, it establishes, in my opinion, a strong presumption of murder against some person who may have obtained access to the house."

This point in the discussion brought us to the ruined house, which stood at the corner of two small streets. One of the firemen in charge admitted us, when we had shown our credentials, through a temporary door and down a ladder into the basement, where we found a number of men treading gingerly, ankle deep in white ash, among a litter of charred woodwork, fused glass, warped and broken china, and more or less recognisable metal objects.

"The coroner and the jury," the fireman explained; "come to view the scene of the disaster." He introduced us to the former, who bowed stiffly and continued his investigations.

"These," said the other fireman, "are the springs of the chair that the deceased was sitting in. We found the body—or rather the bones—lying among them under a heap of hot ashes; and we found the buttons of his clothes and the things from his pockets among the ashes, too. You'll see them in the mortuary with the remains."

"It must have been a terrific blaze," one of the jurymen remarked. "Just look at this, sir," and he handed to Thorndyke what looked like part of a gas-fitting, of which the greater part was melted into shapeless lumps and the remainder encrusted into fused porcelain.

"That," said the fireman, "was the gasalier of the first-floor room, where Mr. Bland was sitting. Ah! you won't turn that tap, sir; nobody'll ever turn that tap again."

Thorndyke held the twisted mass of brass towards me in silence, and, glancing up the blackened walls, remarked: "I think we shall have to come here again with the Divisional Officer, but meanwhile, we had better see the remains of the body. It is just possible that we may learn something from them."

He applied to the coroner for the necessary authority to make the inspection, and, having obtained a rather ungracious and grudging permission to examine the remains when the jury had "viewed" them, began to ascend the ladder.

"Our friend would have liked to refuse permission," he remarked when we had emerged into the street, "but he knew that I could and should have insisted."

"So I gathered from his manner," said I. "But what is he doing here? This isn't his district."

"No; he is acting for Bettsford, who is laid up just now; and a very poor substitute he is. A non-medical coroner is an absurdity in any case, and a coroner who is hostile to the medical profession is a public scandal. By the way, that gas-tap offers a curious problem. You noticed that it was turned off?"

"Yes."

"And consequently that the deceased was sitting in the dark when the fire broke out. I don't see the bearing of the fact, but it is certainly rather odd. Here is the mortuary. We had better wait and let the jury go in first."

We had not long to wait. In a couple of minutes or so the "twelve good men and true" made their appearance with a small attendant crowd of ragamuffins. We let them enter first, and then we followed. The mortuary was a good-sized room, well lighted by a glass roof, and having at its centre a long table on which lay the shell containing the remains. There was also a sheet of paper on which had been laid out a set of blackened steel waistcoat buttons, a bunch of keys, a steel-handled pocket-knife, a steel-cased watch on a partly-fused rolled-gold chain, and a pocket corkscrew. The coroner drew the attention of the jury to these objects, and then took possession of them, that they might be identified by witnesses. And meanwhile the jurymen gathered round the shell and stared shudderingly at its gruesome contents.

"I am sorry, gentlemen," said the coroner, "to have to subject you to this painful ordeal. But duty is duty. We must hope, as I think we may, that this poor creature met a painless if in some respects a rather terrible death."

At this point, Thorndyke, who had drawn near to the table, cast a long and steady glance down into the shell; and immediately his ordinarily rather impassive face seemed to congeal; all expression faded from it, leaving it as immovable and uncommunicative as the granite face of an Egyptian statue. I knew the symptom of old and began to speculate on its present significance.

"Are you taking any medical evidence?" he asked.

"Medical evidence!" the coroner repeated, scornfully. "Certainly not, sir! I do not waste the public money by employing so-called experts to tell the jury what each of them can see quite plainly for himself. I imagine," he added, turning to the foreman, "that you will not require a learned doctor to explain to you how that poor fellow mortal met his death?"

And the foreman, glancing askance at the skull, replied, with a pallid and sickly smile, that "he thought not."

"Do you, sir," the coroner continued, with a dramatic wave of the hand towards the plain coffin, "suppose that we shall find any difficulty in determining how that man came by his death?"

"I imagine," replied Thorndyke, without moving a muscle, or, indeed, appearing to have any muscles to move, "I imagine you will find no difficulty what ever."

"So do I," said the coroner.

"Then," retorted Thorndyke, with a faint, inscrutable smile, "we are, for once, in complete agreement."

As the coroner and jury retired, leaving my colleague and me alone in the mortuary, Thorndyke remarked: "I suppose this kind of farce will be repeated periodically so long as these highly technical medical inquiries continue to be conducted by lay persons."

I made no reply, for I had taken a long look into the shell, and was lost in astonishment.

"But my dear Thorndyke!" I exclaimed; "what on earth does it mean? Are we to suppose that a woman can have palmed herself off as a man on the examining medical officer of a London Life Assurance Society?"

Thorndyke shook his head. "I think not," said he. "Our friend, Mr. Bland, may conceivably have been a woman in disguise, but he certainly was not a negress."

"A negress!" I gasped. "By Jove! So it is! I hadn't looked at the skull. But that only makes the mystery more mysterious. Because, you remember, the body was certainly dressed in Bland's clothes."

"Yes, there seems to be no doubt about that. And you may have noticed, as I did," Thorndyke continued dryly, "the remarkably fire-proof character of the waistcoat buttons, watch-case, knife-handle, and other identifiable objects."

"But what a horrible affair!" I exclaimed. "The brute must have gone out and enticed some poor devil of a negress into the house, have murdered her in cold blood and then deliberately dressed the corpse in his own clothes! It is perfectly frightful!"

Again Thorndyke shook his head. "It wasn't as bad as that, Jervis," said he, "though I must confess that I feel strongly tempted to let your hypothesis stand. It would be quite amusing to put Mr. Bland on trial for the murder of an unknown negress, and let him explain the facts himself. But our reputation is at stake. Look at the bones again and a little more critically. You very probably looked for the sex first; then you looked for racial characters. Now carry your investigations a step farther."

"There is the stature," said I. "But that is of no importance, as these are not Bland's bones. The only other point that I notice is that the fire seems to have acted very unequally on the different parts of the body."

"Yes," agreed Thorndyke, "and that is the point. Some parts are more burnt than others; and the parts which are burnt most are the wrong parts. Look at the back-bone, for instance. The vertebrae are as white as chalk. They are mere masses of bone ash. But, of all parts of the skeleton, there is none so completely protected from fire as the back-bone, with the great dorsal muscles behind, and the whole mass of the viscera in front. Then look at the skull. Its appearance is quite inconsistent with the suggested facts.

"The bones of the face are bare and calcined and the orbits contain not a trace of the eyes or other structures; and yet there is a charred mass of what may or may not be scalp adhering to the crown. But the scalp, as the most exposed and the thinnest covering, would be the first to be destroyed, while the last to be consumed would be the structures about the jaws and the base, of which, you see, not a vestige is left."

Here he lifted the skull carefully from the shell, and, peering in through the great foramen at the base, handed it to me.

"Look in," he said, "through the *Foramen Magnum*—you will see better if you hold the orbits towards the skylight—and notice an even more extreme inconsistency with the supposed conditions. The brain and membranes have vanished without leaving a trace. The inside of the skull is as clean as if it had been macerated. But this is impossible. The brain is not only protected from the fire; it is also protected from contact with the air. But without access of oxygen, although it might become carbonised, it could not be consumed. No, Jervis; it won't do."

I replaced the skull in the coffin and looked at him in surprise. "What is it that you are suggesting?" I asked.

"I suggest that this was not a body at all, but merely a dry skeleton."

"But," I objected, "what about those masses of what looks like charred muscle adhering to the bones?"

"Yes," he replied, "I have been noticing them. They do, as you say, look like masses of charred muscle. But they are quite shapeless and structureless; I cannot identify a single muscle or muscular group, and there is not a vestige of any of the tendons. Moreover, the distribution is false. For instance, will you tell me what muscle you think that is?"

He pointed to a thick, charred mass on the inner surface of the left tibia or shin-bone. "Now this portion of the bone—as many a hockey-player has had reason to realise—has no muscular covering at all. It lies immediately under the skin."

"I think you are right, Thorndyke," said I. "That lump of muscle in the wrong place gives the whole fraud away. But it was really a rather smart dodge. This fellow Bland must be an ingenious rascal."

"Yes," agreed Thorndyke; "but an unscrupulous villain too. He might have burned down half the street and killed a score of people. He'll have to pay the piper for this little frolic."

"What shall you do now? Are you going to notify the coroner?"

"No; that is not my business. I think we will verify our conclusions and then inform our clients and the police. We must measure the skull as well as we can without callipers, but it is, fortunately, quite typical. The short, broad, flat nasal bones, with the '*Simian groove*,' and those large, strong teeth, worn flat by hard and gritty food, are highly characteristic." He once more lifted out the skull, and, with a spring tape, made a few measurements, while I noted the lengths of the principal long bones and the width across the hips.

"I make the cranial-nasal index 55," said he, as he replaced the skull, "and the cranial index about 72, which are quite representative numbers; and, as I see that your notes show the usual disproportionate length of arm and the characteristic curve of the tibia, we may be satisfied. But it is fortunate that the specimen is so typical. To the experienced eye, racial types have a physiognomy which is unmistakable on mere inspection. But you cannot transfer the experienced eye. You can only express personal conviction and back it up with measurements.

"And now we will go and look in on Stalker, and inform him that his office has saved three thousand pounds by employing us. After which it will be Westward Ho! for Scotland Yard, to prepare an unpleasant little surprise for Mr. Percival Bland."

There was joy among the journalists on the following day. Each of the morning papers devoted an entire column to an unusually detailed account of the inquest on the late Percival Bland—who, it appeared, met his death by misadventure—and a verbatim report of the coroner's eloquent remarks on the danger of solitary, fireside tippling, and the stupefying effects of port wine. An adjacent column contained an equally detailed account of the appearance of the deceased at Bow Street Police Court to answer complicated charges of arson, fraud and forgery; while a third collated the two accounts with gleeful commentaries.

Mr. Percival Bland, alias Robert Lindsay, now resides on the breezy uplands of Dartmoor, where, in his abundant leisure, he, no doubt, regrets his misdirected ingenuity. But he has not laboured in vain. To the Lord Chancellor he has furnished an admirable illustration of the danger of appointing lay coroners; and to me an unforgettable warning against the effects of suggestion.

Rex V. Burnaby

It is a normal incident in general medical practice that the family doctor soon drifts into the position of a family friend. The Burnabys had been among my earliest patients, and mutual sympathies had quickly brought about the more intimate relationship. It was a pleasant household, pervaded by a quiet geniality and a particularly attractive homely, unaffected culture. It was an interesting household, too, for the disparity in age between the husband and wife made the domestic conditions a little unusual and invited speculative observation. And there were other matters, to be referred to presently.

Frank Burnaby was a somewhat delicate man of about fifty: quiet, rather shy, gentle, kindly, and singularly innocent and trustful. He held a post at the Records Office, and was full of quaint and curious lore derived from the ancient documents on which he worked: selections from which he would retail in the family circle with a picturesque imagination and a fund of quiet, dry humour that made them delightful to listen to. I have never met a more attractive man, or one whom I liked better or respected more.

Equally attractive, in an entirely different way, was his wife: an extremely charming and really beautiful woman of under thirty—little more than a girl, in fact: amiable, high-spirited and full of fun and frolic, but nevertheless an accomplished, cultivated woman with a strong interest in her husband's pursuits. They appeared to me an exceedingly happy and united couple deeply attached to one another and in perfect sympathy. There were four children—three boys and a girl—of Burnaby's by his first wife; and their devotion to their young stepmother spoke volumes for her care of them.

But there was a fly in the domestic ointment: at least, that was what I felt. There was another family friend, a youngish man named Cyril Parker. Not that I had anything against him, personally, but I was not quite happy about the relationship. He was a markedly good-looking man, pleasant, witty, and extremely well informed; for he was a partner in a publishing house and acted as reader for the firm; whence it happened that he, like Mr. Burnaby, gathered stores of interesting matter from his professional reading. But I could not disguise from myself that his admiration and affection for Mrs. Burnaby were definitely inside the danger zone, and that the intimacy—on his side, at any rate—was growing rather ominously. On her side there seemed nothing more than frank, though very pronounced, friendship. But I looked at the relationship askance. She was a woman whom any man might have fallen in love with, and I did not like the expression that I sometimes detected in Parker's eyes when he was looking at her. Still, there was nothing in the conduct of either to which the slightest exception could have been taken or which in any way foreshadowed the terrible disaster which was so shortly to befall.

The starting-point of the tragedy was a comparatively trivial event. By much poring over crabbed manuscripts, Mr. Burnaby developed symptoms of eye-strain which caused me to send him to an oculist for an opinion and a prescription for suitable spectacles. On the evening of the day on which he had consulted the oculist, I received an urgent summons from Mrs. Burnaby, and, on arriving at the house, found her husband somewhat seriously ill. His symptoms were rather puzzling, for they corresponded to no known disease. His face was flushed, his temperature slightly raised, his pulse rapid, though the breathing was slow, his throat was excessively dry, and his pupils widely dilated. It was an extraordinary condition, resembling nothing within my knowledge excepting *atropine* poisoning.

"Has he been taking medicine of any kind?" I asked.

Mrs. Burnaby shook her head. "He never takes any drugs or medicine but what you prescribe; and it couldn't be anything that he has taken, because the attack came on quite soon after he came home, before he had either food or drink."

It was very mysterious and the patient himself could throw no light on the origin of the attack. While I was reflecting on the matter, I happened to glance at the mantelpiece, on which I noticed a drop labelled "The Eye Drops" and a prescription envelope. Opening the latter I found the oculist's prescription for the drops—a very weak solution of *atropine* sulphate.

"Has he had any of these drops?" I asked.

"Yes," replied Mrs. Burnaby. "I dropped some into his eyes as soon as he came in; two drops in each eye, according to the directions."

It was very odd. The amount of *atropine* in those four drops was less than a hundredth of a grain; an impossibly small dose to produce the symptoms. Yet he had all the appearance of having taken a poisonous dose, which he obviously had not, since the drop-bottle was nearly full. I could make nothing of it. However, I treated it as a case of *atropine* poisoning; and as the treatment produced marked improvement, I went home, more mystified than ever.

When I called on the following morning, I learned that he was practically well, and had gone to his office. But that evening I had another urgent message, and on hurrying round to Burnaby's house, found him suffering from an attack similar to, but even more severe than, the one on the previous day. I immediately administered an injection of *pilocarpine* and other appropriate remedies, and had the satisfaction of seeing a rapid improvement in his condition. But whereas the efficacy of the treatment proved that the symptoms were really due to *atropine*, no *atropine* appeared to have been taken excepting the minute quantity contained in the eye-drops.

It was very mysterious. The most exhaustive inquiries failed to suggest any possible source of the poison excepting the drops; and as each attack had occurred a short time after the use of them, it was impossible to ignore the apparent connection, in spite of the absurdly minute dose.

"I can only suppose," said I, addressing Mrs. Burnaby and Mr. Parker, who had called to make inquiries, "that Burnaby is the subject of an idiosyncrasy—that he is abnormally sensitive to this drug."

"Is that a known condition?" asked Parker.

"Oh, yes," I replied. "People vary enormously in the way in which they react to drugs. Some are so intolerant of particular drugs—iodine, for instance—that ordinary medicinal doses produce poisonous effects, while others have the most extraordinary tolerance. Christisori, in his *Treatise on Poisons*, gives a case of a man, unaccustomed to opium, who took nearly an ounce of laudanum without any effect—a dose that would have killed an ordinary man. These drugs are terrible pitfalls for the doctor who doesn't know his patient. Just think what might have happened to Burnaby if someone had given him a full medicinal dose of *belladonna*."

"Does *belladonna* have the same effect as *atropine*?" asked Mrs. Burnaby.

"It is the same," I replied. "*Atropine* is the active principle of *bel-*

171

ladonna."

"What a mercy," she exclaimed, "that we discovered this idiosyncrasy in time. I suppose he had better discontinue the drops?"

"Yes," I answered, "most emphatically; and I will write to Mr. Haines and let him know that the *atropine* is impracticable."

I accordingly wrote to the oculist, who was politely sceptical as to the connection between the drops and the attacks. However, Burnaby settled the matter by refusing point-blank to have any further dealings with *atropine*; and his decision was so far justified that, for the time being, the attacks did not recur.

A couple of months passed. The incident had, to a great extent, faded from my mind. But then it was revived in a way that not only filled me with astonishment but caused me very grave anxiety. I was just about to set out on my morning round when Burnaby's housemaid met me at my door, breathing quickly and carrying a note. It was from Mrs. Burnaby, begging me to call at once and telling me that her husband had been seized by an attack similar to the previous ones. I ran back for my emergency bag and then hurried round to the house, where I found Burnaby lying on a sofa, very flushed, rather alarmed, and exhibiting well-marked symptoms of *atropine* poisoning. The attack, however, was not a very severe one, and the application of the appropriate remedies soon produced a change for the better.

"Now, Burnaby," I said, as he sat up with a sigh of relief, "what have you been up to? Haven't been tinkering with those drops again?"

"No," he replied. "Why should I? Haines has finished with my eyes."

"Well, you've been taking something with *atropine* in it."

"I suppose I have, but I can't imagine what. I have had no medicine of any kind."

"No pills, lozenges, liniment, plaster, or ointment?"

"Nothing medicinal of any sort," he replied. "In fact, I have swallowed nothing today but my breakfast; and the attack came on directly after, though it was a simple enough meal, goodness knows—just a couple of pigeon's eggs and some toast and tea."

"Pigeon's eggs," said I, with a grin, "why not sparrow's?"

"Cyril sent them—as a joke, I think," Mrs. Burnaby explained (Cyril, of course, was Mr. Parker), "but I must say Frank enjoyed them. You see, Cyril has taken lately to keeping pigeons and rabbits and other edible beasts, and I think he has done it principally for Frank's sake, as you have ordered him a special diet. We are constantly getting things from Cyril now—pigeons and rabbits especially; and much younger than we can buy them at the shops."

"Yes," said Burnaby, "he is most generous. I should think he supplies more than half my diet. I hardly like to accept so much from him."

"It gives him pleasure to send these gifts," said Mrs. Burnaby; "but I wish it gave him pleasure to slaughter the creatures first. He always brings or sends them alive, and the cook hates killing them. As to me, I couldn't do it, though I deal with the corpses afterwards. I prepare nearly all Frank's food myself."

"Yes," said Burnaby, with a glance of deep affection at his wife, "Margaret is an artist in kickshaws and I consume the works of art. I can tell you, doctor, I live like a fighting cock."

This was all very well, but it was beside the question; which was, where did the *atropine* come from? If Burnaby had swallowed nothing but his breakfast, it would seem that the *atropine* must have been in that. I pointed this out.

"But you know, doctor," said Burnaby, "that isn't possible. We can write the eggs off. You can't get poison into an egg without making a hole in the shell, and these eggs were intact. And as to the bread and butter, and the tea, we all had the same, and none of the others seem any the worse."

"That isn't very conclusive," said I. "A dose of *atropine* that would be poisonous to you would probably have no appreciable effect on the others. But, of course, the real mystery is how on earth *atropine* could have got into any of the food."

"It couldn't," said Burnaby and that really was my own conviction. But it was an unsatisfactory conclusion, for it left the mystery unexplained; and when a length I took my leave, to continue my rounds of visits, it was with the uncomfortable feeling that I had failed to trace the origin of the danger or to secure my patient against its recurrence.

Nor was my uneasiness unjustified. Little more than a week had passed when a fresh summons brought me to Burnaby's house, full of bewilderment and apprehension. And indeed there was good cause for apprehension; for when I arrived, to find Burnaby lying speechless and sightless his blue eyes turned to blank discs of black, glittering with the unnatural "*belladonna* sparkle,"—when I felt his racing pulse and watched his vain efforts to swallow a sip of water,—I began to ask myself whether he was not beyond recall. The same question was asked mutely by the terrified eyes of his wife, who rose like a ghost from his bedside as I entered the room. But once more he responded to the remedies, though more slowly this time, and at the end of an hour I was relieved to see that the urgent danger was past, although he still remained very ill.

Meanwhile, inquiries failed utterly to elicit any explanation of the attack. The symptoms had set in shortly after dinner; a simple meal, consisting of a pigeon cooked *en casserole* by Mrs. Burnaby herself, vegetables and a light pudding which had been shared by the rest of the family, and a little Chablis from a bottle that I been unsealed and opened in the dining-room. Nothing else had been taken and no medicaments of any kind used. On the other hand, any doubts as to the nature of the attack were set at rest by a chemical test made by me and confirmed by the Clinical Research Association, *atropine* was demonstrably present, though the amount was comparatively small. But its source remained an impenetrable mystery.

It was a profoundly disturbing state of affairs. The last attack had narrowly missed a fatal termination and the poison was still untraced. From the same unknown source a fresh charge might be delivered at any moment, and who could say what the result would be? Poor Burnaby was in a state of chronic terror and his wife began to look haggard and worn with constant anxiety and apprehension. Nor was I in much better case myself, for, whatever should befall, the responsibility was mine. I racked my brains for some possible explanation, but could think of none, though there were times when a horrible thought would creep into my mind, only to be indignantly cast out.

One evening a few days after the last attack, I received a visit from Burnaby's brother, a pathologist attached to one of the London hospitals, but not in practice. Very different was Dr. Burnaby from his gentle, amiable brother; a strong, resolute, energetic man and none too suave in manner. We were already acquainted, so no introductions were necessary, and he came to the point with characteristic directness.

"You can guess what I have come about, Jardine—this *atropine* business. What is being done in the matter?"

"I don't know that anything is being done," I answered lamely. "I can make nothing of it."

"Waiting for the next attack and the inquest, h'm? Well, that won't do, you know. This affair has got to be stopped before it is too late. If you don't know where the poison comes from, somebody does. H'm! And it is time to find out who that somebody is. There aren't many to choose from. I am going there now to have a look round and make a few inquiries. You'd better come with me."

"Are they expecting you?" I asked.

"No," he answered gruffly; "but I'm not a stranger and neither are you."

I decided to go round with him, though I didn't much like his manner. This was evidently meant to be a surprise visit, and I had no great difficulty in guessing at what was in his mind. On the other hand, I was not sorry to share the responsibility with a man of his position and a relative of the patient. Accordingly, I set forth with him willingly enough; and it is significant of my state of mind at this time, that I took my emergency bag with me.

When we arrived Burnaby and his wife were just sitting down to dinner—the children took their evening meal by themselves—and they welcomed us with the ready hospitality that made this such a pleasant household. Dr. Burnaby's place was laid opposite mine, and I was faintly amused to note his eye furtively travelling over the table, evidently assessing each article of food as a possible vehicle of *atropine*. "If you had only let us know you were coming, Jim," said Mrs. Burnaby when the joint made its appearance, "we would have had something better than saddle of mutton. As it is, you must take pot-luck."

"Saddle of mutton is good enough for me," replied Dr. Burnaby. "But what on earth is that stuff that Frank has got?" he added, as Burnaby lifted the lid from a little casserole.

"That," she answered, "is a *fricassee* of rabbit. Such a tiny creature it was; a mere infant. Cook nearly wept at having to kill it."

"Kill it!" exclaimed the doctor; "do you buy your rabbits alive?"

"We didn't buy this one," she replied. "It was brought by Cyril—Mr. Parker, you know," she added hastily and with a slight flush, as she caught a grim glance of interrogation. "He sends quite a lot of poultry and rabbits and things for Frank from his little farm."

"Ha!" said the doctor with a reflective eye on the casserole. "H'm! Breeds them himself, hey? Whereabouts is his farm?"

"At Eltham. But it isn't really a farm. He just keeps rabbits and fowls and pigeons in a place at the back of his garden."

"Is your cook English?" Dr. Burnaby asked, glancing again at the casserole. "That affair of Frank's has rather a French look."

"Bless you, Jim," said Burnaby, "I am not dependent on mere cooks. I am a pampered gourmet. Margaret prepares most of my food with her own sacred hands. Cooks can't do this sort of thing;" and he helped himself afresh from the casserole.

Dr. Burnaby seemed to reflect profoundly upon this explanation. Then he abruptly changed the subject from cookery to the Lindisfarne Gospels and thereby set his brother's chin wagging to a new tune. For Burnaby's affections as a scholar were set on seventh- and eighth-century manuscripts and his knowledge of them was as great as his enthusiasm.

"Oh, get on with your dinner, Frank, you old windbag," exclaimed Mrs. Burnaby. "You are letting everything get cold."

"So I am, dear," he admitted, "but—I won't be a minute. I just want Jim to see those collotypes of the Durham Book. Excuse me."

He sprang up from the table and darted into the adjoining library, whence he returned almost immediately carrying a small portfolio.

"These are the plates," he said, handing the portfolio to his brother. "Have a look at them while I dispose of the arrears."

He took up his knife and fork and made as if to resume his meal. Then he laid them down and leaned back in his chair. "I don't think I want any more, after all," he said.

The tone in which he spoke caused me to look at him critically; for my talk with his brother had made me a little nervous and apprehensive of further trouble. What I now saw was by no means reassuring. A slight flush and a trace of anxiety in his expression made me ask, with outward composure but inward alarm: "You are feeling quite fit, I hope, Burnaby?"

"Well, not so very," he replied. "My eyes are going a bit misty and my throat—" Here he worked his lips and swallowed as if with some effort.

I rose hastily, and, catching a terrified glance from his wife, went to him and looked into his eyes. And thereupon my heart sank. For already his pupils were twice their natural size and the darkened eyes exhibited the too-familiar sparkle. I was sensible of a thrill of terror, and, as I looked into Burnaby's now distinctly alarmed face, his brother's ominous words echoed in my ears. Had I waited "for the next attack and the inquest"?

The symptoms, once started, developed apace. From moment to moment he grew worse, and the rapid enlargement of the pupils gave an alarming hint as to the intensity of the poisoning. I darted out into the hall for my bag, and as I re-entered, I saw him rise, groping blindly with his hands, until his wife, ashen-faced and trembling, took his arm and led him to the door.

"I had better give him a dose of *pilocarpine* at once," I said, getting out my hypodermic syringe and glancing at Dr. Burnaby, who watched me with stony composure.

"Yes," he agreed, "and a little morphine, too! and he will probably need some stimulant. I won't come up; only be in the way."

I followed the patient up to the bedroom and administered the antidotes forthwith. Then, while he was getting partially undressed with his wife's help, I went downstairs in search of brandy and hot water, I was about to enter the dining-room when, through the partly-open door, I saw Dr. Burnaby standing by the fireplace with his open hand-bag—which he had fetched in from the hall—on the table before him, and in his hand a little Bohemian glass jar from the mantelpiece. Involuntarily, I halted for a moment; and as I did so, he carefully deposited the little ornament in the bag and closed the latter, locking it with a small key which he then put in his pocket.

It was an excessively odd proceeding, but, of course, it was no concern of mine. Nevertheless, instead of entering the dining-room, I stole softly towards the kitchen and fetched the hot water myself. When I returned, the bag was back on the hall table and I found Dr. Burnaby grimly pacing up and down the dining room. He asked me a few questions while I was looking for the brandy, and then, somewhat to my surprise, proposed to come up and lend a hand with the patient.

On entering the bedroom, we found poor Burnaby lying half-undressed on the bed and in a very pitiable state; terrified, physically distressed and inclined to ramble mentally. His wife knelt by the bed, white-faced, red-eyed and evidently panic-stricken, though she was quite quiet and self-restrained. As we entered, she rose to make way for us, and while we were examining the patient's pulse and listening to his racing heart, she silently busied herself with the preparations for administering the stimulants.

"You don't think he is going to die, do you?" she whispered, as Dr. Burnaby handed me back my stethoscope.

"It is no use thinking," he replied dryly—and I thought rather callously—"we shall see;" and with this he turned his back to her and looked at his brother with a gloomy frown.

For more than an hour that question was an open one. From moment to moment I expected to feel the wildly-racing pulse flicker out; to hear the troubled breathing die away in an expiring rattle. From time to time we cautiously increased the antidotes and administered restoratives, but I must confess that I had little hope. Dr. Burnaby was undisguisedly pessimistic. And as the weary minutes dragged on, and

I looked momentarily for the arrival of the dread messenger, there would keep stealing into my mind a question that I hardly dared to entertain. What was the meaning of it all? Whence had the poison come? And why, in this household, had it found its way to Burnaby alone—the one inmate to whom it was specially deadly?

At last—at long last—there came a change; hardly perceptible at first, and viewed with little confidence. But after a time it became more pronounced; and then, quite rapidly, the symptoms began to clear up. The patient swallowed with ease, and great relish, a cup of coffee; the heart slowed down, the breathing became natural, and presently, as the morphine began to take effect, he sank into a doze which passed by degrees into a quiet sleep.

"I think he will do now," said Dr. Burnaby, "so I won't stay any longer. But it was a near thing, Jardine; most uncomfortably near."

He walked to the door, where, as he went out, he turned and bowed stiffly to his sister-in-law. I followed him down the stairs, rather expecting him to revert to the subject of his visit to me. But he made no reference to it, nor, indeed, did he say anything until he stood on the doorstep with his bag in his hand. Then he made a somewhat cryptic remark: "Well, Jardine," he said, "the Durham Book saved him. But for those collotypes, he would be a dead man;" and with that he walked away, leaving me to interpret as best I could this decidedly obscure remark.

A quarter of an hour later, as Burnaby was peacefully asleep and apparently out of all danger, I took my own departure, and as soon as I was outside the house, I proceeded to put into execution a plan that had been forming in my mind during the last hour. There was some mystery in this case that was evidently beyond my powers to solve. But solved it had to be, if Burnaby's life was to be saved, to say nothing of my own reputation; so I had decided to put the facts before my friend and former teacher, Dr. Thorndyke, and seek his advice, and if necessary, his assistance.

It was now past ten o'clock, but I determined to take my chance of finding him at his chambers, and accordingly, having found a taxi, I directed the driver to set me down at the gate of Inner Temple Lane. My former experience of Thorndyke's habits led me to be hopeful, and my hopes were not unjustified on this occasion, for when I had mounted to the first pair landing of No. 5A King's Bench Walk, and assaulted the knocker of the inner door, I was relieved to find him not only at home, but alone and disengaged. "It's a deuce of a time to come knocking you up," I said, as he shook my hand, "but I am in rather a hole, and the matter is urgent, so—"

"So you paid me the compliment of treating me as a friend," said he. "Very proper of you. What is the nature of your difficulty?"

"Why, I've got a case of recurrent *atropine* poisoning and I can make absolutely nothing of it."

Here I began to give a brief outline sketch of the facts, but after a minute or two he stopped me.

"It is of no use being sketchy, Jardine," said he. "The night is young. Let us have a complete history of the case, with particulars of all the persons concerned and their mutual relations. And don't spare detail."

He seated himself with a notebook on his knee, and when he had lighted his pipe, I plunged into the narrative of the case, beginning with the eye-drop incident and finishing with the alarming events of the present evening.

He listened with close attention, refraining from interrupting me excepting occasionally to ask for a date, which he jotted down with a few other notes. When I had finished, he laid aside his notebook, and, as he knocked out his pipe, observed: "A very remarkable case, Jardine, and interesting by reason of the unusual nature of the poison."

"Oh, hang the interest!" I exclaimed. "I am not a toxicologist. I am a general practitioner; and I want to know what the deuce I ought to do."

"I think," said he, "that your duty is perfectly obvious. You ought to communicate with the police, either alone or in conjunction with some member of the family."

I looked at him in dismay. "But," I faltered, "what have I got to tell the police?"

"What you have told me," he replied; "which, put in a nutshell, amounts to this: Frank Burnaby has had three attacks of *atropine* poisoning, disregarding the eye-drops. Each attack has appeared to be associated with some article of food prepared by Mrs. Burnaby and supplied by Mr. Cyril Parker."

"But, good God!" I exclaimed, "you don't suspect Mrs. Burnaby?"

"I suspect nobody," he replied. "It may not be criminal poisoning at all. But Mr. Burnaby has to be protected, and the case certainly needs investigation."

"You don't think I could make a few inquiries myself first?" I suggested.

He shook his head. "The risk is too great," he replied. "The man might die before you reached a conclusion; whereas a few inquiries made by the police would probably put a stop to the affair, unless the poisoning is in some inconceivable way inadvertent."

That was what his advice amounted to, and I felt that he was right. But it put on me a horribly unpleasant duty; and as I wended homewards I tried to devise some means of mitigating its unpleasantness. Finally I decided to try to persuade Mrs. Burnaby to make a joint communication with me.

But the necessity never arose. When I made my morning visit, I found a taxicab drawn up opposite the door and the housemaid who admitted me looked as if she had seen a ghost.

"Why, what is the matter, Mabel?" I asked, as she ushered me funereally into the drawing-room.

She shook her head. "I don't know, sir. Something awful, I'm afraid. I'll tell them you are here." With this she shut the door and departed.

The housemaid's manner and the unusually formal reception filled me with vague forebodings. But even as I was wondering what could have happened, the question was answered by the entry of a tall man who looked like a guardsman in mufti.

"Dr. Jardine?" he asked; and as I nodded, he explained, presenting his card, "I am Detective Lane. I have been instructed to make some inquiries in respect of certain information which we have received. It is stated that Mr. Frank Burnaby is suffering from the effects of poison. So far as you know, is that true?"

"I hope he is recovered now," I replied, "but he was suffering last night from what appeared to be *atropine* poisoning."

"Have there been any previous attacks of the same kind?" the sergeant asked.

"Yes," I answered. "This was the fifth attack; but the first two were evidently due to some eye-drops that he had used."

"And in the case of the other three; have you any idea as to how the poison came to be taken? Whether it was in the food, for instance?"

"I have no idea, sergeant. I know nothing more than what I have told you; and, of course, I am not going to make any guesses. Is it admissible to ask who gave the information?"

"I am afraid not, sir," he replied. "But you will soon know. There is a definite charge against Mrs. Burnaby—I have just made the arrest— and we shall want your evidence for the prosecution."

I stared at him in utter consternation. "Do you mean," I gasped, "that you have arrested Mrs. Burnaby?"

"Yes," he replied; "on a charge of having administered poison to her husband."

I was absolutely thunderstruck. And yet, when I remembered Thorndyke's words and recalled my own dim and hastily-dismissed surmises, there was nothing so very surprising in this shocking turn of events.

"Could I have a few words with Mrs. Burnaby?" I asked.

"Not alone," he replied, "and better not at all. Still, if you have any business—"

"I have," said I; whereupon he led the way to the dining-room, where I found Mrs. Burnaby seated rigidly in a chair, pale as death, but quite calm though rather dazed. Opposite her a military-looking man sat stiffly by the table with an air of being unconscious of her presence, and he took no notice as I walked over to his prisoner and silently pressed her hand.

"I've come, Mrs. Burnaby," said I, "to ask if there is anything that you want me to do. Does Burnaby know about this horrible affair?"

"No," she answered. "You will have to tell him if he is fit to hear it; and if not, I want you to let my father know as soon as you can. That is all; and you had better go now, as we mustn't detain these gentlemen. Goodbye."

She shook my hand unemotionally, and when I had faltered a few words of vague encouragement and sympathy, I went out of the room, but waited in the hall to see the last of her.

The police officers were most polite and considerate. When she came out, they attended her in quite a deferential manner. As the sergeant was in the act of opening the street door, the bell rang; and when the door opened it disclosed Mr. Parker standing on threshold. He was about to address Mrs. Burnaby but she passed him with a slight bow, and descended the steps, preceded by the sergeant and followed by the detective. The former held the door of the cab open while she entered, when he entered also and shut the door. The detective took his seat beside the driver and the cab moved off.

"What is in the wind, Jardine?" Parker asked looking at me with a distinctly alarmed expression. "Those fellows look like plain-clothes policemen."

"They are," said I. "They have just arrest Mrs. Burnaby on a charge of having attempted to poison her husband."

I thought Parker would have fallen. As it was, he staggered to a hall chair and dropped on it in a state of collapse. "Good God!" he gasped. "What a frightful thing! But there can't possibly be any evidence—any real grounds for suspecting her. It must be just a wild guess. I wonder who started it."

On this subject I had pretty strong suspicions, but I did not mention them; and when I had seen Parker into the dining-room and explained matters a little further I went upstairs, bracing myself for my very disagreeable task.

Burnaby was quite recovered, though rather torpid from the effects of the morphine. But my news roused him most effectually. In a moment he was out of bed, hurriedly preparing to dress; and though his pale, set face told how deeply the catastrophe had shocked him, he was quite collected and had all his wits about him.

"It's of no use letting our emotions loose, doctor," said he, in reply to my expressions of sympathy. "Margaret is in a very dangerous position. You have only to consider what she is—a young, beautiful woman—and what I am, to realise that. We must act promptly. I shall go and see her father; he is a very capable lawyer; and we must get a first-class counsel."

This seemed to be an opportunity for mentioning Thorndyke's peculiar qualifications in a case of this kind, and I did so. Burnaby listened attentively, apparently not unimpressed; but he replied cautiously: "We shall have to leave the choice of the counsel to Harratt; but if you care, meanwhile, to consult with Dr. Thorndyke, you have my authority. I will tell Harratt."

On this I took my departure, not a little relieved at the way he had taken the evil tidings; and as soon as I had disposed of the more urgent part of my work, I betook myself to Thorndyke's chambers, just in time to catch him on his return from the Courts.

"Well, Jardine," he said, when I had brought the history up to date, "what is it that you want me to do?"

"I want you to do what you can to establish Mrs. Burnaby's innocence," I replied.

He looked at me reflectively for a few moments; then he said, quietly but rather significantly: "It is not my practice to give *ex parte* evidence. An expert witness cannot act as an advocate. If I investigate the evidence in this case, it will have to be at your risk, as representing the accused, since any fact, no matter how damaging, which is in the possession of the witness must be disclosed in accordance with the terms of the oath, to say nothing of the obvious duty of every person to further the ends of justice. Speaking as a lawyer, and taking the known facts at their face value, I do not advise you to employ me to investigate the case at large. You might find that you had merely strengthened the hand of the prosecution.

"But I will make a suggestion. There seems to me to be in this case a very curious and interesting possibility. Let me investigate that independently. If my inquiries yield a positive result, I will let you know and you can call me as a witness. If they yield a negative result, you had better leave me out of the case."

To this suggestion I necessarily agreed; but when I took my leave of Thorndyke I went away with a sense of discouragement and failure. His reference to "the face value of the known facts" clearly implied that those facts were adverse to the accused; while the "curious possibility" suggested nothing but a forlorn hope from which he had no great expectations.

I need not follow the weary business in detail. At the first hearing before the magistrate the police merely stated the charge and gave evidence of arrest, both they and the defence asking for a remand and neither apparently desiring to show their hand. Accordingly the case was adjourned for seven days, and as bail was refused, the prisoner was detained in custody.

During those seven dreary days I spent as much time as I could with Burnaby, and though I was filled with admiration of his fortitude and self his drawn and pallid face wrung my heart. In those few days he seemed to have changed into an old man. At his house I also met Mr. Harratt, Mrs. Burnaby's father, a fine, dignified man and a typical old lawyer; and it was unspeakably pathetic to see the father and the husband of the accused woman each trying to support the courage of the other while both were torn with anxiety and apprehension. On one occasion Mr. Parker was present and looked more haggard and depressed than either. But Mr. Harratt's manner towards him was so frigid and forbidding that he did not repeat his visit. At these meetings we discussed the case freely, which was a further affliction to me. For even I could not fail to see that any evidence that I could give directly supported the case for the prosecution.

So six of the seven days ran out, and all the time there was no word from Thorndyke. But on the evening of the sixth day I received a letter from him, curt and dry, but still giving out a ray of hope. This was the brief message:

"I have gone into the question of which I spoke to you and consider that the point is worth raising. I have accordingly written to Mr. Harratt advising him to that effect."

It was a somewhat colourless communication. But I knew Thorndyke well enough to realise that his promises usually understated his intentions. And when, on the following morning, I met Mr. Harratt and Burnaby at the court, something in their manner—a new vivacity and expectancy—suggested that Thorndyke had been more explicit in his communication to the lawyer. But, all the same, their anxiety, for all their outward courage, was enough to have touched a heart of stone.

The spectacle that that court presented when the case was called forms a tableau that is painted on my memory in indelible colours. The mingling of squalor and tragedy, of frivolity and dread solemnity—the grave magistrate on the bench, the stolid policemen, the busy, preoccupied lawyers, and the gibbering crowd of spectators, greedy for sensation, with eager eyes riveted on the figure in the dock—offered such a medley of contrasts as I hope never to look upon again.

As to the prisoner herself, her appearance brought my heart into my mouth. Rigid as a marble statue and nearly as void of colour, she stood in the dock, guarded by two constables, looking with stony bewilderment on the motley scene, outwardly calm, but with the calm of one who looks death in the face; and when the prosecuting counsel rose to open the case for the police, she looked at him as a victim on the scaffold might look upon the executioner.

As I listened to the brief opening address, my heart sank, though the counsel, Sir Harold Layton, K.C., presented his case with that scrupulous fairness to the accused that makes an English court of justice a thing without parallel in the world. But the mere facts, baldly stated without comment, were appalling. No persuasive rhetoric was needed to show that they led direct to the damning conclusion.

Frank Burnaby, an elderly man, married to a young and beautiful woman, had on three separate occasions had administered to him a certain deadly poison, to wit, *atropine*. It would be proved that he had suffered from the effects of that poison; that the symptoms followed the taking of certain articles of food of which he alone had partaken; that the said food did actually contain the said poison; and that the food which contained the poison was specially prepared for his sole consumption by his wife, the accused, with her own hands. No evidence was at present available as to how the accused obtained the poison or that she had any such poison in her possession, nor would any suggestion be offered as to the motive of the crime. But, on the evidence of the actual administration of the poison, he would ask that the prisoner be committed for trial. He then proceeded to call the witnesses, of whom I was naturally the first. When I had been sworn and given my description, the counsel asked a few questions which elicited the history of the case and which I need not repeat. He then continued:

"Have you any doubt as to the cause of Mr. Burnaby's symptoms?"

"No. They were certainly due to *atropine* poisoning."

"Has Mr. Burnaby any constitutional peculiarity in respect of *atropine?*"

"Yes. He is abnormally susceptible to the effects of *atropine.*"

"Was this peculiar susceptibility known to the accused?"

"Yes. It was communicated to her by me."

"Was it known, so far as you are aware, to any other persons?"

"Mr. Parker was present when I told her, and Mr. Burnaby and his brother, Dr. Burnaby, were also informed."

"Is there any way, so far as you know, in which the accused could have obtained possession of *atropine?*"

"Only by having the oculist's prescription for the eye-drops made up."

"Do you know of any medium, other than the food, by which *atropine* might have been taken by Mr. Burnaby?"

"I do not," I replied; and this concluded my evidence. But as I stepped out of the witness-box, I reflected gloomily that every word that I had spoken was a rivet in the fetters of the silent figure in the dock.

The next witness was the cook. She testified that she had killed and skinned the rabbit and had then handed it to the accused, who made it into a *fricassee* and prepared it for the table. Witness took no part in the preparation and she was absent from the kitchen on one occasion for several minutes, leaving the accused there alone.

When the cook had concluded her evidence, the name of James Burnaby was called, and the doctor entered the witness-box, looking distinctly uncomfortable, but grim and resolute. The first few questions elicited the circumstances of his visit to his brother's house and of the sudden attack of illness. That illness he had at once recognised as acute *atropine* poisoning, and had assumed that the poison was in the specially prepared food.

"Did you take any measures to verify this opinion?" counsel asked.

"Yes. As soon as I was alone, I took part of the remainder of the rabbit and put it in a glass jar which I found on the mantelpiece and which I first rinsed out with water. Later, I carried the sample of food to Professor Berry, who analysed it in my presence and found it to contain *atropine*. He obtained from it a thirtieth of a grain of *atropine* sulphate."

"Is that a poisonous dose?"

"Not to an ordinary person, though it is considerably beyond the medicinal dose. But it would have been a poisonous dose to Frank Burnaby. If he had swallowed this, in addition to what he had already taken, I feel no doubt that it would have killed him."

This concluded the case for the prosecution, and a black case it undoubtedly looked. There was no cross-examination; and as Thorndyke had arrived some time previously and conferred with Mr. Harratt and his counsel, I concluded that the defence would take the form of a counter-attack by the raising of a fresh issue. And so it turned out. When Thorndyke entered the witness-box and had disposed of the preliminaries, the counsel for the defence "gave him his head."

"You have made certain investigations in regard to this case, I believe?" Thorndyke assented, and the counsel continued: "I will not ask you specific questions, but will request you to describe your investigations and their result, and tell us what caused you to make them."

"This case," Thorndyke began, "was brought to my notice by Dr. Jardine, who gave me all the facts known to him. These facts were very remarkable, and, taken together, they suggested a possible explanation of the poisoning. There were four striking points in the case. First, there was the very unusual nature of the poison. Second, the abnormal susceptibility of Mr. Burnaby to this particular poison. Third, the fact that all the food in which the poison appeared to have been conveyed came from the same source: it was sent by Mr. Cyril Parker. Fourth, that food consisted of pigeon's eggs, pigeon's flesh, and rabbit's flesh."

"What is there remarkable about that?" the counsel asked.

"The remarkable point is that the pigeon and the rabbit have an extraordinary immunity to *atropine*. Most vegetable-feeding birds and animals are more or less immune to vegetable poisons. Many birds and animals are largely immune to *atropine*; but among birds the pigeon is exceptionally immune, while the rabbit is the most extreme instance among animals. A single rabbit can take without the slightest harm more than a hundred times the quantity of *atropine* that would kill a man; and rabbits habitually feed freely on the leaves and berries of the *belladonna* or deadly nightshade."

"Does the deadly nightshade contain *atropine*?" the counsel asked.

"Yes. *Atropine* is the active principle of the *belladonna* plant and gives to it its poisonous properties."

"And if an animal, such as a rabbit, were to feed on the nightshade plant, would its flesh be poisonous?"

"Yes. Cases of *belladonna* poisoning from eating rabbit have been recorded—by Firth and Bentley, for instance."

"And you suspected that the poison in this case had been contained in the pigeon and the rabbit themselves?"

"Yes. It was a striking coincidence that the poisoning should follow the consumption of these two specially immune animals. But there was a further reason for connecting them. The symptoms were strictly proportionate to the probable amount of poison in each case. Thus the symptoms were only slight after eating the pigeon's eggs. But the eggs of a poisoned pigeon could contain only a minute quantity of the poison. After eating the pigeon the symptoms were much more severe, and the body of a pigeon which had fed on *belladonna* would contain much more *atropine* than could be contained in an egg. Finally, after eating the rabbit, the symptoms were extremely violent; but a rabbit has the greatest immunity and is the most likely to have eaten large quantities of *belladonna* leaves."

"Did you take any measures to put your theory to the test?"

"Yes. Last Monday I went to Eltham, where I had ascertained that Mr. Cyril Parker lives, and inspected his premises from the outside. At the end of his garden is a small paddock enclosed by a wall. Approaching this across a meadow and looking over the wall, I saw that the enclosure was provided with small fowl-houses, pigeon-cotes, and rabbit hutches. All these were open and their inmates were roaming about the paddock. On one side of the enclosure, by the wall was a dense mass of deadly nightshade plants, extending the whole length of the wall and about a couple of yards in width. At one part of this was a ring fence of wire netting, and inside it were five half-grown rabbits. There was a basket containing a small quantity of cabbage leaves and other green stuff, but as I watched, I saw the young rabbits browsing freely on the nightshade plants in preference to the food provided for them.

"On the following day I went to Eltham again taking with me an assistant who carried a young rabbit in a small hamper. We watched the paddock until the coast was clear. Then my assistant got over the wall and abstracted a young rabbit from inside the ring fence and handed it to me. He then took the rabbit from the hamper and dropped it inside the fence. As soon as we were clear of the meadow, we killed the captured rabbit—to prevent any possible elimination of any poison that it might have swallowed. On arriving in London, I at once took the dead rabbit to St. Margaret's Hospital, where, in the chemical laboratory, and in the presence of Dr. Woodford, the Professor of Chemistry, I skinned it and prepared it as if for cooking by removing the viscera. I then separated the flesh from the bones and handed the former to Dr. Woodford, who, in my presence, carried out an exhaustive chemical test for *atropine*. The result was that *atropine* was found to be present in all the muscles; and, on making a quantitative test, the muscles alone yielded no less than .93 grain."

"Is that a poisonous dose?" the counsel asked.

"Yes; it is a poisonous dose for a normal man. In the case of an abnormally susceptible person like Mr. Burnaby it would certainly be a fatal dose."

This completed Thorndyke's evidence. There was no cross and the magistrate put no questions. When Dr. Woodford had been called and had given confirmatory evidence, Mrs. Burnaby's counsel proceeded to address the bench. But the magistrate cut him short.

"There is really no case to argue," said he. "The evidence of the expert witnesses makes it perfectly clear that the poison was already in the food when it came into the hands of the accused. Consequently the charge against her of introducing the poison falls to the ground and the case must be dismissed. I am sure everyone will sympathise with the unfortunate lady who has been the victim of these extraordinary circumstances, and will rejoice, as I do, at the clearing up of the mystery. The prisoner is discharged."

It was a dramatic moment when, amidst the applause of the spectators, Mrs. Burnaby stepped down from the dock and clasped her husband's outstretched hand But, overwhelmed as they both were by the sudden relief, I thought it best not to linger, but, after congratulations, to take myself off with Thorndyke. But one pleasant incident I witnessed before I went Dr. Burnaby had been standing apart, evidently some what embarrassed, when suddenly Mrs. Burnaby ran to him and held out her hand.

"I suppose, Margaret," he said gruffly, "you think I'm an old beast?"

"Indeed I don't," she replied. "You acted quite properly, and I respect you for having the moral courage to do it. And don't forget, Jim, that you action has saved Frank's life. But for you, there would have been no Dr. Thorndyke; and but for Dr. Thorndyke, there would have been another poisoned rabbit."

"What do you make of this case?" I asked, as Thorndyke and I walked away from the court. "Do you suppose the poisoning was accidental?"

He shook his head. "No, Jardine," he replied. "There are too many coincidences. You notice that the poisoned animals did not appear until after Mr Parker had learned from you that Burnaby was abnormally sensitive to *atropine* and could consequently be poisoned by an ordinary medicinal dose. Then the sending of the animals alive looks like a precaution divert suspicion from himself and confuse the issue. Again, that ring fence among the *belladonna* plans has a fishy look, and the plants themselves were not only abnormally numerous but many of them very young and looked as if they had been planted. Further, I happen to know that Parker's firm published, only last year, a book on toxicology in which the immunity of pigeons and rabbits was mentioned and which Parker probably read."

"Then do you believe that he intended to let Mrs. Burnaby—the woman with whom he was in love—bear the brunt of his crime? It seems incredibly villainous and cowardly."

"I do not," he replied. "I imagine that the rabbit that I captured, or one of the others, would have been sent to Burnaby in a few days' time. The cook would probably have prepared it for him and it would almost certainly have killed him; and his death would have been proof of Mrs. Burnaby's innocence. Suspicion would have been transferred to the cook. But I don't suppose any action will be taken against him, for it is practically certain that no jury would convict him on my evidence."

Thorndyke was right in his opinion. No proceedings were taken against Parker. But the house of the Burnabys knew him no more.

The Anthropologist at Large

Thorndyke was not a newspaper reader. He viewed with extreme disfavour all scrappy and miscellaneous forms of literature, which, by presenting a disorderly series of unrelated items of information, tended, as he considered, to destroy the habit of consecutive mental effort.

"It is most important," he once remarked to me, "habitually to pursue a definite train of thought, and to pursue it to a finish, instead of flitting indolently from one uncompleted topic to another, as the newspaper reader is so apt to do. Still, there is no harm in a daily paper—so long as you don't read it."

Accordingly, he patronized a morning paper, and his method of dealing with it was characteristic. The paper was laid on the table after breakfast, together with a blue pencil and a pair of office shears. A preliminary glance through the sheets enabled him to mark with the pencil those paragraphs that were to be read, and these were presently cut out and looked through, after which they were either thrown away or set aside to be pasted in an indexed book.

The whole proceeding occupied, on an average, a quarter of an hour.

On the morning of which I am now speaking he was thus engaged. The pencil had done its work, and the snick of the shears announced the final stage. Presently he paused with a newly-excised cutting between his fingers, and, after glancing at it for a moment, he handed it to me.

"Another art robbery," he remarked. "Mysterious affairs, these—as to motive, I mean. You can't melt down a picture or an ivory carving, and you can't put them on the market as they stand. The very qualities that give them their value make them totally unnegotiable."

"Yet I suppose," said I, "the really inveterate collector—the pottery or stamp maniac, for instance—will buy these contraband goods even

191

though he dare not show them."

"Probably. No doubt the *cupiditas habendi*, the mere desire to possess, is the motive force rather than any intelligent purpose—"

The discussion was at this point interrupted by a knock at the door, and a moment later my colleague admitted two gentlemen. One of these I recognised as a Mr. Marchmont, a solicitor, for whom we had occasionally acted; the other was a stranger—a typical Hebrew of the blonde type—good-looking, faultlessly dressed, carrying a bandbox, and obviously in a state of the most extreme agitation.

"Good-morning to you, gentlemen," said Mr. Marchmont, shaking hands cordially. "I have brought a client of mine to see you, and when I tell you that his name is Solomon Loewe, it will be unnecessary for me to say what our business is."

"Oddly enough," replied Thorndyke, "we were, at the very moment when you knocked, discussing the bearings of his case."

"It is a horrible affair!" burst in Mr. Loewe. "I am distracted! I am ruined! I am in despair!"

He banged the bandbox down on the table, and flinging himself into a chair, buried his face in his hands.

"Come, come," remonstrated Marchmont, "we must be brave, we must be composed. Tell Dr. Thorndyke your story, and let us hear what he thinks of it."

He leaned back in his chair, and looked at his client with that air of patient fortitude that comes to us all so easily when we contemplate the misfortunes of other people.

"You must help us, sir," exclaimed Loewe, starting up again—"you must, indeed, or I shall go mad. But I shall tell you what has happened, and then you must act at once. Spare no effort and no expense. Money is no object—at least, not in reason," he added, with native caution. He sat down once more, and in perfect English, though with a slight German accent, proceeded volubly: "My brother Isaac is probably known to you by name."

Thorndyke nodded.

"He is a great collector, and to some extent a dealer—that is to say, he makes his hobby a profitable hobby."

"What does he collect?" asked Thorndyke.

"Everything," replied our visitor, flinging his hands apart with a comprehensive gesture—"everything that is precious and beautiful—pictures, ivories, jewels, watches, objects of art and *vertu*—everything. He is a Jew, and he has that passion for things that are rich and costly that has distinguished our race from the time of my namesake Solomon onwards. His house in Howard Street, Piccadilly, is at once a museum and an art gallery. The rooms are filled with cases of gems, of antique jewellery, of coins and historic relics—some of priceless value—and the walls are covered with paintings, every one of which is a masterpiece.

"There is a fine collection of ancient weapons and armour, both European and Oriental; rare books, manuscripts, papyri, and valuable antiquities from Egypt, Assyria, Cyprus, and elsewhere. You see, his taste is quite catholic, and his knowledge of rare and curious things is probably greater than that of any other living man. He is never mistaken. No forgery deceives him, and hence the great prices that he obtains; for a work of art purchased from Isaac Loewe is a work certified as genuine beyond all cavil."

He paused to mop his face with a silk handkerchief, and then, with the same plaintive volubility, continued:

"My brother is unmarried. He lives for his collection, and he lives with it. The house is not a very large one, and the collection takes up most of it; but he keeps a suite of rooms for his own occupation, and has two servants—a man and wife—to look after him. The man, who is a retired police sergeant, acts as caretaker and watchman; the woman as housekeeper and cook, if required, but my brother lives largely at his club. And now I come to this present catastrophe."

He ran his fingers through his hair, took a deep breath, and continued:

"Yesterday morning Isaac started for Florence by way of Paris, but his route was not certain, and he intended to break his journey at various points as circumstances determined. Before leaving, he put his collection in my charge, and it was arranged that I should occupy his rooms in his absence. Accordingly, I sent my things round and took possession.

"Now, Dr. Thorndyke, I am closely connected with the drama, and it is my custom to spend my evenings at my club, of which most of the members are actors. Consequently, I am rather late in my habits; but last night I was earlier than usual in leaving my club, for I started for my brother's house before half-past twelve. I felt, as you may suppose, the responsibility of the great charge I had undertaken; and you may, therefore, imagine my horror, my consternation, my despair, when, on letting myself in with my latchkey, I found a police-inspector, a sergeant, and a constable in the hall. There had been a robbery, sir, in my brief absence, and the account that the inspector gave of the affair was briefly this:

"While taking the round of his district, he had noticed an empty hansom proceeding in leisurely fashion along Howard Street. There was nothing remarkable in this, but when, about ten minutes later, he was returning, and met a hansom, which he believed to be the same, proceeding along the same street in the same direction, and at the same easy pace, the circumstance struck him as odd, and he made a note of the number of the cab in his pocket-book. It was 72,863, and the time was 11.35.

"At 11.45 a constable coming up Howard Street noticed a hansom standing opposite the door of my brother's house, and, while he was looking at it, a man came out of the house carrying something, which he put in the cab. On this the constable quickened his pace, and when the man returned to the house and reappeared carrying what looked like a portmanteau, and closing the door softly behind him, the policeman's suspicions were aroused, and he hurried forward, hailing the cabman to stop.

"The man put his burden into the cab, and sprang in himself. The cabman lashed his horse, which started off at a gallop, and the policeman broke into a run, blowing his whistle and flashing his lantern on to the cab. He followed it round the two turnings into Albemarle Street, and was just in time to see it turn into Piccadilly, where, of course, it was lost. However, he managed to note the number of the cab, which was 72,863, and he describes the man as short and thickset, and thinks he was not wearing any hat.

"As he was returning, he met the inspector and the sergeant, who had heard the whistle, and on his report the three officers hurried to the house, where they knocked and rang for some minutes without any result. Being now more than suspicious, they went to the back of the house, through the mews, where, with great difficulty, they managed to force a window and effect an entrance into the house.

"Here their suspicions were soon changed to certainty, for, on reaching the first-floor, they heard strange muffled groans proceeding from one of the rooms, the door of which was locked, though the key had not been removed. They opened the door, and found the caretaker and his wife sitting on the floor, with their backs against the wall. Both were bound hand and foot, and the head of each was enveloped in a green-baize bag; and when the bags were taken off, each was found to be lightly but effectively gagged.

"Each told the same story. The caretaker, fancying he heard a noise, armed himself with a truncheon, and came downstairs to the first-floor, where he found the door of one of the rooms open, and a light burning inside. He stepped on tiptoe to the open door, and was peering in, when he was seized from behind, half suffocated by a pad held over his mouth, pinioned, gagged, and blindfolded with the bag.

"His assailant—whom he never saw—was amazingly strong and skilful, and handled him with perfect ease, although he—the caretaker—is a powerful man, and a good boxer and wrestler. The same thing happened to the wife, who had come down to look for her husband. She walked into the same trap, and was gagged, pinioned, and blindfolded without ever having seen the robber. So the only description that we have of this villain is that furnished by the constable."

"And the caretaker had no chance of using his truncheon?" said Thorndyke.

"Well, he got in one backhanded blow over his right shoulder, which he thinks caught the burglar in the face; but the fellow caught him by the elbow, and gave his arm such a twist that he dropped the truncheon on the floor."

"Is the robbery a very extensive one?"

"Ah!" exclaimed Mr. Loewe, "that is just what we cannot say. But I fear it is. It seems that my brother had quite recently drawn out of his bank four thousand pounds in notes and gold. These little transactions are often carried out in cash rather than by cheque"—here I caught a twinkle in Thorndyke's eye—"and the caretaker says that a few days ago Isaac brought home several parcels, which were put away temporarily in a strong cupboard. He seemed to be very pleased with his new acquisitions, and gave the caretaker to understand that they were of extraordinary rarity and value.

"Now, this cupboard has been cleared out. Not a vestige is left in it but the wrappings of the parcels, so, although nothing else has been touched, it is pretty clear that goods to the value of four thousand pounds have been taken; but when we consider what an excellent buyer my brother is, it becomes highly probable that the actual value of those things is two or three times that amount, or even more. It is a dreadful, dreadful business, and Isaac will hold me responsible for it all."

"Is there no further clue?" asked Thorndyke. "What about the cab, for instance?"

"Oh, the cab," groaned Loewe—"that clue failed. The police must have mistaken the number. They telephoned immediately to all the police stations, and a watch was set, with the result that number 72,863 was stopped as it was going home for the night. But it then turned out that the cab had not been off the rank since eleven o'clock, and the driver had been in the shelter all the time with several other men. But there is a clue; I have it here."

Mr. Loewe's face brightened for once as he reached out for the bandbox.

"The houses in Howard Street," he explained, as he untied the fastening, "have small balconies to the first-floor windows at the back. Now, the thief entered by one of these windows, having climbed up a rain-water pipe to the balcony. It was a gusty night, as you will remember, and this morning, as I was leaving the house, the butler next door called to me and gave me this; he had found it lying in the balcony of his house."

He opened the bandbox with a flourish, and brought forth a rather shabby billycock hat.

"I understand," said he, "that by examining a hat it is possible to deduce from it, not only the bodily characteristics of the wearer, but also his mental and moral qualities, his state of health, his pecuniary position, his past history, and even his domestic relations and the peculiarities of his place of abode. Am I right in this supposition?"

The ghost of a smile flitted across Thorndyke's face as he laid the hat upon the remains of the newspaper. "We must not expect too much," he observed. "Hats, as you know, have a way of changing owners. Your own hat, for instance" (a very spruce, hard felt), "is a new one, I think."

"Got it last week," said Mr. Loewe.

"Exactly. It is an expensive hat, by Lincoln and Bennett, and I see you have judiciously written your name in indelible marking-ink on the lining. Now, a new hat suggests a discarded predecessor. What do you do with your old hats?"

"My man has them, but they don't fit him. I suppose he sells them or gives them away."

"Very well. Now, a good hat like yours has a long life, and remains serviceable long after it has become shabby; and the probability is that many of your hats pass from owner to owner; from you to the shabby-genteel, and from them to the shabby ungenteel. And it is a fair assumption that there are, at this moment, an appreciable number of tramps and casuals wearing hats by Lincoln and Bennett, marked in indelible ink with the name S. Loewe; and anyone who should examine those hats, as you suggest, might draw some very misleading deductions as to the personal habits of S. Loewe."

Mr. Marchmont chuckled audibly, and then, remembering the gravity of the occasion, suddenly became portentously solemn.

"So you think that the hat is of no use, after all?" said Mr. Loewe, in a tone of deep disappointment.

"I won't say that," replied Thorndyke. "We may learn something from it. Leave it with me, at any rate; but you must let the police know that I have it. They will want to see it, of course."

"And you will try to get those things, won't you?" pleaded Loewe.

"I will think over the case. But you understand, or Mr. Marchmont does, that this is hardly in my province. I am a medical jurist, and this is not a medico-legal case."

"Just what I told him," said Marchmont. "But you will do me a great kindness if you will look into the matter. Make it a medico-legal case," he added persuasively.

Thorndyke repeated his promise, and the two men took their departure.

For some time after they had left, my colleague remained silent, regarding the hat with a quizzical smile. "It is like a game of forfeits," he remarked at length, "and we have to find the owner of 'this very pretty thing.'" He lifted it with a pair of forceps into a better light, and began to look at it more closely.

"Perhaps," said he, "we have done Mr. Loewe an injustice, after all. This is certainly a very remarkable hat."

"It is as round as a basin," I exclaimed. "Why, the fellow's head must have been turned in a lathe!"

Thorndyke laughed. "The point," said he, "is this. This is a hard hat, and so must have fitted fairly, or it could not have been worn; and it was a cheap hat, and so was not made to measure. But a man with a head that shape has got to come to a clear understanding with his hat. No ordinary hat would go on at all.

"Now, you see what he has done—no doubt on the advice of some friendly hatter. He has bought a hat of a suitable size, and he has made it hot—probably steamed it. Then he has jammed it, while still hot and soft, on to his head, and allowed it to cool and set before removing it. That is evident from the distortion of the brim. The important corollary is, that this hat fits his head exactly—is, in fact, a perfect mould of it; and this fact, together with the cheap quality of the hat, furnishes the further corollary that it has probably only had a single owner.

"And now let us turn it over and look at the outside. You notice at once the absence of old dust. Allowing for the circumstance that it had been out all night, it is decidedly clean. Its owner has been in the habit of brushing it, and is therefore presumably a decent, orderly man. But if you look at it in a good light, you see a kind of bloom on the felt, and through this lens you can make out particles of a fine white powder which has worked into the surface."

He handed me his lens, through which I could distinctly see the particles to which he referred.

"Then," he continued, "under the curl of the brim and in the folds of the hatband, where the brush has not been able to reach it, the powder has collected quite thickly, and we can see that it is a very fine powder, and very white, like flour. What do you make of that?"

"I should say that it is connected with some industry. He may be engaged in some factory or works, or, at any rate, may live near a factory, and have to pass it frequently."

"Yes; and I think we can distinguish between the two possibilities. For, if he only passes the factory, the dust will be on the outside of the hat only; the inside will be protected by his head. But if he is engaged in the works, the dust will be inside, too, as the hat will hang on a peg in the dust-laden atmosphere, and his head will also be powdered, and so convey the dust to the inside."

He turned the hat over once more, and as I brought the powerful lens to bear upon the dark lining, I could clearly distinguish a number of white particles in the interstices of the fabric.

"The powder is on the inside, too," I said.

He took the lens from me, and, having verified my statement, proceeded with the examination. "You notice," he said, "that the leather head-lining is stained with grease, and this staining is more pronounced at the sides and back. His hair, therefore, is naturally greasy, or he greases it artificially; for if the staining were caused by perspiration, it would be most marked opposite the forehead."

He peered anxiously into the interior of the hat, and eventually turned down the head-lining; and immediately there broke out upon his face a gleam of satisfaction.

"Ha!" he exclaimed. "This is a stroke of luck. I was afraid our neat and orderly friend had defeated us with his brush. Pass me the small dissecting forceps, Jervis."

I handed him the instrument, and he proceeded to pick out daintily from the space behind the head-lining some half a dozen short pieces of hair, which he laid, with infinite tenderness, on a sheet of white paper.

"There are several more on the other side," I said, pointing them out to him.

"Yes, but we must leave some for the police," he answered, with a smile. "They must have the same chance as ourselves, you know."

"But surely," I said, as I bent down over the paper, "these are pieces of horsehair!"

"I think not," he replied; "but the microscope will show. At any rate, this is the kind of hair I should expect to find with a head of that shape."

"Well, it is extraordinarily coarse," said I, "and two of the hairs are nearly white."

"Yes; black hairs beginning to turn grey. And now, as our preliminary survey has given such encouraging results, we will proceed to more exact methods; and we must waste no time, for we shall have the police here presently to rob us of our treasure."

He folded up carefully the paper containing the hairs, and taking the hat in both hands, as though it were some sacred vessel, ascended with me to the laboratory on the next floor.

"Now, Polton," he said to his laboratory assistant, "we have here a specimen for examination, and time is precious. First of all, we want your patent dust-extractor."

The little man bustled to a cupboard and brought forth a singular appliance, of his own manufacture, somewhat like a miniature vacuum cleaner. It had been made from a bicycle foot-pump, by reversing the piston-valve, and was fitted with a glass nozzle and a small detachable glass receiver for collecting the dust, at the end of a flexible metal tube.

"We will sample the dust from the outside first," said Thorndyke, laying the hat upon the work-bench. "Are you ready, Polton?"

The assistant slipped his foot into the stirrup of the pump and worked the handle vigorously, while Thorndyke drew the glass nozzle slowly along the hat-brim under the curled edge. And as the nozzle passed along, the white coating vanished as if by magic, leaving the felt absolutely clean and black, and simultaneously the glass receiver became clouded over with a white deposit.

"We will leave the other side for the police," said Thorndyke, and as Polton ceased pumping he detached the receiver, and laid it on a sheet of paper, on which he wrote in pencil, "Outside," and covered it with a small bell-glass. A fresh receiver having been fitted on, the nozzle was now drawn over the silk lining of the hat, and then through the space behind the leather head-lining on one side; and now the dust that collected in the receiver was much of the usual grey colour and fluffy texture, and included two more hairs.

"And now," said Thorndyke, when the second receiver had been detached and set aside, "we want a mould of the inside of the hat, and we must make it by the quickest method; there is no time to make a paper mould. It is a most astonishing head," he added, reaching down from a nail a pair of large callipers, which he applied to the inside of the hat; "six inches and nine-tenths long by six and six-tenths broad, which gives us"—he made a rapid calculation on a scrap of paper—"the extraordinarily high cephalic index of 95.6."

Polton now took possession of the hat, and, having stuck a band of wet tissue-paper round the inside, mixed a small bowl of plaster-of-Paris, and very dexterously ran a stream of the thick liquid on to the tissue-paper, where it quickly solidified. A second and third application resulted in a broad ring of solid plaster an inch thick, forming a perfect mould of the inside of the hat, and in a few minutes the slight contraction of the plaster in setting rendered the mould sufficiently loose to allow of its being slipped out on to a board to dry.

We were none too soon, for even as Polton was removing the mould, the electric bell, which I had switched on to the laboratory, announced a visitor, and when I went down I found a police-sergeant waiting with a note from Superintendent Miller, requesting the immediate transfer of the hat.

"The next thing to be done," said Thorndyke, when the sergeant had departed with the bandbox, "is to measure the thickness of the hairs, and make a transverse section of one, and examine the dust. The section we will leave to Polton—as time is an object, Polton, you had better imbed the hair in thick gum and freeze it hard on the microtome, and be very careful to cut the section at right angles to the length of the hair—meanwhile, we will get to work with the microscope."

The hairs proved on measurement to have the surprisingly large diameter of one one-hundred-and-thirty-fifth of an inch—fully double that of ordinary hairs, although they were unquestionably human. As to the white dust, it presented a problem that even Thorndyke was unable to solve. The application of reagents showed it to be carbonate

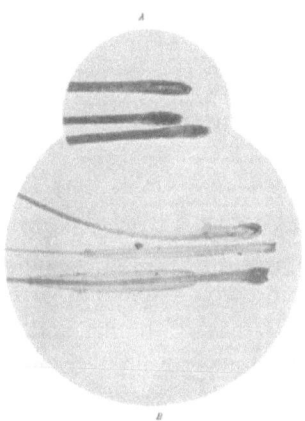

of lime, but its source for a time remained a mystery.

"The larger particles," said Thorndyke, with his eye applied to the microscope, "appear to be transparent, crystalline, and distinctly laminated in structure. It is not chalk, it is not whiting, it is not any kind of cement. What can it be?"

"Could it be any kind of shell?" I suggested. "For instance—"

"Of course!" he exclaimed, starting up; "you have hit it, Jervis, as you always do. It must be mother-of-pearl. Polton, give me a pearl shirt-button out of your oddments box."

The button was duly produced by the thrifty Polton, dropped into an agate mortar, and speedily reduced to powder, a tiny pinch of which Thorndyke placed under the microscope.

"This powder," said he, "is, naturally, much coarser than our specimen, but the identity of character is unmistakable. Jervis, you are a treasure. Just look at it."

I glanced down the microscope, and then pulled out my watch. "Yes," I said, "there is no doubt about it, I think; but I must be off. Anstey urged me to be in court by 11.30 at the latest."

With infinite reluctance I collected my notes and papers and departed, leaving Thorndyke diligently copying addresses out of the Post Office Directory.

My business at the court detained me the whole of the day, and it was near upon dinner-time when I reached our chambers. Thorndyke had not yet come in, but he arrived half an hour later, tired and hungry, and not very communicative.

"What have I done?" he repeated, in answer to my inquiries. "I have walked miles of dirty pavement, and I have visited every pearl-shell cutter's in London, with one exception, and I have not found what I was looking for. The one mother-of-pearl factory that remains, however, is the most likely, and I propose to look in there tomorrow morning. Meanwhile, we have completed our data, with Polton's assistance.

"Here is a tracing of our friend's skull taken from the mould; you see it is an extreme type of *brachycephalic* skull, and markedly unsymmetrical. Here is a transverse section of his hair, which is quite circular—unlike yours or mine, which would be oval. We have the mother-of-pearl dust from the outside of the hat, and from the inside similar dust mixed with various fibres and a few granules of rice starch. Those are our data."

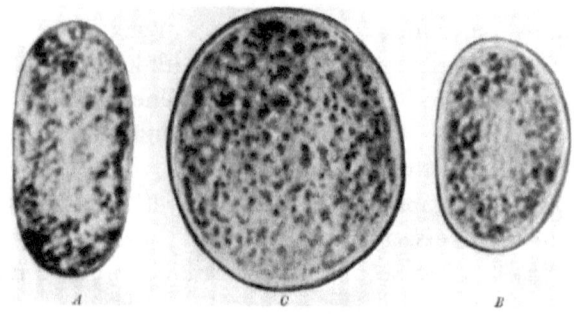

TRANSVERSE SECTIONS OF HUMAN HAIR:
A, OF A NEGRO; B, OF AN ENGLISHMAN; C, OF THE BURGLAR.
ALL MAGNIFIED 600 DIAMETERS.

"Supposing the hat should not be that of the burglar after all?" I suggested.

"That would be annoying. But I think it is his, and I think I can guess at the nature of the art treasures that were stolen."

"And you don't intend to enlighten me?"

"My dear fellow," he replied, "you have all the data. Enlighten yourself by the exercise of your own brilliant faculties. Don't give way to mental indolence."

I endeavoured, from the facts in my possession, to construct the personality of the mysterious burglar, and failed utterly; nor was I more successful in my endeavour to guess at the nature of the stolen property; and it was not until the following morning, when we had set out on our quest and were approaching Limehouse, that Thorndyke would revert to the subject.

"We are now," he said, "going to the factory of Badcomb and Martin, shell importers and cutters, in the West India Dock Road. If I don't find my man there, I shall hand the facts over to the police, and waste no more time over the case."

"What is your man like?" I asked.

"I am looking for an elderly Japanese, wearing a new hat or, more probably, a cap, and having a bruise on his right cheek or temple. I am also looking for a cab-yard; but here we are at the works, and as it is now close on the dinner-hour, we will wait and see the hands come out before making any inquiries."

We walked slowly past the tall, blank-faced building, and were just turning to re-pass it when a steam whistle sounded, a wicket opened in the main gate, and a stream of workmen—each powdered with white, like a miller—emerged into the street. We halted to watch the men as they came out, one by one, through the wicket, and turned to the right or left towards their homes or some adjacent coffee-shop; but none of them answered to the description that my friend had given.

The outcoming stream grew thinner, and at length ceased; the wicket was shut with a bang, and once more Thorndyke's quest appeared to have failed.

"Is that all of them, I wonder?" he said, with a shade of disappointment in his tone; but even as he spoke the wicket opened again, and a leg protruded. The leg was followed by a back and a curious globular head, covered with iron-grey hair, and surmounted by a cloth cap, the whole appertaining to a short, very thick-set man, who remained thus, evidently talking to someone inside.

Suddenly he turned his head to look across the street; and immediately I recognised, by the pallid yellow complexion and narrow eye-slits, the physiognomy of a typical Japanese. The man remained talking for nearly another minute; then, drawing out his other leg, he turned towards us; and now I perceived that the right side of his face, over the prominent cheekbone, was discoloured as though by a severe bruise.

"Ha!" said Thorndyke, turning round sharply as the man approached, "either this is our man or it is an incredible coincidence." He walked away at a moderate pace, allowing the Japanese to overtake us slowly, and when the man had at length passed us, he increased his speed somewhat, so as to maintain the distance.

Our friend stepped along briskly, and presently turned up a side street, whither we followed at a respectful distance, Thorndyke holding open his pocket-book, and appearing to engage me in an earnest discussion, but keeping a sharp eye on his quarry.

"There he goes!" said my colleague, as the man suddenly disappeared—"the house with the green window-sashes. That will be number thirteen."

It was; and, having verified the fact, we passed on, and took the next turning that would lead us back to the main road.

Some twenty minutes later, as we were strolling past the door of a coffee-shop, a man came out, and began to fill his pipe with an air of leisurely satisfaction. His hat and clothes were powdered with white like those of the workmen whom we had seen come out of the factory. Thorndyke accosted him.

"Is that a flour-mill up the road there?"

"No, sir; pearl-shell. I work there myself."

"Pearl-shell, eh?" said Thorndyke. "I suppose that will be an industry that will tend to attract the aliens. Do you find it so?"

"No, sir; not at all. The work's too hard. We've only got one foreigner in the place, and he ain't an alien—he's a Jap."

"A Jap!" exclaimed Thorndyke. "Really. Now, I wonder if that would chance to be our old friend Kotei—you remember Kotei?" he added, turning to me.

"No, sir; this man's name is Futashima. There was another Jap in the works, a chap named Itu, a pal of Futashima's, but he's left."

"Ah! I don't know either of them. By the way, usen't there to be a cab-yard just about here?"

"There's a yard up Rankin Street where they keep vans and one or two cabs. That chap Itu works there now. Taken to horseflesh. Drives a van sometimes. Queer start for a Jap."

"Very." Thorndyke thanked the man for his information, and we sauntered on towards Rankin Street. The yard was at this time nearly deserted, being occupied only by an ancient and crazy four-wheeler and a very shabby hansom.

"Curious old houses, these that back on to the yard," said Thorndyke, strolling into the enclosure. "That timber gable, now," pointing to a house, from a window of which a man was watching us suspiciously, "is quite an interesting survival."

"What's your business, mister?" demanded the man in a gruff tone.

"We are just having a look at these quaint old houses," replied Thorndyke, edging towards the back of the hansom, and opening his pocket-book, as though to make a sketch.

"Well, you can see 'em from outside," said the man.

"So we can," said Thorndyke suavely, "but not so well, you know."

At this moment the pocket-book slipped from his hand and fell, scattering a number of loose papers about the ground under the hansom, and our friend at the window laughed joyously.

"No hurry," murmured Thorndyke, as I stooped to help him to gather up the papers—which he did in the most surprisingly slow and clumsy manner. "It is fortunate that the ground is dry." He stood up with the rescued papers in his hand, and, having scribbled down a brief note, slipped the book in his pocket.

"Now you'd better mizzle," observed the man at the window.

"Thank you," replied Thorndyke, "I think we had;" and, with a pleasant nod at the custodian, he proceeded to adopt the hospitable suggestion.

"Mr. Marchmont has been here, sir, with Inspector Badger and another gentleman," said Polton, as we entered our chambers. "They said they would call again about five."

"Then," replied Thorndyke, "as it is now a quarter to five, there is just time for us to have a wash while you get the tea ready. The particles that float in the atmosphere of Limehouse are not all mother-of-pearl."

Our visitors arrived punctually, the third gentleman being, as we had supposed, Mr. Solomon Loewe. Inspector Badger I had not seen before, and he now impressed me as showing a tendency to invert the significance of his own name by endeavouring to "draw" Thorndyke; in which, however, he was not brilliantly successful.

"I hope you are not going to disappoint Mr. Loewe, sir," he commenced facetiously. "You have had a good look at that hat—we saw your marks on it—and he expects that you will be able to point us out the man, name and address all complete." He grinned patronizingly at our unfortunate client, who was looking even more haggard and worn than he had been on the previous morning.

"Have you—have you made any—discovery?" Mr Loewe asked with pathetic eagerness.

"We examined the hat very carefully, and I think we have established a few facts of some interest."

"Did your examination of the hat furnish any information as to the nature of the stolen property, sir?" inquired the humorous inspector.

Thorndyke turned to the officer with a face as expressionless as a wooden mask.

"We thought it possible," said he, "that it might consist of works of Japanese art, such as netsukes, paintings, and such like."

Mr. Loewe uttered an exclamation of delighted astonishment, and the facetiousness faded rather suddenly from the inspector's countenance.

"I don't know how you can have found out," said he. "We have only known it half an hour ourselves, and the wire came direct from Florence to Scotland Yard."

"Perhaps you can describe the thief to us," said Mr. Loewe, in the same eager tone.

"I dare say the inspector can do that," replied Thorndyke.

"Yes, I think so," replied the officer. "He is a short strong man, with a dark complexion and hair turning grey. He has a very round head, and he is probably a workman engaged at some whiting or cement works. That is all we know; if you can tell us any more, sir, we shall be very glad to hear it."

"I can only offer a few suggestions," said Thorndyke, "but perhaps you may find them useful. For instance, at 13, Birket Street, Limehouse, there is living a Japanese gentleman named Futashima, who works at Badcomb and Martin's mother-of-pearl factory. I think that if you were to call on him, and let him try on the hat that you have, it would probably fit him."

The inspector scribbled ravenously in his notebook, and Mr. Marchmont—an old admirer of Thorndyke's—leaned back in his chair, chuckling softly and rubbing his hands.

"Then," continued my colleague, "there is in Rankin Street, Limehouse, a cab-yard, where another Japanese gentleman named Itu is employed. You might find out where Itu was the night before last; and if you should chance to see a hansom cab there—number 22,481—have a good look at it. In the frame of the number-plate you will find six small holes. Those holes may have held brads, and the brads may have held a false number card. At any rate, you might ascertain where that cab was at 11.30 the night before last. That is all I have to suggest."

Mr. Loewe leaped from his chair. "Let us go—now—at once—there is no time to be lost. A thousand thanks to you, doctor—a thousand million thanks. Come!"

He seized the inspector by the arm and forcibly dragged him towards the door, and a few moments later we heard the footsteps of our visitors clattering down the stairs.

"It was not worth while to enter into explanations with them," said Thorndyke, as the footsteps died away—"nor perhaps with you?"

"On the contrary," I replied, "I am waiting to be fully enlightened."

"Well, then, my inferences in this case were perfectly simple ones, drawn from well-known anthropological facts. The human race, as you know, is roughly divided into three groups—the black, the white, and the yellow races. But apart from the variable quality of colour, these races have certain fixed characteristics associated especially with the shape of the skull, of the eye-sockets, and the hair.

"Thus in the black races the skull is long and narrow, the eye-sockets are long and narrow, and the hair is flat and ribbon-like, and usually coiled up like a watch-spring. In the white races the skull is oval, the eye-sockets are oval, and the hair is slightly flattened or oval in section, and tends to be wavy; while in the yellow or Mongol races, the skull is short and round, the eye-sockets are short and round, and the hair is straight and circular in section. So that we have, in the black races, long skull, long orbits, flat hair; in the white races, oval skull, oval orbits, oval hair; and in the yellow races, round skull, round orbits, round hair.

"Now, in this case we had to deal with a very short round skull. But you cannot argue from races to individuals; there are many short-skulled Englishmen. But when I found, associated with that skull, hairs which were circular in section, it became practically certain that the individual was a Mongol of some kind. The mother-of-pearl dust and the granules of rice starch from the inside of the hat favoured this view, for the pearl-shell industry is specially connected with China and Japan, while starch granules from the hat of an Englishman would probably be wheat starch.

"Then as to the hair: it was, as I mentioned to you, circular in section, and of very large diameter. Now, I have examined many thousands of hairs, and the thickest that I have ever seen came from the heads of Japanese; but the hairs from this hat were as thick as any of them. But the hypothesis that the burglar was a Japanese received confirmation in various ways. Thus, he was short, though strong and active, and the Japanese are the shortest of the Mongol races, and very strong and active.

"Then his remarkable skill in handling the powerful caretaker—a retired police-sergeant—suggested the Japanese art of *ju-jitsu*, while the nature of the robbery was consistent with the value set by the Japanese on works of art. Finally, the fact that only a particular collection was taken, suggested a special, and probably national, character in the things stolen, while their portability—you will remember that goods of the value of from eight to twelve thousand pounds were taken away in two hand-packages—was much more consistent with Japanese than Chinese works, of which the latter tend rather to be bulky and ponderous. Still, it was nothing but a bare hypothesis until we had seen Futashima—and, indeed, is no more now. I may, after all, be entirely mistaken."

He was not, however; and at this moment there reposes in my drawing-room an ancient *netsuke*, which came as a thank-offering from Mr. Isaac Loewe on the recovery of the booty from a back room in No. 13, Birket Street, Limehouse. The treasure, of course, was given in the first place to Thorndyke, but transferred by him to my wife on the pretence that but for my suggestion of shell-dust the robber would never have been traced. Which is, on the face of it, preposterous.

The Apparition of Burling Court

Thorndyke seldom took a formal holiday. He did not seem to need one. As he himself put it, "A holiday implies the exchange of a less pleasurable occupation for one more pleasurable. But there is no occupation more pleasurable than the practice of Medical Jurisprudence." Moreover, his work was less affected by terms and vacations than that of an ordinary barrister, and the Long Vacation often found him with his hands full. Even when he did appear to take a holiday the appearance tended to be misleading, and it was apt to turn out that his disappearance from his usual haunts was associated with a case of unusual interest at a distance.

Thus it was on the occasion when our old friend, Mr. Brodribb, of Lincoln's Inn, beguiled him into a fortnight's change at St. David's-at-Cliffe, a seaside hamlet on the Kentish coast. There was a case in the background, and a very curious case it turned out to be, though at first it appeared to me quite a commonplace affair; and the manner of its introduction was as follows.

One hot afternoon in the early part of the Long Vacation the old solicitor dropped in for a cup of tea and a chat. That, at least, was how he explained his visit; but my experience of Mr. Brodribb led me to suspect some ulterior purpose in the call, and as he sat by the open window, teacup in hand, looking, with his fine pink complexion, his silky white hair and his faultless "turn out," the very type of the courtly, old-fashioned lawyer, I waited expectantly for the matter of his visit to transpire. And, presently, out it came.

"I am going to take a little holiday down at St. David's," said he. "Just a quiet spell by the sea, you know. Delightful place. So quiet and restful and so breezy and fresh. Ever been there?"

"No," replied Thorndyke. "I only just know the name."

"Well, why shouldn't you come down for a week or so? Both of you. I shall stay at Burling Court, the Lumleys' place. I can't invite you there as I'm only a guest, but I know of some comfortable rooms in the village that I could get for you. I wish you would come down, Thorndyke," he added after a pause. "I'm rather unhappy about young Lumley—I'm the family lawyer, you know, and so was my father and my grandfather, so I feel almost as if the Lumleys were my own kin— and I should like to have your advice and help."

"Why not have it now?" suggested Thorndyke.

"I will," he replied; "but I should like your help on the spot too. I'd like you to see Lumley have a talk with him and tell me what you think of him."

"What is amiss with him?" Thorndyke asked.

"Well," answered Brodribb, "it looks uncomfortably like insanity. He has delusions—sees apparitions and that sort of thing. And there is some insanity in the family. But I had better give you the facts in their natural order.

"About four months ago Giles Lumley of Burling Court died; and as he was a widower without issue, the estate passed to his nearest male relative, my present client, Frank Lumley, who was also the principal beneficiary under the will. At the time of Giles' death Frank was abroad, but a cousin of his, Lewis Price, was staying at the house with his wife as a more or less permanent guest; and as Price's circumstances were not very flourishing, and as he is the next heir to the estate, Frank—who is a bachelor—wrote to him at once telling him to look upon Burling Court as his home for as long as he pleased."

"That was extremely generous of him," I remarked

"Yes," Brodribb agreed; "Frank is a good fellow; a very high-minded gentleman and a very sweet man but a little queer—very queer just now. Well, Frank came back from abroad and took up his abode at the house; and for a time all went well. Then, one day, Price called on me and gave me some very unpleasant news. It seemed that Frank, who had always been rather neurotic and imaginative, had been interesting himself a good deal in psychical research and—and balderdash of that kind, you know. Well, there was no great harm in that, perhaps. But just lately he had taken to seeing visions and—what was worse— talking about them; so much so that Price got uneasy and privately invited a mental specialist down to lunch; and the specialist, having had a longish talk with Frank Price confidentially that he (Frank) was obviously suffering from insane delusions. Thereupon Price called me and begged me to see Frank myself and what ought to be done; so I made an occasion for him to come and see me at the office."

"And what did you think of him?" asked Thorndyke.

"I was horrified—horrified," said Mr. Brodribb. "I assure you, Thorndyke, that that poor young man sat in my office and talked like a stark lunatic. Quite quietly, you know. No excitement, though he was evidently anxious and unhappy. But there he sat gravely talking the damnedest nonsense you ever heard."

"As, for instance—?"

"Well, his infernal visions. Luminous birds flying about in the dark, and a human head suspended in mid air—upside down, too. But I had better give you his story as he told it. I made full shorthand notes as he was talking, and I've brought them with me, though I hardly need them.

"His trouble seems to have begun soon after he took up his quarters at Burling Court. Being a bookish sort of fellow, he started to go through his library systematically; and presently he came across a small manuscript book, which turned out to be a sort of family history, or rather a collection of episodes. It was rather a lurid little book, for it apparently dwelt chiefly on the family crime, the family spectre and the family madness."

"Did you know about these heirlooms?" Thorndyke asked.

"No; it was the first I'd heard of 'em. Price knew there was some soft of family superstition, but he didn't know what it was; and Giles knew about it—so Price tells me—but didn't care to talk about it. He never mentioned it to me."

"What is the nature of the tradition?" inquired Thorndyke.

"I'll tell you," said Brodribb, taking out his notes. "I've got it all down, and poor Frank reeled the stuff off as if he had learned it by heart. The book, which is dated 1819, was apparently written by a Walter Lumley and the story of the crime and the spook runs thus:

"About 1720 the property passed to a Gilbert Lumley, a naval officer, who then gave up the sea, married and settled down at Burling Court. A year or two later some trouble arose about his wife and a man named Glynn, a neighbouring squire. With or without cause, Lumley became violently jealous, and the end of it was that he lured Glynn to a large cavern in the cliffs and there murdered him. It was a most ferocious and vindictive crime. The cavern, which was then used by smugglers, had a beam across the roof bearing a tackle for hoisting out boat cargoes, and this tackle Lumley fastened to Glynn's ankles—having first pinioned him—and hoisted him up so that he hung head downwards a foot or so clear of the floor of the cave. And there he left him hanging until the rising tide flowed into the cave and drowned him.

"The very next day the murder was discovered, and as Lumley was the nearest justice of the peace, the discoverers reported to him and took him to the cave to the body. When he entered the cave the corpse was still hanging as he had left the living man, and a bat was flittering round and round the dead man's head. He had the body taken down and carried to Glynn's house and took the necessary measures for the inquest. Of course, everyone suspected him of the murder, but there was no evidence against him. The verdict was murder by some person unknown, and as Gilbert Lumley was not sensitive, everything seemed to have gone quite satisfactorily.

"But it hadn't. One night, exactly a month after murder, Gilbert retired to his bedroom in the dark. He was in the act of feeling along the mantelpiece for the tinder-box, when he became aware of a dim light moving about the room. He turned round quickly and then saw that it was a bat—a most uncanny and abnormal bat that seemed to give out a greenish ghostly light—flitting round and round his bed. On this, remembering the bat in the cavern, he rushed out of the room in the very devil of a fright. Presently he returned with one of the servants and a couple of candles; but the bat had disappeared.

"From that time onward, the luminous bat haunted Gilbert, appearing in dark rooms, on staircases and passages and corridors, until his nerves were all on end and he did not dare to move about the house at night without a candle or a lantern. But that was not the worst. Exactly two months after the murder the next stage of the haunting began. He had retired to his bedroom and was just about to get into bed when he remembered that he had left his watch in the little dressing-room that adjoined his chamber. With a candle in his hand he went to the dressing-room and flung open the door. And then he stopped dead and stood as if turned into stone; for, within a couple of yards of him, suspended in mid-air, was a man's head hanging upside down.

"For some seconds he stood rooted to the spot, unable to move. Then he uttered a cry of horror and rushed back to his room and down to the hall. There was no doubt whose head it was, strange and horrible as it looked in that unnatural, inverted position; for he had seen it twice before in that very position hanging in the cavern. Evidently he had not got rid of Glynn.

212

"That night, and every night henceforward, he slept in his wife's room. And all through the night he was conscious of a strange and dreadful impulse to rise and go down to the shore; to steal into the cavern and wait for the flowing tide. He lay awake, fighting against the invisible power that seemed to be drawing him to destruction, and by the morning the horrid impulse began to weaken. But he went about in terror, not daring to go near the shore and afraid to trust himself alone.

"A month passed. The effect of the apparition grew daily weaker and an abundance of lights in the house protected him from the visitation of the bat. Then, exactly three months after the murder, he saw the head again. This time it was in the library, where he had gone to fetch a book. He was standing by the book shelves and had just taken out a volume, when, as he turned away, there the hideous thing was, hanging in hat awful, grotesque posture, chin upwards and the scanty hair dropping down like wet fringe. Gilbert dropped the book that he was holding and fled from the room with a shriek; and all that night invisible hands seemed to be plucking at him to draw him away to where the voices of the waves were reverberating in the cavern.

"This second visitation affected him profoundly. He could not shake off that sinister impulse to steal away to the shore. He was a broken man, the victim of an abiding terror, clinging for protection to the very servants, creeping abroad with shaking limbs and an apprehensive eye towards the sea. And ever in his ears was the murmur of the surf and the hollow echoes of the cavern.

"Already he had sought forgetfulness in drink; and sought it in vain. Now he took refuge in opiates. Every night, before retiring to the dreaded bed, he mingled *laudanum* with the brandy that brought him stupor if not repose. And brandy and opium began to leave their traces in the tremulous hand, the sallow cheek and the bloodshot eye. And so another month passed.

"As the day approached that would mark the fourth month, his terror of the visitation that he now anticipated reduced him to a state of utter prostration. Sleep—even drugged sleep—appeared that night to be out of the question, and he decided to sit up with his family, hoping by that means to escape the dreaded visitor. But it was a vain hope. Hour after hour he sat in his elbow chair by the fire, while his wife dozed in her chair opposite, until the clock in the hall struck twelve. He listened and counted the strokes of the bell, leaning back with his eyes closed. Half the weary night was gone. As the last stroke sounded and a deep silence fell on the house, he opened his eyes—and looked into the face of Glynn within a few inches of his own.

"For some moments he sat with dropped jaw and dilated eyes staring in silent horror at this awful thing; then with an agonised screech he slid from his chair into a heap on the floor.

"At noon on the following day he was missed from the house. A search was made in the grounds and in the neighbourhood, but he was nowhere to be found. At last someone thought of the cavern, of which he had spoken in his wild mutterings and a party of searchers made their way thither. And there they found him when the tide went out, lying on the wet sand with the brown sea-tangle wreathed about his limbs and the *laudanum* bottle—now full of sea water—by his side.

"With the death of Gilbert Lumley it seemed that the murdered man's spirit was appeased. During the lifetime of Gilbert's son, Thomas, the departed Glynn made no sign. But on his death and the succession of his son Arthur—then a middle-aged man—the visitations began again, and in the same order. At the end of the first month the luminous bat appeared; at the end of the second, the inverted head made its entry, and again at the third and the fourth months; and within twenty-four hours of the last visitation, the body of Arthur Lumley was found in the cavern. And so it has been from that time onward. One generation escapes untouched by the curse; but in the next, Glynn and the sea claim their own."

"Is that true, so far as you know?" asked Thorndyke.

"I can't say," answered Brodribb. "I am now only quoting Walter Lumley's infernal little book. But I remember that, in fact, Giles' father was drowned. I understood that his boat capsized, but that may have been only a story to cover the suicide.

"Well now, I have given you the gruesome history from this book that poor Frank had the misfortune to find. You see that had had it all off by heart and had evidently read it again and again. Now I come to his own story, which he told me very quietly but with intense conviction and very evident forebodings.

"He found this damned book a few days after his arrival at Burling Court, and it was clear to him that, if the story was true, he was the next victim, since his predecessor, Giles, had been left in peace. And so it turned out. Exactly a month after his arrival, going up to his bedroom in the dark—no doubt expecting this apparition—as soon as he opened the door he saw a thing like a big glow-worm or firefly flitting round the room. It is evident that he was a good deal upset, for he rushed downstairs in a state of great agitation and fetched Price up to see it. But the strange thing was—though perhaps not so very strange, after all—that, although the thing was still there, flitting about the room, Price could see nothing. However, he pulled up the blind—the window was wide open—and the bat flopped out and disappeared.

"During the next month the bat reappeared several times, in the bedroom, in corridors and once in a garret, when it flew out as Frank opened the door."

"What was he doing in the garret?" asked Thorndyke.

"He went up to fetch an ancient coffin-stool that Mrs. Price had seen there and was telling him about. Well, this went on until the end of the second month. And then came the second act. It seems that by some infernal stupidity, he was occupying the bedroom that had been used by Gilbert. Now on this night, as soon as he had gone up, he must needs pay a visit to the little dressing-room, which is now known as Gilbert's cabin'—so he tells me, for I was not aware of it—and where Gilbert's cutlass, telescope, quadrant and the old navigator's watch are kept."

"Did he take a light with him?" inquired Thorndyke.

"I think not. There is a gas jet in the corridor and presumably he lit that. Then he opened the door of the cabin; and immediately he saw, a few feet in front of him, a man's head, upside down, apparently hanging in mid-air. It gave him a fearful shock—the more so, perhaps, because he half expected it—and, as before, he ran downstairs, all of a tremble. Price had gone to bed but Mrs. Price came up with him, and he showed her the horrible thing which was still hanging in the middle of the dark room.

"But Mrs. Price could see nothing. She assured him that it was all his imagination; and in proof of it, she walked into the room, right through the head, as it seemed, and when she had found the matches, she lit the gas. Of course, there was nothing whatever in the room.

"Another month passed. The bat appeared at intervals and kept poor Frank's nerves in a state of constant tension. On the night of the appointed day, as you will anticipate, Frank went again to Gilbert's cabin, drawn there by an attraction that one can quite understand. And there, of course, was the confounded head as before. That was a fort-night ago. So, you see, the affair is getting urgent. Either there is some truth in this weird story—which I don't believe for a moment—or poor old Frank is ripe for the asylum. But in any case something will have to be done."

"You spoke just now," said Thorndyke, "of some insanity in the family. What does it amount to, leaving these apparitions out of the question?"

"Well, a cousin of Frank's committed suicide in an asylum."

"And Frank's parents?"

"They were quite sane. The cousin was the son of Frank's mother's sister; and she was all right, too. But the boy's father had to be put away."

"Then," said Thorndyke, "the insanity doesn't seem to be in Frank's family at all, in a medical sense. Legal inheritance and physiological inheritance do not follow the same lines. If his mother's sister married a lunatic, he might inherit that lunatic's property, but he could not inherit his insanity. There was no blood relationship."

"No, that's true," Brodribb admitted, "though Frank certainly seems as mad as a hatter. But now, to come back to the holiday question, what do you say to a week or so at St. David's?"

Thorndyke looked at me interrogatively. "What says my learned friend?" he asked.

"I say: Let us put up the shutters and leave Polton in charge," I replied; and Thorndyke assented without a murmur.

Less than a week later, we were installed in the very comfortable rooms that Mr. Brodribb had found for us in the hamlet of St. David's, within five minutes' walk of the steep gap-way that led down to the beach. Thorndyke entered into the holiday with an enthusiasm that would have astonished the denizens of King Bench Walk. He explored the village, he examined the church, inside and out, he sampled all the footpaths with the aid of the Ordnance map, he foregathered with the fishermen on the beach and renewed his acquaintance with boat-craft, and he made a pilgrimage to the historic cavern—it was less than a mile along the shore—and inspected its dark and chilly interior with the most lively curiosity.

We had not been at St. David's twenty-four hours before we made the acquaintance of Frank Lumley. Mr. Brodribb saw to that. For the old solicitor was profoundly anxious about his client—he took his responsibilities very seriously, did Mr. Brodribb. His "family" clients were to him as his own kin, and their interests his own interests—and his confidence in Thorndyke's wisdom was unbounded. We were very favourably impressed by the quiet, gentle, rather frail young man, and for my part, I found him, for a certifiable lunatic, a singularly reasonable and intelligent person. Indeed, apart from his delusions—or rather hallucinations—he seemed perfectly sane; for a somewhat eager interest in psychical and supernormal phenomena (of which he made no secret) is hardly enough to create a suspicion of a man's sanity.

But he was clearly uneasy about his own mental condition. He realised that the apparitions might be the products of a disordered brain, though that was not his own view of them; and he discussed them with us in the most open and ingenuous manner.

"You don't think," Thorndyke suggested, "that these apparitions may possibly be natural appearances which you have misinterpreted or exaggerated in consequence of having read that very circumstantial story?"

Lumley shook his head emphatically. "It is impossible," said he. "How could I? Take the case of the bat. I have seen it on several occasions quite distinctly. It was obviously a bat; but yet it seemed full of a ghostly, greenish light like that of a glow-worm. If it was not what it appeared, what was it? And then the head. There it was, perfectly clear and solid and real, hanging in mid-air within three or four feet of me. I could have touched it if I had dared."

"What size did it appear?" asked Thorndyke.

Lumley reflected. "It was not quite life-size. I should say about two-thirds the size of an ordinary head."

"Should you recognise the face if you saw it again?

"I can't say," replied Lumley. "You see, it was upside down. I haven't a very clear picture of it—I mean as to what the face would have been like the right way up."

"Was the room quite dark on both occasions?" Thorndyke asked.

"Yes, quite. The gas jet in the corridor is just above the door and does not any light into the room."

"And what is there opposite the door?"

"There is a small window, but that is usually kept shuttered nowadays. Under the window is a small folding dressing-table that belonged to Gilbert Lumley. He had it made when he came home from sea."

Thus Lumley was quite lucid and coherent in his answers. His manner was perfectly sane; it was only the matter that was abnormal. Of the reality of the apparitions he had not the slightest doubt, and he never varied in the smallest degree in his description of their appearance. The fact that they had been invisible both to Mr. Price and his wife he explained by pointing out that the curse applied only to the direct descendants of Gilbert Lumley, and to those only in alternate generations.

After one of our conversations, Thorndyke expressed a wish to see the little manuscript book that had been the cause of all the trouble—or at least had been the forerunner; and Lumley promised to bring it to our rooms on the following afternoon. But then came an interruption to our holiday, not entirely unexpected; an urgent telegram from one of our solicitor friends asking consultation on an important and intricate case that had just been put into his hands, and making it necessary for us to go up to town by an early train on the following morning.

We sent a note to Brodribb, telling him that we should be away from St. David's for perhaps a day or two, and on our way to the station he overtook us.

"I am sorry you have had to break your holiday," he said; "but I hope you will be back before Thursday."

"Why Thursday, in particular?" inquired Thorndyke.

"Because Thursday is the day on which that damned head is due to make its third appearance. It will be an anxious time. Frank hasn't said anything, but I know his nerves are strung up to concert pitch."

"You must watch him," said Thorndyke. "Don't let him out of your sight if you can help it."

"That's all very well," said Brodribb, "but he isn't a child, and I am not his keeper. He is the master of the house and I am just his guest. I can't follow him about if he wants to be alone."

"You mustn't stand on politeness, Brodribb," rejoined Thorndyke. "It will be a critical time and you must keep him in sight."

"I shall do my best," Brodribb said anxiously, "but I do hope you will be back by then."

He accompanied us dejectedly to the platform and stayed with us until our train came in. Suddenly, just as we were entering our carriage, he thrust his hand into his pocket.

"God bless me!" he exclaimed, "I had nearly forgotten this book. Frank asked me to give it to you." As he spoke, he drew out a little rusty calf-bound volume and handed it to Thorndyke. "You can look through it at your leisure," said he, "and if you think it best to chuck the infernal thing out of the window, do so. I suspect poor Frank is none the better for conning it over perpetually as he does."

I thought there was a good deal of reason in Brodribb's opinion. If Lumley's illusions were, as I suspected, the result of suggestion produced by reading the narrative, that suggestion would certainly tend to be reinforced by conning it over and over again. But the old lawyer's proposal was hardly practicable.

As soon as the train had fairly started, Thorndyke proceeded to inspect the little volume; and his manner of doing so was highly characteristic. An ordinary person would have opened the book and looked through the contents, probably seeking out at once the sinister history of Gilbert Lumley.

Not so Thorndyke. His inspection began at the very beginning and proceeded systematically to deal with every fact that the book had to disclose. First he made an exhaustive examination of the cover; scrutinised the corners; inspected the bottom edges and compared them with the top edges; and compared the top and bottom headcaps. Then he brought out his lens and examined the tooling, which was simple in character and worked in "blind"—i.e. not gilt. He also inspected the head-bands through the glass, and then he turned his attention to the interior. He looked carefully at both end-papers, he opened the sections and examined the sewing-thread, he held the leaves up to the light and tested the paper by eye and by touch and he viewed the writing in several places through his lens. Finally he handed the book and the lens to me without remark.

It was a quaint little volume, with a curiously antique air, though it was but a century old. The cover was of rusty calf, a good deal rubbed, but not in bad condition; for the joints were perfectly sound; but then it had probably had comparatively little use. The paper—a laid paper with very distinct wire-lines but no watermark—had turned with age to a pale, creamy buff; the writing had faded to a warm brown, but was easily legible and very clearly and carefully written. Having noted these points, I turned over the leaves until I came to the story of Gilbert Lumley and the ill-fated Glynn, which I read through attentively, observing that Mr. Brodribb's notes had given the whole substance of the narrative with singular completeness.

"This story," I said, as I handed the book back to Thorndyke, "strikes me as rather unreal and unconvincing. One doesn't see how Walter Lumley got his information."

"No," agreed Thorndyke. "It is on the plane of fiction. The narrator speaks in the manner of a novelist with complete knowledge of events and actions which were apparently known only to the actors."

"Do you think it possible that Walter Lumley was simply romancing?"

"I think it quite possible, and in fact very probable that the whole narrative is fictitious," he replied. "We shall have to go into that question later on. For the present, I suppose, we had better give our attention to the case that we have in hand at the moment."

The little volume was accordingly put away, and for the rest of the journey our conversation was occupied with the matter of the consultation that formed our immediate business. As this, however, had no connection with the present history, I need make no further reference to it beyond stating that it kept us both busy for three days and that we finished with it on the evening of the third.

"Do you propose to go down to St. David's tonight or tomorrow?" I asked, as we let ourselves into our chambers.

"Tonight," replied Thorndyke. "This is Thursday, you know, and Brodribb was anxious that we should be back some time today. I have sent him a telegram saying that we shall go down by the train that arrives about ten o'clock. So if he wants us, he can meet us it the station or send a message."

"I wonder," said I, "if the apparition of Glynn's head will make its expected visitation tonight."

"It probably will if there is an opportunity," Thorndyke replied. "But I hope that Brodribb will manage to prevent the opportunity from occurring. And, talking of Lumley, as we have an hour to spare, we may as well finish our inspection of his book. I snipped off a corner of one of the leaves and gave it to Polton to boil up in weak caustic soda. It will be ready for examination by now."

"You don't suspect that the book has been faked, do you?" said I.

"I view that book with the deepest suspicion," he replied, opening a drawer and producing the little volume. "Just look at it, Jervis. Look at the cover, for instance."

"Well," I said, turning the book over in my hand, "the cover looks ancient enough to me; typical old, rusty calf with a century's wear on it."

"Oh, there's no doubt that it is old calf," said he; "just the sort of leather that you could skin off the cover of an old *quarto* or folio. But don't you see that the signs of wear are all in the wrong places? How does a book wear in use? Well, first there are the bottom edges, which rub on the shelf. Then the corners, which are the thinnest leather and the most exposed. Then the top head-cap, which the finger hooks into in pulling the book from the shelf. Then the joint or hinge, which wears through from frequent opening and shutting. The sides get the least wear of all. But in this book, the bottom edges, the corners, the top head-cap and the joints are perfectly sound. They are not more worn than the sides; and the tooling is modern in character. It looks quite fresh and the tool-marks are impressed on the marks of wear instead of being themselves worn. The appearances suggest to me a new binding with old leather.

"Then look at the paper. It professes to be discoloured by age. But the discoloration of the leaves of an old book occurs principally at the edges, where the paper has become oxidised by exposure to the air. The leaves of this book are equally discoloured all over. To me they suggest a bath of weak tea rather than old age.

"Again, there is the writing. Its appearance is that of faded writing done with the old-fashioned writing ink—made with iron sulphate and oak-galls. But it doesn't look quite the right colour. However, we can easily test that. If it is old iron-gall ink, a drop of ammonium sulphide will turn it black. Let us take the book up to the laboratory and try it—and we had better have a "control" to compare it with."

He ran his eye along the book-shelves and took down a rusty-looking volume of *Humphry Clinker*, the end-paper of which bore several brown and faded signatures.

"Here is a signature dated 1803," said he. "That will be near enough;" and with the two books in his hand he led the way upstairs to the laboratory. Here he took down the ammonium sulphide bottle, and dipping up a little of the liquid in a fine glass tube, opened the cover of *Humphry Clinker* and carefully deposited a tiny drop on the figure 3 in the date. Almost immediately the ghostly brown began to darken until it at length became jet black. Then, in the same way, he opened Walter Lumley's manuscript book and on the 9th of the date, 1819, he deposited a drop of the solution. But this time there was no darkening of the pale brown writing; on the contrary, it faded rapidly to a faint and muddy violet.

"It is not an iron ink," said Thorndyke, "and it looks suspiciously like an aniline brown. But let us see what the paper is made of. Have you boiled up that fragment, Polton?"

"Yes, sir," answered our laboratory assistant, "and I've washed the soda out of it, so it's all ready."

He produced a labelled test-tube containing a tiny corner of paper floating in water, which he carefully emptied into a large watch-glass. From this Thorndyke transferred the little pulpy fragment to a microscope slide and, with a pair of mounted needles, broke it up into its constituent fibres. Then he dropped on it a drop of aniline stain, removed the surplus with blotting-paper, added a drop of glycerine and put on it a large cover-slip.

"There, Jervis," said he, handing me the slide, "let us have your opinion on Walter Lumley's paper."

I placed the slide on the stage of the microscope and proceeded to inspect the specimen. But no exhaustive examination was necessary. The first glance settled the matter.

"It is nearly all wood," I said. "Mechanical wood fibre, with some esparto, a little cotton and a few linen fibres."

"Then," said Thorndyke, "it is a modern paper. Mechanical wood-pulp—prepared by Keller's process—was first used in paper-making in 1840. 'Chemical wood-pulp' came in later; and *esparto* was not used until 1860. So we can say with confidence that this paper was not made until more than twenty years after the date that is written on it. Probably it is of quite recent manufacture."

"In that case," said I, "this book is a counterfeit—presumably fraudulent."

"Yes. In effect it is a forgery."

"But that seems to suggest a conspiracy."

"It does," Thorndyke agreed; "especially if it is considered in conjunction with the apparitions. The suggestion is that this book was prepared for the purpose of inducing a state of mind favourable to the acceptance of supernatural appearances. The obvious inference is that the apparitions themselves were an imposture produced for fraudulent purposes. But it is time for us to go."

We shook hands with Polton, and, having collected our suit-cases from the sitting-room, set forth for the station.

During the journey down I reflected on the new turn that Frank Lumley's affairs had taken. Apparently, Brodribb had done his client an injustice. Lumley was not so mad as the old lawyer had supposed. He was merely credulous and highly suggestible. The "hallucinations" were real phenomena which he had simply misinterpreted. But who was behind these sham illusions? And what was it all about? I tried to open the question with Thorndyke; but though he was willing to discuss the sham manuscript book and the technique of its production, he would commit himself to nothing further.

On our arrival at St. David's, Thorndyke looked up and down the platform and again up the station approach. "No sign of Brodribb or any messenger," he remarked, "so we may assume that all is well at Burling Court up to the present. Let us hope that Brodribb's presence has had an inhibitory effect on the apparitions."

Nevertheless, it was evident that he was not quite easy in his mind. During supper he appeared watchful and preoccupied, and when, after the meal, he proposed a stroll down to the beach, he left word with our landlady as to where he was to be found if he should be wanted.

It was about a quarter to eleven when we arrived at the shore, and the tide was beginning to run out. The beach was deserted with the exception of a couple of fishermen who had apparently come in with the tide and who were making their boat secure for the night before going home. Thorndyke approached them, and addressing the older fisherman, remarked: "That is a big, powerful boat. Pretty fast, too, isn't she?"

"Ay, sir," was the reply; "fast and weatherly, she is. What we calls a galley-punt. Built at Deal for the hovelling trade—salvage, you know, sir—but there ain't no hovelling nowadays, not to speak of."

"Are you going out tomorrow?" asked Thorndyke.

"Not as I knows of, sir. Was you thinking of a bit of fishing?"

"If you are free," said Thorndyke, "I should like to charter the boat for tomorrow. I don't know what time I shall be able to start, but if you will stand by ready to put off at once when I come down we can count the waiting as sailing."

"Very well, sir," said the fisherman; "the boat's yours for the day tomorrow. Any time after six, or earlier, if you like, if you come down here you'll find me and my mate standing by with a stock of bait and the boat ready to push off."

"That will do admirably," said Thorndyke; and the morrow's programme being thus settled, we wished the fishermen goodnight and walked slowly back to our lodgings, where, after a final pipe, we turned in.

On the following morning, just as we were finishing a rather leisurely breakfast, we saw from our window our friend Mr. Brodribb hurrying down the street towards our house. I ran out and opened the door, and as he entered I conducted him into our sitting-room. From his anxious and flustered manner it was obvious that something had gone wrong, and his first words confirmed the sinister impression.

"I'm afraid we're in for trouble, Thorndyke," said he. "Frank is missing."

"Since when?" asked Thorndyke.

"Since about eight o'clock this morning. He is nowhere about the house and he hasn't had any breakfast."

"When was he last seen?" Thorndyke asked. "And where?"

"About eight o'clock, in the breakfast-room. Apparently he went in there to say "goodbye" to the Prices—they have gone on a visit for the day to Folkestone and were having an early breakfast so as to catch the eight-thirty train. But he didn't have breakfast with them. He just went in and wished them a pleasant journey and then it appears that he went out for a stroll in the grounds. When I came down to breakfast at half-past eight, the Prices had gone and Frank hadn't come in. The maid sounded the gong, and as Frank still did not appear, she went out into the grounds to look for him; and presently I went out myself. But he wasn't there and he wasn't anywhere in the house. I don't like the look of it at all. He is usually very regular and punctual at meals. What do you think we had better do, Thorndyke?"

My colleague looked at his watch and rang the bell.

"I think, Brodribb," said he, "that we must act on the obvious probabilities and provide against the one great danger that is known to us. Mrs. Robinson," he added, addressing the landlady, who, had answered the bell in person, "can you let us have a jug of strong coffee at once?"

Mrs. Robinson could, and bustled away to prepare it, while Thorndyke produced from a cupboard a large vacuum flask.

"I don't quite follow you, Thorndyke," said Mr. Brodribb. "What probabilities and what danger do you mean?"

"I mean that, up to the present, Frank Lumley has exactly reproduced in his experiences and his actions the experiences and actions of Gilbert Lumley as set forth in Walter Lumley's narrative. The overwhelming probability is that he will continue to reproduce the story of Gilbert to the end. He probably saw the apparition for the third time last night, and is even now preparing for the final act."

"Good God!" gasped Brodribb. "What a fool I am! You mean the cave? But we can never get there now. It will be high water in an hour and the beach at St. David's Head will be covered already. Unless we can get a boat," he added despairingly.

"We have got a boat," said Thorndyke. "I chartered one last night."

"Thank the Lord!" exclaimed Brodribb. "But you always think of everything—though I don't know what you want that coffee for."

"We may not want it at all," said Thorndyke, as he poured the coffee, which the landlady had just brought, into the vacuum flask, "but on the other hand we may."

He deposited the flask in a hand-bag, in which I observed a small emergency-case, and then turned to Brodribb.

"We had better get down to the beach now," said he.

As we emerged from the bottom of the gap-way we saw our friends of the previous night laying a double line of planks across the beach from the boat to the margin of the surf; for the long galley-punt, with her load of ballast, was too heavy, over the shingle. They had just got the last plank laid as we reached the boat, and as they observed us they came running back with half a dozen of their mates.

"Jump aboard, gentlemen," said our skipper, with a slightly dubious eye on Mr. Brodribb—for the boat's gunwale was a good four feet above the beach. "We'll have her afloat in a jiffy."

We climbed in and hauled Mr. Brodribb in after us. The tall mast was already stepped—against the middle thwart in the odd fashion of galley-punts—and the great sail was hooked to the traveller and the tack-hook ready for hoisting. The party of boatmen gathered round and each took a tenacious hold of gunwale or thole. The skipper gave time with a jovial "Yo-ho!" His mates joined in with a responsive howl and heaved as one man. The great boat moved forward, and gathering way, slid swiftly along the greased planks towards the edge of the surf. Then her nose splashed into the sea; the skipper and his mate sprang in over the transom; the tall lug-sail soared up the mast and filled and the skipper let the rudder slide down its pintles and grasped the tiller.

"Did you want to go anywheres in particklar?" he inquired.

"We want to make for the big cave round St. David's Head," said Thorndyke, " and we want to get there well before high water."

"We'll do that easy enough, sir," said the skipper "with this breeze. 'Tis but about a mile and we've got three-quarters of an hour to do it in."

He took a pull at the main sheet and, putting the helm down, brought the boat on a course parallel to the coast. Quietly but swiftly the water slipped past, one after another fresh headlands opened out till, in about a quarter of an hour, we were abreast of St. David's Head with the sinister black shape of the cavern in full view over the port bow. Shortly afterwards the sail was lowered and our crew, reinforced by Thorndyke and me, took to the oars, pulling straight towards the shore with the cavern directly ahead.

As the boat grounded on the beach Thorndyke, Brodribb and I sprang out and hurried across the sand and shingle to the gloomy and forbidding hole in white cliff. At first, coming out of the bright sunlight we seemed to be plunged in absolute darkness, and groped our way insecurely over the heaps of slippery sea-tangle that littered

225

the floor. Presently our eyes grew accustomed to the dim light, and we could trace faintly the narrow, tunnel-like passage with its slimy green and the jagged roof nearly black with age. At the farther end it grew higher; and here I could see the small, dark bodies of bats hanging from the roof and clinging to the walls, and one or two fluttering blindly and noiselessly like large moths in the hollows of the vault above. But it was not the bats that engrossed my attention.

Far away, at the extreme end, I could dimly discern the prostrate figure of a man lying motionless on a patch of smooth sand; a dreadful shape that seemed to sound the final note of tragedy to which the darkness, the clammy chill of the cavern and the ghostly forms of he bats had been a fitting prelude.

"My God!" gasped Brodribb, "we're too late!" He broke into a shambling run and Thorndyke and I darted on ahead. The man was Frank Lumley, of course, and a glance at him gave us at least a ray of hope. He was lying in an easy posture with closed eyes and was still breathing, though his respiration was shallow and slow. Beside him on the sand lay a little bottle and near it a cork. I picked up the former and read on the label "*Laudanum*: Poison" and a local druggist's name and address. But it was empty save for a few drops, the appearance and smell of which confirmed the label.

Thorndyke, who had been examining the unconscious man's eyes with a little electric lamp, glanced at the bottle.

"Well," said he, "we know the worst. That is a two-*drachm* phial, so if he took the lot his condition is not hopeless."

As he spoke he opened the hand-bag, and taking out the emergency-case, produced from it a hypodermic syringe and a tiny bottle of *atropine* solution. I drew up Lumley's sleeve while the syringe was filled and Thorndyke then administered the injection.

"It is opium poisoning, I suppose?" said I.

"Yes," was the answer. "His pupils are like pin points; but his pulse is not so bad. I think we can safely move him down to the boat."

Thereupon we lifted him, and with Brodribb supporting his feet, we moved in melancholy procession down the cave. Already the waves were lapping the beach at the entrance and even trickling in amongst the seaweed; and the boat, following the rising tide, had her bows within the cavern. The two fishermen, who were steadying the boat with their oars, greeted our appearance, carrying the body, with exclamations of astonishment. But they asked no questions, simply taking the unconscious man from us and laying him gently on the grating in the stern-sheets.

"Why, 'tis Mr. Lumley!" exclaimed the skipper.

"Yes," said Thorndyke; and having given them a few words of explanation, he added: "I look to you to keep this affair to yourselves."

To this the two men agreed heartily, and the boat having been pushed off and the sail hoisted, the skipper asked: "Do we sail straight back, sir?"

"Yes," replied Thorndyke, "but we won't land yet. Stand on and off opposite the gap-way."

Already, as a result of the movement, the patient's stupor appeared less profound. And now Thorndyke took definite measures to rouse him, shaking him gently and constantly changing his position. Presently Lumley drew a deep sighing breath, and opened his eyes for a moment. Then Thorndyke sat him up, and producing the vacuum-flask, made him swallow a few teaspoonful of coffee. This procedure was continued for over an hour while the boat cruised up and down opposite the landing-place half a mile or so from the shore. Constantly our patient relapsed into stuporous sleep, only to be roused again and given a sip of coffee.

At length he recovered so far as to be able to sit up—lurching from side to side as the boat rolled—and drowsily answer questions spoken loudly in his ears. A quarter of an hour later, as he still continued to improve, Thorndyke ordered the skipper to bring the boat to the landing-place.

"I think he could walk now," said he, "and the exercise will rouse him more completely."

The boat was accordingly beached and Lumley assisted to climb out; and though at first he staggered as if he would fall, after a few paces he was able to walk fairly steadily, supported on either side by me and Thorndyke. The effort of ascending the steep gap-way revived him further; and by the time we reached the gate of Burling Court— half a mile across the fields—he was almost able to stand alone.

But even when he had arrived home he was not allowed to rest, earnestly as he begged to be left in peace. First Thorndyke insisted on his taking a light meal, and then proceeded to question him as to the events of the previous night.

"I presume, Lumley," said he, "that you saw the apparition of Glynn's head?"

"Yes. After Mr. Brodribb had seen me to bed, I got up and went to Gilbert's cabin. Something seemed to draw me to it. And as soon as I opened the door, there was the head hanging in the air within three feet of me. Then I knew that Glynn was calling me, and—well, you know the rest."

"I understand," said Thorndyke. "But now I want you to come to Gilbert's cabin with me and show me exactly where you were and where the head was."

Lumley was profoundly reluctant and tried to postpone the demonstration. But Thorndyke would listen to no refusal, and at last Lumley rose wearily and conducted his tormentor up the stairs, followed by Brodribb and me.

We went first to Lumley's bedroom and from that into a corridor, into which some other bedrooms opened. The corridor was dimly lighted by a single window, and when Thorndyke had drawn the thick curtain over this, the place was almost completely dark. At one end of the corridor was the small, narrow door of the "cabin," over which was a gas bracket. Thorndyke lighted the gas and opened the door and we then saw that the room was in total darkness, its only window being closely shuttered and the curtains drawn. Thorndyke struck a match and lit the gas and we then looked curiously about the little room.

It was a quaint little apartment, to which its antique furniture and contents gave an old-world air. An ancient hanger, quadrant and spy-glass hung on the wall, a large, dropsical-looking watch, inscribed "Thomas Tompion, *Londini fecit*," reposed on a little velvet cushion in the middle of a small, black mahogany table by the window, and a couple of Cromwellian chairs stood against the wall. Thorndyke looked curiously at the table, which was raised on wooden blocks, and Lumley explained: "That was Gilbert's dressing-table. He had it made for his cabin on board ship."

"Indeed," said Thorndyke. "Then Gilbert was a rather up-to-date gentleman. There wasn't much mahogany furniture before 1720. Let us have a look I at the interior arrangements."

He lifted the watch, and having placed it on a chair, raised the lid of the table, disclosing a small wash basin, a little squat ewer and other toilet appliances. The table lid, which was held upright by a brass strut, held a rather large dressing-mirror enclosed in a projecting case.

"I wonder," said I, "why the table was stood on those blocks."

"Apparently," said Thorndyke, "for the purpose of bringing the mirror to the eye-level of a person standing up."

The answer gave Brodribb an idea. "I suppose, Frank," said he, "it was not your own reflection in the mirror that you saw?"

"How could it be?" demanded Lumley. "The head was upside down, and besides, it was quite near to me."

"No, that's true," said Brodribb; and turning away from the table he picked up the old navigator's watch. "A queer old timepiece, this," he remarked.

"Yes," said Lumley; "but it's beautifully made. Let me show you the inside."

He took off the outer case and opened the inner one, exhibiting the delicate workmanship of the interior to Brodribb and me, while Thorndyke continued to pore over the inner fittings of the table. Suddenly my colleague said: "Just go outside, you three, and shut the door. I want to try an experiment."

Obediently we all filed out and closed the door, waiting expectantly in the corridor. In a couple of minutes Thorndyke came out and before he shut the door I noticed that the little room was now in darkness. He walked us a short distance down the corridor and then, halting, said:

"Now, Lumley, I want you to go into the cabin and tell us what you see."

Lumley appeared a little reluctant to go in alone, but eventually he walked towards the cabin and opened the door. Instantly he uttered a cry of horror, and closing the door, ran back to us, trembling, agitated, wild-eyed.

"It is there now!" he exclaimed. "I saw it distinctly."

"Very well," said Thorndyke. "Now you go and look, Brodribb."

Mr. Brodribb showed no eagerness. With very obvious trepidation he advanced to the door and threw it open with a jerk. Then, with a sharp exclamation, he slammed it to, and came hurrying back, his usually pink complexion paled down to a delicate mauve.

"Horrible! Horrible!" he exclaimed. "What the devil is it, Thorndyke?"

A sudden suspicion flashed into my mind. I strode forward, and turning the handle of the door, pulled it open. And then I was not surprised that Brodribb had been startled. Within a yard of my face, clear, distinct and solid, was an inverted head, floating in mid-air in the pitch-dark room. Of course, being prepared for it, I saw at a glance what it was; recognised my own features, strangely and horribly altered as they were by their inverted position. But even now that I knew what it was, the thing had a most appalling, uncanny aspect.

"Now," said Thorndyke, "let us go in and explode the mystery. Just stand outside the door, Jervis, while I demonstrate."

He produced a sheet of white paper from his pocket, and smoothing it out, let our two friends into the room.

First," said he, holding the paper out flat at the eye-level, "you see on this paper a picture of Dr. Jervis's head upside down."

"So there is," said Brodribb; "like a magic-lantern picture."

"Exactly like," agreed Thorndyke; "and of exactly the same nature. Now let us see how it is produced."

He struck a match and lit the gas; and instantly all our eyes turned towards the open dressing-table.

"But that is not the same mirror that we saw just now," said Brodribb.

"No," replied Thorndyke. "The frame is reversible on a sliding hinge and I have turned it round. On one side is the ordinary flat looking-glass which you saw before; on the other is this concave shaving-mirror. You observe that, if you stand close to it, you see your face the right way up and magnified; if you go back to the door, you see your head upside down and smaller."

"But," objected Lumley, "the head looked quite solid and seemed to be right out in the room."

"So it was, and is still. But the effect of reality is destroyed by the fact that you can now see the frame of the mirror enclosing the image, so that the head appears to be in the mirror. But in the dark, you could only see the image. The mirror was invisible."

Brodribb reflected on this explanation. Presently he said: "I don't think I quite understand it now."

Thorndyke took a pencil from his pocket and began to draw a diagram on the sheet of paper that he still held.

"The figure that you see in an ordinary flat looking glass," he explained, "is what is called a 'virtual image.' It appears to be behind the mirror, but of course it is not there. It is an optical illusion. But the image from a concave mirror is in front of the mirror and is a real image like that of a magic-lantern or a camera, and, like them, inverted. This diagram will explain matters. Here is Lumley standing at the open door of the room. His figure is well lighted by the gas over the door (which, however, throws no light into the room) and is clearly reflected by the mirror, which throws forward a bright inverted image. But, as the room is dark and the mirror invisible, he sees only the image, which looks like—and in fact is—a real object standing in mid-air."

"But why did I see only the head?" asked Lumley.

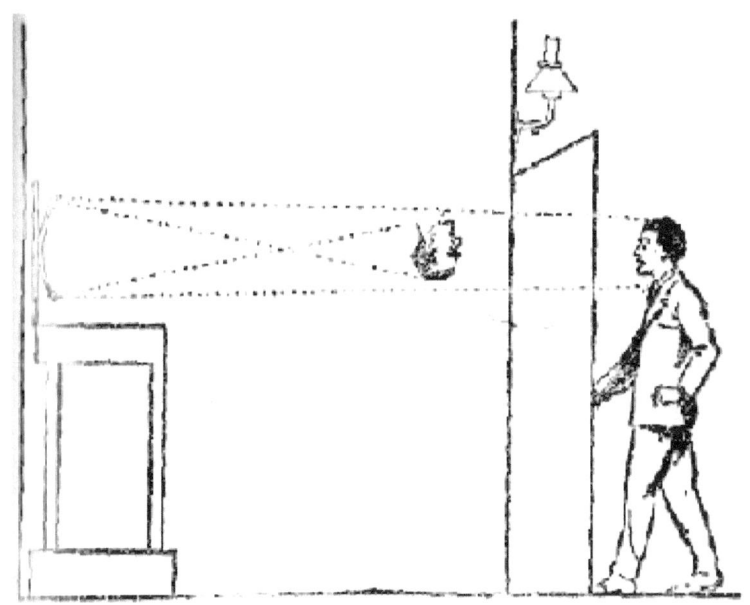

THE APPARITION OF BURLING COURT.

"Because the head occupied the whole of the mirror. If the mirror had been large enough you would have seen the full-length figure."

Lumley reflected for a moment. "It almost looks if this had been arranged," he said at length.

"Of course it has been arranged," said Thorndyke "and very cleverly arranged, too. And now let us go and see if anything else has been arranged. Which is Mr. Price's room?"

"He has three rooms, which open out of this corridor," said Lumley; and he conducted us to a door at the farther end, which Thorndyke tried and found locked.

"It is a case for the smoker's companion," said he, producing from his pocket an instrument that went by that name, but which looked suspiciously like a lock-pick. At any rate, after one or two trials—which Mr Brodribb watched with an appreciative smile—the bolt shot back and the door opened.

We entered what was evidently the bedroom, around which Thorndyke cast a rapid glance and then asked: "What are the other rooms?"

"I think he uses them to tinker in," said Lumley, "but I don't quite know what he does in them. All three rooms communicate."

We advanced to the door of communication and, finding it un-

231

locked, passed through into the next room. Here, on a large table by the window, was a litter of various tools and appliances.

"What is that thing with the wooden screws?" Brodribb asked.

"A bookbinder's sewing-press," replied Thorndyke. "And here are some boxes of finishing tools. Let us look over them."

He took up the boxes one after the other and inspected the ends of the tools—brass stamps for impressing the ornaments on book covers. Presently he lifted out two, a leaf and a flower. Then he produced from his coat pocket the little manuscript book, and laying it on the table, picked up from the floor a little fragment of leather. Placing this also on the table, he pressed two of the tools on it, leaving a clear impression of a leaf and a flower. Finally he laid the scrap of leather on the book, when it was obvious that the leaf and flower were identical replicas of the leaves and flowers which formed the decoration of the book cover.

"This is very curious," said Lumley. "They seem to be exactly alike."

"They are exactly alike," said Thorndyke. "I affirm that the tooling on that book was done with these tools, and the leaves sewn on that press."

"But the book is a hundred years old," objected Lumley.

Thorndyke shook his head. "The leather is old," said he, "but the book is new. We have tested the paper and found it to be of recent manufacture. But now let us see what is in that little cupboard. There seem to be some bottles there."

He ran his eye along the shelves, crowded with bottles and jars of varnish, glair, oil, cement and other material.

"Here," he said, taking down a small bottle of dark-coloured powder, "is some aniline brown. That probably produced the ancient and faded writing. But this is more illuminating—in more senses than one." He picked out a little, wide-mouthed bottle labelled "Radium Paint for the hands and figures of luminous watches."

"Ha!" exclaimed Brodribb; "a very illuminating discovery, as you say."

"And that," said Thorndyke, looking keenly round the room, "seems to be all there is here. Shall we take a glance at the third room?"

We passed through the communicating doorway and found ourselves in a small apartment practically unfurnished and littered with trunks, bags and various lumber. As we stood looking about us, Thorndyke sniffed suspiciously.

"I seem to detect a sort of mousy odour," said he, glancing round inquisitively. "Do you notice it, Jervis?"

I did; and with the obvious idea in my mind began I to prowl round the room in search of the source, Suddenly my eye lighted on a smallish box, in the top of which a number of gimlet-holes had been bored. I raised the lid and peered in. The interior was covered with filth and on the bottom lay a dead bat.

We all stood for a few seconds looking in silence at the little corpse. Then Thorndyke closed the box and tucked it under his arm.

"This completes the case, I think," said he. "What time does Price return?"

"He is expected home about seven o'clock," said Lumley. Then he added with a troubled expression: "I don't understand all this. What does it mean?"

"It is very simple," replied Thorndyke. "You have a sham ancient book containing an evidently fabulous story of supernatural events; and you have a series of appliances and arrangements for producing illusions which seem to repeat those events. The book was planted where it was certain to be found and read, and the illusions began after it was known that it actually had been read. It is a conspiracy."

"But why?" demanded Lumley. "What was the object?"

"My dear Frank," said Brodribb, "you seem forget that Price is the next of kin and the heir to your estate on your death."

Lumley's eyes filled. He seemed overcome with grief and disgust. "It is incredible," he murmured huskily. "The baseness of it is beyond belief."

Price and his wife arrived home at about seven o'clock, A meal had been prepared for them, and when they had finished, a servant was sent in to ask Mr. Price to speak with Mr. Brodribb in the study. There we all awaited him, Lumley being present by his own wish; and on the table were deposited the little book, the scrap of leather, the two finishing tools, the pot of radium paint and the box containing the dead bat. Presently Price entered, accompanied by his wife; and at the sight of the objects on the table they both turned deathly pale. Mr. Brodribb placed chairs for them, and when they were seated he began in a dry, stern voice:

"I have sent for you, Mr. Price, to give you certain information. These two gentlemen, Dr. Thorndyke and Dr. Jervis, are eminent criminal lawyers whom I have commissioned to make investigations and to advise me in this matter. Their investigations have disclosed the existence of a forged manuscript, a dead bat, a pot of luminous paint and a concave mirror. I need not enlarge on those discoveries. My intention is to prosecute you and your wife for conspiracy to procure the suicide of Mr. Frank Lumley. But, at Mr. Lumley's request, I have consented to delay the proceedings for forty-eight hours. During that period you will be at liberty to act as you think best."

For some seconds there was a tense silence. The two crestfallen conspirators sat with their eyes fixed on the floor, and Mrs. Price choked down a half-hysterical sob. Then they rose; and Price, without looking at any of us, said in a low voice: "Very well. Then I suppose we had better clear out."

"And the best thing, too," remarked Brodribb, when they had gone; "for I doubt if we could have carried our bluff into court."

On the wall of our sitting-room in the Temple there hang, to this day, two keys. One is that of the postern gate of Burling Court, and the other belongs to the suite of rooms that were once occupied by Mr. Lewis Price; and they hang there, by Frank Lumley's wish, as a token that Burling Court is a country home to which we have access at all hours and seasons as tenants in virtue of an inalienable right.

The Blue Sequin

Thorndyke stood looking up and down the platform with anxiety that increased as the time drew near for the departure of the train.

"This is very unfortunate," he said, reluctantly stepping into an empty smoking compartment as the guard executed a flourish with his green flag. "I am afraid we have missed our friend." He closed the door, and, as the train began to move, thrust his head out of the window.

"Now I wonder if that will be he," he continued. "If so, he has caught the train by the skin of his teeth, and is now in one of the rear compartments."

The subject of Thorndyke's speculations was Mr. Edward Stopford, of the firm of Stopford and Myers, of Portugal Street, solicitors, and his connection with us at present arose out of a telegram that had reached our chambers on the preceding evening. It was reply-paid, and ran thus:

Can you come here tomorrow to direct defence? Important case. All costs undertaken by us.—Stopford and Myers.

Thorndyke's reply had been in the affirmative, and early on this present morning a further telegram—evidently posted overnight— had been delivered:

Shall leave for Woldhurst by 8.25 from Charing Cross. Will call for you if possible. Edward Stopford.

He had not called, however, and, since he was unknown personally to us both, we could not judge whether or not he had been among the passengers on the platform.

"It is most unfortunate," Thorndyke repeated, "for it deprives us of that preliminary consideration of the case which is so invaluable."

235

He filled his pipe thoughtfully, and, having made a fruitless inspection of the platform at London Bridge, took up the paper that he had bought at the bookstall, and began to turn over the leaves, running his eye quickly down the columns, unmindful of the journalistic baits in paragraph or article.

"It is a great disadvantage," he observed, while still glancing through the paper, "to come plump into an inquiry without preparation—to be confronted with the details before one has a chance of considering the case in general terms. For instance—"

He paused, leaving the sentence unfinished, and as I looked up inquiringly I saw that he had turned over another page, and was now reading attentively.

"This looks like our case, Jervis," he said presently, handing me the paper and indicating a paragraph at the top of the page. It was quite brief, and was headed "Terrible Murder in Kent," the account being as follows:

A shocking crime was discovered yesterday morning at the little town of Woldhurst, which lies on the branch line from Halbury Junction. The discovery was made by a porter who was inspecting the carriages of the train which had just come in. On opening the door of a first-class compartment, he was horrified to find the body of a fashionably-dressed woman stretched upon the floor. Medical aid was immediately summoned, and on the arrival of the divisional surgeon, Dr. Morton, it was ascertained that the woman had not been dead more than a few minutes. The state of the corpse leaves no doubt that a murder of a most brutal kind has been perpetrated, the cause of death being a penetrating wound of the head, inflicted with some pointed implement, which must have been used with terrible violence, since it has perforated the skull and entered the brain. That robbery was not the motive of the crime is made clear by the fact that an expensively fitted dressing-bag was found on the rack, and that the dead woman's jewellery, including several valuable diamond rings, was untouched. It is rumoured that an arrest has been made by the local police.

"A gruesome affair," I remarked, as I handed back the paper, "but the report does not give us much information."

"It does not," Thorndyke agreed, "and yet it gives us something to consider. Here is a perforating wound of the skull, inflicted with some pointed implement—that is, assuming that it is not a bullet wound. Now, what kind of implement would be capable of inflicting such an injury? How would such an implement be used in the confined space of a railway-carriage, and what sort of person would be in possession of such an implement? These are preliminary questions that are worth considering, and I commend them to you, together with the further problems of the possible motive—excluding robbery—and any circumstances other than murder which might account for the injury."

"The choice of suitable implements is not very great," I observed.

"It is very limited, and most of them, such as a plasterer's pick or a geological hammer, are associated with certain definite occupations. You have a notebook?"

I had, and, accepting the hint, I produced it and pursued my further reflections in silence, while my companion, with his notebook also on his knee, gazed steadily out of the window. And thus he remained, wrapped in thought, jotting down an entry now and again in his book, until the train slowed down at Halbury Junction, where we had to change on to a branch line.

As we stepped out, I noticed a well-dressed man hurrying up the platform from the rear and eagerly scanning the faces of the few passengers who had alighted. Soon he espied us, and, approaching quickly, asked, as he looked from one of us to the other:

"Dr. Thorndyke?"

"Yes," replied my colleague, adding: "And you, I presume, are Mr. Edward Stopford?"

The solicitor bowed. "This is a dreadful affair," he said, in an agitated manner. "I see you have the paper. A most shocking affair. I am immensely relieved to find you here. Nearly missed the train, and feared I should miss you."

"There appears to have been an arrest," Thorndyke began.

"Yes—my brother. Terrible business. Let us walk up the platform; our train won't start for a quarter of an hour yet."

We deposited our joint Gladstone and Thorndyke's travelling-case in an empty first-class compartment, and then, with the solicitor between us, strolled up to the unfrequented end of the platform.

"My brother's position," said Mr. Stopford, "fills me with dismay—but let me give you the facts in order, and you shall judge for yourself. This poor creature who has been murdered so brutally was a Miss Edith Grant. She was formerly an artist's model, and as such was a good deal employed by my brother, who is a painter—Harold Stopford, you know, A.R.A. now—"

"I know his work very well, and charming work it is."

"I think so, too. Well, in those days he was quite a youngster—about twenty—and he became very intimate with Miss Grant, in quite an innocent way, though not very discreet; but she was a nice respectable girl, as most English models are, and no one thought any harm. However, a good many letters passed between them, and some little presents, amongst which was a beaded chain carrying a locket, and in this he was fool enough to put his portrait and the inscription, 'Edith, from Harold.'

"Later on Miss Grant, who had a rather good voice, went on the stage, in the comic opera line, and, in consequence, her habits and associates changed somewhat; and, as Harold had meanwhile become engaged, he was naturally anxious to get his letters back, and especially to exchange the locket for some less compromising gift. The letters she eventually sent him, but refused absolutely to part with the locket.

"Now, for the last month Harold has been staying at Halbury, making sketching excursions into the surrounding country, and yesterday morning he took the train to Shinglehurst, the third station from here, and the one before Woldhurst.

"On the platform here he met Miss Grant, who had come down from London, and was going on to Worthing. They entered the branch train together, having a first-class compartment to themselves. It seems she was wearing his locket at the time, and he made another appeal to her to make an exchange, which she refused, as before. The discussion appears to have become rather heated and angry on both sides, for the guard and a porter at Munsden both noticed that they seemed to be quarrelling; but the upshot of the affair was that the lady snapped the chain, and tossed it together with the locket to my brother, and they parted quite amiably at Shinglehurst, where Harold got out. He was then carrying his full sketching kit, including a large holland umbrella, the lower joint of which is an ash staff fitted with a powerful steel spike for driving into the ground.

"It was about half-past ten when he got out at Shinglehurst; by eleven he had reached his pitch and got to work, and he painted steadily for three hours. Then he packed up his traps, and was just starting on his way back to the station, when he was met by the police and arrested.

"And now, observe the accumulation of circumstantial evidence against him. He was the last person seen in company with the murdered woman—for no one seems to have seen her after they left Munsden; he appeared to be quarrelling with her when she was last seen alive, he had a reason for possibly wishing for her death, he was provided with an implement—a spiked staff—capable of inflicting the injury which caused her death, and, when he was searched, there was found in his possession the locket and broken chain, apparently removed from her person with violence.

"Against all this is, of course, his known character—he is the gentlest and most amiable of men—and his subsequent conduct—imbecile to the last degree if he had been guilty; but, as a lawyer, I can't help seeing that appearances are almost hopelessly against him."

"We won't say 'hopelessly,'" replied Thorndyke, as we took our places in the carriage, "though I expect the police are pretty cocksure. When does the inquest open?"

"Today at four. I have obtained an order from the coroner for you to examine the body and be present at the post-mortem."

"Do you happen to know the exact position of the wound?"

"Yes; it is a little above and behind the left ear—a horrible round hole, with a ragged cut or tear running from it to the side of the forehead."

"And how was the body lying?"

"Right along the floor, with the feet close to the off-side door."

"Was the wound on the head the only one?"

"No; there was a long cut or bruise on the right cheek—a contused wound the police surgeon called it, which he believes to have been inflicted with a heavy and rather blunt weapon. I have not heard of any other wounds or bruises."

"Did anyone enter the train yesterday at Shinglehurst?" Thorndyke asked.

"No one entered the train after it left Halbury."

Thorndyke considered these statements in silence, and presently fell into a brown study, from which he roused only as the train moved out of Shinglehurst station.

"It would be about here that the murder was committed," said Mr. Stopford; "at least, between here and Woldhurst."

Thorndyke nodded rather abstractedly, being engaged at the moment in observing with great attention the objects that were visible from the windows.

"I notice," he remarked presently, "a number of chips scattered about between the rails, and some of the chair-wedges look new. Have there been any platelayers at work lately?"

"Yes," answered Stopford, "they are on the line now, I believe—at least, I saw a gang working near Woldhurst yesterday, and they are said to have set a rick on fire; I saw it smoking when I came down."

"Indeed; and this middle line of rails is, I suppose, a sort of siding?"

"Yes; they shunt the goods trains and empty trucks on to it. There are the remains of the rick—still smouldering, you see."

Thorndyke gazed absently at the blackened heap until an empty cattle-truck on the middle track hid it from view. This was succeeded by a line of goods-waggons, and these by a passenger coach, one compartment of which—a first-class—was closed up and sealed. The train now began to slow down rather suddenly, and a couple of minutes later we brought up in Woldhurst station.

It was evident that rumours of Thorndyke's advent had preceded us, for the entire staff—two porters, an inspector, and the station-master—were waiting expectantly on the platform, and the latter came forward, regardless of his dignity, to help us with our luggage.

"Do you think I could see the carriage?" Thorndyke asked the solicitor.

"Not the inside, sir," said the station-master, on being appealed to. "The police have sealed it up. You would have to ask the inspector."

"Well, I can have a look at the outside, I suppose?" said Thorndyke, and to this the station-master readily agreed, and offered to accompany us.

"What other first-class passengers were there?" Thorndyke asked.

"None, sir. There was only one first-class coach, and the deceased was the only person in it. It has given us all a dreadful turn, this affair has," he continued, as we set off up the line. "I was on the platform when the train came in. We were watching a rick that was burning up the line, and a rare blaze it made, too; and I was just saying that we should have to move the cattle-truck that was on the mid-track, because, you see, sir, the smoke and sparks were blowing across, and I thought it would frighten the poor beasts. And Mr. Felton he don't like his beasts handled roughly. He says it spoils the meat."

"No doubt he is right," said Thorndyke. "But now, tell me, do you think it is possible for any person to board or leave the train on the off-side unobserved? Could a man, for instance, enter a compartment on the off-side at one station and drop off as the train was slowing down at the next, without being seen?"

"I doubt it," replied the station-master. "Still, I wouldn't say it is impossible."

"Thank you. Oh, and there's another question. You have a gang of men at work on the line, I see. Now, do those men belong to the district?"

"No, sir; they are strangers, every one, and pretty rough diamonds some of 'em are. But I shouldn't say there was any real harm in 'em. If you was suspecting any of 'em of being mixed up in this—"

"I am not," interrupted Thorndyke rather shortly. "I suspect nobody; but I wish to get all the facts of the case at the outset."

"Naturally, sir," replied the abashed official; and we pursued our way in silence.

"Do you remember, by the way," said Thorndyke, as we approached the empty coach, "whether the off-side door of the compartment was closed and locked when the body was discovered?"

"It was closed, sir, but not locked. Why, sir, did you think—?"

"Nothing, nothing. The sealed compartment is the one, of course?"

Without waiting for a reply, he commenced his survey of the coach, while I gently restrained our two companions from shadowing him, as they were disposed to do. The off-side footboard occupied his attention specially, and when he had scrutinized minutely the part opposite the fatal compartment, he walked slowly from end to end with his eyes but a few inches from its surface, as though he was searching for something.

Near what had been the rear end he stopped, and drew from his pocket a piece of paper; then, with a moistened finger-tip he picked up from the footboard some evidently minute object, which he carefully transferred to the paper, folding the latter and placing it in his pocket-book.

He next mounted the footboard, and, having peered in through the window of the sealed compartment, produced from his pocket a small insufflator or powder-blower, with which he blew a stream of impalpable smoke-like powder on to the edges of the middle window, bestowing the closest attention on the irregular dusty patches in which it settled, and even measuring one on the jamb of the window with a pocket-rule. At length he stepped down, and, having carefully looked over the near-side footboard, announced that he had finished for the present.

As we were returning down the line, we passed a working man, who seemed to be viewing the chairs and sleepers with more than casual interest.

"That, I suppose, is one of the plate-layers?" Thorndyke suggested to the station-master.

"Yes, the foreman of the gang," was the reply.

"I'll just step back and have a word with him, if you will walk on slowly." And my colleague turned back briskly and overtook the man, with whom he remained in conversation for some minutes.

"I think I see the police inspector on the platform," remarked Thorndyke, as we approached the station.

"Yes, there he is," said our guide. "Come down to see what you are after, sir, I expect." Which was doubtless the case, although the officer professed to be there by the merest chance.

"You would like to see the weapon, sir, I suppose?" he remarked, when he had introduced himself.

"The umbrella-spike," Thorndyke corrected. "Yes, if I may. We are going to the mortuary now."

"Then you'll pass the station on the way; so, if you care to look in, I will walk up with you."

This proposition being agreed to, we all proceeded to the police-station, including the station-master, who was on the very tiptoe of curiosity.

"There you are, sir," said the inspector, unlocking his office, and ushering us in. "Don't say we haven't given every facility to the defence. There are all the effects of the accused, including the very weapon the deed was done with."

"Come, come," protested Thorndyke; "we mustn't be premature." He took the stout ash staff from the officer, and, having examined the formidable spike through a lens, drew from his pocket a steel calliper-gauge, with which he carefully measured the diameter of the spike, and the staff to which it was fixed. "And now," he said, when he had made a note of the measurements in his book, "we will look at the colour-box and the sketch. Ha! a very orderly man, your brother, Mr. Stopford. Tubes all in their places, palette-knives wiped clean, palette cleaned off and rubbed bright, brushes wiped—they ought to be washed before they stiffen—all this is very significant." He unstrapped the sketch from the blank canvas to which it was pinned, and, standing it on a chair in a good light, stepped back to look at it.

"And you tell me that that is only three hours' work!" he exclaimed, looking at the lawyer. "It is really a marvellous achievement."

"My brother is a very rapid worker," replied Stopford dejectedly.

"Yes, but this is not only amazingly rapid; it is in his very happiest vein—full of spirit and feeling. But we mustn't stay to look at it longer." He replaced the canvas on its pins, and having glanced at the locket and some other articles that lay in a drawer, thanked the inspector for his courtesy and withdrew.

"That sketch and the colour-box appear very suggestive to me," he remarked, as we walked up the street.

"To me also," said Stopford gloomily, "for they are under lock and key, like their owner, poor old fellow."

He sighed heavily, and we walked on in silence.

The mortuary-keeper had evidently heard of our arrival, for he was waiting at the door with the key in his hand, and, on being shown the coroner's order, unlocked the door, and we entered together; but, after a momentary glance at the ghostly, shrouded figure lying upon the slate table, Stopford turned pale and retreated, saying that he would wait for us outside with the mortuary-keeper.

As soon as the door was closed and locked on the inside, Thorndyke glanced curiously round the bare, whitewashed building. A stream of sunlight poured in through the skylight, and fell upon the silent form that lay so still under its covering-sheet, and one stray beam glanced into a corner by the door, where, on a row of pegs and a deal table, the dead woman's clothing was displayed.

"There is something unspeakably sad in these poor relics, Jervis," said Thorndyke, as we stood before them. "To me they are more tragic, more full of pathetic suggestion, than the corpse itself. See the smart, jaunty hat, and the costly skirts hanging there, so desolate and forlorn; the dainty lingerie on the table, neatly folded—by the mortuary-man's wife, I hope—the little French shoes and open-work silk stockings. How pathetically eloquent they are of harmless, womanly vanity, and the gay, careless life, snapped short in the twinkling of an eye. But we must not give way to sentiment. There is another life threatened, and it is in our keeping."

He lifted the hat from its peg, and turned it over in his hand. It was, I think, what is called a "picture-hat"—a huge, flat, shapeless mass of gauze and ribbon and feather, spangled over freely with dark-blue sequins. In one part of the brim was a ragged hole, and from this the glittering sequins dropped off in little showers when the hat was moved.

"This will have been worn tilted over on the left side," said Thorndyke, "judging by the general shape and the position of the hole."

"Yes," I agreed. "Like that of the Duchess of Devonshire in Gainsborough's portrait."

"Exactly."

He shook a few of the sequins into the palm of his hand, and, replacing the hat on its peg, dropped the little discs into an envelope, on which he wrote, "From the hat," and slipped it into his pocket. Then, stepping over to the table, he drew back the sheet reverently and even tenderly from the dead woman's face, and looked down at it with grave pity. It was a comely face, white as marble, serene and peaceful in expression, with half-closed eyes, and framed with a mass of brassy, yellow hair; but its beauty was marred by a long linear wound, half cut, half bruise, running down the right cheek from the eye to the chin.

"A handsome girl," Thorndyke commented—"a dark-haired blonde. What a sin to have disfigured herself so with that horrible peroxide." He smoothed the hair back from her forehead, and added: "She seems to have applied the stuff last about ten days ago. There is about a quarter of an inch of dark hair at the roots. What do you make of that wound on the cheek?"

"It looks as if she had struck some sharp angle in falling, though, as the seats are padded in first-class carriages, I don't see what she could have struck."

"No. And now let us look at the other wound. Will you note down the description?" He handed me his notebook, and I wrote down as he dictated: "A clean-punched circular hole in skull, an inch behind and above margin of left ear—diameter, an inch and seven-sixteenths; starred fracture of parietal bone; membranes perforated, and brain entered deeply; ragged scalp-wound, extending forward to margin of left orbit; fragments of gauze and sequins in edges of wound. That will do for the present. Dr. Morton will give us further details if we want them."

He pocketed his callipers and rule, drew from the bruised scalp one or two loose hairs, which he placed in the envelope with the sequins, and, having looked over the body for other wounds or bruises (of which there were none), replaced the sheet, and prepared to depart.

As we walked away from the mortuary, Thorndyke was silent and deeply thoughtful, and I gathered that he was piecing together the facts that he had acquired. At length Mr. Stopford, who had several times looked at him curiously, said:

"The post-mortem will take place at three, and it is now only half-past eleven. What would you like to do next?"

Thorndyke, who, in spite of his mental preoccupation, had been looking about him in his usual keen, attentive way, halted suddenly.

"Your reference to the post-mortem," said he, "reminds me that I forgot to put the ox-gall into my case."

"Ox-gall!" I exclaimed, endeavouring vainly to connect this substance with the technique of the pathologist. "What were you going to do with—"

But here I broke off, remembering my friend's dislike of any discussion of his methods before strangers.

"I suppose," he continued, "there would hardly be an artist's colourman in a place of this size?"

"I should think not," said Stopford. "But couldn't you get the stuff from a butcher? There's a shop just across the road."

"So there is," agreed Thorndyke, who had already observed the shop. "The gall ought, of course, to be prepared, but we can filter it ourselves—that is, if the butcher has any. We will try him, at any rate."

He crossed the road towards the shop, over which the name "Felton" appeared in gilt lettering, and, addressing himself to the proprietor, who stood at the door, introduced himself and explained his wants.

"Ox-gall?" said the butcher. "No, sir, I haven't any just now; but I am having a beast killed this afternoon, and I can let you have some then. In fact," he added, after a pause, "as the matter is of importance, I can have one killed at once if you wish it."

"That is very kind of you," said Thorndyke, "and it would greatly oblige me. Is the beast perfectly healthy?"

"They're in splendid condition, sir. I picked them out of the herd myself. But you shall see them—ay, and choose the one that you'd like killed."

"You are really very good," said Thorndyke warmly. "I will just run into the chemist's next door, and get a suitable bottle, and then I will avail myself of your exceedingly kind offer."

He hurried into the chemist's shop, from which he presently emerged, carrying a white paper parcel; and we then followed the butcher down a narrow lane by the side of his shop. It led to an enclosure containing a small pen, in which were confined three handsome steers, whose glossy, black coats contrasted in a very striking manner with their long, greyish-white, nearly straight horns.

"These are certainly very fine beasts, Mr. Felton," said Thorndyke, as we drew up beside the pen, "and in excellent condition, too."

He leaned over the pen and examined the beasts critically, especially as to their eyes and horns; then, approaching the nearest one, he raised his stick and bestowed a smart tap on the under-side of the right horn, following it by a similar tap on the left one, a proceeding that the beast viewed with stolid surprise.

"The state of the horns," explained Thorndyke, as he moved on to the next steer, "enables one to judge, to some extent, of the beast's health."

"Lord bless you, sir," laughed Mr. Felton, "they haven't got no feeling in their horns, else what good 'ud their horns be to 'em?"

Apparently he was right, for the second steer was as indifferent to a sounding rap on either horn as the first. Nevertheless, when Thorndyke approached the third steer, I unconsciously drew nearer to watch; and I noticed that, as the stick struck the horn, the beast drew back in evident alarm, and that when the blow was repeated, it became manifestly uneasy.

"He don't seem to like that," said the butcher. "Seems as if—Hullo, that's queer!"

Thorndyke had just brought his stick up against the left horn, and immediately the beast had winced and started back, shaking his head and moaning. There was not, however, room for him to back out of reach, and Thorndyke, by leaning into the pen, was able to inspect the sensitive horn, which he did with the closest attention, while the butcher looked on with obvious perturbation.

"You don't think there's anything wrong with this beast, sir, I hope," said he.

"I can't say without a further examination," replied Thorndyke. "It may be the horn only that is affected. If you will have it sawn off close to the head, and sent up to me at the hotel, I will look at it and tell you. And, by way of preventing any mistakes, I will mark it and cover it up, to protect it from injury in the slaughter-house."

He opened his parcel and produced from it a wide-mouthed bottle labelled "Ox-gall," a sheet of *gutta-percha* tissue, a roller bandage, and a stick of sealing-wax. Handing the bottle to Mr. Felton, he encased the distal half of the horn in a covering by means of the tissue and the bandage, which he fixed securely with the sealing-wax.

"I'll saw the horn off and bring it up to the hotel myself, with the ox-gall," said Mr. Felton. "You shall have them in half an hour."

He was as good as his word, for in half an hour Thorndyke was seated at a small table by the window of our private sitting-room in the Black Bull Hotel. The table was covered with newspaper, and on it lay the long grey horn and Thorndyke's travelling-case, now open and displaying a small microscope and its accessories. The butcher was seated solidly in an armchair waiting, with a half-suspicious eye on Thorndyke for the report; and I was endeavouring by cheerful talk to keep Mr. Stopford from sinking into utter despondency, though I, too, kept a furtive watch on my colleague's rather mysterious proceedings.

I saw him unwind the bandage and apply the horn to his ear, bending it slightly to and fro. I watched him, as he scanned the surface closely through a lens, and observed him as he scraped some substance from the pointed end on to a glass slide, and, having applied a drop of some reagent, began to tease out the scraping with a pair of mounted needles. Presently he placed the slide under the microscope, and, having observed it attentively for a minute or two, turned round sharply.

"Come and look at this, Jervis," said he.

I wanted no second bidding, being on tenterhooks of curiosity, but came over and applied my eye to the instrument.

"Well, what is it?" he asked.

"A multipolar nerve corpuscle—very shrivelled, but unmistakable."

"And this?"

He moved the slide to a fresh spot.

"Two pyramidal nerve corpuscles and some portions of fibres."

"And what do you say the tissue is?"

"Cortical brain substance, I should say, without a doubt."

"I entirely agree with you. And that being so," he added, turning to Mr. Stopford, "we may say that the case for the defence is practically complete."

"What, in Heaven's name, do you mean?" exclaimed Stopford, starting up.

"I mean that we can now prove when and where and how Miss Grant met her death. Come and sit down here, and I will explain. No, you needn't go away, Mr. Felton. We shall have to *subpoena* you. Perhaps," he continued, "we had better go over the facts and see what they suggest. And first we note the position of the body, lying with the feet close to the off-side door, showing that, when she fell, the deceased was sitting, or more probably standing, close to that door. Next there is this." He drew from his pocket a folded paper, which he opened, displaying a tiny blue disc. "It is one of the sequins with which her hat was trimmed, and I have in this envelope several more which I took from the hat itself.

"This single sequin I picked up on the rear end of the off side foot-board, and its presence there makes it nearly certain that at some time Miss Grant had put her head out of the window on that side.

"The next item of evidence I obtained by dusting the margins of the off-side window with a light powder, which made visible a greasy impression three and a quarter inches long on the sharp corner of the right-hand jamb (right-hand from the inside, I mean).

"And now as to the evidence furnished by the body. The wound in the skull is behind and above the left ear, is roughly circular, and measures one inch and seven-sixteenths at most, and a ragged scalp-wound runs from it towards the left eye. On the right cheek is a linear contused wound three and a quarter inches long. There are no other injuries.

"Our next facts are furnished by this." He took up the horn and tapped it with his finger, while the solicitor and Mr. Felton stared at him in speechless wonder. "You notice it is a left horn, and you remember that it was highly sensitive. If you put your ear to it while I strain it, you will hear the grating of a fracture in the bony core. Now look at the pointed end, and you will see several deep scratches running lengthwise, and where those scratches end the diameter of the horn is, as you see by this calliper-gauge, one inch and seven-sixteenths. Covering the scratches is a dry bloodstain, and at the extreme tip is a small mass of a dried substance which Dr. Jervis and I have examined with the microscope and are satisfied is brain tissue."

"Good God!" exclaimed Stopford eagerly. "Do you mean to say—"

"Let us finish with the facts, Mr. Stopford," Thorndyke interrupted. "Now, if you look closely at that bloodstain, you will see a short piece of hair stuck to the horn, and through this lens you can make out the root-bulb. It is a golden hair, you notice, but near the root it is black, and our calliper-gauge shows us that the black portion is fourteen sixty-fourths of an inch long. Now, in this envelope are some hairs that I removed from the dead woman's head. They also are golden hairs, black at the roots, and when I measure the black portion I find it to be fourteen sixty-fourths of an inch long. Then, finally, there is this."

He turned the horn over, and pointed to a small patch of dried blood. Embedded in it was a blue sequin.

Mr. Stopford and the butcher both gazed at the horn in silent amazement; then the former drew a deep breath and looked up at Thorndyke.

"No doubt," said he, "you can explain this mystery, but for my part I am utterly bewildered, though you are filling me with hope."

"And yet the matter is quite simple," returned Thorndyke, "even with these few facts before us, which are only a selection from the body of evidence in our possession. But I will state my theory, and you shall judge." He rapidly sketched a rough plan on a sheet of paper, and continued: "These were the conditions when the train was approaching Woldhurst: Here was the passenger-coach, here was the burning rick, and here was a cattle-truck. This steer was in that truck. Now my hypothesis is that at that time Miss Grant was standing with her head out of the off-side window, watching the burning rick. Her wide hat, worn on the left side, hid from her view the cattle-truck which she was approaching, and then this is what happened."

He sketched another plan to a larger scale. "One of the steers—this one—had thrust its long horn out through the bars. The point of that horn struck the deceased's head, driving her face violently against the corner of the window, and then, in disengaging, ploughed its way through the scalp, and suffered a fracture of its core from the violence of the wrench. This hypothesis is inherently probable, it fits all the facts, and those facts admit of no other explanation."

The solicitor sat for a moment as though dazed; then he rose impulsively and seized Thorndyke's hands. "I don't know what to say to you," he exclaimed huskily, "except that you have saved my brother's life, and for that may God reward you!"

The butcher rose from his chair with a slow grin.

"It seems to me," said he, "as if that ox-gall was what you might call a blind, eh, sir?"

And Thorndyke smiled an inscrutable smile.

When we returned to town on the following day we were a party of four, which included Mr. Harold Stopford. The verdict of "Death by misadventure," promptly returned by the coroner's jury, had been shortly followed by his release from custody, and he now sat with his brother and me, listening with rapt attention to Thorndyke's analysis of the case.

"So, you see," the latter concluded, "I had six possible theories of the cause of death worked out before I reached Halbury, and it only remained to select the one that fitted the facts. And when I had seen the cattle-truck, had picked up that sequin, had heard the description of the steers, and had seen the hat and the wounds, there was nothing left to do but the filling in of details."

"And you never doubted my innocence?" asked Harold Stopford. Thorndyke smiled at his quondam client.

"Not after I had seen your colour-box and your sketch," said he, "to say nothing of the spike."

The Funeral Pyre

Thorndyke did not often indulge in an evening paper, and was even disposed to view that modern institution with some disfavour; whence it happened that when I entered our chambers shortly before dinner time with a copy of the *Evening Gazette* in my hand, he fixed upon the folded news-sheet an inquiring and slightly disapproving eye.

"'Orrible discovery near Dartford," I announced, quoting the juvenile vendor.

The disapproval faded from his face, but the inquiring expression remained.

"What is it?" he asked.

"I don't know," I replied; "but it seems to be something in our line."

"My learned friend does us an injustice," he rejoined, with his eye riveted on the paper. "Still, if you are going to make my flesh creep, I will try to endure it."

Thus invited, I opened the paper and read out as follows:

"A shocking tragedy has come to light in a meadow about a mile from Dartford. About two o'clock this morning, a rural constable observed a rick on fire out on the marshes near the creek. By the time he reached it the upper half of the rick was burning fiercely in the strong wind, and as he could do nothing alone, he went to the adjacent farm-house and gave the alarm. The farmer and two of his sons accompanied the constable to the scene of the conflagration, but the rick was now a blazing mass, roaring in the wind and giving out an intense heat. As it was obviously impossible to save any part of it, and as there were no other ricks near, the farmer decided to abandon it to its fate and went home.

"At eight o'clock he returned to the spot and found the rick still

251

burning, though reduced to a heap of glowing cinders and ashes, and approaching it, he was horrified to perceive a human skull grinning out from the cindery mass. Closer examination showed other bones— all calcined white and chalky—and close to the skull a stumpy clay pipe. The explanation of this dreadful occurrence seems quite simple. The rick was not quite finished, and when the farm hands knocked off work they left the ladder in position. It is assumed that some tramp, in search of a night's lodging, observed the ladder, and climbing up it, made himself comfortable in the loose hay at the top of the rick, where he fell asleep with his lighted pipe in his mouth. This ignited the hay and the man must have been suffocated by the fumes without awakening from his sleep."

"A reasonable explanation," was Thorndyke's comment, "and quite probable; but of course it is pure hypothesis. As a matter of fact, any one of the three conceivable causes of violent death is possible in this case—accident, suicide or homicide."

"I should have supposed," said I, "that we could almost exclude suicide. It is difficult to imagine a man electing to roast himself to death."

"I cannot agree with my learned friend," Thorndyke rejoined. "I can imagine a case—and one of great medico-legal interest—that would exactly fit the present circumstances. Let us suppose a man, hopelessly insolvent, desperate and disgusted with life, who decides to provide for his family by investing the few pounds that he has left in insuring his life heavily and then making away with himself. How would he proceed? If he should commit suicide by any of the orthodox methods he would simply invalidate his policy.

"But now, suppose he knows of a likely rick; that he provides himself with some rapidly-acting poison, such as potassium cyanide—he could even use prussic acid if he carried it in a rubber or celluloid bottle, which would be consumed in the fire; that he climbs on to the rick; sets fire to it, and as soon as it is fairly alight, takes his dose of poison and falls back dead among the hay. Who is to contest his family's claim? The fire will have destroyed all traces of the poison, even if they should be sought for. But it is practically certain that the question would never be raised. The claim would be paid without demur."

I could not help smiling at this calm exposition of a practicable crime. "It is a mercy, Thorndyke," I remarked, "that you are an honest man. If you were not—"

"I think," he retorted, "that I should find some better means of livelihood than suicide. But with regard to this case: it will be worth watching. The tramp hypothesis is certainly the most probable; but its very probability makes an alternative hypothesis at least possible. No one is likely to suspect fraudulent suicide; but that immunity from suspicion is a factor that increases the probability of fraudulent suicide. And so, to a less extent, with homicide. We must watch the case and see if there are any further developments."

Further developments were not very long in appearing. The report in the morning paper disposed effectually of the tramp theory without offering any other, it said,:

The tragedy of the burning rick is taking a some what mysterious turn. It is now clear that the unknown man, who was assumed to have been a tramp, must have been a person of some social position, for careful examination of the ashes by the police have brought to light various articles which would have been carried only by a man of fair means. The clay pipe was evidently one of a pair—of which the second one has been recovered—probably silver-mounted and carried in a case, the steel frame of which has been found. Both pipes are of the 'Burns Cutty' pattern and have neatly scratched on the bowls the initials 'R. R.'

The following articles have also been found:—Remains of a watch, probably gold, and a rather singular watch-chain, having alternate links of platinum and gold. The gold links have partly disappeared, but numerous beads of gold have been found, derived apparently from the watch and chain. The platinum links are intact and are fashioned of twisted square wire. A bunch of keys, partly fused; a rock crystal seal, apparently from a ring; a little porcelain mascot figure, with a hole for suspension—possibly from the watch-chain—and a number of artificial teeth.

In connection with the latter, a puzzling and slightly sinister aspect has been given to the case by the finding of an upper dental plate by a ditch some two hundred yards from the rick. The plate has two gaps and, on comparison with the skull of the unknown man, these have been found by the police surgeon to correspond with two groups of remaining teeth. Moreover, the artificial teeth found in the ashes all seem to belong to a lower plate. The presence of this plate, so far from the scene of the man's death, is extremely difficult to account for.

As Thorndyke finished reading the extract he looked at me as if inviting some comment.

"It is a most remarkable and mysterious affair," said I, "and naturally recalls to my mind the hypothetical case that you suggested yesterday. If that case was possible then, it is actually probable now. It fits these new facts perfectly not only in respect of the abundant means of identification but even to this dental plate—if we assume that he took the poison as he was approaching the rick, and that the poison was of an acrid or irritating character which caused him to cough or retch. And I can think of no other plausible explanation."

"There are other possibilities," said Thorndyke, "but fraudulent suicide is certainly the most probable theory on the known facts. But we shall see. As you say, the body can hardly fail to be identified at a pretty early date."

As a matter of fact it was identified in the course of that same day. Both Thorndyke and I were busily engaged until evening in the courts and elsewhere and had not had time to give this curious case any consideration. But as we walked home together, we encountered Mr. Stalker of the Griffin Life Assurance Company pacing up and down King's Bench Walk near the entry of our chambers.

"Ha!" he exclaimed, striding forward to meet us near the Mitre Court gateway, "you are just the very men I wanted to see. There is a little matter that I want to consult you about. I shan't detain you long."

"It won't matter much if you do," said Thorndyke. "We have finished our routine work for the day and our time is now our own." He led the way up to our chambers, where, having given the fire a stir, he drew up three arm-chairs.

"Now, Stalker," said he. "Warm your toes and tell us your troubles."

Mr. Stalker spread out his hands to the blaze began reflectively:

"It will be enough, I think, if I give you the facts—and most of them you probably know already. You have heard about this man whose remains were found in the ashes of a burnt rick? Well, it turns out that he was a certain Mr. Reginald Reed, an outside broker, as I understand; but what is of more interest to us is that he was a client of ours. We have issued a policy on his life for three thousand pounds. I thought I remembered the name when I saw it in the paper this afternoon, so I looked up our files and there it was, sure enough."

"When was the policy issued?" Thorndyke asked.

"Ah!" exclaimed Stalker. "That's the exasperating feature of the case. The policy was issued less than a year ago. He has only paid a single premium. So we stand to drop practically the whole three thousand. Of course, we have to take the fat with the lean, but we don't like to take it in such precious large lumps."

"Of course you don't," agreed Thorndyke. "But now you have come to consult me—about what?"

"Well," replied Stalker, "I put it to you: isn't there something obviously fishy about the case? Are the circumstances normal? For instance, how the devil came a respectable city gentleman to be smoking his pipe in a haystack out in a lonely meadow at two o'clock in the morning, or thereabouts?"

"I agree," said Thorndyke, "that the circumstances are highly abnormal. But there is no doubt that the man is dead. Extremely dead, if I may use the expression. What is the point that you wish to raise?"

"I am not raising any point," replied Stalker. "We should like you to attend the inquest and watch the case for us. Of course, in our policies, as you know, suicide is expressly ruled out; and if this should turn out to have been a case of suicide—"

"What is there to suggest that it was?" asked Thorndyke.

"What is there to suggest that it wasn't?" retorted Stalker.

"Nothing," rejoined Thorndyke. "But a negative plea is of no use to you. You will have to furnish positive proof of suicide, or else pay the claim."

"Yes, I realise that," said Stalker, "and I am not suggesting—But there, it is of no use discussing the matter while we know so little. I leave the case in your hands. Can you attend the inquest?"

"I shall make it my business to do so," replied Thorndyke.

"Very well," said Stalker, rising and putting on his gloves, "then we will leave it at that; and we couldn't leave it in better case."

When our visitor had gone I remarked to Thorndyke: "Stalker seems to have conceived the same idea as my learned senior—fraudulent suicide."

"It is not surprising," he replied. "Stalker is a shrewd man and he perceives that when an abnormal thing has happened we may look for an abnormal explanation. Fraudulent suicide was a speculative possibility yesterday: today, in the light of these new facts, it is the most probable theory. But mere probabilities won't help Stalker. If there is no direct evidence of suicide—and there is not likely to be any—the verdict will be Death by Misadventure, and the Griffin Company will have to pay."

"I suppose you won't do anything until you have heard what transpires at the inquest?"

"Yes," he replied. "I think we should do well to go down and just go over the ground. At present we have the facts at third hand, and we don't know what may have been overlooked. As tomorrow is fairly free I propose that we make an early start and see the place ourselves."

"Is there any particular point that you want to clear up?"

"No; I have nothing definite in view. The circumstances are compatible with either accident, suicide or homicide, with an undoubted leaning towards suicide. But, at present, I have a completely open mind. I am, in fact, going down to Dartford in the hope of getting a lead in some definite direction."

When we alighted at Dartford Station on the following morning, Thorndyke looked inquiringly up and down the platform until he espied an inspector, when he approached the official and asked for a direction to the site of the burnt rick.

The official glanced at Thorndyke's canvas-covrered research-case and at my binocular and camera as he replied with a smile: "You are not the first, by a long way, that has asked that question. There has been a regular procession of Press gentlemen that way this morning. The place is about a mile from here. You take the foot-path to Joyce Green and turn off towards the creek opposite Temple Farm. This is about where the rick stood," he added, as Thorndyke produced his one-inch Ordnance Map and a pencil, "a few yards from that dyke."

With this direction and the open map we set forth from the station, and taking our way along the unfrequented path soon left the town behind. As we crossed the second stile, where the path rejoined the road, Thorndyke paused to survey the prospect.

"Stalker's question," he remarked, "was not unreasonable. This road leads nowhere but to the river, and one does rather wonder what a city man can have been doing out on these marshes in the small hours of the morning. I think that will be our objective, where you see those men at work by the shepherd's hut, or whatever it is."

We struck off across the level meadows, out of which arose the red sails of a couple of barges, creeping down the invisible creek; and as we approached our objective the shepherd's hut resolved itself into a contractor's office van, and the men were seen to be working with shovels and sieves on the ashes of the rick. A police inspector was superintending the operations, and when we drew near he accosted us with a civil inquiry as to our business.

Thorndyke presented his card and explained that he was watching the case in the interests of the Griffin Insurance Company. "I suppose," he added, "I shall be given the necessary facilities?"

"Certainly," replied the officer, glancing at my colleague with an odd mixture of respect and suspicion, "and if you can spot anything that we've overlooked, you are very welcome. It's all for the public good. Is there anything in particular that you want to see?"

"I should like to see everything that has been recovered so far. The remains of the body have been removed, I suppose?"

"Yes, sir. To the mortuary. But I have got all the effects here."

He led the way to the office—a wooden hut on low wheels—and unlocking the door, invited us to enter. "Here are the things that we have salved," he said, indicating a table covered with white paper on which the various articles were neatly set out, "and I think it's about the lot. We haven't come on anything fresh for the last hour or so."

Thorndyke looked over the collection thoughtfully; picked up and examined successively the two clay pipes—each with the initials "R. R." neatly incised on the bowl—the absurd little mascot figure, so incongruous with its grim surroundings and the tragic circumstances, the distorted keys, the platinum chain-links to several of which shapeless blobs of gold adhered, and the crystal seal; and then, collecting the artificial teeth, arranged them in what appeared to be their correct order and compared them with the dental plate.

"I think," said he, holding the latter in his fingers, "that as the body is not here, I should like to secure the means of comparison of these teeth with the skull. There will be no objection to that, I presume?"

"What did you wish to do?" the inspector asked.

"I should like to take a cast of the plate and a wax impression of the loose teeth. No damage will be done to the originals, of course."

The inspector hesitated, his natural, official tendency to refuse permission apparently contending with a desire to see with his own eyes how the famous expert carried out his mysterious methods of research. In the end the latter prevailed and the official sanction was given, subject to a proviso. "You won't mind my looking on while you do it?"

"Of course not," replied Thorndyke. "Why should I?"

"I thought that perhaps your methods were a sort of trade secret."

Thorndyke laughed softly as he opened the research case. "My dear inspector," said he, "the people who have trade secrets are those who make a profound mystery of simple processes that any schoolboy could carry out with once showing. That is the necessity for the secrecy."

As he was speaking he half-filled a tiny aluminium saucepan with water, and having dropped into it a couple of cakes of dentist's moulding composition, put it to heat over a spirit-lamp. While it was heating he greased the dental plate and the loose teeth, and prepared the little rubber basin and the other appliances for mixing the plaster.

The inspector was deeply interested. With almost ravenous attention he followed these proceedings, and eagerly watched Thorndyke roll the softened composition into the semblance of a small sausage and press it firmly on the teeth of the plate; peered into the plaster tin, and when the liquid plaster was mixed and applied, first to the top and then to the lower surface of the plate, not only observed the process closely but put a number of very pertinent questions.

While the plaster and composition were setting Thorndyke renewed his inspection of the salvage from the rick, picking out a number of iron boot protectors which he placed apart in a little heap.

Then he proceeded to roll out two flat strips of softened composition, into one of which he pressed the loose teeth in what appeared to be their proper order, and into the other the boot protectors—eight in number—after first dusting the surface with powdered French chalk. By this time the plaster had set hard enough to allow of the mould being opened and the dental plate taken out. Then Thorndyke, having painted the surfaces of the plaster pieces with knotting, put the mould together again and tied it firmly with string, mixed a fresh bowl of plaster and poured it into the mould.

While this was setting Thorndyke made a careful inventory, with my assistance, of the articles found in the ashes and put a few discreet questions to the inspector. But the latter knew very little about the case. His duty was merely to examine and report on the rick for the information of the coroner. The investigation of the case was evidently being conducted from headquarters. There being no information to be gleaned from the officer, we went out and inspected the site of the rick. But here, also, there was nothing to be learned; the surface of the ground was now laid bare and the men who were working with the sieves reported no further discoveries.

We accordingly returned to the hut, and as the plaster had now set hard Thorndyke proceeded with infinite care to open the mould. The operation was a complete success, and as my colleague extracted the cast—a perfect replica, in plaster, of the dental plate—the inspector's admiration was unbounded. "Why," he exclaimed, "excepting for the colour you couldn't tell one from the other; but all the same, I don't quite see what you want it for."

"I want it to compare with the skull," replied Thorndyke, "if I have time to call at the mortuary. As I can't take the original plate with me, I shall need this copy to make the comparison. Obviously, it is important to make sure that this is Reed's plate and not that of some other person. By the way, can you show us the spot where the plate was picked up?"

"Yes," replied the inspector. "You can see the place from here. It was just by that gate at the crossing of the ditch."

"Thank you, inspector," said Thorndyke. "I think we will walk down and have a look at the place." He wrapped the new cast in a soft cloth, and having repacked his research—case, shook hands with the officer and prepared to depart.

"You will notice, Jervis," he remarked as we walked towards the gate, "that this denture was picked up at a spot beyond the rick—farther from the town, I mean. Consequently, if the plate is Reed's, he must have dropped it while he was approaching the rick from the direction of the river. It will be worthwhile to see if we can find out whence he came."

"Yes," I agreed. "But the dropping of the plate is a rather mysterious affair. It must have happened when he took the poison—assuming that he really did poison himself; but one would have expected that he would wait until he got to the rick to take his dose."

"We had better not make too many assumptions while we have so few facts," said Thorndyke. He put down his case beside the gate, which guarded a bridge across a broad ditch, or drainage dyke, and opened his map.

"The question is," said he, "did he come through this gate or was he only passing it? This dyke, you see, opens into the creek about three-quarters of a mile farther down. The probability is, therefore, that if he came up from the river across the marshes he would be on this side of the ditch and would pass the gate. But we had better try both sides. Let us leave our things by the gate and explore the ground for a few hundred yards, one on either side of the ditch. Which side will you take?"

I elected to take the side nearer the creek, and, having put my camera down by the research-case, climbed over the padlocked gate and began to walk slowly along by the side of the ditch, scanning the ground for footprints showing the impression of boot-protectors. At first the surface was far from favourable for imprints of any kind, being, like that immediately around the gate, covered with thick turf. About a hundred and fifty yards down, however, I came upon a heap of worm-casts on which was plainly visible the print of a heel with a clear impression of a kidney-shaped protector such as I had seen in the hut. Thereupon I hailed Thorndyke and, having stuck my stick in the ground beside the heel-print, went back to meet him at the gate.

"This is rather interesting, Jervis," he remarked, when I had described my find. "The inference seems to be that he came from the creek—unless there is another gate farther down. We had better have our compo impressions handy for comparison." He opened his case and taking from it the strip of composition—now as hard as bone—on which were the impressions of the boot-protectors, slipped it into his outer pocket. We then took up the case and the camera and proceeded to the spot marked by my stick.

"Well," said Thorndyke, "it is not very conclusive, seeing that so many people use boot-protectors, but it is probably Reed's foot-print. Let us hope that we shall find something more distinctive farther on."

We resumed our march, keeping a few yards apart and examining the ground closely as we went. For a full quarter of a mile we went on without detecting any trace of a foot-print on the thick turf. Suddenly we perceived ahead of us a stretch of yellow mud occupying a slight hollow, across which the creek had apparently overflowed at the last spring tide. When we reached it we found that the mud was nearly dry, but still soft enough to take an impression; and the surface was covered with a maze of foot-prints.

We halted at the edge of the patch and surveyed the complicated pattern; and then it became evident that the whole group of prints had been produced by two pairs of feet, with the addition of a row of sheep-tracks.

"This seems to raise an entirely new issue," I remarked.

"It does," Thorndyke agreed. "I think we now begin to see a definite light on the case. But we must go cautiously. Here are two sets of foot-prints of which one is apparently Reed's—to judge by the boot-protectors—while the other prints have been made by a man, whom we will call X, who wore boots or shoes with rubber soles and heels. We had better begin by verifying Reed's."

He produced the composition strip from his pocket, and, stooping over one pair of footprints, continued: "I think we may assume that these are Reed's feet. We have on the compo strip impressions of eight protectors from the rick, and on each footprint there are four protectors. Moreover, the individual protectors are the same on the compo and on the foot-prints. Thus the compo shows two pairs of half-protectors, two single edge-pieces, and two kidney-shaped protectors; while each foot-print shows a pair of half-protectors on the outside of the sole, a single one on the inside and a kidney-shaped piece on the heel. Furthermore, in both cases the protectors are nearly new and show no appreciable signs of wear. The agreement is complete."

"Don't you think," said I, "that we ought to take plaster records of them?"

"I do," he replied, "seeing that a heavy shower or a high tide would obliterate them. If you will make the casts I will, meanwhile, make a careful drawing of the whole group to show the order of imposition."

We fell to work forthwith upon our respective tasks, and by the time I had filled four of the clearest of the foot-prints with plaster, Thorndyke had completed his drawing with the aid of a set of coloured pencils from the research-case. While the plaster was setting he exhibited and explained the drawing.

"You see, Jervis, that there are four lines of prints and a set of sheep-tracks. The first in order of time are these prints of X, drawn in blue. Then come the sheep, which trod on X's foot-prints. Next comes Reed, alone and after some interval, for he has trodden both on the sheep-tracks and on the tracks of X. Both men were going towards the river. Then we have the tracks of the two men coming back. This time they were together, for their tracks are parallel and neither treads into the prints of the other.

"Both tracks are rather sinuous as if the men were walking unsteadily, and both have trodden on the sheep-tracks and on the preceding tracks. Next, we have the tracks of X going alone towards the river and treading on all the others excepting number four, which is the tracks of X coming from the river and turning off towards that gate, which opens on to the road. The sequence of events is therefore pretty clear.

"First, X came along here alone to some destination which we have yet to discover. Later—how much later we cannot judge—came Reed, alone. The two men seem to have met, and later returned together, apparently the worse for drink. That is the last we see of Reed. Next comes X, walking back—quite steadily, you notice—towards the river. Later, he returns; but this time, for some reason—perhaps to avoid the neighbourhood of the rick—he crosses the ditch at that gate, apparently to get on the road, though you see by the map that the road is much the longer route to the town. And now we had better get on and see if we can discover the rendezvous to and from which these two men went and came."

As the plaster had now set quite hard I picked up the casts, and when I had carefully packed them in the case we resumed our progress riverwards. I had already noticed, some distance ahead, the mast of what looked like a small cutter yacht standing up above the marshes, and I now drew Thorndyke's attention to it. But he had already observed it and, like me, had marked it as the probable rendezvous of the two men. In a few minutes the probability became a certainty, for a bend in the creek showed us the little vessel—with the name *Moonbeam* newly painted on the bow—made fast alongside a small wooden staging; and when we reached this the bare earth opposite the gangway was seen to be covered with the foot-prints of both men.

"I wonder," said I, "which of them was the owner of the yacht."

"It is pretty obvious, I think," said Thorndyke, "that X was the owner if either of them was. He came to the yacht alone, and he wore rubber-soled shoes such as yachtsmen favour; whereas Reed came when the other man was there, and he wore iron boot-protectors, which no yacht owner would do if he had any respect for his deck-planks. But they may have had a joint interest; appearances suggest that they were painting the woodwork when they were here together, as some of the paint is fresh and some of it old and shabby." He gazed at the yacht reflectively for some time and then remarked: "It would be interesting—and perhaps instructive—to have a look at the inside."

"It would be a flagrant trespass, to put it mildly," said I.

"It would be more than trespass if that padlock is locked," he replied. "But we need not take a pedantic view of the legal position. My learned friend has a serviceable pair of glasses and commands an unobstructed view of a mile or so; and if he maintains an observant attitude while I make an inspection of the premises any trifling irregularity will be of no consequence."

As he spoke he felt in his pocket and produced the instrument which our laboratory assistant, Polton, had made from a few pieces of stiff steel wire, and which was euphemistically known as a smoker's companion. With this appliance in his hand he dropped down on to the yacht's deck, and after a quick look round, tried the padlock. Finding it locked he proceeded to operate on it with the smoker's companion, and in a few moments it fell open, when he pushed back the sliding hatch and stepped down into the little cabin.

His exploration did not take long. In a few minutes he reappeared and climbed the short ladder to the staging. "There isn't much to see," he reported, "but what there is is highly suggestive. If you slip down and have a look round, I think you will have no difficulty in forming a plausible reconstruction of the recent events. You had better take the camera. There is light enough for a time exposure."

I handed him the glasses, and dropping on to the deck, stepped down through the open hatch into the cabin. It was an absurd little cave, barely four feet high from the floor to the coach-roof, open to the fore-peak and lighted by a little skylight and two portholes. Of the two sleeping berths, one had evidently been used as a seat, while the other appeared to have been slept in, to judge by the indented pillow and the tumbled blankets, left just as the occupant had crawled out of them.

But the whole interior was in a stale of squalid disorder. Paint-pots and unwashed brushes lay about the floor, in company with a couple of whisky-bottles—one empty and one half-full—two tumblers, a pair of empty siphons and a litter of playing cards scattered broadcast and evidently derived from two packs. It was, as Thorndyke had said, easy to reconstruct the scene of sordid debauchery that the light of the two candles—each in its congealed pool of grease—must have displayed on that night of horror whose dreadful secret had been disclosed by the ashes of the rick. But I could see nothing that would enable me to give a name to the dead man's mysterious companion.

When I had completed my inspection and taken a photograph of the interior, I rejoined Thorndyke, who then descended and replaced the padlock on the closed hatch, relocking it with the invaluable smoker's companion.

"Well, Jervis," said he, as we turned our faces towards the town, "it seems as if we had accomplished our task, so far as Stalker is concerned. It is still possible that this was a case of suicide, but it is no longer probable. All the appearances point to homicide. I think my learned friend will agree with me in that."

"Undoubtedly," I replied. "And to me there is a strong suggestion of premeditation. I take it that X, the owner of the yacht, enticed Reed out here, possibly to prepare for a cruise; that the two men worked at the repainting while the daylight lasted and then spent the evening drinking and gambling. The fact that they used several packs of cards suggests that they played for pretty heavy stakes.

"Then, I think, Reed became drunk and X offered to see him safely off the marshes. It is evident that X was not drunk, because, although both tracks appear unsteady when the men were walking together, the tracks of X returning to the yacht are quite steady and straight. I should say that the actual murder took place just after they had got over the gate; that Reed's false teeth fell out while his body was being dragged to the rick, and that this was unnoticed by X owing to the darkness. Then X dragged the body up the ladder and laid it in the middle of the rick at the top, set fire to the rick—probably on the lee side-and at once made off back to the yacht. There he passed the night, and in the morning he returned to the town along the road, giving the neighbourhood of the rick a wide berth. That is my reading of the evidence."

"Yes," said Thorndyke, "that seems to be the interpretation of the facts. And now all that remains is to give a name to the mysterious X, and I should think that will present no difficulties."

"Are you proposing to inspect the remains at the mortuary?" I asked.

"No," he replied. "It would be interesting, but it is not necessary. We have all the available data for identification, and our concern is now not with Reed but with X. We had better get back to London."

On our arrival at the station, we found the bookstall keeper in the act of sticking up a placard of the evening paper on which was the legend: "Rick tragedy; Sensational development."

We immediately provided ourselves each with a copy of the paper, and sitting down on a seat, proceeded to read the heavily-leaded report.

"A new and startling aspect has been given to the rick tragedy by some further inquiries that the police have made. It seems that the dead man, Reed, was a member of the firm of Reed and Jarman, outside brokers, and it now transpires that his partner, Walter Jarman, is also missing. There has been no one at the office this week, but the caretaker states that on Monday evening at about eight o'clock, he saw Mr. Jarman let himself into the office with his key (the rick was first seen to be on fire at two o'clock on Monday morning).

"It appears that three cheques, payable to the firm and endorsed by Jarman, were paid into the bank—Patmore's—by the first post on Tuesday morning, and that, also on Tuesday morning, Jarman purchased a parcel of diamonds of just over a thousand pounds in value from a diamond merchant in Hatton Garden, who accepted a cheque in payment after telephoning to the bank.

"It further appears that on the previous Saturday morning, Reed and Jarman visited the bank together and drew out in cash practically their whole balance, leaving only thirty-two pounds. The diamond merchant's cheque was met by the cheques that had just been paid in. It is premature to make any comments, but we may expect some strange disclosures at the inquest, which will be held at Dartford the day after tomorrow."

"I assume," said I, "that the identity of X is no longer a mystery. It looks as if these two men had agreed to realise their assets and abscond, and had then spent the night gambling for the swag, and, oddly enough, Reed appears to have been the winner, for otherwise there would have been no need to murder him."

"That is so," Thorndyke agreed, "assuming that X is Jarman, which is probable, though not certain. But we mustn't go beyond our facts, and we mustn't construct theories from newspaper reports. I think we had better call at Scotland Yard on our way home and verify those particulars."

The report and our own observations occupied us during the journey to London, though our discussion produced no further conclusions. As soon as we arrived at Charing Cross, Thorndyke sprang out of the train, and emerging from the station, walked swiftly towards Whitehall.

Our visit was fortunately timed, for as we approached the entrance to the headquarters, our old friend, Superintendent Miller, came out. He smiled as he saw us and halted to utter the laconic query:

"Rick Case?"

"Yes," replied Thorndyke. "We have come to verify the particulars given in the evening paper. Have you seen the report?"

"Yes; and you may take it as correct. Anything else?"

"I should have liked to look over a series of the cheques drawn by the firm. The last two, I suppose, are inaccessible?"

"Yes. They will be at the bank, and we couldn't inspect them without an order of the court. But, as to the others, if they are at the office, I think you could see them. I'll come along with you now if you like, and have a look round myself. Our people are in possession."

We at once closed with the superintendent's offer and proceeded with him by the Underground Railway to the Mansion House, from whence we made our way to Queen Victoria Street, where Reed and Jarman had their offices. A sergeant was in charge at the moment, and to him the superintendent addressed himself.

"Have you found any returned cheques?"

"Yes, sir," replied the sergeant; "lots of 'em. We've been through them all."

As he spoke he produced several bundles of cheques and laid them on a desk, the drawers of which all stood open.

"Well," said Miller, "there they are, doctor. I don't know what you want to find out, but I expect you do." He placed a chair by the desk, and as Thorndyke sat down and proceeded to turn the cheques over, he watched him with politely-suppressed curiosity.

"It appears," said Thorndyke, "as if these two men had mixed up their private affairs with the business account. Here, for instance, is a cheque drawn by Reed for the Picardy Wine Company. But that company could hardly have been a client. And this one of Jarman's for the Secretary of the St. John's Nursing Home must be a private cheque, and so I should say are these two for F. Waller, Esq., F.R.C.S., and for Andrew Darton, Esq., L.D.S. They are drawn for professional men and both are—like the Nursing Home cheque—stated in even amounts of guineas, whereas the business cheques are in uneven amounts of pounds, shillings and pence."

"I think you are right, sir," said Miller. "The business seems to have been conducted in a very casual manner. And just look at those signatures! Never twice alike. The banks hate that sort of thing, naturally. When a customer signs in the signature book he has given a specimen for reference and he ought to keep to it strictly. A man who varies his signature is asking for trouble."

"He is," Thorndyke agreed, as he rapidly entered a few particulars of the cheques in his notebook; "particularly in the case of a firm with a staff of clerks."

He stood up, and having pocketed his notebook, held out his hand.

"I am very much obliged to you, superintendent," he said.

"Seen all that you wanted to see?" Miller asked.

"Thank you, yes," Thorndyke replied.

"I should very much like to know what you have seen," Miller rejoined; to which my colleague replied by waving his hand towards the cheques, as he turned to go.

"I don't quite see the bearing of those cheques on our inquiry," I said, as we took our way homeward along Cheapside.

"It is not very direct," Thorndyke replied, "but the cheques help us to understand the characters of these two men and their relations with one another; which may be very necessary when we come to the inquest."

During the following day I saw very little of Thorndyke, for our excursion to Dartford had put our work somewhat in arrears and we had to secure a free day for the inquest on the morrow. We met at dinner after the day's work, but, beyond settling the programme for the next day nothing of importance passed with reference to the "Rick Case."

The opening phases of the inquest, though of thrilling interest to the numerous spectators and Press men, did not particularly concern us. The evidence of the rural constable, the farmer and the police inspector—with whom Thorndyke had a little confidential talk and apparently surprised the officer considerably—merely amplified what we knew already. Of more interest was that of a local dentist who testified to having examined the dental plate and to having compared it with the skull of the dead man. "The plate and the jaw of deceased," he said, "agree completely. The jaw contains five natural teeth in two groups, and the plate has two spaces which exactly correspond to those two groups of teeth. I have tried the plate on the jaw and have no doubt whatever that it belonged to deceased."

"That is a very important fact," Thorndyke remarked to me as the witness retired. "It is the indispensable link in the chain."

"But surely it was obvious?" said I.

"No doubt," he replied. "But now it is proved and in evidence."

I was somewhat puzzled by Thorndyke's remark, but the appearance of a new witness forbade discussion. Mr. Arthur Gerrard was an alert-looking, rather tall man, with bushy, Mephistophelian eyebrows and a small, dark moustache, who wore a pair of large bifocal spectacles, and to whom a small mole at the corner of the mouth imparted the effect of a permanent one-sided smile.

"It was on your information," said the coroner, "that the identity of the deceased was established."

"Yes," replied the witness, who spoke with a slight, but perceptible, Irish accent. "I saw the description in the papers of the things that had been found in the rick and at once recognised them as Reed's. I knew deceased intimately and had often noticed his peculiar watch-chain and the little china mascot and seen him smoking the clay pipe with his initials scratched on it; and I knew that he wore false teeth."

"Did you meet him frequently?"

"Oh, yes. For more than a year he was my partner in business, and we remained friends after I had dissolved the partnership."

"Why did you dissolve the partnership?"

"I had to. Reed was impossible in a business sense. He gambled incessantly in stocks and I had to pay his losses. I lent him, for this purpose, at one time and another, over two thousand pounds. He gave me bills for the loans, but he was never able to meet them, and in the end, when we dissolved, I got him to insure his life for three thousand pounds and to draw up a document making his debt to me the first charge on his estate in the event of his death."

"Had you ever any reason to suppose that he contemplated suicide?

"None whatever. After he left me, he entered into partnership with a Mr. Walter Jarman, and whenever I met him, he seemed to be quite happy and contented, though I gathered that he was still gambling a good deal. I saw him a week ago today and he then told me that he proposed to take a short yachting holiday with his partner, who owned a small cutter. That was the last time that I saw him alive."

As the witness was about to retire, Thorndyke rose, and having obtained the coroner's permission to cross-examine, asked: "You have spoken of a yacht. Do you know what her name is and where she has been kept lately?"

"Her name is the *Moonbeam*, and I believe Jarman kept her somewhere in the Thames, but I don't know where."

"And as to Jarman himself: what do you know about him, as to his character, for instance?"

"I knew him very slightly. He appeared to be rather a dissipated man. Drank a good deal, I should say, and I think he was a bit of a gambler."

"Do you know if he was a heavy smoker?"

"He didn't smoke at all, but he was an inveterate snuff-taker."

At this point the foreman of the jury interposed with the audible remark that "he didn't see what this had to do with the inquiry," and the coroner looked dubiously at Thorndyke; but as my colleague sat down, the objection was not pursued.

The next witness was the caretaker of the building in which Reed and Jarman's office was situated. His evidence was to the effect that on the previous Monday evening at about eight o'clock, he saw Mr. Jarman let himself into the office with his key. "I don't know how long he stayed there," he continued, in reply to the coroner's question. "I had finished my work and was going up to my rooms at the top of the building. I didn't see him again."

"Did you notice anything unusual in his appearance?" asked

Thorndyke, rising to cross-examine. "Was his face at all flushed, for instance?"

"I couldn't say. I was going up the stairs and I just looked back over my shoulder when I heard him. His face was turned away from me."

"But you had no difficult in recognising him?"

"No: I should have known him a mile off. He had his overcoat on, and it is a very peculiar overcoat—light brown with a sort of greenish check. You couldn't possibly mistake it."

"What should you say was Mr. Jarman's height?"

"About five feet nine or ten, I should say."

Here the foreman of the jury again interposed. "Aren't we wasting time, sir?" he inquired impatiently. "These details about Jarman may be very important to the police, but they don't concern us. We are inquiring into the death of Mr. Reginald Reed."

The coroner looked deprecatingly at Thorndyke and remarked, "There is some truth in what the foreman says."

"I submit, sir," replied Thorndyke, "that there is no truth in it at all. We are not inquiring into the death of Reginald Reed, but into that of a man whose remains were found in a burned rick."

"But the body has been identified as that of Reginald Reed."

"Then," said Thorndyke, "I submit that it has been wrongly identified. I suggest that the body is that of Walter Jarman and I am prepared to produce witnesses who will prove that it is."

"But," exclaimed the coroner, "we have just heard the evidence of a witness who states that he saw Jarman alive eighteen hours after the rick was fired."

"I beg your pardon, sir," said Thorndyke. "We have heard the witness say that he saw Jarman's overcoat. He expressly stated that he did not see the man's face."

The coroner hastily conferred with the jury—who openly scoffed at Thorndyke's suggestion—and then said: "I find what you say perfectly incredible and so do the jury. It is utterly irreconcilable with the facts. You had better call your witnesses and let us dispose of this extraordinary suggestion."

Thorndyke bowed to the coroner and called Mr. Andrew Darton; whereupon a middle-aged man of markedly professional aspect came forward and, having been sworn, gave evidence as follows: "I am a dental surgeon. A little over two years ago, Mr. Walter Jarman was under my care. I extracted some loose teeth from both jaws and made him two plates—an upper and a lower."

"Could you identify those plates?"

"Yes. I have with me the plaster model on which those plates were made." He opened a bag and produced a plaster cast of a pair of jaws fitted with a brass hinge so that the jaws could be opened and shut. On the upper jaw were two groups of teeth separated by a space of bare gums, while the lower jaw bore a single group of four front teeth.

"This model," the witness explained, "is an exact replica of the patient's jaws, and the two plates were actually moulded on it." He picked up the dental plate from the table and, amidst a hush of breathless expectancy, opened the mouth of the model and applied the plate to the upper jaw. At a glance, it was obvious that it fitted perfectly. The two groups of the plaster teeth slipped exactly into the spaces on the plate, making a complete row of teeth. Then the witness covered the lower gums with strips of plastic wax, and taking the loose teeth from the table, attached them to the wax; and again the correspondence was evident. The teeth thus applied exactly filled the vacant spaces.

"Can you now identify that plate?" Thorndyke asked.

"Yes," was the reply. "I am quite certain that this is the plate I made for Mr. Jarman and that those loose teeth are from his lower plate."

Thorndyke looked at the coroner, who nodded emphatically. "This evidence seems perfectly conclusive," he admitted. "What do you say, gentlemen?" he added, turning to the jury.

There was no doubt as to their sentiments. With one voice they declared their complete conviction. Had they not seen the demonstration with their own eyes?

"And now, sir," said the coroner, "as you appear to know more than anyone else about this case, and as it is perfectly incomprehensible to me, and probably also to the jury, I suggest that you give us an explanation. And you had better make it a sworn statement, so that it can go into the depositions."

"Yes," Thorndyke agreed, "especially as I have some evidence to give." He was accordingly sworn and then proceeded to make the following statement:

"The first thing that struck me on reading the report of this case was the very remarkable character of the objects found in the ashes of the rick. They included objects composed of platinum, of pipe-clay, of iron and of porcelain—all substances practically indestructible by fire. And these imperishable objects were all highly distinctive and easily identifiable, and two of them actually bore the initials of their owner. There was almost a suggestion of the body having been prepared for identification after burning. This mere suggestion, however, gave place to definite suspicion when I saw the dental plate. That plate presented a most striking discrepancy. Here it is, sir, and you see that it is a clean polished plate of red vulcanite, with not a trace of stain or discoloration. But associated with that plate were two clay pipes.

"Now, the man who smokes a clay pipe is not only—as a rule—a heavy smoker, but he smokes strong and dark-coloured tobacco. And if he wears a dental plate, that plate becomes encrusted with a black deposit which is very difficult to remove. There is, as you see, no trace of any such deposit, or of any tobacco stain in the interstices of the teeth. It appeared to be almost certainly the plate of a non-smoker. But if that were so, it could not be Reed's. But it had been ascertained by the police surgeon that it fitted the jaw of the skull and undoubtedly belonged to the burned body. Consequently if the plate was not Reed's plate, the skull was not Reed's skull, and the body was not Reed's body.

"But the watch-chain was Reed's, the pipes were his and the mascot was his. That is to say that the very identifiable and fire-proof property of Reed was associated with the burned body of some other person; that, in other words, the body of some unknown person had been deliberately prepared to counterfeit the body of Reed. This offered a further suggestion and raised a question. The suggestion was that the unknown person had been murdered—presumably somewhere near the spot where the dental plate was found. The question was—What was the object of causing the body to counterfeit that of Reed?

"Now, I knew, from the insurance company, that Reed had insured his life for three thousand pounds. Therefore, somebody stood to gain three thousand pounds by his death. The question was—Who was that somebody? I proceeded to make certain investigations on the spot;"—and here Thorndyke gave a summary of our discoveries on the marsh and on the yacht. "It thus appeared," he continued, "that there were two men on the marshes that night, going towards the rick. One of them was the person whose body was found in the ashes; the other, who went back alone to the yacht, was presumably the person who stood to gain three thousand pounds by Reed's death."

"Have you formed any opinion as to who that person was?" the coroner asked.

"Yes," replied Thorndyke. "I have very little doubt that he was Reginald Reed."

"But," exclaimed the coroner, "we have heard in evidence that it was Mr. Arthur Gerrard who stood to gain the three thousand pounds!"

"Precisely," said Thorndyke; and for a while he and the coroner looked at one another without speaking.

Suddenly the latter cast a searching look around the court. "Where is Mr. Gerrard?" he demanded.

"He left the court about ten minutes ago," said Thorndyke; "and a police inspector left immediately afterwards. I had advised him not to lose sight of Mr. Gerrard."

"Then I take it that you suspect Gerrard of being in collusion with Reed?"

"I suspect that Arthur Gerrard and Reginald Reed are one and the same person."

As Thorndyke made this statement, a murmur of astonishment arose from the jurymen and the spectators. The coroner, after a few moments' puzzled reflection, remarked: "You are not forgetting that Reed's caretaker was present while Gerrard was giving his evidence?" Then, turning to the caretaker, he asked: "What do you say? Was that Mr. Reed who gave evidence under the name of Gerrard?"

The caretaker, who had evidently been thinking furiously, was by no means confident. "I should say not," he replied, "unless he was made up a good deal. He was certainly about the same height and build and colour; but he had a moustache, whereas Mr. Reed was clean-shaved; he had a mole on his face, which Mr. Reed hadn't; he had bushy eyebrows, whereas Mr. Reed had hardly any eyebrows to speak of; and he wore spectacles, which Mr. Reed didn't, and he spoke like an Irishman, whereas Mr. Reed was English. Still it is possible—"

Before he could finish, the door rattled to a heavy concussion. Then it flew open, and Mr. Gerrard staggered into the room, thrust forward by the police inspector. His appearance was marvellously changed, for he had lost his spectacles, and one of his eyebrows had disappeared, as had also the mole and a portion of the built-up moustache. The caretaker started up with an exclamation, but at this moment Gerrard, with a violent effort, wrenched himself free. The inspector sprang forward to recapture him. But he was too late. The prisoner's hand flew upwards; there was a ringing report; and Arthur Gerrard—or Reginald Reed—fell back across a bench with a trickle of blood on his temple and a pistol still clutched in his hand.

"And so," said Stalker, when he called on us the next day for details, "it was a suicide after all. Very lucky, too, seeing that there was no provision in the policy for death by judicial hanging."

The Contents of a Mare's Nest

"It is very unsatisfactory," said Mr. Stalker, of the Griffin Life Assurance Company, at the close of a consultation on a doubtful claim. "I suppose we shall have to pay up."

"I am sure you will," said Thorndyke. "The death was properly certified, the deceased is buried, and you have not a single fact with which to support an application for further inquiry."

"No," Stalker agreed. "But I am not satisfied. I don't believe that doctor really knew what she died from. I wish cremation were more usual."

"So, I have no doubt, has many a poisoner," Thorndyke remarked dryly.

Stalker laughed, but stuck to his point. "I know you don't agree," said he, "but from our point of view it is much more satisfactory to know that the extra precautions have been taken. In a cremation case, you have not to depend on the mere death certificate; you have the cause of death verified by an independent authority, and it is difficult to see how any miscarriage can occur."

Thorndyke shook his head. "It is a delusion, Stalker. You can't provide in advance for unknown contingencies. In practice, your special precautions degenerate into mere formalities. If the circumstances of a death appear normal, the independent authority will certify; if they appear abnormal, you won't get a certificate at all. And if suspicion arises only after the cremation has taken place, it can neither be confirmed nor rebutted."

"My point is," said Stalker, "that the searching examination would lead to discovery of a crime before cremation."

"That is the intention," Thorndyke admitted. "But no examination, short of an exhaustive post-mortem, would make it safe to destroy a body so that no reconsideration of the cause of death would be possible."

Stalker smiled as he picked up his hat. "Well," he said, "to a cobbler there is nothing like leather, and I suppose that to a toxicologist there is nothing like an exhumation," and with this parting shot he took his leave.

We had not seen the last of him, however. In the course of the same week he looked in to consult us on a fresh matter.

"A rather queer case has turned up," said he. "I don't know that we are deeply concerned in it, but we should like to have your opinion as to how we stand. The position is this: Eighteen months ago, a man named Ingle insured with us for fifteen hundred pounds, and he was then accepted as a first-class life. He has recently died—apparently from heart failure, the heart being described as fatty and dilated—and his wife, Sibyl, who is the sole legatee and *executrix*, has claimed payment.

"But just as we were making arrangements to pay, a caveat has been entered by a certain Margaret Ingle, who declares that she is the wife of the deceased and claims the estate as next-of-kin. She states that the alleged wife, Sibyl, is a widow named Huggard who contracted a bigamous marriage with the deceased, knowing that he had a wife living."

"An interesting situation," commented Thorndyke, "but, as you say, it doesn't particularly concern you. It is a matter for the Probate Court."

"Yes," agreed Stalker. "But that is not all. Margaret Ingle not only charges the other woman with bigamy; she accuses her of having made away with the deceased."

"On what grounds?"

"Well, the reasons she gives are rather shadowy. She states that Sibyl's husband, James Huggard, died under suspicious circumstances—there seems to have been some suspicion that he had been poisoned—and she asserts that Ingle was a healthy, sound man and could not have died from the causes alleged."

"There is some reason in that," said Thorndyke, "if he was really a first-class life only eighteen months ago. As to the first husband, Huggard, we should want some particulars: as to whether there was an inquest what was the alleged cause of death, and what grounds there were for suspecting that he had been poisoned. If there really were any suspicious circumstances, it would be advisable to apply to the Home Office for an order to exhume the body of Ingle and verify the cause of death."

Stalker smiled somewhat sheepishly. "Unfortunately," said he, "that is not possible. Ingle was cremated."

"Ah!" said Thorndyke, "that is, as you say, unfortunate. It clearly increases the suspicion of poisoning, but destroys the means of verifying that suspicion."

"I should tell you," said Stalker, "that the cremation was in accordance with the provisions of the will."

"That is not very material," replied Thorndyke. "In fact, it rather accentuates the suspicious aspect of the case; for the knowledge that the death of the deceased would be followed by cremation might act as a further inducement to get rid of him by poison. There were two death certificates, of course?"

"Yes. The confirmatory certificate was given by Dr. Halbury, of Wimpole Street. The medical attendant was a Dr. Barber, of Howland Street. The deceased lived in Stock-Orchard Crescent, Holloway."

"A good distance from Howland Street," Thorndyke remarked. "Do you know if Halbury made a post-mortem? I don't suppose he did."

"No, he didn't," replied Stalker.

"Then," said Thorndyke, "his certificate is worthless. You can't tell whether a man has died from heart failure by looking at his dead body. He must have just accepted the opinion of the medical attendant. Do I understand that you want me to look into this case?"

"If you will. It is not really our concern whether or not the man was poisoned, though I suppose we should have a claim on the estate of the murderer. But we should like you to investigate the case; though how the deuce you are going to do it I don't quite see."

"Neither do I," said Thorndyke. "However, we must get into touch with the doctors who signed the certificates, and possibly they may be able to clear the whole matter up."

"Of course," said I, "there is the other body—that of Huggard—which might be exhumed—unless he was cremated, too."

"Yes," agreed Thorndyke; "and for the purposes of the criminal law, evidence of poisoning in that case would be sufficient. But it would hardly help the Griffin Company, which is concerned exclusively with Ingle deceased. Can you let us have a *précis* of the facts relating to this case, Stalker?"

"I have brought one with me," was the reply; "a short statement, giving names, addresses, dates, and other particulars. Here it is;" and he handed Thorndyke a sheet of paper bearing a tabulated statement.

When Stalker had gone Thorndyke glanced rapidly through the *précis* and then looked at his watch. "If we make our way to Wimpole Street at once," said he, "we ought to catch Halbury. That is obviously the first thing to do. He signed the 'C' certificate, and we shall be able to judge from what he tells us whether there is any possibility of foul play. Shall we start now?"

As I assented, he slipped the *précis* in his pocket and we set forth. At the top of Middle Temple Lane we chartered a taxi by which we were shortly deposited at Dr. Halbury's door and a few minutes later were ushered into his consulting room, and found him shovelling a pile of letters into the waste-paper basket.

"How d'ye do?" he said briskly, holding out his hand. "I'm up to my eyes in arrears, you see. Just back from my holiday. What can I do for you?"

"We have called," said Thorndyke, "about a man named Ingle."

"Ingle—Ingle," repeated Halbury. "Now, let me see—"

"Stock-Orchard Crescent, Holloway," Thorndyke explained.

"Oh, yes. I remember him. Well, how is he?"

"He's dead," replied Thorndyke.

"Is he really?" exclaimed Halbury. "Now that shows how careful one should be in one's judgments. I half suspected that fellow of malingering. He was supposed to have a dilated heart, but I couldn't make out any appreciable dilatation. There was excited, irregular action. That was all. I had a suspicion that he had been dosing himself with *trinitrine*. Reminded me of the cases of cordite chewing that I used to meet with in South Africa. So he's dead, after all. Well, it's queer. Do you know what the exact cause of death was?"

"Failure of a dilated heart is the cause stated on the certificates—the body was cremated; and the 'C' Certificate was signed by you."

"By me!" exclaimed the physician. "Nonsense! It's a mistake. I signed a certificate for a Friendly Society. Ingle brought it here for me to sign—but I didn't even know he was dead. Besides, I went away for my holiday a few days after I saw the man and only came back yesterday. What makes you think I signed the death certificate?"

Thorndyke produced Stalker's *précis* and handed it to Halbury, who read out his own name and address with a puzzled frown. "This is an extraordinary affair," said he. "It will have to be looked into."

"It will, indeed," assented Thorndyke; "especially as a suspicion of poisoning has been raised."

"Ha!" exclaimed Halbury. "Then it was *trinitrine*, you may depend. But I suspected him unjustly. It was somebody else who was dosing him; perhaps that sly-looking baggage of a wife of his. Is anyone in particular suspected?

"Yes. The accusation, such as it is, is against the wife."

"H'm. Probably a true bill. But she's done us. Artful devil. You can't get much evidence out of an urnful of ashes. Still, somebody has forged my signature. I suppose that is what the hussy wanted that certificate for—to get a specimen of my handwriting. I see the 'B' certificate was signed by a man named Meeking. Who's he? It was Barber who called me in for an opinion."

"I must find out who he is," replied Thorndyke. "Possibly Dr. Barber will know. I shall go and call on him now."

"Yes," said Dr. Halbury, shaking hands as we rose to depart, "you ought to see Barber. He knows the history of the case, at any rate."

From Wimpole Street we steered a course for Howland Street, and here we had the good fortune to arrive just as Dr. Barber's car drew up at the door. Thorndyke introduced himself and me, and then introduced the subject of his visit, but said nothing, at first, about our call on Dr. Halbury.

"Ingle," repeated Dr. Barber. "Oh, yes, I remember him. And you say he is dead. Well, I'm rather surprised. I didn't regard his condition as serious."

"Was his heart dilated?" Thorndyke asked.

"Not appreciably. I found nothing organic; no valvular disease. It was more like a tobacco heart. But it's odd that Meeking didn't mention the matter to me—he was my locum, you know. I handed the case over to him when I went on my holiday. And you say he signed the death certificate?"

"Yes; and the 'B' certificate for cremation, too."

"Very odd," said Dr. Barber. "Just come in and let us have a look at the day book."

We followed him into the consulting room, and there, while he was turning over the leaves of the day book, I ran my eye along the shelf over the writing-table from which he had taken it; on which I observed the usual collection of case books and books of certificates and notification forms, including the book of death certificates.

"Yes;" said Dr. Barber, "here we are; 'Ingle, Mr., Stock-Orchard Crescent.' The last visit was on the 4th of September, and Meeking seems to have given some sort of certificate. Wonder if he used a printed form." He took down two of the books and turned over the counterfoils.

"Here we are," he said presently; "'Ingle, Jonathan, 4 September. Now recovered and able to resume duties.' That doesn't look like dying, does it? Still, we may as well make sure."

He reached down the book of death certificates and began to glance through the most recent entries.

"No," he said, turning over the leaves, "there doesn't seem to be—Hullo! What's this? Two blank counterfoils; and about the date, too; between the 2nd and 13th of September. Extraordinary! Meeking is such a careful, reliable man."

He turned back to the day book and read through the fortnight's entries. Then he looked up with an anxious frown.

"I can't make this out," he said. "There is no record of any patient having died in that period."

"Where is Dr. Meeking at present?" I asked.

"Somewhere in the South Atlantic," replied Barber. "He left here three weeks ago to take up a post on a Royal Mail Boat. So he couldn't have signed the certificate in any case."

That was all that Dr. Barber had to tell us, and a few minutes later we took our departure.

"This case looks pretty fishy," I remarked, as we turned down Tottenham Court Road.

"Yes," Thorndyke agreed. "There is evidently something radically wrong. And what strikes me especially is the cleverness of the fraud; the knowledge and judgment and foresight that are displayed."

"She took pretty considerable risks," I observed.

"Yes, but only the risks that were unavoidable. Everything that could be foreseen has been provided for. All the formalities have been complied with—in appearance. And you must notice, Jervis, that the scheme did actually succeed. The cremation has taken place. Nothing but the incalculable accident of the appearance of the real Mrs. Ingle, and her vague and apparently groundless suspicions, prevented the success from being final. If she had not come on the scene, no questions would ever have been asked."

"No," I agreed. "The discovery of the plot is a matter of sheer bad luck. But what do you suppose has really happened?"

Thorndyke shook his head.

"It is very difficult to say. The mechanism of the affair is obvious enough, but the motives and purpose are rather incomprehensible.

The illness was apparently a sham, the symptoms being produced by nitroglycerine or some similar heart poison. The doctors were called in, partly for the sake of appearances and partly to get specimens of their handwriting. The fact that both the doctors happened to be away from home and one of them at sea at the time when verbal questions might have been asked—by the undertaker, for instance—suggests that this had been ascertained in advance.

"The death certificate forms were pretty certainly stolen by the woman when she was left alone in Barber's consulting-room, and, of course, the cremation certificates could be obtained on application to the crematorium authorities. That is all plain sailing. The mystery is, what is it all about? Barber or Meeking would almost certainly have given a death certificate, although the death was unexpected, and I don't suppose Halbury would have refused to confirm it. They would have assumed that their diagnosis had been at fault."

"Do you think it could have been suicide, or an in advertent over-dose of *trinitrine*?"

"Hardly. If it was suicide, it was deliberate, for the purpose of get-ting the insurance money for the woman, unless there was some fur-ther motive behind. And the cremation, with all its fuss and formali-ties, is against suicide; while the careful preparation seems to exclude inadvertent poisoning. Then, what was the motive for the sham illness except as a preparation for an abnormal death?"

"That is true," said I. "But if you reject suicide, isn't it rather re-markable that the victim should have provided for his own crema-tion?"

"We don't know that he did," replied Thorndyke. "There is a sug-gestion of a capable forger in this business. It is quite possible that the will itself is a forgery."

"So it is!" I exclaimed. "I hadn't thought of that."

"You see," continued Thorndyke, "the appearances suggest that cremation was a necessary part of the programme; otherwise these extraordinary risks would not have been taken. The woman was sole *executrix* and could have ignored the cremation clause. But if the cre-mation was necessary, why was it necessary? The suggestion is that there was something suspicious in the appearance of the body; some-thing that the doctors, would certainly have observed or that would have been discovered if an exhumation had taken place."

"You mean some injury or visible signs of poisoning?"

"I mean something discoverable by examination even after burial."

"But what about the undertaker? Wouldn't he have noticed anything palpably abnormal?"

"An excellent suggestion, Jervis. We must see the undertaker. We have his address: Kentish Town Road—a long way from deceased's house, by the way. We had better get on a bus and go there now."

A yellow omnibus was approaching as he spoke. We hailed it and sprang on, continuing our discussion as we were borne northward.

Mr. Burrell, the undertaker, was a pensive-looking, profoundly civil man who was evidently in a small way, for he combined with his funeral functions general carpentry and cabinet making. He was perfectly willing to give any required information, but he seemed to have very little to give.

"I never really saw the deceased gentleman," he said in reply to Thorndyke's cautious inquiries. "When I took the measurements, the corpse was covered with a sheet; and as Mrs. Ingle was in the room, I made the business as short as possible."

"You didn't put the body in the coffin, then?"

"No. I left the coffin at the house, but Mrs. Ingle said that she and the deceased gentleman's brother would lay the body in it."

"But didn't you see the corpse when you screwed the coffin-lid down?"

"I didn't screw it down. When I got there it was screwed down already. Mrs. Ingle said they had to close up the coffin, and I dare say it was necessary. The weather was rather warm; and I noticed a strong smell of *formalin*."

"Well," I said, as we walked back down the Kentish Town Road, "we haven't got much more forward."

"I wouldn't say that," replied Thorndyke. "We have a further instance of the extraordinary adroitness with which this scheme was carried out; and we have confirmation of our suspicion that there was something unusual in the appearance of the body. It is evident that this woman did not dare to let even the undertaker see it. But one can hardly help admiring the combination of daring and caution, the boldness with which these risks were taken, and the care and judgment with which they were provided against. And again I point out that the risks were justified by the result. The secret of that man's death appears to have been made secure for all time."

It certainly looked as if the mystery with which we were concerned were beyond the reach of investigation. Of course, the woman could be prosecuted for having forged the death certificates, to say nothing of the charge of bigamy. But that was no concern of ours or Stalker's. Jonathan Ingle was dead, and no one could say how he died.

On our arrival at our chambers we found a telegram that had just arrived, announcing that Stalker would call on us in the evening; and as this seemed to suggest that he had some fresh information we looked forward to his visit with considerable interest. Punctually at six o'clock he made his appearance and at once opened the subject.

"There are some new developments in this Ingle case," said he. "In the first place, the woman, Huggard, has bolted. I went to the house to make a few inquiries and found the police in possession. They had come to arrest her on the bigamy charge, but she had got wind of their intentions and cleared out. They made a search of the premises, but I don't think they found anything of interest except a number of rifle cartridges; and I don't know that they are of much interest either, for she could hardly have shot him with a rifle."

"What kind of cartridges were they?" Thorndyke asked.

Stalker put his hand in his pocket.

"The inspector let me have one to show you," said he; and he laid on the table a military cartridge of the pattern of some twenty years ago. Thorndyke picked it up, and taking from a drawer a pair of pliers drew the bullet out of the case and inserted into the latter a pair of dissecting forceps. When he withdrew the forceps, their points grasped one or two short strings of what looked like cat-gut.

"Cordite!" said I. "So Halbury was probably right, and this is how she got her supply." Then, as Stalker looked at me inquiringly, I gave him a short account of the results of our investigations.

"Ha!" he exclaimed, "the plot thickens. This juggling with the death certificates seems to connect itself with another kind of juggling that I came to tell you about. You know that Ingle was Secretary and Treasurer to a company that bought and sold land for building estates. Well, I called at their office after I left you and had a little talk with the chairman. From him I learned that Ingle had practically complete control of the financial affairs of the company, that he received and paid all moneys and kept the books.

"Of late, however, some of the directors have had a suspicion that all was not well with the finances, and at last it was decided to have the affairs of the company thoroughly overhauled by a firm of chartered accountants. This decision was communicated to Ingle, and a couple of days later a letter arrived from his wife saying that he had had a severe heart attack and asking that the audit of the books might be postponed until he recovered and was able to attend at the office."

"And was it postponed?" I asked.

"No," replied Stalker. "The accountants were asked to get to work at once, which they did; with the result that they discovered a number of discrepancies in the books and a sum of about three thousand pounds unaccounted for. It isn't quite obvious how the frauds were carried out, but it is suspected that some of the returned cheques are fakes with forged endorsements."

"Did the company communicate with Ingle on the subject?" asked Thorndyke.

"No. They had a further letter from Mrs. Ingle—that is, Huggard—saying that Ingle's condition was very serious; so they decided to wait until he had recovered. Then, of course, came the announcement of his death, on which the matter was postponed pending the probate of the will. I suppose a claim will be made on the estate, but as the *executrix* has absconded, the affair has become rather complicated."

"You were saying," said Thorndyke, "that the fraudulent death certificates seem to be connected with these frauds on the company. What kind of connection do you assume?"

"I assume—or at least, suggest," replied Stalker, "that this was a case of suicide. The man, Ingle, saw that his frauds were discovered, or were going to be, and that he was in for a long term of penal servitude, so he just made away with himself. And I think that if the murder charge could be dropped, Mrs. Huggard might be induced to come forward and give evidence as to the suicide."

Thorndyke shook his head.

"The murder charge couldn't be dropped," said he, "if it was suicide, Huggard was certainly an accessory; and in law, an accessory to suicide is an accessory to murder. But, in fact, no official charge of murder has been made, and at present there are no means of sustaining such a charge. The identity of the ashes might be assumed to be that stated in the cremation order, but the difficulty is the cause of death. Ingle was admittedly ill. He was attended for heart disease by three doctors. There is no evidence that he did not die from that illness."

"But the illness was due to cordite poisoning," said I, "That is what we believe. But no one could swear to it. And we certainly could not swear that he died from cordite poisoning."

"Then," said Stalker, "apparently there is no means of finding out whether his death was due to natural causes, suicide, or murder?"

"There is only one chance," replied Thorndyke. "It is just barely possible that the cause of death might be ascertainable by an examination of the ashes."

"That doesn't seem very hopeful," said I. "Cordite poisoning would certainly leave no trace."

"We mustn't assume that he died from cordite poisoning," said Thorndyke. "Probably he did not. That may have masked the action of a less obvious poison, or death might have been produced by some new agent."

"But," I objected, "how many poisons are there that could be detected in the ashes? No organic poison would leave any traces, nor would metallic poisons such as mercury, antimony, or arsenic."

"No," Thorndyke agreed. "But there are other metallic poisons which could be easily recovered from the ashes; lead, tin, gold, and silver, for instance. But it is useless to discuss speculative probabilities. The only chance that we have of obtaining any new facts is by an examination of the ashes. It seems infinitely improbable that we shall learn anything from it, but there is the bare possibility and we ought not to leave it untried."

Neither Stalker nor I made any further remark, but I could see that the same thought was in both our minds. It was not often that Thorndyke was "gravelled;" but apparently the resourceful Mrs. Huggard had set him a problem that was beyond even his powers. When an investigator of crime is reduced to the necessity of examining a potful of ashes in the wild hope of ascertaining from them how the deceased met his death, one may assume that he is at the very end of his tether. It is a forlorn hope indeed.

Nevertheless, Thorndyke seemed to view the matter quite cheerfully, his only anxiety being lest the Home Secretary should refuse to make the order authorising the examination. And this anxiety was dispelled a day or two later by the arrival of a letter giving the necessary authority, and informing him that a Dr. Hemming—known to us both as an expert pathologist—had been deputed to be present at the examination and to confer with him as to the necessity for a chemical analysis.

On the appointed day Dr. Hemming called at our chambers and we set forth together for Liverpool Street; and as we drove thither it became evident to me that his view of our mission was very similar to my own. For, though he talked freely enough, and on professional topics, he maintained a most discreet silence on the subject of the forthcoming inspection; indeed, the first reference to the subject was made by Thorndyke himself just as the train was approaching Corfield, where the crematorium was situated.

"I presume," said he, "you have made all necessary arrangements, Hemming?"

"Yes," was the reply. "The superintendent will meet us and will conduct us to the catacombs, and there, in our presence, will take the casket from its niche in the columbarium and have it conveyed to the office, where the examination will be made. I thought it best to use these formalities, though, as the casket is sealed and bears the name of the deceased, there is not much point in them."

"No," said Thorndyke, "but I think you were right. It would be easy to challenge the identity of a mass of ashes if all precautions were not taken, seeing that the ashes themselves are unidentifiable."

"That was what I felt," said Hemming; and then, as the train slowed down, he added: "This is our station, and that gentleman on the platform, I suspect, is the superintendent."

The surmise turned out to be correct; but the cemetery official was not the only one present bearing that title; for as we were mutually introducing ourselves, a familiar tall figure approached up the platform from the rear of the train—our old friend Superintendent Miller of the Criminal Investigation Department.

"I don't wish to intrude," said he, as he joined the group and was presented by Thorndyke to the strangers, "but we were notified by the Home Office that an investigation was to be made, so I thought I would be on the spot to pick up any crumbs of information that you may drop. Of course, I am not asking to be present at the examination."

"You may as well be present as an additional witness to the removal of the urn," said Thorndyke; and Miller accordingly joined the party, which now made its way from the station to the cemetery.

The catacombs were in a long, low arcaded building at the end of the pleasantly-wooded grounds, and on our way thither we passed the crematorium, a smallish, church-like edifice with a perforated chimney-shaft partly concealed by the low spire. Entering the catacombs, we were conducted to the "columbarium," the walls of which were occupied by a multitude of niches or pigeon-holes, each niche accommodating a *terra-cotta* urn or casket.

The superintendent proceeded to near the end of the gallery, where he halted, and opening the register, which he had brought with him, read out a number and the name "Jonathan Ingle," and then led us to a niche bearing that number and name, in which reposed a square casket, on which was inscribed the name and date of death. When we had verified these particulars, the casket was tenderly lifted from its place by two attendants, who carried it to a well-lighted room at the end of the building, where a large table by a window had been covered with white paper. Having placed the casket on the table, the attendants retired, and the superintendent then broke the seals and removed the cover.

For a while we all stood looking in at the contents of the casket without speaking; and I found myself contrasting them with what would have been revealed by the lifting of a coffin-lid. Truly corruption had put on incorruption. The mass of snow-white, coral-like fragments, delicate, fragile, and lace-like in texture, so far from being repulsive in aspect, were almost attractive. I ran my eye, with an anatomist's curiosity, over these dazzling remnants of what had lately been a man, half-unconsciously seeking to identify and give a name to particular fragments, and a little surprised at the difficulty of determining that this or that irregularly-shaped white object was a part of any one of the bones with which I had thought myself so familiar.

Presently Hemming looked up at Thorndyke and asked: "Do you observe anything abnormal in the appearance of these ashes? I don't."

"Perhaps," replied Thorndyke, "we had better turn them out on to the table, so that we can see the whole of them."

This was done very gently, and then Thorndyke proceeded to spread out the heap, touching the fragments with the utmost delicacy—for they were extremely fragile and brittle—until the whole collection was visible.

"Well," said Hemming, when we had once more looked them over critically, "what do you say? I can see no trace of any foreign substance. Can you?"

"No," replied Thorndyke. "And there are some other things that I can't see. For instance, the medical referee reported that the proposer had a good set of sound teeth. Where are they? I have not seen a single fragment of a tooth. Yet teeth are far more resistant to fire than bones, especially the enamel caps."

Hemming ran a searching glance over the mass of fragments and looked up with a perplexed frown.

"I certainly can't see any sign of teeth," he admitted, "and it is rather curious, as you say. Does the fact suggest any particular significance to you?"

By way of reply, Thorndyke delicately picked up a flat fragment and silently held it out towards us. I looked at it and said nothing; for a very strange suspicion was beginning to creep into my mind.

"A piece of a rib," said Hemming. "Very odd that it should have broken across so cleanly. It might have been cut with a saw."

Thorndyke laid it down and picked up another, larger fragment, which I had already noticed.

"Here is another example," said he, handing it to our colleague.

"Yes," agreed Hemming. "It is really rather extraordinary. It looks exactly as if it had been sawn across."

"It does," agreed Thorndyke. "What bone should you say it is?"

"That is what I was just asking myself," replied Hemming, looking at the fragment with a sort of half-vexed smile. "It seems ridiculous that a competent anatomist should be in any doubt with as large a portion as this, but really I can't confidently give it a name. The shape seems to me to suggest a tibia, but of course it is much too small. Is it the upper end of the ulna?"

"I should say no," answered Thorndyke. Then he picked out another of the larger fragments, and handing it to Hemming, asked him to name it.

Our friend began to look somewhat worried.

"It is an extraordinary thing, you know," said he, "but I can't tell you what bone it is part of. It is clearly the shaft of a long bone, but I'm hanged if I can say which. It is too big for a metatarsal and too small for any of the main limb bones. It reminds one of a diminutive thigh bone."

"It does," agreed Thorndyke, "very strongly." While Hemming had been speaking he had picked out four more large fragments, and these he now laid in a row with the one that had seemed to resemble a tibia in shape. Placed thus together, the five fragments bore an obvious resemblance.

"Now," said he, "look at these. There are five of them. They are parts of limb bones, and the bones of which they are parts were evidently exactly alike, excepting that three were apparently from the left side and two from the right. Now, you know, Hemming, a man has only four limbs and of those only two contain similar bones. Then two of them show distinct traces of what looks like a saw-cut."

Hemming gazed at the row of fragments with a frown of deep cogitation.

"It is very mysterious," he said. "And looking at them in a row they

286

strike me as curiously like tibia in shape; not in size."

"The size," said Thorndyke is about that of a sheep's tibia."

"A sheep's?" exclaimed Hemming, staring in amazement, first at the calcined bones and then at my colleague.

"Yes; the upper half, sawn across in the middle of the shank."

Hemming was thunderstruck. "It is an astounding affair!" he exclaimed. "You mean to suggest—"

"I suggest," said Thorndyke, "that there is not a sign of a human bone in the whole collection. But there are very evident traces of at least five legs of mutton."

For a few moments there was a profound silence, broken only by a murmur of astonishment from the cemetery official and a low chuckle from Superintendent Miller, who had been listening with absorbed interest. At length Hemming spoke.

"Then, apparently, there was no corpse in the coffin at all?"

"No," answered Thorndyke. "The weight was made up, and the ashes furnished, by joints of butcher's meat. I dare say, if we go over the ashes carefully, we shall be able to judge what they were. But it is hardly necessary. The presence of five legs of mutton and the absence of a single recognisable fragment of a human skeleton, together with the forged certificates, gives us a pretty I conclusive case. The rest, I think we can leave to Superintendent Miller."

★★★★★★★★

"I take it, Thorndyke," said I, as the train moved out of the station, "that you came here expecting to find what you did find?"

"Yes," he replied. "It seemed to me the only possibility, having regard to all the known facts."

"When did it first occur to you?"

"It occurred to me as a possibility as soon as we discovered that the cremation certificates had been forged; but it was the undertaker's statement that seemed to clench the matter."

"But he distinctly stated that he measured the body."

"True. But there was nothing to show that it was a dead body. What was perfectly clear was that there was something that must on no account be seen; and when Stalker told us of the embezzlement we had a body of evidence that could point to only one conclusion. Just consider that evidence.

"Here we had a death, preceded by an obviously sham illness and followed by cremation with forged certificates. Now, what was it that had happened? There were four possible hypotheses. Normal death, suicide, murder, and fictitious death. Which of these hypotheses fitted the facts?

"Normal death was apparently excluded by the forged certificates.

"The theory of suicide did not account for the facts. It did not agree with the careful, elaborate preparation. And why the forged certificates? If Ingle had really died, Meeking would have certified the death. And why the cremation? There was no purpose in taking those enormous risks.

"The theory of murder was unthinkable. These certificates were almost certainly forged by Ingle himself, who we know was a practised forger. But the idea of the victim arranging for his own cremation is an absurdity.

"There remained only the theory of fictitious death; and that theory fitted all the facts perfectly. First, as to the motive. Ingle had committed a felony. He had to disappear. But what kind of disappearance could be so effectual as death and cremation? Both the prosecutors and the police would forthwith write him off and forget him. Then there was the bigamy—a criminal offence in itself. But death would not only wipe that off; after 'death' he could marry Huggard regularly under another name, and he would have shaken off his deserted wife for ever.

"And he stood to gain fifteen hundred pounds from the Insurance Company. Then see how this theory explained the other facts. A fictitious death made necessary a fictitious illness. It necessitated the forged certificates, since there was no corpse. It made cremation highly desirable; for suspicion might easily have arisen, and then the exhumation of a coffin containing a dummy would have exploded the fraud. But successful cremation would cover up the fraud for ever. It explained the concealment of the corpse from the undertaker, and it even explained the smell of *formalin* which he noticed."

"How did it?" I asked.

"Consider, Jervis," he replied. "The dummy in this coffin had to be a dummy of flesh and bone which would yield the correct kind of ash. Joints of butcher's meat would fulfil the conditions. But the quantity required would be from a hundred and fifty to two hundred pounds. Now Ingle could not go to the butcher and order a whole sheep to be sent the day before the funeral. The joints would have to be bought gradually and stored. But the storage of meat in warm weather calls for some kind of preservative; and *formalin* is highly effective, as it leaves no trace after burning.

"So you see that the theory of fictitious death agreed with all the known circumstances, whereas the alternative theories presented inexplicable discrepancies and contradictions. Logically, it was the only possible theory, and, as you have seen, experiment proved it to be the true one."

As he concluded, Dr. Hemming took his pipe from his mouth and laughed softly.

"When I came down today," said he, "I had all the facts which you had communicated to the Home Office, and I was absolutely convinced that we were coming to examine a mare's nest. And yet, now I have heard your exposition, the whole thing looks perfectly obvious."

"That is usually the case with Thorndyke's conclusions," said I. "They are perfectly obvious—when you have heard the explanation."

Within a week of our expedition, Ingle was in the hands of the police. The apparent success of the cremation adventure had misled him to a sense of such complete security that he had neglected to cover his tracks, and he had accordingly fallen an easy prey to our friend Superintendent Miller. The police were highly gratified, and so were the directors of the Griffin Life Assurance Company.

The Magic Casket

It was in the near neighbourhood of King's Road, Chelsea, that chance, aided by Thorndyke's sharp and observant eyes, introduced us to the dramatic story of the Magic Casket. Not that there was anything strikingly dramatic in the opening phase of the affair, nor even in the story of the casket itself. It was Thorndyke who added the dramatic touch, and most of the magic, too; and I record the affair principally as an illustration of his extraordinary capacity for producing odd items of out-of-the-way knowledge and instantly applying them in the most unexpected manner.

Eight o'clock had struck on a misty November night when we turned out of the main road, and, leaving behind the glare of the shop windows, plunged into the maze of dark and narrow streets to the north. The abrupt change impressed us both, and Thorndyke proceeded to moralise on it in his pleasant, reflective fashion.

"London is an inexhaustible place," he mused. "Its variety is infinite. A minute ago we walked in a glare of light, jostled by a multitude. And now look at this little street. It is as dim as a tunnel, and we have got it absolutely to ourselves. Anything might happen in a place like this."

Suddenly he stopped. We were, at the moment, passing a small church or chapel, the west door of which was enclosed in an open porch; and as my observant friend stepped into the latter and stooped, I perceived in the deep shadow against the wall, the object which had evidently caught his eye.

"What is it?" I asked, following him in.

"It is a handbag," he replied; "and the question is, what is it doing here?"

He tried the church door, which was obviously locked, and coming out, looked at the windows.

"There are no lights in the church." said he; "the place is locked up, and there is nobody in sight. Apparently the bag is derelict. Shall we have a look at it?"

Without waiting for an answer, he picked it up and brought it out into the mitigated darkness of the street, where we proceeded to inspect it. But at the first glance it told its own tale; for it had evidently been locked, and it bore unmistakable traces of having been forced open.

"It isn't empty," said Thorndyke. "I think we had better see what is in it. Just catch hold while I get a light."

He handed me the bag while he felt in his pocket for the tiny electric lamp which he made a habit of carrying, and an excellent habit it is. I held the mouth of the bag open while he illuminated the interior, which we then saw to be occupied by several objects neatly wrapped in brown paper. One of these Thorndyke lifted out, and untying the string and removing the paper, displayed a Chinese stoneware jar. Attached to it was a label, bearing the stamp of the Victoria and Albert Museum, on which was written:

Miss MABEL BONNET,
168 Willow Walk,
Fulham Road, W.

"That tells us all that we want to know," said Thorndyke, re-wrapping the jar and tenderly replacing it in the bag. "We can't do wrong in delivering the things to their owner, especially as the bag itself is evidently her property, too," and he pointed to the gilt initials, "M. B.," stamped on the morocco.

It took us but a few minutes to reach the Fulham Road, but we then had to walk nearly a mile along that thoroughfare before we arrived at Willow Walk—to which an obliging shopkeeper had directed us—and, naturally, No. 168 was at the farther end.

As we turned into the quiet street we almost collided with two men, who were walking at a rapid pace, but both looking back over their shoulders. I noticed that they were both Japanese—well-dressed, gentlemanly-looking men—but I gave them little attention, being interested, rather, in what they were looking at. This was a taxicab which was dimly visible by the light of a street lamp at the farther end of the "Walk," and from which four persons had just alighted. Two of these had hurried ahead to knock at a door, while the other two walked very slowly across the pavement and up the steps to the threshold.

Almost immediately the door was opened; two of the shadowy figures entered, and the other two returned slowly to the cab and as we came nearer, I could see that these latter were policemen in uniform. I had just time to note this fact when they both got into the cab and were forthwith spirited away.

"Looks like a street accident of some kind," I remarked; and then, as I glanced at the number of the house we were passing, I added: "Now, I wonder if that house happens to be—yes, by Jove! it is. It is 168! Things have been happening, and this bag of ours is one of the *dramatis personae.*"

The response to our knock was by no means prompt. I was, in fact, in the act of raising my hand to the knocker to repeat the summons when the door opened and revealed an elderly servant-maid, who regarded us inquiringly, and, as I thought, with something approaching alarm.

"Does Miss Mabel Bonney live here?" Thorndyke asked.

"Yes, sir," was the reply; "but I am afraid you can't see her just now, unless it is something urgent. She is rather upset, and particularly engaged at present."

"There is no occasion whatever to disturb her," said Thorndyke. "We have merely called to restore this bag, which seemed to have been lost;" and with this he held it out towards her. She grasped it eagerly with a cry of surprise, and as the mouth fell open, she peered into it.

"Why," she exclaimed, "they don't seem to have taken anything, after all. Where did you find it, sir?"

"In the porch of a church in Spelton Street," Thorndyke replied, and was turning away when the servant said earnestly: "Would you kindly give me your name and address, sir? Miss Bonney will wish to write and thank you."

"There is really no need," said he; but she interrupted anxiously: "If you would be so kind, sir. Miss Bonney will be so vexed if she is unable to thank you; and besides, she may want to ask you some questions about it."

"That is true," said Thorndyke (who was restrained only by good manners from asking one or two questions, himself). He produced his card-case, and having handed one of his cards to the maid, wished her "good-evening" and retired.

"That bag had evidently been pinched," I remarked, as we walked back towards the Fulham Road.

"Evidently," he agreed, and was about to enlarge on the matter when our attention was attracted to a taxi, which was approaching from the direction of the main road. A man's head was thrust out of the window, and as the vehicle passed a street lamp, I observed that the head appertained to an elderly gentleman with very white hair and a very fresh face.

"Did you see who that was?" Thorndyke asked.

"It looked like old Brodribb," I replied.

"It did; very much. I wonder where he is off to."

He turned and followed, with a speculative eye, the receding taxi, which presently swept alongside the kerb and stopped, apparently opposite the house from where we had just come. As the vehicle came to rest, the door flew open and the passenger shot out like an elderly, but agile, Jack-in-the-box, and bounced up the steps.

"That is Brodribb's knock, sure enough," said I, as the old-fashioned flourish reverberated up the quiet street. "I have heard it too often on our own knocker to mistake it. But we had better not let him see us watching him."

As we went once more on our way, I took a sly glance, now and again, at my friend, noting with a certain malicious enjoyment his profoundly cogitative air. I knew quite well what was happening in his mind for his mind reacted to observed facts in an invariable manner. And here was a group of related facts: the bag, stolen, but deposited intact; the museum label; the injured or sick person—probably Miss Bonney, herself—brought home under police escort; and the arrival, post-haste, of the old lawyer; a significant group of facts.

And there was Thorndyke, under my amused and attentive observation, fitting them together in various combinations to see what general conclusion emerged. Apparently my own mental state was equally clear to him, for he remarked, presently, as if response to an unspoken comment: "Well, I expect we shall know all about it before many days have passed if Brodribb sees my card, as he most probably will. Here comes an omnibus that will suit us. Shall we hop on?"

He stood at the kerb and raised his stick; and as the accommodation on the omnibus was such that our seats were separated, there was no opportunity to pursue the subject further, even if there had been anything to discuss.

But Thorndyke's prediction was justified sooner than I had expected. For we had not long finished our supper, and had not yet closed the "oak," when there was heard a mighty flourish on the knocker of our inner door.

"Brodribb, by Jingo!" I exclaimed, and hurried across the room to let him in.

"No, Jervis," he said as I invited him to enter, "I am not coming in. Don't want to disturb you at this time of night. I've just called to make an appointment for tomorrow with a client."

"Is the client's name Bonney?" I asked.

He started and gazed at me in astonishment. "Gad, Jervis!" he exclaimed, "you are getting as bad as Thorndyke. How the deuce did you know that she was my client?"

"Never mind how I know. It is our business to know everything in these chambers. But if your appointment concerns Miss Mabel Bonney, for the Lord's sake come in and give Thorndyke a chance of a night's rest. At present, he is on broken bottles, as Mr. Bumble would express it."

On this persuasion, Mr. Brodribb entered, nothing loath—very much the reverse, in fact—and having bestowed a jovial greeting on Thorndyke, glanced approvingly round the room.

"Ha!" said he, "you look very cosy. If you are really sure I am not—"

I cut him short by propelling him gently towards the fire, beside which I deposited him in an easy chair, while Thorndyke pressed the electric bell which rang up in the laboratory.

"Well," said Brodribb, spreading himself out comfortably before the fire like a handsome old Tom-cat, "if you are going to let me give you a few particulars—but perhaps you would rather that I should not talk shop?"

"Now you know perfectly well, Brodribb," said Thorndyke, "that 'shop' is the breath of life to us all. Let us have those particulars."

Brodribb sighed contentedly and placed his toes on the fender (and at this moment the door opened softly and Polton looked into the room. He took a single, understanding glance at our visitor, and withdrew, shutting the door without a sound).

"I am glad," pursued Brodribb, "to have this opportunity of a preliminary chat, because there are certain things that one can say better when the client is not present; and I am deeply interested in Bonney's affairs. The crisis in those affairs which has brought me here is of quite recent date—in fact, it dates from this evening. But I know your partiality for having events related in their proper sequence, so I will leave today's happenings for the moment and tell you the story—the whole of which is material to the case—from the beginning."

Here there was a slight interruption, due to Polton's noiseless entry with a tray on which was a decanter, a biscuit box, and three port glasses. This he deposited, on a small table, which he placed within convenient reach of our guest. Then, with a glance of altruistic satisfaction at our old friend, he stole out like a benevolent ghost.

"Dear, dear!" exclaimed Brodribb, beaming on the decanter, "this is really too bad. You ought not to indulge me in this way."

"My dear Brodribb," replied Thorndyke, "you are a benefactor to us. You give us a pretext for taking a glass of port. We can't drink alone, you know."

"I should, if I had a cellar like yours," chuckled Brodribb, sniffing ecstatically at his glass. He took a sip, with his eyes closed, savoured it solemnly, shook his head, and set the glass down on the table.

"To return to our case," he resumed; "Miss Bonney is the daughter of a solicitor, Harold Bonney—you may remember him. He had offices in Bedford Row; and there, one morning, a client came to him and asked him to take care of some property while he, the said client, ran over to Paris, where he had some urgent business. The property in question was a collection of pearls of most unusual size and value, forming a great necklace, which had been unstrung for the sake of portability. It is not clear where they came from, but as the transaction occurred soon after the Russian Revolution, we may make a guess. At any rate, there they were, packed loosely in a leather bag, the string of which was sealed with the owner's seal.

"Bonney seems to have been rather casual about the affair. He gave the client a receipt for the bag, stating the nature of the contents, which he had not seen, and deposited it, in the client's presence, in the safe in his private office. Perhaps he intended to take it to the bank or transfer it to his strong-room, but it is evident that he did neither; for his managing clerk, who kept the second key of the strong-room without which the room could not be opened—knew nothing of the transaction. When he went home at about seven o'clock, he left Bonney hard at work in his office, and there is no doubt that the pearls were still in the safe.

"That night, at about a quarter to nine, it happened that a couple of C.I.D. officers were walking up Bedford Row when they saw three men come out of one of the houses. Two of them turned up towards Theobald's Road, but the third came south, towards them. As he passed them, they both recognised him as a Japanese named Uyenishi, who was believed to be a member of a cosmopolitan gang and whom the police were keeping under observation. Naturally, their suspicions were aroused. The first two men had hurried round the corner and were out of sight; and when they turned to look after Uyenishi, he had mended his pace considerably and was looking back at them. Thereupon one of the officers, named Barker, decided to follow the Jap, while the other, Holt, reconnoitred the premises.

"Now, as soon as Barker turned, the Japanese broke into a run. It was just such a night as this dark and, slightly foggy. In order to keep his man in sight, he had to run, too; and he found that he had a sprinter to deal with. From the bottom of Bedford Row, Uyenishi darted across and shot down Hand Court like a lamp-lighter. Barker followed, but at the Holborn end his man was nowhere to be seen. However, he presently learned from a man at a shop door that the fugitive had run past and turned up Brownlow Street, so off he went again in pursuit. But when he got to the top of the street, back in Bedford Row, he was done. There was no sign of the man, and no one about from whom he could make inquiries. All he could do was to cross the road and walk up Bedford Row to see if Holt had made any discoveries.

"As he was trying to identify the house, his colleague came out on to the doorstep and beckoned him in and this was the story that he told. He had recognised the house by the big lamp-standard; and as the place was all dark, he had gone into the entry and tried the office door. Finding it unlocked, he had entered the clerks' office, lit the gas, and tried the door of the private office, but found it locked. He knocked at it, but getting no answer, had a good look round the clerk's office; and there, presently, on the floor in a dark corner, he found a key. This he tried in the door of the private office, and finding that it fitted, turned it and opened the door. As he did so, the light from the outer office fell on the body of a man lying on the floor just inside.

"A moment's inspection showed that the man had been murdered—first knocked on the head and then finished with a knife. Examination of the pockets showed that the dead man was Harold Bonney, and also that no robbery from the person seemed to have been committed. Nor was there any sign of any other kind of robbery. Nothing seemed to have been disturbed, and the safe had not been broken into, though that was not very conclusive, as the safe key was in the dead man's pocket. However, a murder had been committed, and obviously Uyenishi was either the murderer or an accessory; so

Holt had, at once, rung up Scotland Yard on the office telephone, giving all the particulars.

"I may say at once that Uyenishi disappeared completely and at once. He never went to his lodgings at Limehouse, for the police were there before he could have arrived. A lively hue and cry was kept up. Photographs of the wanted man were posted outside every police-station, and a watch was set at all the ports. But he was never found. He must have got away at once on some outward-bound tramp from the Thames. And there we will leave him for the moment.

"At first it was thought that nothing had been stolen, since the managing clerk could not discover that anything was missing. But a few days later the client returned from Paris, and presenting his receipt, asked for his pearls. But the pearls had vanished. Clearly they had been the object of the crime. The robbers must have known about them and traced them to the office. Of course the safe had been opened with its own key, which was then replaced in the dead man's pocket.

"Now, I was poor Bonney's executor, and in that capacity I denied his liability in respect of the pearls on the ground that he was a *gratuitous bailee*—there being no evidence that any consideration had been demanded—and that being murdered cannot be construed as negligence. But Miss Mabel, who was practically the sole legatee, insisted on accepting liability. She said that the pearls could have been secured in the bank or the strong-room, and that she was morally, if not legally, liable for their loss; and she insisted on handing to the owner the full amount at which he valued them. It was a wildly foolish proceeding, for he would certainly have accepted half the sum. But still I take my hat off to a person—man or woman—who can accept poverty in preference to a broken covenant;" and here Brodribb, being in fact that sort of person himself, had to be consoled with a replenished glass.

"And mind you," he resumed, "when I speak of poverty, I wish to be taken literally. The estimated value of those pearls was fifty thousand pounds—if you can imagine anyone out of Bedlam giving such a sum for a parcel of trash like that; and when poor Mabel Bonney had paid it, she was left with the prospect of having to spread her butter mighty thin for the rest of her life. As a matter of fact, she has had to sell one after another of her little treasures to pay just her current expenses, and I'm hanged if I can see how she is going to carry on when she has sold the last of them. But there, I mustn't take up your time with her private troubles. Let us return to our muttons.

"First, as to the pearls They were never traced, and it seems probable that they were never disposed of. For, you see, pearls are different from any other kind of gems. You can cut up a big diamond, but you can't cut up a big pearl. And the great value of this necklace was due not only to the size, the perfect shape and 'orient' of the separate pearls, but to the fact that the whole set was perfectly matched. To break up the necklace was to destroy a good part of its value.

"And now as to our friend Uyenishi. He disappeared, as I have said; but he reappeared at Los Angeles, in custody of the police, charged with robbery and murder. He was taken red-handed and was duly convicted and sentenced to death; but for some reason—or more probably, for no reason, as we should think—the sentence was commuted to imprisonment for life. Under these circumstances, the English police naturally took no action, especially as they really had no evidence against him.

"Now Uyenishi was, by trade, a metal-worker; a maker of those pretty trifles that are so dear to the artistic Japanese, and when he was in prison he was allowed to set up a little workshop and practise his trade on a small scale. Among other things that he made was a little casket in the form of a seated figure, which he said he wanted to give to his brother as a keepsake. I don't know whether any permission was granted for him to make this gift, but that is of no consequence; for Uyenishi got influenza and was carried off in a few days by pneumonia; and the prison authorities learned that his brother had been killed, a week or two previously, in a shooting affair at San Francisco. So the casket remained on their hands.

"About this time, Miss Bonney was invited to accompany an American lady on a visit to California, and accepted gratefully. While she was there she paid a visit to the prison to inquire whether Uyenishi had ever made any kind of statement concerning the missing pearls. Here she heard of Uyenishi's recent death; and the governor of the prison, as he could not give her any information, handed over to her the casket as a sort of memento. This transaction came to the knowledge of the press, and—well, you know what the Californian press is like. There were 'some comments,' as they would say, and quite an assortment of Japanese, of shady antecedents, applied to the prison to have the casket 'restored' to them as Uyenishi's heirs.

"Then Miss Bonney's rooms at the hotel were raided by burglars—but the casket was in the hotel strong-room—and Miss Bonney and her hostess were shadowed by various undesirables in such a disturbing fashion that the two ladies became alarmed and secretly made their way to New York. But there another burglary occurred, with the same unsuccessful result, and the shadowing began again. Finally, Miss Bonney, feeling that her presence was a danger to her friend, decided to return to England, and managed to get on board the ship without letting her departure be known in advance.

"But even in England she has not been left in peace. She has had an uncomfortable feeling of being watched and attended, and has seemed to be constantly meeting Japanese men in the streets, especially in the vicinity of her house. Of course, all the fuss is about this infernal casket; and when she told me what was happening, I promptly popped the thing in my pocket and took it, to my office, where I stowed it in the strong-room. And there, of course, it ought to have remained, but it didn't. One day Miss Bonney told me that she was sending some small things to a loan exhibition of oriental works of art at the South Kensington Museum, and she wished to include the casket. I urged her strongly to do nothing of the kind, but she persisted; and the end of it was that we went to the museum together, with her pottery and stuff in a handbag and the casket in my pocket.

"It was a most imprudent thing to do, for there the beastly casket was, for several months, exposed in a glass case for anyone to see, with her name on the label; and what was worse, full particulars of the origin of the thing. However, nothing happened while it was there—the museum is not an easy place to steal from—and all went well until it was time to remove the things after the close of the exhibition.

"Now, today was the appointed day, and, as on the previous occasion, she and I went to the museum together. But the unfortunate thing is that we didn't come away together. Her other exhibits were all pottery, and these were dealt with first, so that she had her handbag packed and was ready to go before they had begun on the metal work cases. As we were not going the same way, it didn't seem necessary for her to wait; so she went off with her bag and I stayed behind until the casket was released, when I put it in my pocket and went home, where I locked the thing up again in the strong-room.

"It was about seven when I got home. A little after eight I heard the telephone ring down in the office, and down I went, cursing the untimely ringer, who turned out to be a policeman at St. George's Hospital. He said he had found Miss Bonney lying unconscious in the street and had taken her to the hospital, where she had been detained for a while, but she was now recovered and he was taking her home. She would like me, if possible, to go and see her at once. Well, of course, I set off forthwith and got to her house a few minutes after her arrival, and just after you had left.

"She was a good deal upset, so I didn't worry her with many questions, but she gave me a short account of her misadventure, which amounted to this: She had started to walk home from the museum along the Brompton Road, and she was passing down a quiet street between that and Fulham Road when she heard soft footsteps behind her. The next moment, a scarf or shawl was thrown over her head and drawn tightly round her neck. At the same moment, the bag was snatched from her hand. That is all that she remembers, for she was so terrified that she fainted, and knew no more until she found herself in a cab with two policemen who were taking her to the hospital.

"Now it is obvious that her assailants were in search of that damned casket, for the bag had been broken open and searched, but nothing taken or damaged; which suggests the Japanese again, for a British thief would have smashed the crockery. I found your card there, and I put it to Miss Bonney that we had better ask you to help us—I told her all about you—and she agreed emphatically. So that is why I am here, drinking your port and robbing you of your night's rest."

"And what do you want me to do?" Thorndyke asked.

"Whatever you think best," was the cheerful reply. "In the first place, this nuisance must be put a stop to—this shadowing and hanging about. But apart from that, you must see that there is something queer about this accursed casket. The beastly thing is of no intrinsic value. The museum man turned up his nose at it. But it evidently has some extrinsic value, and no small value either. If it is good enough for these devils to follow it all the way from the States, as they seem to have done, it is good enough for us to try to find out what its value is. That is where you come in. I propose to bring Miss Bonney to see you tomorrow, and I will bring the infernal casket, too. Then you will ask her a few questions, take a look at the casket—through the microscope, if necessary—and tell us all about it in your usual necromantic way."

Thorndyke laughed as he refilled our friend's glass. "If faith will move mountains, Brodribb," said he, "you ought to have been a civil engineer. But it is certainly a rather intriguing problem."

"Ha!" exclaimed the old solicitor; "then it's all right. I've known you a good many years, but I've never known you to be stumped; and you are not going to be stumped now. What time shall I bring her? Afternoon or evening would suit her best."

"Very well," replied Thorndyke; "bring her to tea—say, five o'clock. How will that do?"

"Excellently; and here's good luck to the adventure." He drained his glass, and the decanter being now empty, he rose, shook our hands warmly, and took his departure in high spirits.

It was with a very lively interest that I looked forward to the prospective visit. Like Thorndyke, I found the case rather intriguing. For it was quite clear, as our shrewd old friend had said, that there was something more than met the eye in the matter of this casket.

Hence, on the following afternoon, when, on the stroke of five, footsteps became audible on our stairs, I awaited the arrival of our new client with keen curiosity, both as to herself and her mysterious property.

To tell the truth, the lady was better worth looking at than the casket. At the first glance, I was strongly prepossessed in her favour, and so, I think, was Thorndyke. Not that she was a beauty, though comely enough. But she was an example of a type that seems to be growing rarer; quiet, gentle, soft-spoken, and a lady to her finger-tips; a little sad-faced and care worn, with a streak or two of white in her prettily-disposed black hair, though she could not have been much over thirty-five. Altogether a very gracious and winning personality.

When we had been presented to her by Brodribb—who treated her as if she had been a royal personage—and had enthroned her in the most comfortable easy-chair, we inquired as to her health, and were duly thanked for the salvage of the bag. Then Polton brought in the tray, with an air that seemed to demand an escort of choristers; the tea was poured out, and the informal proceedings began.

She had not, however, much to tell; for she had not seen her assailants, and the essential facts of the case had been fully presented in Brodribb's excellent summary. After a very few questions, therefore, we came to the next stage; which was introduced by Brodribb's taking from his pocket a small parcel which he proceeded to open.

"There," said he, "that is the *fons et origo mali*. Not much to look at, I think you will agree." He set the object down on the table and glared at it malevolently, while Thorndyke and I regarded it with a more impersonal interest. It was not much to look at. Just an ordinary Japanese casket in the form of a squat, shapeless figure with a silly little grinning face, of which the head and shoulders opened on a hinge; a pleasant enough object, with its quiet, warm colouring, but certainly not a masterpiece of art.

Thorndyke picked it up and turned it over slowly for preliminary inspection; then he went on to examine it detail by detail, watched closely, in his turn, by Brodribb and me. Slowly and methodically, his eye—fortified by a watchmaker's eyeglass—travelled over every part of the exterior. Then he opened it, and I having examined the inside of the lid, scrutinised the bottom from within, long and attentively. Finally, he turned the casket upside down and examined the bottom from without, giving to it the longest and most rigorous inspection of all—which puzzled me somewhat, for the bottom was absolutely plain At length, he passed the casket and the eyeglass to me without comment.

"Well," said Brodribb, "what is the verdict?"

"It is of no value as a work of art," replied Thorndyke. "The body and lid are just castings of common white metal—an antimony alloy, I should say. The bronze colour is lacquer."

"So the museum man remarked," said Brodribb.

"But," continued Thorndyke, "there is one very odd thing about it. The only piece of fine metal in it is in the part which matters least. The bottom is a separate plate of the alloy known to the Japanese as *Shakudo*—an alloy of copper and gold."

"Yes," said Brodribb, "the museum man noted that, too, and couldn't make out why it had been put there."

"Then," Thorndyke continued, "there is another anomalous feature; the inside of the bottom is covered with elaborate decoration—just the place where decoration is most inappropriate, since it would be covered up by the contents of the casket. And, again, this decoration is etched; not engraved or chased. But etching is a very unusual process for this purpose, if it is ever used at all by Japanese metalworkers. My impression is that it is not; for it is most unsuitable for decorative purposes. That is all that I observe, so far."

"And what do you infer from your observations?" Brodribb asked.

"I should like to think the matter over," was the reply. "There is an obvious anomaly, which must have some significance. But I won't embark on speculative opinions at this stage. I should like, however, to take one or two photographs of the casket, for reference; but that will occupy some time. You will hardly want to wait so long."

"No," said Brodribb. "But Miss Bonney is coming with me to my office to go over some documents and discuss a little business. When we have finished, I will come back and fetch the confounded thing."

"There is no need for that," replied Thorndyke. "As soon as I have done what is necessary, I will bring it up to your place."

To this arrangement Brodribb agreed readily, and he and his client prepared to depart. I rose, too, and as I happened to have a call to make in Old Square, Lincoln's Inn, I asked permission to walk with them.

As we came out into King's Bench Walk I noticed a smallish, gentlemanly-looking man who had just passed our entry and now turned in at the one next door; and by the light of the lamp in the entry he looked to me like a Japanese. I thought Miss Bonney had observed him, too, but she made no remark, and neither did I. But, passing up Inner Temple Lane, we nearly overtook two other men, who—though I got but a back view of them and the light was feeble enough—aroused my suspicions by their neat, small figures. As we approached, they quickened their pace, and one of them looked back over his shoulder; and then my suspicions were confirmed, for it was an unmistakable Japanese face that looked round at us. Miss Bonney saw that I had observed the men, for she remarked, as they turned sharply at the Cloisters and entered Pump Court: "You see, I am still haunted by Japanese."

"I noticed them," said Brodribb. "They are probably law students. But we may as well be companionable;" and with this, he, too, headed for Pump Court.

We followed our oriental friends across the Lane into Fountain Court, and through that and Devereux Court out to Temple Bar, where we parted from them; they turning westward and we crossing to Bell Yard, up which we walked, entering New Square by the Carey Street gate. At Brodribb's doorway we halted and looked back, but no one was in sight. I accordingly went my way, promising to return *anon* to hear Thorndyke's report, and the lawyer and his client disappeared through the portal.

My business occupied me longer than I had expected, but nevertheless, when I arrived at Brodribb's premises—where he lived in chambers over his office—Thorndyke had not yet made his appearance. A quarter of an hour later, however, we heard his brisk step on the stairs, and as Brodribb threw the door open, he entered and produced the casket from his pocket.

"Well," said Brodribb, taking it from him and locking it, for the time being, in a drawer, "has the oracle spoken; and if so, what did he say?"

"Oracles," replied Thorndyke, "have a way of being more concise than explicit. Before I attempt to interpret the message, I should like to view the scene of the escape; to see if there was any intelligible reason why this man Uyenishi should have returned up Brownlow Street into what must have been the danger zone. I think that is a material question."

"Then," said Brodribb, with evident eagerness, "let us all walk up and have a look at the confounded place. It is quite close by."

We all agreed instantly, two of us, at least, being on the tip-toe of expectation. For Thorndyke, who habitually understated his results, had virtually admitted that the casket had told him something; and as we walked up the Square to the gate in Lincoln's Inn Fields, I watched him furtively, trying to gather from his impassive face a hint as to what the something amounted to, and wondering how the movements of the fugitive bore on the solution of the mystery. Brodribb was similarly occupied, and as we crossed from Great Turnstile and took our way up Brownlow Street, I could see that his excitement was approaching bursting-point.

At the top of the street Thorndyke paused and looked up and down the rather dismal thoroughfare which forms a continuation of Bedford Row and bears its name. Then he crossed to the paved island surrounding the pump which stands in the middle of the road, and from thence surveyed the entrances to Brownlow Street and Hand Court; and then he turned and looked thoughtfully at the pump.

"A quaint old survivor, this," he remarked, tapping the iron shell with his knuckles. "There is a similar one, you may remember, in Queen Square, and another at Aldgate. But that is still in use."

"Yes," Brodribb assented, almost dancing with impatience and inwardly damning the pump, as I could see, "I've noticed it."

"I suppose," Thorndyke proceeded, in a reflective tone, "they had to remove the handle. But it was rather a pity."

"Perhaps it was," growled Brodribb, whose complexion was rapidly developing affinities to that of a pickled cabbage, "but what the d—"

Here he broke off short and glared silently at Thorndyke, who had raised his arm and squeezed his hand into the opening once occupied by the handle. He groped in the interior with an expression of placid interest, and presently reported: "The barrel is still there, and so, apparently, is the plunger"—(Here I heard Brodribb mutter huskily, "Damn the barrel and the plunger too!")—"but my hand is rather large for the exploration. Would you, Miss Bonney, mind slipping your hand in and telling me if I am right?"

We all gazed at Thorndyke in dismay, but in a moment Miss Bonney recovered from her astonishment, and with a deprecating smile, half shy, half amused, she slipped off her glove, and reaching up—it was rather high for her—inserted her hand into the narrow slit. Brodribb glared at her and gobbled like a turkey-cock, and I watched her with a sudden suspicion that something was going to happen. Nor was I mistaken. For, as I looked, the shy, puzzled smile faded from her face and was succeeded by an expression of incredulous astonishment. Slowly she withdrew her hand, and as it came out of the slit it dragged something after it. I started forward, and by the light of the lamp above the pump I could see that the object was a leather bag secured by a string from which hung a broken seal.

"It can't be!" she gasped as, with trembling fingers, she untied the string. Then, as she peered into the open mouth, she uttered a little cry. "It is! It is! It is the necklace!"

Brodribb was speechless with amazement. So was I; and I was still gazing open-mouthed at the bag in Miss Bonney's hands when I felt Thorndyke touch my arm. I turned quickly and found him offering me an automatic pistol. "Stand by, Jervis," he said quietly, looking towards Gray's Inn.

I looked in the same direction, and then perceived three men stealing round the corner from Jockey's Fields. Brodribb saw them, too, and snatching the bag of pearls from his client's hands, buttoned it into his breast pocket and placed himself before its owner, grasping his stick with a war-like air. The three men filed along the pavement until they were opposite us, when they turned simultaneously and bore down on the pump, each man, as I noticed, holding his right hand behind him. In a moment, Thorndyke's hand, grasping a pistol, flew up—as did mine, also—and he called out sharply: "Stop! If any man moves a hand, I fire."

The challenge brought them up short, evidently unprepared for this kind of reception. What would have happened next it is impossible to guess. But at this moment a police whistle sounded and two constables ran out from Hand Court. The whistle was instantly echoed from the direction of Warwick Court, whence two more constabulary figures appeared through the postern gate of Gray's Inn. Our three attendants hesitated but for an instant. Then, with one accord, they turned tail and flew like the wind round into Jockey's Fields, with the whole posse of constables close on their heels.

"Remarkable coincidence," said Brodribb, "that those policemen should happen to be on the look-out. Or isn't it a coincidence?"

"I telephoned to the station superintendent before I started," replied Thorndyke, "warning him of a possible breach of the peace at this spot."

Brodribb chuckled. "You're a wonderful man, Thorndyke. You think of everything. I wonder if the police will catch those fellows."

"It is no concern of ours," replied Thorndyke. "We've got the pearls, and that finishes the business. There will be no more shadowing, in any case."

Miss Bonney heaved a comfortable little sigh and glanced gratefully at Thorndyke. "You can have no idea what a relief that is!" she exclaimed; "to say nothing of the treasure-trove."

We waited some time, but as neither the fugitives nor the constables reappeared, we presently made our way back down Brownlow Street. And there it was that Brodribb had an inspiration.

"I'll tell you what," said he. "I will just pop these things in my strong-room—they will be perfectly safe there until the bank opens tomorrow—and then we'll go and have a nice little dinner. I'll pay the piper."

"Indeed you won't!" exclaimed Miss Bonney. "This is my thanksgiving festival, and the benevolent wizard shall be the guest of the evening."

"Very well, my dear," agreed Brodribb. "I will pay and charge it to the estate. But I stipulate that the benevolent wizard shall tell us exactly what the oracle said. That is essential to the preservation of my sanity."

"You shall have his *ipsissima verba*," Thorndyke promised; and the resolution was carried, *nem. con.*

An hour and a half later we were seated around a table in a private room of a *café* to which Mr. Brodribb had conducted us. I may not divulge its whereabouts, though I may, perhaps, hint that we approached it by way of Wardour Street. At any rate, we had dined, even to the fulfilment of Brodribb's ideal, and coffee and liqueurs furnished a sort of gastronomic doxology. Brodribb had lighted a cigar and Thorndyke had produced a vicious-looking little black cheroot, which he regarded fondly and then returned to its abiding-place as unsuited to the present company.

"Now," said Brodribb, watching Thorndyke fill his pipe (as understudy of the cheroot aforesaid), "we are waiting to hear the words of the oracle."

"You shall hear them," Thorndyke replied. "There were only five

307

of them. But first, there are certain introductory matters to be disposed of. The solution of this problem is based on two well-known physical facts, one metallurgical and the other optical."

"Ha!" said Brodribb. "But you must temper the wind to the shorn lamb, you know, Thorndyke. Miss Bonney and I are not scientists."

"I will put the matter quite simply, but you must have the facts. The first relates to the properties of malleable metals—excepting iron and steel—and especially of copper and its alloys. If a plate of such metal or alloy—say, bronze, for instance—is made red-hot and quenched in water, it becomes quite soft and flexible—the reverse of what happens in the case of iron. Now, if such a plate of softened metal be placed on a steel anvil and hammered, it becomes extremely hard and brittle."

"I follow that," said Brodribb.

"Then see what follows. If, instead of hammering the soft plate, you put on it the edge of a blunt chisel and strike on that chisel a sharp blow, you produce an indented line. Now the plate remains soft; but the metal forming the indented line has been hammered and has become hard. There is now a line of hard metal on the soft plate. Is that clear?"

"Perfectly," replied Brodribb; and Thorndyke accordingly continued: "The second fact is this: If a beam of light falls on a polished surface which reflects it, and if that surface is turned through a given angle, the beam of light is deflected through double that angle."

"H'm!" grunted Brodribb. "Yes. No doubt. I hope we are not going to get into any deeper waters, Thorndyke."

"We are not," replied the latter, smiling urbanely. "We are now going to consider the application of these facts. Have you ever seen a Japanese magic mirror?

"Never; nor even heard of such a thing."

"They are bronze mirrors, just like the ancient Greek or Etruscan mirrors—which are probably 'magic' mirrors, too. A typical specimen consists of a circular or oval plate of bronze, highly polished on the face and decorated on the back with chased ornament—commonly a dragon or some such device—and furnished with a handle. The ornament is, as I have said, chased; that is to say, it is executed in indented lines made with chasing tools, which are, in effect, small chisels, more or less blunt, which are struck with a chasing-hammer.

"Now these mirrors have a very singular property. Although the face is perfectly plain, as a mirror should be, yet, if a beam of sunlight is caught on it and reflected, say, on to a white wall, the round or oval patch of light on the wall is not a plain light patch. It shows quite clearly the ornament on the back of the mirror."

"But how extraordinary!" exclaimed Miss Bonney.

"It sounds quite incredible." I said.

"It does," Thorndyke agreed. "And yet the explanation is quite simple. Professor Sylvanus Thompson pointed it out years ago. It is based on the facts which I have just stated to you. The artist who makes one of these mirrors begins, naturally, by annealing the metal until it is quite soft. Then he chases the design on the back, and this design then shows slightly on the face. But he now grinds the face perfectly flat with fine emery and water so that the traces of the design are complete obliterated. Finally, he polishes the face with rouge on a soft buff.

"But now observe that wherever the chasing-tool has made a line, the metal is hardened right through, so that the design is in hard metal on a soft matrix. But the hardened metal resists the wear of the polishing buffer more than the soft metal does. The result is that the act of polishing causes the design to appear in faint relief on the face. Its projection is infinitesimal—less than the hundred-thousandth of an inch—and totally invisible to the eye. But, minute as it is, owing to the optical law which I mentioned—which, in effect, doubles the projection—it is enough to influence the reflection of light. As a consequence, every chased line appears on the patch of light as a dark line with a bright border, and so the whole design is visible. I think that is quite clear."

"Perfectly clear," Miss Bonney and Brodribb agreed.

"But now," pursued Thorndyke, "before we come to the casket, there is a very curious corollary which I must mention. Supposing our artist, having finished the mirror, should proceed with a scraper to erase the design from the back; and on the blank, scraped surface to etch a new design. The process of etching does not harden the metal, so the new design does not appear on the reflection. But the old design would. For although it was invisible on the face and had been erased from the back, it would still exist in the substance of the metal and continue to influence the reflection. The odd result would be that the design which would be visible in the patch of light on the wall would be a different one from that on the back of the mirror.

"No doubt, you see what I am leading up to. But I will take the investigation of the casket as it actually occurred. It was obvious, at once, that the value of the thing was extrinsic. It had no intrinsic

309

value, either in material or workmanship. What could that value be? The clear suggestion was that the casket was the vehicle of some secret message or information. It had been made by Uyenishi, who had almost certainly had possession of the missing pearls, and who had been so closely pursued that be never had an opportunity to communicate with his confederates. It was to be given to a man who was almost certainly one of those confederates; and, since the pearls had never been traced, there was a distinct probability that the (presumed) message referred to some hiding-place in which Uyenishi had concealed them during his flight, and where they were probably still hidden.

"With these considerations in my mind, I examined the casket, and this was what I found. The thing, itself, was a common white-metal casting, made presentable by means of lacquer. But the white metal bottom had been cut out and replaced by a plate of fine bronze—*Shakudo*. The inside of this was covered with an etched design, which immediately aroused my suspicions. Turning it over, I saw that the outside of the bottom was not only smooth and polished; it was a true mirror. It gave a perfectly undistorted reflection of my face. At once, I suspected that the mirror held the secret; that the message, whatever it was, had been chased on the back, had then been scraped away and an etched design worked on it to hide the traces of the scraper.

"As soon as you were gone, I took the casket up to the laboratory and threw a strong beam of parallel light from a condenser on the bottom, catching the reflection on a sheet of white paper. The result was just what I had expected. On the bright oval patch on the paper could be seen the shadowy, but quite distinct, forms of five words in the Japanese character.

"I was in somewhat of a dilemma, for I have no knowledge of Japanese, whereas the circumstances were such as to make it rather unsafe to employ a translator. However, as I do just know the Japanese characters and possess a Japanese dictionary, I determined to make an attempt to fudge out the words myself. If I failed, I could then look for a discreet translator.

"However, it proved to be easier than I had expected, for the words were detached; they did not form a sentence, and so involved no questions of grammar. I spelt out the first word and then looked it up in the dictionary. The translation was 'pearls.' This looked hopeful, and I went on to the next, of which the translation was 'pump.' The third word floored me. It seemed to be 'jokkis,' or 'jokkish,' but there was no such word in the dictionary; so I turned to the next word, hoping that it would explain its predecessor. And it did. The fourth word was 'fields,' and the last word was evidently 'London.' So the entire group read 'Pearls, Pump, Jokkis, Fields, London.'

"Now, there is no pump, so far as I know, in Jockey Fields, but there is one in Bedford Row close to the corner of the Fields, and exactly opposite the end of Brownlow Street And by Mr. Brodribb's account, Uyenishi, in his flight, ran down Hand Court and returned up Brownlow Street, as if he were making for the pump. As the latter is disused and the handle-hole is high up, well out of the way of children, it offers quite a good temporary hiding-place, and I had no doubt that the bag of pearls had been poked into it and was probably there still.

"I was tempted to go at once and explore; but I was anxious that the discovery should be made by Miss Bonney, herself, and I did not dare to make a preliminary exploration for fear of being shadowed. If I had found the treasure I should have had to take it and give it to her; which would have been a flat ending to the adventure. So I had to dissemble and be the occasion of much smothered objurgation on the part of my friend Brodribb. And that is the whole story of my interview with the oracle."

Our mantelpiece is becoming a veritable museum of trophies of victory, the gifts of grateful clients. Among them is a squat, shapeless figure of a Japanese gentleman of the old school, with a silly grinning little face—The Magic Casket. But its possession is no longer a menace. Its sting has been drawn; its magic is exploded; its secret is exposed, and its glory departed.

The Dead Hand

About half-past eight on a fine, sunny June morning a small yacht crept out of Sennen Cove, near the Land's End, and headed for the open sea. On the shelving beach of the Cove two women and a man, evidently visitors (or "foreigners," to use the local term), stood watching her departure with valedictory waving of cap or handkerchief; and the boatman who had put the crew on board, aided by two of his comrades, was hauling his boat up above the tide-mark.

A light northerly breeze filled the yacht's sails and drew her gradually seaward. The figures of her crew dwindled to the size of a doll's, shrank with the increasing distance to the magnitude of insects, and at last, losing all individuality, became mere specks merged in the form of the fabric that bore them. At this point the visitors turned their faces inland and walked away up the beach, and the boatman, having opined that "she be fetchin' a tidy offing," dismissed the yacht from his mind and reverted to the consideration of a heap of netting and some invalid lobster-pots.

On board the receding craft two men sat in the little cockpit. They formed the entire crew, for the *Sandhopper* was only a ship's lifeboat, timber and decked, of light draught, and, in the matter of spars and canvas, what the art critics would call "reticent."

Both men, despite the fineness of the weather, wore yellow oilskins and sou'westers, and that was about all they had in common. In other respects, they made a curious contrast: the one small, slender, sharp-featured, dark almost to swarthiness, and restless and quick in his movements; the other large, massive, red-faced, blue-eyed, with the rounded outlines suggestive of ponderous strength—a great ox of a man, heavy, stolid, but much less unwieldy than he looked.

The conversation incidental to getting the yacht under way had ceased, and silence had fallen on the occupants of the cockpit. The big

313

man grasped the tiller and looked sulky, which was probably his usual aspect, and the small man watched him furtively. The land was nearly two miles distant when the latter broke the silence with a remark very similar to that of the boatman on the beach.

"You're not going to take the shore on board, Purcell. Where are we supposed to be going to?"

"I am going outside the Longships," was the stolid answer.

"So, I see," rejoined the other. "It's hardly the shortest course for Penzance, though."

"I like to keep an offing on this coast," said Purcell; and once more the conversation languished.

Presently the smaller man spoke again, this time in a more cheerful and friendly tone.

"Joan Haygarth has come on wonderfully the last few months; getting quite a fine-looking girl. Don't you think so?"

"Yes," answered Purcell, "and so does Phil Rodney."

"You're right," agreed the other. "But she isn't a patch on her sister, though, and never will be. I was looking at Maggie as we came down the beach this morning and thinking what a handsome girl she is. Don't you agree with me?"

Purcell stooped to look under the boom, and answered without turning his head:

"Yes, she's all right."

"All right!" exclaimed the other. "Is that the way?"

"Look here, Varney," interrupted Purcell, "I don't want to discuss my wife's looks with you or any other man. She'll do for me, or I shouldn't have married her."

A deep coppery flush stole into Varney's cheeks. But he had brought the rather brutal snub on himself, and apparently had the fairness to recognise the fact, for he mumbled an apology and relapsed into silence.

When he next spoke he did so with a manner diffident and uneasy, as though approaching a disagreeable or difficult subject.

"There's a little matter, Dan, that I've been wanting to speak to you about when we got a chance of a private talk." He glanced a little anxiously at his stolid companion, who grunted, and then, without removing his gaze from the horizon ahead, replied: "You've a pretty fair chance now, seeing that we shall be bottled up together for another five or six hours. And it's private enough, unless you bawl loud enough to be heard at the Longships."

It was not a gracious invitation. But that Varney had hardly expected; and if he resented the rebuff he showed no signs of annoyance,
for reasons which appeared when he opened his subject.

"What I wanted to say," he resumed, "was this. We're both doing pretty well now on the square. You must be positively piling up
the *shekels*, and I can earn a decent living, which is all I want. Why
shouldn't we drop this flash note business?"

Purcell kept his blue eye fixed on the horizon, and appeared to ignore the question; but after an interval, and without moving a muscle,
he said gruffly, "Go on," and Varney continued:

"The lay isn't what it was, you know. At first it was all plain sailing.
The notes were first-class copies, and not a soul suspected anything
until they were presented at the bank. Then the murder was out, and
the next little trip that I made was a very different affair. Two or three
of the notes were suspected quite soon after I had changed them, and
I had to be precious fly, I can tell you, to avoid complications. And
now that the second batch has come into the bank, the planting of
fresh specimens is no sinecure. There isn't a money changer on the
Continent of Europe that isn't keeping his weather eyeball peeled, to
say nothing of the detectives that the bank people have sent abroad."

He paused and looked appealingly at his companion. But Purcell,
still minding his helm, only growled: "Well?"

"Well, I want to chuck it, Dan. When you've had a run of luck and
pocketed your winnings is the time to stop play."

"You've come into some money then, I take it," said Purcell.

"No, I haven't. But I can make a living now by safe and respectable
means, and I'm sick of all this scheming and dodging with the gaol
everlastingly under my lee."

"The reason I asked," said Purcell, "is that there is a trifle outstand-
ing. You hadn't forgotten that, I suppose?"

"No, I hadn't forgotten it, but I thought that perhaps you might be
willing to let me down a bit easily."

The other man pursed up his thick lips, but continued to gaze
stonily over the bow.

"Oh, that's what you thought, hey?" he said; and then, after a pause,
he continued: "I fancy you must have lost sight of some of the facts
when you thought that. Let me just remind you how the case stands.
To begin with, you start your career with a little playful forgery and
embezzlement; you blue the proceeds, and you are mug enough to be
found out. Then I come in. I compound the affair with old Marston

315

for a couple of thousand, and practically clean myself out of every penny I possess, and he consents to regard your temporary absence in the light of a holiday.

"Now why do I do this? Am I a philanthropist? Devil a bit. I'm a man of business. Before I ladle out that two thousand, I make a business contract with you. I happen to possess the means of making and the skill to make a passable imitation of the Bank of England paper; you are a skilled engraver and a plausible scamp. I am to supply you with paper blanks; you are to engrave plates, print the notes, and get them changed. I am to take two-thirds of the proceeds, and, although I have done the most difficult part of the work, I agree to regard my share of the profits as constituting repayment of the loan. Our contract amounts to this: I lend you two thousand without security—with an infernal amount of insecurity, in fact—you 'promise, covenant, and agree,' as the lawyers say, to hand me back ten thousand in instalments, being the products of our joint industry. It is a verbal contract which I have no means of enforcing; but I trust you to keep your word, and up to the present you have kept it. You have paid me a little over four thousand. Now you want to cry off and leave the balance unpaid. Isn't that the position?"

"Not exactly," said Varney. "I'm not crying off the debt; I only want time. Look here, Dan: I'm making about five-fifty a year now. That isn't much, but I'll manage to let you have a hundred a year out of it. What do you say to that?"

Purcell laughed scornfully. "A hundred a year to pay off six thousand! That'll take just sixty years, and as I'm now forty-three, I shall be exactly a hundred and three years of age when the last instalment is paid. I think, Varney, you'll admit that a man of a hundred and three is getting a bit past his prime."

"Well, I'll pay you something down to start. I've saved about eighteen hundred pounds out of the note business. You can have that now, and I'll pay off as much as I can at a time until I'm clear. Remember that if I should happen to get clapped in chokee for twenty years or so you won't get anything. And, I tell you, it's getting a risky business."

"I'm willing to take the risk," said Purcell.

"I dare say you are!" Varney retorted passionately, "because it's my risk. If I am grabbed, it's my racket. You sit out. It's I who passed the notes, and I'm known to be a skilled engraver. That'll be good enough for them. They won't trouble about who made the paper."

"I hope not," said Purcell.

"Of course they wouldn't, and you know I shouldn't give you away."

"Naturally. Why should you? Wouldn't do you any good."

"Well, give me a chance, Dan," Varney pleaded. "This business is getting on my nerves. I want to be quit of it. You've had four thousand; that's a hundred *per cent*. You haven't done so badly."

"I didn't expect to do badly. I took a big risk. I gambled two thousand for ten."

"Yes, and you got me out of the way while you put the screw on to poor old Haygarth to make his daughter marry you."

It was an indiscreet thing to say, but Purcell's stolid indifference to his danger and distress had ruffled Varney's temper somewhat.

Purcell, however, was unmoved. "I don't know," he said, "what you mean by getting you out of the way. You were never in the way. You were always hankering after Maggie, but I could never see that she wanted you."

"Well, she certainly didn't want you," Varney retorted, "and, for that matter, I don't much think she wants you now."

For the first time Purcell withdrew his eye from the horizon to turn it on his companion. And an evil eye it was, set in the great sensual face, now purple with anger.

"What the devil do you mean?" he exclaimed furiously, "you infernal sallow-faced little whipper snapper! If you mention my wife's name again I'll knock you on the head and pitch you over board."

Varney's face flushed darkly, and for a moment he was inclined to try the wager of battle. But the odds were impossible, and if Varney was not a coward, neither was he a fool. But the discussion was at an end. Nothing was to be hoped for now. Those indiscreet words of provocation had rendered further pleading impossible; and as Varney relapsed into sullen silence, it was with the knowledge that, for weary years to come, he was doomed, at best, to tread the perilous path of crime, or, more probably, to waste the brightest years of his life in a convict prison. For it is a strange fact, and a curious commentary on our current ethical notions, that neither of these rascals even contemplated as a possibility the breach of a merely verbal covenant. A promise had been given. That was enough. Without a specific release, the terms of that promise must be fulfilled to the letter. How many righteous men—prim lawyers or strait-laced, church-going men of business—would have looked at the matter in the same way?

The silence that settled down on the yacht and the aloofness that encompassed the two men were conducive to reflection. Each of the men ignored the presence of the other. When the course was altered southerly, Purcell slacked out the sheets with his own hand as he put up the helm. He might have been sailing single-handed. And Varney watched him askance, but made no move, sitting hunched up on the locker, nursing a slowly matured hatred and thinking his thoughts.

Very queer thoughts they were, rambling, but yet connected and very vivid. He was following out the train of events that might have happened, pursuing them to their possible consequences. Supposing Purcell had carried out his threat? Well, there would have been a pretty tough struggle, for Varney was no weakling. But a struggle with that solid fifteen stone of flesh could end only in one way. He glanced at the great purple, shiny hand that grasped the knob of the tiller. Not the sort of hand that you would want at your throat! No, there was no doubt; he would have gone overboard.

And what then? Would Purcell have gone back to Sennen Cove, or sailed alone into Penzance? In either case, he would have had to make up some sort of story, and no one could have contradicted him, whether the story was believed or not. But it would have been awkward for Purcell.

Then there was the body: That would have washed up sooner or later, as much of it as the lobsters had left. Well, lobsters don't eat clothes or bones, and a dent in the skull might take some accounting for. Very awkward, this, for Purcell. He would probably have had to clear out—to make a bolt for it, in short.

The mental picture of this great bully fleeing in terror from the vengeance of the law gave Varney appreciable pleasure. Most of his life he had been borne down by the moral and physical weight of this domineering brute. At school Purcell had fagged him; he had even bullied him up at Cambridge; and now he had fastened on for ever like the Old Man of the Sea. And Purcell always got the best of it. When he, Varney, had come back from Italy after that unfortunate little affair, behold! the girl whom they had both wanted (and who had wanted neither of them) had changed from Maggie Haygarth into Maggie Purcell. And so, it was even unto this day. Purcell, once a book-keeper in a paper-mill, now a prosperous "financier"—a moneylender, as Varney more than suspected—spent a part of his secret leisure making, in absolute safety, those paper blanks, which he, Varney, must risk his liberty to change into money. Yes, it was quite pleasant to think of Purcell sneaking from town to town, from country to country, with the police at his heels.

But in these days of telegraphs and extradition there isn't much chance for a fugitive. Purcell would have been caught to a certainty, and he would have been hanged; no doubt of it. The imagined picture of the execution gave him quite a lengthy entertainment. Then his errant thoughts began to spread out in search of other possibilities. For after all, it was not an absolute certainty that Purcell could have got him overboard. There was just the chance that Purcell might have gone overboard himself. That would have been a very different affair.

Varney settled himself composedly to consider the new and interesting train of consequences that would thus have been set going. They were more agreeable to contemplate than the others, because they did not include his own demise. The execution scene made no appearance in this version. The salient fact was that his oppressor would have vanished; that the intolerable burden of his servitude would have been lifted for ever; that he would have been free.

It was mere idle speculation to while away a dull hour with an uncongenial companion, and he let his thoughts ramble at large. One moment he was dreamily wondering whether Maggie would ever have listened to him, ever have come to care for him; the next, he was back in the yacht's cabin, where hung from a hook on the bulkhead the revolver that the Rodneys used to practise at floating bottles. It was usually loaded, he knew, but if not, there was a canvas bag full of cartridges in the starboard locker. Again, he found himself dreaming of the home that he would have had, a home very different from the cheerless lodgings in which he moped at present; and then his thoughts had flitted back to the yacht's hold, and were busying themselves with the row, of half-hundredweights that rested on the on either side of the kelson.

When Varney had thus brought his mental picture, so to speak, to a finish, its completeness surprised him. It was so simple, so secure. He had actually planned out the scheme of a murder; and he found himself wondering whether many murders passed undetected. They well might if murders were as easy and as safe as this—a dangerous reflection for an injured and angry man. And at this critical point his meditations were interrupted by Purcell, continuing the conversation as if there had been no pause.

"So, you can take it from me, Varney, that I expect you to stick to your bargain. I paid down my money, and I'm going to have my pound of flesh."

It was a brutal thing to say, and it was brutally said. But more than that: it was inopportune—or opportune, as you will. For it came as a sort of infernal doxology to the devil's anthem that had been, all unknown, ringing in Varney's soul.

Purcell had spoken without looking round. That was his unpleasant habit. Had he looked at his companion, he might have been startled. A change in Varney's face might have given him pause: a warm flush, a sparkle of the eye, a look of elation, of settled purpose, deadly, inexorable—the look of a man who has made a fateful resolution.

It was so simple, so secure! That was the burden of the song that echoed in Varney's brain.

He glanced over the sea. They had opened the South Coast now, and he could see, afar off, a fleet of black-sailed luggers heading east. They wouldn't be in his way. Nor would the big four-master that was creeping away to the west, for she was hull down already; and other ships there were none.

There was one hindrance, though. Dead ahead the Wolf Rock lighthouse rose from the blue water, its red-and-white-ringed tower looking like some gaudily painted toy. The keepers of lonely light houses have a natural habit of watching the passing shipping through their glasses, and it was possible that one of their telescopes might be pointed at the yacht at this very moment. That was a complication.

Suddenly there came down the wind a sharp report like the firing of a gun, quickly followed by a second. Both men recognised the duplicate report and both looked round. It was the explosive signal from the Longships lighthouse; but when they looked there was no lighthouse to be seen, and the dark blue heaving water faded away at the foot of an advancing wall of vapour.

Purcell cursed volubly. A pretty place, this, to be caught in a fog! And then, as his eye lighted on his companion, he demanded angrily: "What the devil are you grinning at?"

For Varney, drunk with suppressed excitement, snapped his fingers at rocks and shoals; he was thinking only of the light-keeper's telescope and of the revolver that hung on the bulkhead. He must make some excuse presently to go below and secure that revolver.

But no excuse was necessary. The opportunity came of itself. After a hasty glance at the vanishing land and another at the compass, Purcell put up the helm to jibe the yacht round on to an easterly course.

As she came round, the single headsail that she carried in place of jib and foresail shivered for a few seconds and then filled suddenly on the opposite tack. And at this moment the halyard parted with a loud snap, the end of the rope flew through the blocks, and, in an instant, the sail was down and its upper half trailing in the water alongside.

Purcell swore furiously, but kept an eye to business. "Run below, Varney," said he, "and fetch up that coil of new rope out of the starboard locker while I haul the sail on board. And look alive. We don't want to drift down on to the Wolf."

Varney obeyed with silent alacrity and a curious feeling of elation. It was going to be even easier and safer than he had thought. He slipped through the hatch into the cabin, and, as he heard Purcell scrambling along the side-deck overhead, he quietly took the revolver from its hook and examined the chambers.

Finding them all loaded, he cocked the hammer and slipped the weapon carefully into the inside breast-pocket of his oilskin coat. Then he took the coil of rope from the locker and went on deck.

As he emerged from the hatch he perceived that the yacht was already enveloped in fog, which drifted past in steamy clouds and swirling streamers, and that she had come up head to wind. Purcell was kneeling on the forecastle, tugging at the sail, which had caught under the forefoot, and punctuating his efforts with deep-voiced curses.

Varney stole silently along the deck, steadying himself by mast and shroud, softly laid down the coil of rope, and approached. Purcell was quite engrossed with his task; his back was towards Varney, his face over the side, intent on the entangled sail. It was a chance in a thousand.

With scarcely a moment's hesitation Varney stooped forward, steadying himself with a hand on the little windlass, and, softly drawing forth the revolver, pointed it at the back of Purcell's head, at the spot where the back seam of his sou'wester met the brim.

The report rang out, but weak and flat in that open space, and a cloud of smoke mingled with the fog; but it blew away immediately, and showed Purcell almost unchanged in posture, crouching on the sail with his chin resting on the little rim of bulwark, while behind him his murderer, as if turned into bronze, still stood stooping forward, one hand grasping the windlass, the other still pointing the revolver.

Thus, the two figures remained for some seconds motionless like some horrible waxworks, until the little yacht, lifting to the swell, gave a more than usually lively curvet, when Purcell rolled over on to his back, and Varney relaxed the rigidity of his posture like a golf player who has watched his ball drop.

Purcell was dead. That was the salient fact. The head wagged to and fro as the yacht pitched and rolled, the limp arms and legs seemed to twitch, the limp body to writhe uneasily. But Varney was not disturbed. Lifeless things will move on an unsteady deck. He was only interested to notice how the passive movements produced the illusion of life. But it was only illusion. Purcell was dead. There was no doubt of that.

The double report from the Longships came down the wind, and then, as if in answer, a prolonged deep bellow. That was the fog-horn of the lighthouse on the Wolf Rock, and it sounded surprisingly near. But, of course, these signals were meant to be heard at a distance. Then a stream of hot sunshine, pouring down on deck, startled him and made him hurry. The body must be got overboard before the fog lifted.

With an uneasy glance at the clear sky over head, he hastily cast off the broken halyard from its cleat and cut off a couple of fathoms. Then he hurried below and, lifting the trap in the cabin floor, hoisted out one of the iron half-hundredweights with which the yacht was ballasted.

As he stepped on deck with the weight in his hand the sun was shining overhead; but the fog was still thick below, and the horn sounded once more from the Wolf. And again, it struck him as surprisingly near.

He passed the length of rope that he had cut off twice round Purcell's body, hauled it tight, and secured it with a knot. Then he made the ends fast to the handle of the iron weight.

Not much fear of Purcell drifting ashore now! That weight would hold him as long as there was anything to hold. But it had taken some time to do, and the warning bellow from the Wolf seemed to draw nearer and nearer. He was about to heave the body over when his eye fell on the dead man's sou' wester, which had fallen off when the body rolled over.

That hat must be got rid of, for Purcell's name was worked in silk on the lining, and there was an unmistakable bullet-hole through the back. It must be destroyed, or, which would be simpler and quicker, lashed securely on the dead man's head.

Hurriedly, Varney ran aft and descended to the cabin. He had noticed a new ball of spun-yarn in the locker when he had fetched the rope. This would be the very thing.

He was back again in a few moments with the ball in his hand, unwinding it as he came, and without wasting time he knelt down by the body and fell to work.

And every half minute the deep-voiced growl of the Wolf came to him out of the fog, and each time it sounded nearer and yet nearer.

By the time he had made the sou'wester secure, the dead man's face and chin were encaged in a web of spun-yarn that made him look like some old-time, grotesque-vizored Samurai warrior.

Varney rose to his feet. But his task was not finished yet. There was Purcell's suitcase. That must be sunk, too; and there was something in it that had figured in the detailed picture that his imagination had drawn. He ran to the cockpit, where the suitcase lay, and having tried its fastenings and found it unlocked, he opened it and took out with his right hand—the clean one—a letter that lay on top of the other contents. This he tossed through the hatch into the cabin. Then his eye caught Purcell's fountain-pen, slipped neatly through a loop in the lid. It was filled, he knew, with the peculiar black ink that Purcell always used. The thought passed swiftly through his mind that perchance it might be of use to him. In a moment he had drawn it from its loop and slipped it into his pocket. Then, having closed and fastened the suit case, he carried it forward and made it fast to the iron weight with a half-dozen turns of spun-yarn.

That was really all, and, indeed, it was time. As he rose, once more, to his feet, the growl of the fog horn burst out, as it seemed, right over the stern of the yacht, and she was drifting stern foremost, who could say how fast? Now, too, he caught a more ominous sound, which he might have heard sooner had he listened—the wash of water, the boom of breakers bursting on a rock.

A revulsion came over him. He burst into a wild sardonic laugh. And had it come to this, after all? Had he schemed and laboured only to leave himself alone on an unmanageable craft drifting down to shipwreck and certain death? Had he taken all this thought and care to secure Purcell's body, when his own might be resting beside it on the sea bottom within an hour?

But his reverie was brief. Suddenly from the white void over his very head, as it seemed, there issued a stunning, thunderous roar that shook the very deck-under his feet. The water around him boiled into a foamy chaos, the din of bursting waves was in his ears, the yacht plunged and wallowed amidst clouds of spray, and, for an instant, a dim; gigantic shadow loomed through the fog and was gone.

In that moment his nerve had come back. Holding on, with one hand, to the windlass, he dragged the body to the edge of the fore-castle, hoisted the weight out-board, and then, taking advantage of a heavy lurch, gave the corpse a vigorous shove. There was a rattle and a hollow splash, and corpse and weight and suitcase had vanished into the seething water.

He clung to the swinging mast and waited. Breathlessly he told out the allotted seconds until, once again, the invisible Titan belched forth his thunderous warning. But this time the roar came over the yacht's bow. She had drifted past the Rock, then. The danger was over, and Purcell would have to go down to Davy Jones's Locker companion-less after all.

Very soon the water around ceased to boil and tumble, and as the yacht's wild plunging settled down once more into the normal rise and fall on the long swell, Varney turned his attention to the refitting of the halyard. But what was this on the creamy duck sail? A pool of blood and a gory imprint of his own hand! That wouldn't do at all. He would have to clear that away before he could hoist the sail, which was annoying, as the yacht was helpless without her head-sail and was evidently drifting out to sea.

He fetched a bucket, a swab, and a scrubbing brush, and set to work. The bulk of the large blood stain cleared off pretty completely after he had drenched the sail with a bucketful or two and given it a good scrubbing. But the edge of the stain, where the heat of the deck had dried it, remained like the painted boundary on a map; and the two hand-prints—which had also dried, though they faded to a pale buff—continued clearly visible.

Varney began to grow uneasy. If those stains would not come out—especially the hand-prints—it would be very awkward; they would take such a deal of explaining. He decided to try the effect of marine soap, and fetched a cake from the cabin; but even this did not obliterate the stains completely, though it turned them a faint greenish brown, very unlike the colour of blood. Still, he scrubbed on, until at last the hand-print faded away entirely and the large stain was reduced to a faint green wavy line, and that was the best he could do—and quite good enough, for if that faint line should ever be noticed, no one would ever suspect its origin.

He put away the bucket and proceeded with the refitting. The sea had disengaged the sail from the forefoot, and he hauled it on board without difficulty. Then there was the reeving of the new halyard, a troublesome business, involving the necessity of his going aloft, where his weight—small man as he was—made the yacht roll most infernally, and set him swinging to and fro like the bob of a metronome. But he was a smart yachtsman and active, though not powerful, and a few minutes' strenuous exertion ended in his sliding down the shrouds with the new halyard running fairly through the upper block. A vigorous haul or two at the new hairy rope sent the head of the dripping sail aloft, and the yacht was once more under control.

The rig of the *Sandhopper* was not smart, but it was handy. She carried a short bowsprit to accommodate the single head-sail and a relatively large mizzen, of which the advantage was that by judicious management of the mizzen-sheet the yacht would sail with very little attention to the helm. Of this advantage Varney was keenly appreciative just now, for he had several things to do before entering port. The excitement of the last hour and the bodily exertions had left him shaky and faint. He wanted refreshment, he wanted a wash, and the various traces of recent events had to be removed. Also, there was that letter to be attended to. So that it was convenient to be able to leave the helm in charge of a lashing for a minute now and again.

When he had washed, he put the kettle on the spirit-stove, and, while it was heating, busied himself in cleaning the revolver, flinging the empty cartridge-case overboard, and replacing it with a cartridge from the bag in the locker. Then he picked up the letter that he had taken from Purcell's suitcase and examined it. It was addressed to "Joseph Penfield, Esq., George Yard, Lombard Street," and was unstamped, though the envelope was fastened up. He affixed a stamp from his pocket-book, and, when the kettle began to boil, he held the envelope in the steam that issued from spout. Very soon the flap of the envelope loosened and curled back, when he laid it aside to mix himself a mug of hot grog, which, together with the letter and a biscuit-tin, he took out into the cockpit.

The fog was still dense, and the hoot of a steamer's whistle from somewhere to the westward caused him to reach the fog-horn out of the locker and blow a long blast on it. As if in answer to his treble squeak came the deep bass note from the Wolf, and, unconsciously, he looked round. He turned automatically, as one does towards a sudden noise, not expecting to see anything but fog, and what he did see startled him not a little.

For there was the lighthouse—or half of it, rather—standing up above the fogbank, clear, distinct, and hardly a mile away. The gilded vane, the sparkling lantern, the gallery, and the upper half of the red-and-white-ringed tower, stood sharp against the pallid sky, but the lower half was invisible. It was a strange apparition—like half a lighthouse suspended in mid-air—and uncommonly disturbing, too. It raised a very awkward question. If he could see the lantern the light-keepers could see him. But how long had the lantern been clear of the fog? That was the question, and the answer to it might come in a highly disagreeable form.

Thus, he meditated as, with one hand on the tiller, he munched his biscuit and sipped his grog. Presently he picked up the stamped envelope and drew from it a letter, which he tore into fragments and dropped overboard. Then, from his pocket-book, he took a similar but unaddressed envelope, from which he drew out its contents, and very curious those contents were.

There was a letter, brief and laconic, which he read thoughtfully. "These," it ran, "are all I have by me, but they will do for the present, and when you have planted them, I will let you have a fresh supply." There was no date and no signature, but the rather peculiar handwriting, in jet-black ink, was similar to that on the envelope addressed to Joseph Penfield, Esq.

The other contents consisted of a dozen sheets of blank paper, each of the size of a Bank of England note. But they were not quite blank, for each bore an elaborate water-mark, identical with that of a twenty-pound banknote. They were, in fact, the "paper blanks" of which Purcell had spoken. The envelope with its contents had been slipped into his hand by Purcell, without remark, only three days ago.

Varney refolded the "blanks," enclosed them within the letter, and slipped letter and "blanks" together into the stamped envelope, the flap of which he licked and reclosed.

"I should like to see old Penfield's face when he opens that envelope," was his reflection as, with a grim smile, he put it away in his pocket-book "And I wonder what he will do," he added mentally; "however, I shall see before many days are over."

Varney looked at his watch. He was to meet Jack Rodney on Penzance Pier at a quarter to three. He would never do it at this rate, for when he opened Mount's Bay, Penzance would be right in the wind's eye. That would mean a long beat to windward. Then Rodney would be there first, waiting for him. Deuced awkward, this. He would have to account for his being alone on board, would have to invent some lie about having put Purcell ashore at Mousehole or Newlyn. But a lie is a very pernicious thing. Its effects are cumulative. You never know when you have done with it. Apart from moral considerations, lies should be avoided at all cost of present inconvenience; that is, unless they are absolutely unavoidable, and then they should be as probable as can be managed, and not calculated to provoke inquiry. Now, if he had reached Penzance before Rodney, he need have said nothing about Purcell—for the present, at any rate, and that would have been so much safer.

When the yacht was about abreast of Lamorna Cove, though some seven miles to the south, the breeze began to draw ahead, and the fog cleared off quite suddenly. The change of wind was unfavourable for the moment, but when it veered round yet a little more until it blew from east-north-east, Varney brightened up considerably. There was still a chance of reaching Penzance before Rodney arrived; for now, as soon as he had fairly opened Mount's Bay, he could head straight for his destination and make it on a single board.

Between two and three hours later the *Sandhopper* entered Penzance Harbour, and, threading her way among an assemblage of luggers and small coasters, brought up alongside the Albert Pier, at the foot of a vacant ladder. Having made the yacht fast to a couple of rings, Varney divested himself of his oilskins, locked the cabin scuttle, and climbed the ladder. The change of wind had saved him after all, and as he strode away along the pier he glanced complacently at his watch. He still had nearly half an hour to the good.

He seemed to know the place well and to have a definite objective, for he struck out briskly from the foot of the pier into Market Jew Street, and from thence, by a somewhat zigzag route, to a road which eventually brought him out about the middle of the esplanade. Continuing westward, he entered the Newlyn Road, along which he walked rapidly for about a third of a mile, when he drew up opposite a small letter-box, which was let into a wall. Here he stopped to read the tablet, on which was printed the hours of collection, and then, having glanced at his watch, he walked on again, but at a less rapid pace.

When he reached the outskirts of Newlyn, he turned and began slowly to retrace his steps, looking at his watch from time to time with a certain air of impatience. Presently a quick step behind him caused him to look round. The newcomer was a postman, striding along, bag on shoulder, with the noisy tread of a heavily shod man and evidently collecting letters. Varney let him pass, watched him halt at the little letter-box, unlock the door, gather up the letters, and stow them in his bag, heard the clang of the iron door, and finally saw the man set forth again on his pilgrimage. Then he brought forth his pocket-book, and drawing from it the letter addressed to Joseph Penfield, Esq., stepped up to the letter-box. The tablet now announced that the next collection would be at 8.30 p.m. Varney read the announcement with a faint smile, glanced again at his watch, which stood at two minutes past four, and dropped the letter into the box.

As he walked up the pier with a large paper bag under his arm, he became aware of a tall man who was doing sentry-go before a Gladstone bag that stood on the coping opposite the ladder, and who, observing his approach, came forward to meet him.

"Here you are, then, Rodney," was Varney's rather unoriginal greeting.

"Yes," replied Rodney, "and here I've been for nearly half an hour. Purcell gone?"

"Bless you! yes, long ago," answered Varney.

"I didn't see him at the station. What train was he going by?"

"I don't know. He said something about taking Falmouth on the way; had some business or other there. But I expect he's gone to have a feed at one of the hotels. We got hung up in a fog; that's why I'm so late. I've been up to buy some grog."

"Well," said Rodney, "bring it on board. It's time we were under way. As soon as we are outside, I'll take charge, and you can go below and stoke up at your ease."

The two men descended the ladder and proceeded at once to hoist the sails and cast off the shore ropes. A few strokes of an oar sent them clear of the lee of the pier, and in a few minutes the yacht *Sandhopper* was once more outside, heading south with a steady breeze from east-north-east.

2.—THE UNRAVELLING OF THE MYSTERY

Romance lurks in unsuspected places. As we go our daily round, we are apt to look distastefully upon the scenes made dull by familiarity, and to seek distraction by letting our thoughts ramble far away into time and space, to ages and regions in which life seems more full of colour. In fancy, perchance, we thread the ghostly aisles of some tropical forest, or linger on the white beach of some lonely coral island, where the coconut palms, shivering in the sea breeze, patter a refrain to the song of the surf; or we wander by moonlight through the narrow streets of some Southern city and hear the thrum of the guitar serenading to the shrouded balcony; and behold! all Romance is at our very doors.

It was on a bright afternoon early in March that I sat beside my friend Thorndyke on one of the lower benches of the lecture theatre of the Royal College of Surgeons. Not a likely place, this, to encounter Romance. Yet there it was, if we had only known it, lying unnoticed at present on the green baize cover of the lecturer's table, But, for the moment, we were thinking of nothing but the lecture

The theatre was nearly full. It usually was when Professor D'Arcy lectured; for that genial *savant* had the magnetic gift of infusing his own enthusiasm into the lecture and so into his audience, even when, as on this occasion, his subject lay on the outside edge of medical science. Today he was lecturing on the epidermic appendages of the marine worms, and from the opening sentence he held his audience as by a spell, standing before the great blackboard with a bunch of coloured chalks in either hand, talking with easy eloquence—mostly over his shoulder—while he covered the black surface with those delightful drawings that added so much to the charm of his lectures.

I watched his flying fingers with fascination, dividing my attention between him and a young man on the bench below me, who was frantically copying the diagrams in a large notebook assisted by an older friend, who sat by him and handed him the coloured pencils as he needed them.

The latter part of the lecture dealt with those beautiful sea worms that build themselves tubes to live in—worms like the *Serpula*, that make their shelly or stony tubes by secretion from their own bodies, or, like the *Sabella* or *Terebella*, build them up with sand-grains, little stones or fragments of shell.

When the lecture came to an end, we trooped down into the arena to look at the exhibits and exchange a few words with the genial professor. Thorndyke knew him very well, and was welcomed with a warm handshake and a facetious question.

"What are you doing here, Thorndyke?" asked Professor D'Arcy. "Is it possible that there are medico-legal possibilities even in a marine worm?"

"Oh, come!" protested Thorndyke, "don't make me such a hidebound specialist. May I have no rational interests in life? Must I live for ever in the witness-box like a marine worm in its tube?"

"I suspect you don't get very far out of your tube," said the professor, with a smile at my colleague. "And that reminds me that I have something in your line. What do you make of this? Let us hear you extract its history."

Here, with a mischievous twinkle, he handed Thorndyke a small round object, which my friend inspected as it lay in the palm of his hand.

"In the first place," said he, "it is a cork; the cork of a small jar."

"Right," said the professor—"full marks. What else?"

"The cork has been saturated with paraffin wax."

"Right again."

"Then some Robinson Crusoe seems to have used it as a button, judging by the two holes in it, and an end of what looks like cat-gut."

"Yes.".

"Finally, a marine worm of some kind—a *Terebella*, I think—has built a tube on it."

"Quite right. And now tell us the history of the cork or button."

"I should like to know something more about the worm first," said Thorndyke.

"The worm," said Professor D'Arcy, "is *Tereballa Rufescens*. It lives, unlike most other species, on a rocky bottom, and in a depth of water of not less than ten fathoms."

It was at this point that Romance stepped in. The young man whom I had noticed working so strenuously at his notes had edged up alongside, and was staring at the object in Thorndyke's hand, not with mere interest or curiosity, but with the utmost amazement and horror. His expression was so remarkable that we all, with one accord, dropped our conversation to look at him.

"Might I be allowed to examine that specimen?" he asked; and when Thorndyke handed it to him, he held it close to his eyes, scrutinising it with frowning astonishment, turned it over and over, and felt the frayed ends of cat-gut between his fingers. Finally, he beckoned to his friend, and the two whispered together for a while, and watching them I saw the seconds man's eyebrows lift, and the same expression of horrified surprise appear on his face. Then the younger man addressed the professor.

"Would you mind telling me where you got this specimen, sir?"

The professor was quite interested. "It was sent to me," he said, "by a friend, who picked it up on the beach at Morte Hoe, on the coast of North Cornwall."

The two men looked significantly at one another, and after a brief pause the older one asked: "Is this specimen of much value, sir?"

"No," replied the professor, "it only a curiosity. There are several specimens of the worm in our collection. But why do you ask?"

"Because I should like to acquire it. I can't give you particulars—I am a lawyer, I may explain—but from what my brother tells me it appears that this object has a bearing on—er—on a case in which we are both interested. A very important bearing, I may add, on a very important case."

The professor was delighted. "There, now, Thorndyke," he chuckled "What did I tell you? The medico-legal worm has arrived. I told you it was something in your line, and now you've been forestalled. Of course," he added, turning to the lawyer, "you are very welcome to this specimen. I'll give you a box to carry it in with some cotton wool."

The specimen was duly packed in its box, and the latter deposited in the lawyer's pocket; but the two brothers did not immediately leave the theatre. They stood apart, talking earnestly together, until Thorndyke and I had taken our leave of the professor, when the lawyer advanced and addressed my colleague.

"I don't suppose you remember me, Dr. Thorndyke," he began; but my friend interrupted him.

"Yes, I do. You are Mr. Rodney. You were junior to Brooke in Jelks v. Partington. Can I be of any assistance to you?"

"If you would be so kind," replied Rodney. "My brother and I have been talking this over, and we think we should like to have your opinion on the case. The fact is we both jumped to a conclusion at once, and now we've got what the Yankees call 'cold feet'. We think that we may have jumped too soon. Let me introduce my brother, Dr. Philip Rodney."

We shook hands, and, making our way out of the theatre, presently emerged from the big portico into Lincoln's Inn Fields.

"If you will come and take a cup of tea at my chambers in Old Buildings," said Rodney, "we can give you the necessary particulars. There isn't so much to tell, after all. My brother identifies the cork, or button, and that seems to be the only plain fact that we have. Tell Dr. Thorndyke how you identified it, Phil."

"It is a simple matter," said Philip Rodney. "I went out in a boat to do some dredging with a friend named Purcell. We both wore our oil-skins as the sea was choppy and there was a good deal of spray blowing about; but Purcell had lost the top button of his, so that the collar kept blowing open and letting the spray down his neck. We had no spare buttons or needles or thread on board, but it occurred to me that I could rig up a jury button with a cork from one of my little collecting jars; so, I took one out, bored a couple of holes through it with a pipe cleaner, and threaded a piece of cat-gut through the holes."

"Why cat-gut?" asked Thorndyke.

"Because I happened to have it. I play the fiddle, and I generally have a bit of broken string in my pocket; usually an E string—the E strings are always breaking, you know. Well, I had the end of an E string in my pocket then, so I fastened the button on with it. I bored two holes in the coat, passed the ends of the string through, and tied a reef-knot. It was as strong as a house."

"You have no doubt that it is the same cork?"

"None at all. First there is the size, which I know from having ordered the corks separately from the jars. Then I paraffined them myself after sticking on the blank labels. The label is there still, protected by the wax. And lastly there is the cat-gut; the bit that is left is obviously part of an E string."

"Yes," said Thorndyke, "the identification seems to be unimpeachable. Now let us have the story."

"We'll have some tea first," said Rodney. "This is my burrow." As he spoke, he dived into the dark entry of one of the ancient buildings on the south side of the little square, and we followed him up the crabbed, time-worn stairs, so different from our lordly staircase in King's Bench Walk. He let us into his chambers, and, having offered us each an armchair, said: "My brother will spin you the yarn while I make the tea. When you have heard him, you can begin the examination-in-chief. You understand that this is a confidential matter and that we are dealing with it professionally?"

"Certainly," replied Thorndyke, "we quite understand that." And thereupon Philip Rodney began his story.

"One morning last June two men started from Sennen Cove, on the west coast of Corwall to sail to Penzance in a little yacht that belongs to my brother and me. One of them was Purcell, of whom I spoke just now, and the other was a man names Varney. When they started, Purcell was wearing the oilskin coat with this button on it. The yacht arrived at Penzance at about four in the afternoon. Purcell went ashore alone to take the train to London or Falmouth, and was never seen again dead or alive. The following day Purcell's solicitor, a Mr. Penfield, received a letter from him bearing the Penzance postmark and the hour 8.45 p.m. The letter was evidently sent by mistake—put into the wrong envelope—and it appears to have been a highly compromising document. Penfield refuses to give any particulars, but thinks that the letter fully accounts for Purcell's disappearance—thinks, in fact, that Purcell has bolted."

"It was understood that Purcell was going to London from Penzance, but he seems to have told Varney that he intended to call in at Falmouth. Whether or not he went to Falmouth we don't know. Varney saw him go up the ladder on to the pier, and there all traces of him vanished. Varney thinks he may have discovered the mistake about the letter and got on board some outward-bound ship at Falmouth; but that is only a surmise. Still, it is highly probable; and when my brother and I saw that button at the museum, we remembered the suggestion and instantly jumped to the conclusion that poor Purcell had gone overboard."

"And the, said Rodney, handing us our tea-cups, "when we came to talk it over, we rather tended to revise our conclusion."

"Why?" asked Thorndyke.

"Well, there are several other possibilities. Purcell may have found a proper button on the yacht and cut off the cork and thrown it overboard—we must ask Varney if he did—or the coat itself may have gone over or been lost or given away, and so on."

On this Thorndyke made no comment, stirring his tea slowly with an air of deep preoccupation. Presently he looked up and asked "Who saw the yacht start?"

"I did, said Philip. "I and Mrs. Purcell and her sister and some fishermen on the beach. Purcell was steering and he took the yacht right out to sea, outside the Long-ships. A sea fog came down soon after, and we were rather anxious, because the Wolf Rock lay right to the leeward of the yacht."

"Did anyone besides Varney see Purcell at Penzance?"

"Apparently not. But we haven't asked. Varney's statement seemed to settle that question. He couldn't very well have been mistaken you know," Philip added with a smile.

"Besides," said Rodney, "if there were any doubt, there is the letter. It was posted in Penzance after eight o'clock at night. Now I met Varney on the pier at quarter past four, and we sailed out of Penzance a few minutes later to return to Sennan."

"Had Varney been ashore?" asked Thorndyke.

"Yes, he had been up to the town buying some provisions."

"But you said Purcell went ashore alone."

"Yes, but there was nothing in that. Purcell was not a genial man.

It was the sort of thing he would do."

"And that is all you know of the matter?" Thorndyke asked, after a few moments' reflection.

"Yes. But we might see if Varney can remember anything more, and we might try if we can squeeze any more information out of old Penfield."

"You, won't," said Thorndyke. "I know Penfield and I never trouble to ask him questions. Besides there's nothing to ask at present. We have an item of evidence that we have not fully examined. I suggest that we exhaust that, and meanwhile keep our own counsel most completely."

Rodney looked dissatisfied. "If," said he, "the item of evidence that you refer to is the button, it seems to me that we have got all that we are likely to get out of it. We have identified it, and we know that it has been thrown up on the beach at Morte Hoe. What more can we learn from it?"

"That remains to be seen," replied Thorndyke. "We may learn nothing, but, on the other hand, we may be able to trace the course of its travels and learn its recent history. It may give us a hint as to where to start a fresh inquiry."

Rodney laughed sceptically. "You talk like a clairvoyant, as if you had the power to make this bit of cork break out into fluent discourse. Of course, you can look at the thing and speculate and guess, but surely the common sense of the matter is to ask a plain question of the man who probably knows. If it turns out that Varney saw Purcell throw the button overboard, or can tell us how it got into the sea, all your speculations will have been useless. I say, let us ask Varney first, and if he knows nothing, it will be time to start guessing."

But Thorndyke was calmly obdurate. "We are not going to guess, Rodney; we are going to investigate. Let me have the button for a couple of days. If I learn nothing from it, I will return it to you, and you can then refresh your legal soul with verbal testimony. But give scientific methods a chance first."

With evident reluctance Rodney handed him the little box. "I have asked your advice," he said rather ungraciously, "so I suppose I must take it; but your methods appeal more to the sporting than the business instincts."

"We shall see," said Thorndyke, rising with a satisfied air. "But, meanwhile, I stipulate that you make no communication to anybody."

"Vey well," said Rodney; and we took leave of the two brothers.

As we walked down Chancery Lane, I looked at Thorndyke, and detected in him an air of purpose for which I could not quite account. Clearly, he has something in view."

"It seems to me," I said tentatively, "that there was something in what Rodney said. Why shouldn't the button just have been thrown overboard?"

He stopped and looked at me with humourous reproach. "Jervis!" he exclaimed, "I am ashamed of you. You are as bad as Rodney. You have utterly lost sight of the main fact, which is a most impressive one. Here is a cork button. Now an ordinary cork if immersed long enough, will soak up water until it is water-logged, and then sink to the bottom. But this one is impregnated with paraffin wax. It can't get water-logged, and it can't sink. It would float for ever."

"Well?"

"But it *has* sunk. It has been lying at the bottom of the sea for months, long enough for a *Terebella* to build a tube on it. And we have D'Arcy's statement that it has been lying in not less than ten fathom of water. Then, at last, it has broken loose and risen to the surface and drifted ashore. Now, I ask you, what has held it down at the bottom of the sea? Of course, it may have been only the coat, weighted by something in the pocket; but there is a much more probable suggestion."

"Yes, I see," said I.

"I suspect you don't—altogether," he rejoined, with a malicious smile. And in the end, it turned out that he was right.

The air of purpose that I noted was not deceptive. No sooner had we reached our chambers, then he fell to work as if with a definite object. Standing by the window, he scrutinised the button, first with the naked eye and then with a lens, and finally laying it on the stage of the microscope, examined the worm-tube by the light of a condenser with a two-inch objective. And the result seemed to please him amazingly.

His next proceeding was to detach, with a fine pair of forceps, the largest of the tiny fragments of stone of which the worm-tube was built. This fragment he cemented on a slide with Canada balsam; and, fetching from the laboratory a slip of Turkey stone, he proceeded to grind the little fragments to a flat surface. Then he melted the balsam, turned the fragment over, and repeated the grinding process until the little fragment was ground down to a thin film or plate, when he applied fresh balsam and a cover-glass. The specimen was now ready for examination; and it was at this point that I suddenly remembered I had an appointment at six o'clock.

It had struck half-past seven when I returned, and a glance round the room told me that the battle was over—and won. The table was littered with trays of mineralogical sections and open books of reference relating to geology and petrology, and one end was occupied by an outspread geological chart of the British Isles. Thorndyke sat in his armchair, smiling with a bland contentment, and smoking a Trichinopoly cheroot.

"Well," I said cheerfully, "what's the news?"

He removed the cheroot, blew out a cloud of smoke, and replied in a single word:

"Phonolite."

"Thank you," I said. "Brevity is the soul of wit. But would you mind amplifying the joke to the dimensions of intelligibility?"

"Certainly," he replied gravely. "I will endeavour to temper the wind to the shorn lamb. You noticed I suppose, that the fragments of which that worm-tube was built are all alike?"

"All the same kind of rock? No, I did not."

"Well, they are, and I have spent a strenuous hour identifying that rock. It is the peculiar, resonant, volcanic rock known as phonolite or clink-stone."

"That is very interesting," said I. "And now I see the object of your researches. You hope to get a hint as to the locality where the button has been lying."

"I hoped, as you say, to get a hint, but I have succeeded beyond my expectations. I have been able to fix the locality exactly."

"Have you really?" I exclaimed. "How on earth did you manage that?"

"By a very singular chance," he replied. "It happens that phonolite occurs in two places only in the neighbourhood of the British Isles. One is inland and may be disregarded. The other is the Wolf Rock."

"The rock of which Philip Rodney was speaking?"

"Yes. He said, you remember, that he was afraid that the yacht might drift down on it in the fog. Well, this Wolf Rock is a very remarkable structure. It is what is called a 'volcanic neck,' that is, it is a mass of altered lava, that once filled the funnel of the volcano. The volcano has disappeared, but this cast of the funnel remains standing up from the bottom of the sea like a great column.

"It is a single mass of *phonolite*, and thus entirely different in composition from the seabed around or anywhere near these islands. But, of course, immediately at its base, the sea-bottom must be covered with decomposed fragments which have fallen from its sides, and it is from these fragments that our *Terebella* has built its tube. So, you see, we can fix the exact locality in which this button has been lying all the months that the tube was building, and we now have a point of departure for fresh investigations."

"But," I said, "this is a very significant discovery, Thorndyke. Shall you tell Rodney?"

"Certainly, I shall. But there are one or two questions that I shall ask him first. I have sent a note inviting him to drop in tonight with his brother, so we had better round to the club and get some dinner. I said nine o'clock."

It was a quarter to nine when we had finished dinner, and ten minutes later we were back in our chambers. Thorndyke made up the fire, placed the chairs hospitably round the hearth, and laid on the table the notes that he had taken at the late interview. Then the treasury clock struck nine, and within less than a minute our two guests arrived.

"I should apologise," said Thorndyke, as we shook hands, "for my rather peremptory message, but I thought it best to waste no time."

"You certainly have wasted no time," said Rodney, "if you have already extracted its history from the button. Do you keep a tame medium on the premises, or are you a clairvoyant yourself?"

"There is our medium," replied Thorndyke, indicating the microscope standing on a side-table under its bell glass. "The man who uses it becomes to some extent a clairvoyant. But I should like to ask you one or two questions if I may."

Rodney made no secret of his disappointment. "We had hoped," said he, "to hear answers rather than questions. However, as you please."

"Then," said Thorndyke, quite unmoved by Rodney's manner, "I will proceed; and I will begin with the yacht in which Purcell and Varney travelled from Sennen to Penzance. I understand that the yacht belongs to you and was lent by you to these two men?"

Rodney nodded, and Thorndyke then asked: "Has the yacht ever been out of your custody on any other occasion?"

"No," replied Rodney, "excepting on this occasion, one or both of us have always been on board."

Thorndyke made a note of the answer and proceeded: "When you resumed possession of the yacht, did you find her in all respects as you had left her?"

"My dear sir," Rodney exclaimed impatiently, "may I remind you that we are inquiring—if we are inquiring about anything—into the disappearance of a man who was seen to go ashore from this yacht and who certainly never came on board again? The yacht is out of it altogether."

"Nevertheless," said Thorndyke, "I should be glad if you would answer my question."

"Oh, very well," Rodney replied irritably. "Then we found her substantially as we had left her."

"Meaning by 'substantially'?—"

"Well, they had to rig up a new jib halyard. The old one had parted."

"Did you find the old one on board?"

"Yes; in two pieces, of course."

"Was the whole of it there?"

"I suppose so. We never measured the pieces. But really, sir, these questions seem extraordinarily irrelevant."

"They are not," said Thorndyke. "You will see that presently. I want to know if you missed any rope, cordage, or chain."

Here Philip interposed. "There was some spun-yarn missing. They opened a new ball and used up several yards. I meant to ask Varney what they used it for."

Thorndyke jotted down a note and asked: "Was there any of the ironwork missing? Any anchor, chain, or other heavy object?"

Rodney shook his head impatiently, but again Philip broke in.

"You are forgetting the ballast-weight, Jack. You see," he continued, addressing Thorndyke, "the yacht is ballasted with half-hundredweights, and, when we came to take out the ballast to lay her up for the winter, we found one of the weights missing. I have no idea when it disappeared, but there was certainly one short, and neither of us had taken it out."

"Can you," asked Thorndyke, "fix any date on which all the ballast-weights were in place?"

"Yes, I think I can. A few days before Purcell went to Penzance we beached the yacht—she is only a little boat—to give her a scrape. Of course, we had to take out the ballast, and when we launched her again, I helped to put it back. I am certain that all the weights were there then."

Here Jack Rodney, who had been listening with ill-concealed impatience, remarked:

This is all very interesting, sir, but I cannot conceive what bearing

338

it has on the movements of Purcell after he left the yacht."

"It has a most direct and important bearing," said Thorndyke. "Perhaps I had better explain before we go any further. Let me begin by pointing out that this button has been lying for many months at the bottom of the sea at a depth of not less than ten fathom. That is proved by the worm-tube which has been built on it. Now, as this button is a waterproofed cork, it could not have sunk by itself; it has been sunk by some body to which it was attached, and there is evidence that that body was a very heavy one."

"What evidence is there of that?" asked Rodney.

"There is the fact that it has been lying continuously in one place. A body of moderate weight, as you know, moves about the sea-bottom impelled by currents and tide-streams, but this button has been lying unmoved in one place."

"Indeed!" said Rodney, with manifest scepticism. "Perhaps you can point out the spot where it has been lying."

"I can," Thorndyke replied. "That button, Mr. Rodney, has been lying all these months at the base of the Wolf Rock."

The two brothers started very perceptibly. They stared at Thorndyke, then looked at one another, and then the lawyer challenged the statement.

"You make this assertion very confidently," he said. "Can you give us any evidence to support it?"

Thorndyke's reply was to produce the button, the section, the test-specimens, the microscope, and the geological chart. In great detail, and with his incomparable lucidity, he assembled the facts, and explained their connection, evolving the unavoidable conclusion.

The different effect of the demonstration on the two men interested me greatly. To the lawyer, accustomed to dealing with verbal and documentary evidence, it manifestly appeared as a far-fetched, rather fantastic argument, ingenious, amusing, and entirely unconvincing. On Philip, the doctor, it made a profound impression. Accustomed to acting on inferences from facts of his own observing, he gave full weight to each item of evidence, and his thoughts were already stretching out to the as yet unstated corollaries.

The lawyer was the first to speak. "What inference," he asked, "do you wish us to draw from this very ingenious theory of yours?"

"The inference," Thorndyke replied impassively, "I leave to you; but perhaps it would help you if I were to recapitulate the facts."

"Perhaps it would," said Rodney.

"Then," said Thorndyke, "I will take them in their order. This is the case of a man who was seen to start on a voyage for a given destination in company with one other man. His start out to sea was witnessed by a number of persons. From that moment he was never seen again by any person excepting his one companion. He is said to have reached his destination, but his arrival there rests upon the unsupported verbal testimony of one person, the said companion. Thereafter he vanished utterly, and since then has made no sign of being alive; although there are several persons with whom he could have safely communicated."

"Some eight months later a portion of this man's clothing is found. It bears evidence of having been lying at the bottom of the sea for many months, so that it must have sunk to its resting-place within a very short time of the man's disappearance. The place where it has been lying is one over, or near, which the man must have sailed in the yacht. It has been moored to the bottom by some very heavy object, and a very heavy object has disappeared from the yacht. That heavy object had apparently not disappeared when the yacht started, and was not seen on the yacht afterwards. The evidence goes to show that the disappearance of that object coincided in time with the disappearance of the man, and a quantity of cordage disappeared certainly on that day. Those are the facts in our possession at present, Mr. Rodney, and I think the inference emerges automatically."

There was a brief silence, during which the two brothers cogitated profoundly and with very disturbed expressions. Then Rodney spoke:

"I am bound to admit, Thorndyke, that as a scheme of circumstantial evidence, this is extremely ingenious and complete. It is impossible to mistake your meaning. But you would hardly expect us to charge a highly respectable gentleman of our acquaintance with having murdered his friend and made away with the body, on a—well—a rather far-fetched theory."

"Certainly not," replied Thorndyke. "But, on the other hand, with this body of circumstantial evidence before us, it is clearly imperative that some further investigation should be made before we speak of the matter to any human soul."

Rodney agreed somewhat grudgingly. "What do you suggest?" he asked.

"I suggest that we thoroughly overhaul the yacht in the first place. Where is she now?"

"Under a tarpaulin in a yard at Battersea. The gear and stores are in a disused workshop in the yard."

"When could we look over her?"

"Tomorrow morning, if you like," said Rodney.

"Very well," said Thorndyke. "We will call for you at nine, if that will suit."

It suited perfectly, and the arrangement was accordingly made. A few minutes late the two brothers took their leave, but as they were shaking hands, Philip said suddenly:

"There is one little matter that occurs to me. I have only just remembered it, and I don't suppose it is of any consequence, but it is as well to mention everything. You remember my brother saying that one of the jib halyards broke the other day?"

"Yes."

"Well, of course, the jib came down and went partly overboard. Now, the next time I hoisted the sail, I noticed a small stain on it; a greenish stain like that of mud, only it wouldn't wash out, and it is there still. I meant to ask Varney about it. Stains of that kind on the jib usually come from a bit of mud on the fluke of the anchor, but the anchor was quite clean when I examined it, and besides, it hadn't been down on that day. I thought I'd better tell you about it."

"I'm glad you did," said Thorndyke. "We will have a look at that stain tomorrow. Goodnight" Once more he shook hands, and then, re-entering the room, stood for quite a long time with his back to the fire, thoughtfully examining the toes of his boots.

We started forth next morning for our rendezvous considerably earlier than seemed necessary. But I made no comment, for Thorndyke was in that state of extreme taciturnity which characterised him whenever he was engaged on an absorbing case with an insufficiency of evidence. I knew that he was turning over and over the facts that he had, and searching for new openings; but I had no clue to the trend of his thoughts until passing the gateway of Lincoln's Inn, he walked briskly up Chancery Lane into Holburn, and finally halted outside a wholesale druggist's.

"I shan't be more than a few minutes," said he, "are you coming in?"

I was, most emphatically. Questions were forbidden at this stage, but there was no harm in keeping one's ears open; and when I heard his order, I was the richer by a distinct clue to his next movements. Tincture of *Guaicum* and *Ozonic* Ether formed a familiar combination, and the size of the bottles indicated the field of investigation.

We found the brothers waiting for us at Lincoln's Inn. They both looked rather hard at the parcel that I was now carrying, and especially at Thorndyke's green canvas-covered research case; but they made no comment, and we set forth at once on the rather awkward cross-country journey to Battersea. Very little was said on the way, but I noticed both men took our quest more seriously than I had expected, and I judged that they had been talking the case over.

Our journey terminated at a large wooden gate on which Rodney knocked loudly with his stick; whereupon a wicket was opened, and, after a few words of explanation, we passed through into a large yard. Crossing this we came to a wharf beyond which was a small stretch of unreclaimed shore, and ere, drawn up well above high-water mark, a small, double-ended yacht stood on chocks under a tarpaulin cover.

"This is the yacht," said Philip, "The gear and loose fittings are in the workshop behind us. Which will you see first?"

"Let us look at the gear," said Thorndyke; and we turned to the disused workshop into which Rodney admitted us with a key from his pocket. I looked curiously about the long, narrow interior with its prosaic contents, so little suggestive of tragedy or romance. Overhead the yacht's spars rested on the tie-beams, from which hung bunches of blocks; on the floor a long row of neatly painted half-hundred weights, a pile of chain cable, two anchors, a stove, and other oddments such as water-breakers, buckets, mops, etc.; and on the long benches at the side folded sails, locker cushions, sidelight lanterns, the binnacle, the cabin lamp, and other more delicate fittings. Thorndyke, too, glanced round inquisitively, and, depositing his case on the bench, asked, "Have you still got the broken jib halyard of which you were telling me?"

"Yes," said Rodney; "it is here under the bench."

He drew out a coil of rope, and, flinging it on the floor, began to uncoil it, when it separated into two lengths.

"Which are the broken ends?" asked Thorndyke.

"It broke near the middle," said Rodney, "where it chafed on the cleat when the sail was hoisted. This is the one end, you see, frayed out, like a brush in breaking, and the other—" He picked up the second half, and passing it rapidly through his hands held up the end. He did not finish the sentence, but stood, with a frown of surprise, staring at the rope in his hand.

"This is queer," he said, after a pause. "The broken end has been cut off. Did you cut it off, Phil?"

"No," replied Philip; "it is just as I took it from the locker, where, I suppose, you or Varney stowed it."

"The question is," said Thorndyke, "how much has it been cut off. Do you know the original length of the rope?"

"Yes. Forty-two feet. It is not down in the inventory, but I remember working it out. Let us see how much there is here."

He laid the two lengths of rope along the floor, and we measured them with Thorndyke's spring tape. The combined length was exactly thirty-one feet.

"So," said Thorndyke, "there are eleven feet missing without allowing for the lengthening of the rope by stretching. That is a very important fact."

"What made you suspect that part of the halyard might be missing as well as the spunyarn?" Philip asked.

"I did not think," replied Thorndyke, "that a yachtsman would use spunyarn to lash a half-hundredweight to a corpse. I suspected that the spunyarn was used for something else. By the way I see you have a revolver here. Was that on board at the time?"

"Yes," answered Rodney. "It was hanging on the cabin bulkhead. Be careful I don't think it has been unloaded."

Thorndyke opened the breech of the revolver, and, dropping the cartridges into his hand, peered down the barrel and into each chamber separately.

"It is quite clean inside," he remarked. Then, glancing at the ammunition in his hand, "I notice," said he, "that these cartridges are not all alike. There are five Eleys and one Curtis and Harvey. That is quite a suggestive coincidence."

Philip looked with a distinctly startled expression at the little heap of cartridges in Thorndyke's hand, and, picking out the odd one, examined it with knitted brows.

"When did you fire the revolver last, Jack?" he asked, looking up at his brother.

"On the day when we potted at those champagne bottles," was the reply.

Philip raised his eyebrows. "Then," said he, "this is a very remarkable affair. I distinctly remember on that occasion, when we had sunk all the bottles, reloading the revolver with Eleys, and that there were then three cartridges left over in the bag. When I had loaded, I opened the new box of Curtis and Harvey's, tipped them into the bag, and threw the box overboard."

"Did you clean the revolver?" asked Thorndyke.

"No, I didn't. I meant to clean it later, but forgot to."

"But," said Thorndyke, "it has undoubtedly been cleaned, and very thoroughly as to the barrel and one chamber. Shall we check the cartridges in the bag? There ought to be forty-nine Curtis and Harveys and three Eleys if what you have told us is correct."

Philip searched among the raffle on the bench, and presently unearthed a small linen bag. Untying the string, he shot out on the bench a heap of cartridges, which he counted one by one. There were fifty-two in all, and three of them were Eleys.

"Then," said Thorndyke, "it comes to this: since you used that revolver it has been used by someone else. That someone fired only a single shot, after which he carefully cleaned the barrel and the empty chamber and reloaded. Incidentally, he seems to have known where the cartridge-bag was kept, but he did not know about the change in the make of cartridges or that the revolver had not been cleaned. You notice, Rodney," he added, "that the circumstantial evidence accumulates."

"I do, indeed," Rodney replied gloomily. "Is there anything else that you wish to examine?"

"Yes; there is the sail. Philip mentioned a stain on the jib. Shall we see if we can make anything of that?"

I don't think you will make much of it," said Philip. "It is very faint. However, you shall see it and judge for yourself."

He picked out one of the bundles of white duck, and while he was unfolding it Thorndyke dragged an empty bench into the middle of the floor under the skylight. Over this the sail was spread so that the mysterious mark was in the middle of the bench. It was very inconspicuous—just a faint grey-green, wavy line, like the representation of an island on a map. The three men looked at it curiously for a few moments, then Thorndyke asked:

"Would you mind if I made a further stain on the sail? I should like to apply some re-agents."

"Of course, you must do what is necessary," said Rodney. "The evidence is more important than the sail."

Accordingly, Thorndyke unpacked our parcel, and as the two bottles emerged, Philip read out the labels with evident surprise, remarking:

"I shouldn't have thought that the *guaiacum* test would be of any use after all these months."

"It will act, I think, if the pigment or its derivatives is there," said Thorndyke; and as he spoke he poured a quantity of the tincture on the middle of the stained area. The pool of liquid rapidly spread considerably beyond the limits of the stain, growing paler as it extended. Then Thorndyke cautiously dropped small quantities of the *ozonic* ether at various points around the stained area, and watched closely as the two liquids mingled in the fabric of the sail. Gradually the ether spread towards the stain, and, first at one point and then at another, approached and finally crossed the wavy grey line; and at each point the same change occurred: first the faint grey line turned into a strong blue line, and then the colour extended to the enclosed space until the entire area of the stain stood out a conspicuous blue patch.

Philip and Thorndyke looked at one another significantly, and the latter said: "You understand the meaning of this reaction, Rodney; this is a bloodstain, and a very carefully washed bloodstain."

"So, I supposed," Rodney replied; and for a while no one spoke.

There was something very dramatic and solemn, they all felt, in the sudden appearance of this staring blue patch on the sail with the sinister message that it brought. But what followed was more dramatic still. As they stood silently regarding the blue stain, the mingled liquids continued to spread; and suddenly, at the extreme edge of the wet area, they became aware of a new spot of blue. At first a mere speck, it grew slowly, as the liquid spread over the canvas, into a small oval, and then a second spot appeared by its side. At this point Thorndyke poured out a fresh charge of the tincture, and when it had soaked into the cloth cautiously applied a sprinkling of ether. Instantly the blue spots began to elongate; fresh spots and patches appeared, and as they ran together there sprang out of the blank surface the clear impression of a hand—a left hand, complete in all its details excepting the third finger, which was represented by a round spot at some two-thirds of its length.

The dreadful significance of this apparition, and the uncanny and mysterious manner of its emergence from the white surface impressed us so that for a while none of us spoke. At length I ventured to remark on the absence of the impression of the third finger.

"I think," said Thorndyke, "that the impression is there. That small round spot looks like the mark of a finger-tip, and its position rather suggests a finger with a stiff joint."

As he made this statement, both brothers simultaneously uttered a smothered exclamation.

Thorndyke looked at them sharply. "What is it?" he asked.

The two men looked at one another with an expression of awe. Then Rodney said in a hushed voice, hardly above a whisper, "Varney, the man who was with Purcell on the yacht—he has a stiff joint on the third finger of his left hand."

There was nothing more to say. The case was complete. The keystone had been laid in the edifice of circumstantial evidence. The investigation was at an end.

After an interval of silence, during which Thorndyke was busily writing up his notes, Rodney asked, "What is to be done now? Shall I swear an information?"

Thorndyke shook his head. No man was more expert in accumulating circumstantial evidence; none was more loth to rely on it.

"A murder charge," said he, "should be supported by proof of death and, if possible, by production of the body."

"But the body is at the bottom of the sea!"

"True. But we know its whereabouts. It is a small area, with the lighthouse as a landmark. If that area were systematically worked over with a trawl or dredge, or, better still, with a set of creepers attached to a good-sized spar, there should be a very fair chance of recovering the body, or at least the clothing and the weight."

Rodney reflected for a few moments. "I think you are right," he said at length. "The thing is practicable, and it is our duty to do it. I suppose you couldn't come down and help us?"

"Not now. But in a few days the spring vacation will commence, and then Jervis and I could join you, if the weather is suitable."

"Thank you both," replied Rodney. "We will make the arrangements and let you know when we are ready."

It was quite early on a bright April morning when the two Rodneys, Thorndyke and I steamed out of Penzance Harbour in a small open launch. The sea was very calm for the time of year, the sky was of a warm blue, and a gentle breeze stole out of the north-east. Over the launch's side hung a long spar, secured to a tow-rope by a bridle and to the spar were attached a number of creepers—lengths of chain fitted with rows of hooks. The outfit further included a spirit compass, provided with sights, a sextant, and a hand-lead.

"It's lucky we didn't run up against Varney in the town," Philip remarked, as the harbour dwindled in the distance.

"Varney!" exclaimed Thorndyke. "Do you mean that he lives in Penzance?"

"He keeps rooms there, and spends most of his spare time down in this part. He was always keen on sea-fishing, and he's keener than ever now. He keeps a boat of his own, too. It's queer, isn't it, if what we think is true?"

"Very," said Thorndyke; and by his meditative manner I judge that circumstances afforded him matter for curious speculation.

As we passed abreast of the Land's End, and the solitary lighthouse rose ahead on the verge of the horizon, we began to overtake the scattered members of a fleet of luggers, some with lowered mainsails and hand-lines down, others with their black sails set, heading for some distant fishing-ground. Threading our way among them, we suddenly became aware that one of the smaller luggers was heading so as to close in on us. Rodney, observing this, was putting over the helm to avoid her, when a seafaring voice from the little craft hailed us.

"Launch ahoy there! Gentleman aboard wants to speak to you!"

We looked at one another significantly and in some confusion; and meanwhile our solitary "hand"—seaman, engineer, and fireman combined—without waiting for orders, shut off steam. The lugger closed in rapidly and of a sudden there appeared, holding on by the mainstay, a small dark fellow who hailed us cheerfully: "hullo, you fellows! Whither away? What's your game?"

"God!" exclaimed Philip. "It's Varney! Sheer off, skipper! Don't let him come along side."

But it was too late. The boat had lost way and failed to answer her helm. The lugger sheered in, sweeping abreast within a foot, and as she crept past Varney sprang lightly from her gunwale and dropped on the side bench in our stern sheets.

"Where are you off to?" he asked. "You can't be going out to fish in this baked-potato can?"

"No," faltered Rodney, "we're not. We're going to do some dredging—or rather—"

Here Thorndyke came to his assistance. "Marine worms," said he, "are the occasion for this little voyage. There seems to be some very uncommon ones on the bottom at the base of the Wolf Rock. I have seen some in a collection, and I want to get a few more if I can."

It was a skilfully-worded explanation, and I could see that, for the time, Varney accepted it. But from the moment when the Wolf Rock was mentioned all his vivacity of manner died out. In an instant he had become grave, thoughtful, and a trifle uneasy.

The introductions over he reverted to the subject. He questioned us closely, especially as to our proposed methods. And it was impossible to evade his questions. There were the creepers in full view; there was the compass and the sextant; and presently these appliances would have to be put in use. Gradually, as the nature of the exploration dawned on him, his manner changed more and more. A horrible pallor overspread his face, and a terrible restlessness took possession of him.

Rodney, who was navigating, brought the launch to within a quarter of a mile of the rock, and then, taking cross-bearings on the lighthouse and a point of land, directed us to lower the creepers.

It was a most disagreeable experience for us all. Varney, pale and clammy, fidgeted about the boat, now silent and moody, now almost hysterically boisterous. Thorndyke watched him furtively, and, I think, judged by his manner how near they were to the object of our search.

Calm as the day was, the sea was breaking heavily over the rock, and as we worked closer the water around boiled and eddied in an unpleasant and even dangerous manner. The three keepers in the gallery of the lighthouse watched us through their glasses, and one of them bellowed through a megaphone to keep farther away.

"What do you say?" asked Rodney. "It's a bit risky here, with the rock right under our lee. Shall we try another side?"

"Better try one more cast this side," said Thorndyke; and he spoke so definitely that we all, including Varney, looked at him curiously. But no one answered, and the creepers were dropped for a fresh cast still nearer the rock. We were then north of the lighthouse, and headed south, so as to pass the rock on its east side. As we approached, the man with the megaphone bawled out fresh warnings and continued to roar at us until we were abreast of the rock in a wild tumble of confused waves.

At this moment, Philip, who held the tow-line with a single turn round a cleat, said that he had felt a pull, but that it seemed as if the creepers had broken away. As soon, therefore, as the we were out of the backwash into smooth water, we hauled in the linen to examine the creepers.

I looked over the side eagerly, for something new in Thorndyke's manner impressed me. Varney, too, who had hitherto taken little notice of the creepers, now knelt on the side bench, gazing earnestly into the clear water whence the tow-rope was rising.

At length the beam came in sight, and below it, on one of the creepers, a yellowish object, dimly visible through the wavering water. "There's somethin' on this time," said the skipper, craning over the side. He shut off steam, and, with the rest of us, watched the incoming creeper. I looked at Varney kneeling on the bench, not fidgeting now, but still, rigid, pale as wax, staring with dreadful fascination at the slowly rising object.

Suddenly the skipper uttered an exclamation.

"Why, 'tis a sou'wester! And all laced about wi' spun-y'n! Surely 'tis—Hi! Steady, sir; My God!"

There was a heavy splash, and as Rodney rushed forward for the boat-hook I saw Varney rapidly sinking head first through the clear, blue-green water, dragged down by the hand-lead that he had hitched to his waist. By the time Rodney was back he was far out of reach; but for a long time, so it seemed, we could see him sinking, sinking, growing paler, more shadowy, more shapeless, but always steadily following the lead sinker, until at last he faded from our sight into the darkness of the ocean.

Not until he had vanished did we haul on board the creeper with its dreadful burden. Indeed, we never hauled it on board, for as Philip, with an unsteady hand, unhooked the sou'wester hat from the creeper, the encircling coils of spunyarn slipped, and from inside the hat a skull dropped into the water and sank. We watched it grow green and pallid and small, until it vanished into the darkness, as Varney had vanished. Then Philip turned and flung the hat down in the bottom of the boat. Thorndyke picked it up and unwound the spun-yarn.

"Do you identify it?" he asked; and then, as he turned it over, he added: "But I see it identifies itself."

He held it towards me, and I read in embroidered, lettering on the silk lining "Dan Purcell."

LEONAUR

ALSO FROM LEONAUR
AVAILABLE IN SOFTCOVER OR HARDCOVER WITH DUST JACKET

MR MUKERJI'S GHOSTS *by S. Mukerji*—Supernatural tales from the British Raj period by India's Ghost story collector.

KIPLINGS GHOSTS *by Rudyard Kipling*—Twelve stories of Ghosts, Hauntings, Curses, Werewolves & Magic.

THE COLLECTED SUPERNATURAL AND WEIRD FICTION OF WASHINGTON IRVING: VOLUME 1 *by Washington Irving*—Including one novel 'A History of New York', and nine short stories of the Strange and Unusual.

THE COLLECTED SUPERNATURAL AND WEIRD FICTION OF WASHINGTON IRVING: VOLUME 2 *by Washington Irving*—Including three novelettes 'The Legend of the Sleepy Hollow', 'Dolph Heyliger', 'The Adventure of the Black Fisherman' and thirty-two short stories of the Strange and Unusual.

THE COLLECTED SUPERNATURAL AND WEIRD FICTION OF JOHN KENDRICK BANGS: VOLUME 1 *by John Kendrick Bangs*—Including one novel 'Toppleton's Client or A Spirit in Exile', and ten short stories of the Strange and Unusual.

THE COLLECTED SUPERNATURAL AND WEIRD FICTION OF JOHN KENDRICK BANGS: VOLUME 2 *by John Kendrick Bangs*—Including four novellas 'A House-Boat on the Styx', 'The Pursuit of the House-Boat', 'The Enchanted Typewriter' and 'Mr. Munchausen' of the Strange and Unusual.

THE COLLECTED SUPERNATURAL AND WEIRD FICTION OF JOHN KENDRICK BANGS: VOLUME 3 *by John Kendrick Bangs*—Including twor novellas 'Olympian Nights', 'Roger Camerden: A Strange Story', and ten short stories of the Strange and Unusual.

THE COLLECTED SUPERNATURAL AND WEIRD FICTION OF MARY SHELLEY: VOLUME 1 *by Mary Shelley*—Including one novel 'Frankenstein or the Modern Prometheus', and fourteen short stories of the Strange and Unusual.

THE COLLECTED SUPERNATURAL AND WEIRD FICTION OF MARY SHELLEY: VOLUME 2 *by Mary Shelley*—Including one novel 'The Last Man', and three short stories of the Strange and Unusual.

THE COLLECTED SUPERNATURAL AND WEIRD FICTION OF AMELIA B. EDWARDS *by Amelia B. Edwards*—Contains two novelettes 'Monsieur Maurice', and 'The Discovery of the Treasure Isles', one ballad 'A Legend of Boisguilbert' and seventeen short stories to cill the blood.

.